Right from Wrong

Also by Cindy Bonner

Lily
Looking After Lily
The Passion of Dellie O'Barr

Right from Wrong

a novel by
Cindy Bonner

ALGONQUIN BOOKS
OF CHAPEL HILL
1999

Published by
ALGONQUIN BOOKS OF CHAPEL HILL
Post Office Box 2225
Chapel Hill, North Carolina 27515-2225

a division of
Workman Publishing
708 Broadway
New York, New York 10003

Printed in the United States of America.
Published simultaneously in Canada by
Thomas Allen & Son Limited.
Design by Anne Winslow.

This is a work of fiction. While, as in all fiction, the literary perceptions and insights are based on experience, all names, characters, places, and incidents are either products of the author's imagination or are used fictitiously. No reference to any real person is intended or should be inferred.

Library of Congress Cataloging-in-Publication Data
Bonner, Cindy, 1953–
    Right from wrong : a novel / by Cindy Bonner.
        p. cm.
    ISBN 1-56512-104-X
    I. Title.
    PS3552.O6362R54   1999
    813'.54—dc21   98-44870
                                              CIP

10 9 8 7 6 5 4 3 2 1
First Edition

For Hestir Weikel 🖋

dearest Daddy—who has always

been my hero.

1913

*T*HE SEPTEMBER OF SUNNY'S twelfth year, Mama left Papa. She waited until he had gone off to Elgin to sell his yam crop to Mr. England like he did every year right before harvest. Then she packed up her old canvas grip, took Sunny by the hand, and together they walked the mile and a half to the McDade station. Mama had her household money from the jelly jar, mostly all loose change, but it added up to enough for two tickets on the eastbound mail train. Two hours and five stops later, they arrived in Burton.

It was a Friday, bright and hot. Sunny wore her best white dress with the lace hem, a blue grosgrain bow in her hair. Mama was dressed fancy, too, in a pleated-front waist, a skirt and matching jacket of tiny green checks with big ball buttons up the front. She wore a wide-brim, low-on-the-brow hat, high-button shoes with a two-inch heel, gloves, and a string of false pearls around her neck. Mama was twenty-eight that September, fully in her prime. Men standing out in front of the Burton feed store turned to look as she passed by. Sunny noticed the way they scrutinized Mama's trim ankles inside the soft cotton uppers of her high-heeled shoes.

Sunny's given name was Florida Faye. The Faye part was there only to go along with the Florida part, and because Mama liked the sound of those two close-together *F*s. The year Sunny was born the state of Florida had become the latest vacation spot, and Mama had a desire to travel, which being a farmer's wife, of course, she could never do. Not only was money tight, but there were always crops in the fields and animals to tend. Theirs was an old-time farm with chickens and milk cows and draft mules, and even a couple of goats for close-cleaning the fields after harvest. It was Papa who had given Sunny her nickname, partly because he was in the habit of handing out nicknames to people anyway and partly because he said she looked just like a ray of sunshine to him, lying in her crib, little spikes of orange-yellow hair making a halo on her embroidered pillow.

The hill was steep going up from the Burton station to Aunt Prudie's house. Uncle Nolan's blacksmith stood just to the other side. Men and horses milled outside over there, but Mama didn't go that far. She turned onto the path to the house and front porch, and just as they reached the top step, Aunt Prudie opened the screened door.

The minute Mama saw her big sister, tears came flooding down her face. Sobbing and gulping for air out there on the porch, she said, "Oh Prudie, I've just left Dane."

Aunt Prudie came outside to take Mama in her arms. "Well, honey, you just cry if you need to."

Mama buried her face against Aunt Prudie's shoulder. The wide-brim hat started sliding off Mama's head, but Aunt Prudie swooped to save it before it fell to the ground.

"He isn't ever going to change." Mama took the hat from Aunt Prudie's hands and tossed it onto the porch glider. "You'd think it would kill him to part with one red cent." She held out her arms.

Tears had made two clean streaks through her face powder. "Just look at me. Look at these shabby old clothes I've got to wear. Look at Sunny's clothes."

Sunny peered down at her dress. The lace hem was a little tattered and tinged brown from too much ironing. Yet until that moment Sunny had believed it to be a pretty dress, her dress-up dress, and she had thought Mama's clothes fine and beautiful, too.

"You don't have to tell me how he is." Aunt Prudie took hold of Mama again. "If I've said it once, I've said it a thousand times, Dane DeLony's as tight as sheets."

Mama wiped at her face. "Can we stay here with you for a while, Prudie? I don't know where else to go."

"You're always welcome here. You know that. We'll put you up in Calvin's room. Now, come inside this house."

Aunt Prudie reached to open the door and they went in, hugged together like the dancing bears on the music box in the front window at Flaxman's store back home. Sunny was left alone on the porch with the canvas grip right where Mama had dropped it. She didn't know whether she should go inside. She could hear them in there, but she didn't think she wanted to know what they were saying. It seemed rude for them to talk about Papa when he wasn't there to defend himself, calling him stingy just because he took care with money.

She fingered the hem of her dress, wondering if it really looked so ugly. She stepped over to lift Mama's hat off the glider and started to try it on for size until she spotted her cousin Gil walking fast through Uncle Nolan's wagon yard. He was walking toward her and she thought he must have seen her and Mama come up.

Gil spent part of every summer working for Papa around the

farm, so Sunny was well used to his company. In fact, all morning on the train she had been looking forward to seeing him again. Barely three weeks had passed since he'd left McDade to get back to Burton in time for school, but he wasn't a person she got tired of easily.

A headful of dark brown curls tumbled out from under his flat tweed bill-cap, curls Mama always said ought not to have been wasted on a boy. He wore a pair of bib-front coveralls over a yellow shirt rolled to the elbows. When he reached the edge of the porch, he stopped right there, put his hands on his hips, and waited for her to speak first, to say what they were doing in Burton so unexpectedly.

"We left Papa," she said, repeating the words Mama had used to Aunt Prudie. They sounded amazing and unreal.

Gil squinted one eye against the sun's glare. "Forever?"

"I don't know. He took off to Elgin this morning and we caught the mail train here. He probably doesn't even know we're gone yet."

She glanced through the screen but couldn't see anything inside. She could hear Mama in there weeping, and Aunt Prudie sympathizing. Their voices carried. Gil looked at the door, too.

"We can go around to the side window and listen better," he said. "If you care to." And she thought from the way he added the last part that he must understand how confused she felt.

"I don't think I do." She stepped around the canvas grip to the top of the steps. She clutched the porch post for a second, taking in Aunt Prudie's row of puny marigolds growing along the footpath. Papa always said Aunt Prudie was no gardener. "Looks like we're moving in here with y'all for a while."

Gil folded his arms across his middle and tilted his head. He made the most awful grimace she had ever seen, and he hung on to that face long enough to make sure she saw it, too. Then he let go of a wide, teasing grin that showed the front tooth he'd chipped last Christmas cracking Brazil nuts.

"Dang it," he said.

She laughed because he dared to say *dang it* right out loud where anyone could hear, Mama or Aunt Prudie if they had been listening, but also because she knew he was teasing her. So, forgetting all about her shabby dress, she lunged down the stairs to give him a shove. He dodged her, and dodged again when she lunged a second time. He even stuck his arm out and touched the top of her head. She almost caught him then. At least she caused him to lose his cap. But he was quick and he bounded, laughing, toward the wagon yard. Twice he turned back, checking to make sure she was on his heels, which she was.

Gil Dailey was the smartest person Sunny knew who was not a grown-up. He wasn't but two years older than her, but he read a lot more than she did, adventure books with hardly any pictures on the pages. He could climb a tree like a monkey, run like the wind, and during the summer just past, he had learned from Sunny's Uncle Daniel O'Barr how to drive an automobile. Uncle Daniel had a big air-cooled Franklin and Gil had gotten up behind the wheel of that motorcar and steered it right out on the road just as straight as Uncle Daniel could. Gil was fearless. Not only did Sunny envy and admire everything he did, but she spent about half her time wishing she'd been born him, or that she could put on his skin and become him.

Gil's little brother, Calvin, had heard Gil and Sunny's laughing and came slamming out the kitchen door and around the side of the house. Calvin was nine, still in short pants, and he had a bad stutter habit. He always carried a sack of marbles in his pocket, marbles being the only game he considered worth playing, so when he came running outside, he yelled, predictably, "Hey, y'all! Hey! Let's sh-shoot marbles! Want to?"

Gil and Sunny stopped their game of tag and watched Calvin lope toward them, fishing the sack of marbles from his pants pocket. He got as close as the edge of the wagon yard before Gil grabbed Sunny by the arm. They lit out in the opposite direction from Calvin. Sunny didn't know why they ran from Calvin, they just always did. And Calvin knew they would. It was expected. And fun. At least for Gil and Sunny it was fun, thrilling to have somebody chasing them, to have to find a quick place to hide.

The wagon yard was a jumble of upturned buggies, wheel hubs and rims, singletrees and doubletrees, piles of rusty trace chains and worn-out lumber. Gil knew his way through the maze and he dragged Sunny along with him. When they came to an old Studebaker wagon with no wheels and propped longways like a lean-to against the back wall of the blacksmith, Gil scrambled underneath. He reached back to duck Sunny in after him.

They held their breath as Calvin ran past, panting, feet beating hard. He even knocked something—a hand, or his foot, or the sack of marbles—against the Studebaker's shell on his way. Gil silenced a laugh.

Calvin called, "W-where are y'all?"

Sunny almost felt sorry enough to answer out, but Gil saw her about to and grabbed her forearm. He put his finger up to his lips and she kept still and quiet. They listened as Calvin's voice grew more and more faint, fading off to the right, then around toward the front of Uncle Nolan's shop.

"He's gone," Gil whispered.

It was cozy underneath the overturned wagon. A couple of sprigs of colorless grass grew right next to the wall, but otherwise it was bare dirt. A few strands of Gil's rowdy curls touched the wagon hull, held there as if caught by a magnet. His eyes locked on hers. They were light brown, glistening eyes, full of the devil, Mama always said.

He grinned. "You want me to kiss you?"

A kiss from Gil Dailey was nothing new. Mama's whole side of the family were huggers and kissers and touchers. For years Gil had been grabbing her for a smooch on the cheek, usually followed by a tug of her hair so she'd chase him. It was part of his teasing way, like a puppy dashing in to nip his littermate, then darting off on a dead run. What was new was this asking.

He was fourteen, coming fifteen in February, and he had started into his growth. Britches he'd worn just fine in June needed the hem let out by August. His voice had pitched a notch deeper. An Adam's apple had developed in his neck. But there were other changes in him as well, changes you couldn't see. More confusing changes. As if he were in a hurry to get a taste of life.

He held tight to her forearm, eyes directly on her, waiting for her answer. Finally she made a pucker and he leaned forward, closed his eyes, and pressed his lips to her lips, and suddenly all those past kisses, those baby, play-pretend kisses from him, didn't count anymore. It lasted only a few seconds, yet everything about this kiss felt different. Maybe it was how he held his breath, or the way his fingers tensed on her arm—those new man's fingers, long and veiny, a pinch of fuzz budding below each middle knuckle. Maybe it had something to do with her bewilderment over Mama leaving Papa. Or maybe it was just the moon, nearly transparent in the bright afternoon sky. Who knows what will make one kiss ordinary and the next one magical? Who understands about love?

Surely not Sunny. All she knew was that at the first touch of his lips something seeped through her and settled at the base of her spine, where it hummed like the tuning fork Miss Plimper held to her desk every school-day morning for "God Bless America." And when Gil broke away his lips, Sunny felt such a loss that she rose a couple of inches on her knees, reaching for a second kiss, which he obliged her with. In the middle of it, she blinked her eyes open to see his face so close, eyelids blue, dark lashes fluttery against his cheekbones. And it was in that moment that Calvin burst under the upturned wagon bed.

"Found you!" he cried out, then seeing them hurry apart, clamped his hand across his mouth. "Ahhmmm. I'm gonna tell Ma." He backed out from under the wagon and jumped to his feet.

Before Sunny could even think straight, or get a deep breath, Gil had gone out after Calvin. She crawled out, too, dusting off her dress. Her white shoes were scuffed black along both sides. She felt dreamy, dazed, like a mole uncovered at midday. She watched Gil outrace Calvin, catch him by his suspenders, and drag him, kicking and swinging wild punches, back to where Sunny stood.

"Get out your marbles," Gil ordered, and Calvin stopped fighting to dig down in the pocket of his knickers. He grinned and his hand brought up the drawstring tobacco sack full of marbles.

The rest of that afternoon, Sunny sat on the ground in her white lace dress and played marbles with Calvin and Gil in the wagon yard. They played roly-holy and knuckles down and Gil let Calvin win every game. The three of them knew Gil was the best shooter amongst them, but nobody said a thing about his unusual losses. Sunny's eyes met his now and then, and his met hers back, but there was no fun in it anymore. None in the marble games either.

Calvin kept hoarding marbles until he had every last one of them tucked between his knees, and he didn't seem aware of what was going on. Gil never said anything directly or made Calvin swear a promise not to tell about what he'd seen, and Sunny felt too timid to even speak, let alone bring up the subject of that kiss. And so at supper that evening, with everyone washed up and sitting around the table, and not two minutes after Uncle Nolan had finished with grace, Calvin blurted out, clear as day, without a stutter one, "Gil was smooching on Sunny up under that big old wagon in Pop's yard today."

Sunny's face caught fire. Gil rolled his eyes shut, then narrowed them on Calvin sitting straight across the table.

"Right on the lips, too." Calvin sneered back at Gil and wrapped both arms around his own rib cage. "All hugged up together like this."

Except for Mama's lame "What wagon . . . ," a dead silence fell over the table. Sunny could hear the mantel clock from the front room. And then Aunt Prudie's hand shot out and slapped Gil hard across the face. It sounded as loud as gunfire. Gil's head lashed sideways. The skin on his neck flamed a brilliant, blotchy red.

Uncle Nolan said, "Now, Prud—," but he was a slow-talking, sweet-tempered man who didn't have one bit of control over his own household. Aunt Prudie yanked Gil up by his shirt collar. His chair went tumbling over backward.

"Apologize!" she screamed. "You will apologize for your indecent behavior!"

"Praise the Lord, Prudie," Uncle Nolan said, but his scolding words continued to go unnoticed.

The slap mark on Gil's face blazed. His eyes were dark with rage and humiliation. Sunny couldn't stand to see it.

"Apologize!" Aunt Prudie said again, giving him a shake.

Sunny sprang to her feet. "No! Don't you make hi—," but that was as much as she got out before Mama snatched her away from the table, too, half dragging her through the dining room and the front room, down the hall to the back bedroom that belonged to Calvin.

The canvas grip sat on the bed, and with both hands Mama shoved Sunny down there beside it. The bag bounced and nearly went off onto the floor. Mama turned to shut the door, then lingered there, listening to the noises from the other end of the house—slamming noises, some more shouting, a door banging shut so hard the walls shuddered. Mama pushed her bottom lip into her teeth and bit at the skin. She peeped out the door, stretching her head around the corner.

Sunny sat listening, too. A flood of shameful, angry tears hovered on the brink of spilling down her face. The house got quiet and still.

"That poor boy," Mama whispered into the silence, talking mostly to herself. She shook her head. "I never in my life saw Prudie so mad."

"We ought to go help him."

"No! You sit still." Mama shut the door.

Sunny slid her eyes down to her lap. A tear spilled out and fell onto her white dress. She smudged it in.

"I wish your papa was here . . ." Mama paced a couple of steps. "No. No. I'm glad he's not. He wouldn't be any use at all. He never has believed in taking a switch to you. He just lets you do as you please."

"That's not so."

"Don't backtalk." Mama stopped pacing, turned around. Her face had taken on a stricken look. "Sunny? Sunny, *were* you kissing Gilbert the way Calvin said you were? Right on the lips?"

"He was kissing me," Sunny answered, and immediately felt awful for making it sound like Gil was the only one to blame.

Mama took a step toward the bed. "Well, you can't let him do that. You shouldn't be letting any boy do that, but especially not Gilbert. He's your cousin. Your *first* cousin. Do you understand what that means?"

"No," Sunny said, then when Mama's expression soured, "I mean, yes ma'am." She blinked to stave off more tears. She couldn't stop seeing Aunt Prudie's hand slapping Gil's face, or the mortified surprise in his eyes.

"You can't be thinking of Gil Dailey with love notions in your head, do you hear me? Half the blood inside of him is exactly like half the blood inside of you is. So you can't be thinking about him, do you understand me?" Mama's voice lowered. "It's just fine for the two of you to be friends. In fact, I hope you will be, but that's all it can ever amount to. Anything else is unnatural. It's incest, is what it is, and it's against the law." Mama steadied herself. "Is this all clear to you? Have you heard a single word I'm telling you?"

Sunny nodded. She clicked her thumbnails together in her lap. She didn't mean to sit there starstruck dumb, she was just having a hard time concentrating on Mama when Gil might be out there someplace getting whipped. Or worse.

Mama sat down on the bed, sighed deeply. She took Sunny's hand. "You two've been together too much, that's all. I probably should of seen it coming. I should of kept a better eye on you both this summer." Mama rubbed the back of Sunny's hand so hard it chafed. "Child, don't you get started this soon. Not *this* soon, do you hear me? You're too young for boys."

Mama hadn't been but fourteen herself when she got married, a fact that Sunny kept quiet about, since Mama seemed on the verge of tears. Sunny felt her own tears start to flood. She flung her arms around Mama and held on tight.

"Shush now, child." Mama petted Sunny's hair in long strokes. "Just shush up."

"Oh Mama . . . wonder what she's doing to him?"

Mama tipped up Sunny's chin and looked at her eyes, back and forth, one to the other, like she was searching for something. "Who? Prudie? Child, Prudie is not going to hurt Gilbert. He's her pride and joy, don't you know that? She wouldn't hurt him for the world."

But Sunny didn't feel convinced. And she couldn't get that hand-slap to stop ringing in her ears.

SUPPER WAS MISSED THAT night. Sunny didn't want to go in to breakfast the next morning either, except Mama made her. Gil wasn't there. He didn't seem to be around anywhere. Calvin kept his head down, pricking at his flapjacks with the tines of his fork, ears as pink as a mouse's. And Sunny hated him. The smell of blue cane syrup and coffee made her want to vomit.

Mama and Aunt Prudie tried their best to keep up a pleasant conversation while they worked together in the kitchen. They chatted about the new drugstore that had just opened up in Burton, and about the neighbor across the street putting in gasoline pumps, which everybody thought was a silly waste of time and money, since nobody in Burton even owned an automobile. They shared a new recipe for applesauce cake Mama had found in one of Papa's newspapers. Sunny dried the dishes and didn't speak a word to either of them.

Right after they finished cleaning up, just as Sunny was taking the last frying pan from the dish drainer to dry, Papa stepped onto the kitchen porch. His boots thudded hollowly. She thought she recognized the sound of them even before he pressed his face to the back screen door. "Anybody in there?" he hollered out, and Sunny nearly dropped the pan flying to unlatch the door for him.

He lifted her in a giant hug and he didn't let her go for the longest time, not until he spotted Mama standing there behind them with a dishrag in her hand. He set Sunny back on her feet and he said, his voice solemn but with surrender in it, too, "All right, Theresa. It's time for you to come on home now."

In later years, whenever Sunny thought about that time in Burton, she wondered if maybe it wasn't just a little bit her fault that Mama and Papa stayed together. Hers and Gil's.

Gil was out in front of the blacksmith when they all headed off down the hill to the train station. Sunny didn't think either Mama or Papa noticed him there. They were too much concerned with each other, Papa telling Mama the price he'd gotten from Mr. England on the yam crop, and Mama listening, nodding, probably spending that money inside her head. Gil was stooped down beside somebody's shaggy workhorse, pulling off an old shoe from the horse's hoof. He acted busy and like he didn't see them either, except for a glance right at the last second. Sunny wanted to wave good-bye. She started to lift her hand, but a frown slipped over his face and he repositioned himself with his back to the road, and to her.

Sunny kept walking down the hill, but later she wished she'd gone ahead and waved. If she had, then maybe he would have, and she'd have known he still liked her, and that they could stay friends. Just that one missed wave might have made the difference. It might have changed everything.

Part One

PRIDE AND JOY

Chapter One

CRAWLEY LANGE DELONY WAS born on the Fourth of July, 1914. Mama named the new baby after both sides of her family. He had tried to come breech and Doc Rutherford had to be summoned. The doctor managed to turn the baby around in time, but the forceps left a little notch in his right ear, so Papa started calling him Ding. The nickname stuck.

For the two weeks of Mama's convalescence, Aunt Prudie came to help with the baby and the housekeeping, but she left the rest of her family in Burton. She said Uncle Nolan's smithing business was just too busy for him to come, and the boys were both working for their Uncle Walter, Nolan's brother, who farmed a cotton patch outside of Brenham. She didn't mention Gil by name, but just her saying *the boys* was enough to cause Sunny's heart to bloom. She knew Gil was there, inside that phrase.

The families didn't get together at Thanksgiving or Christmas either. Uncle Nolan had his Dailey relatives close around Burton to share the holidays with and Papa had family all over McDade. And as Mama said, Ding was still too little to do much traveling.

Mama fussed over Ding like he was a little prince. After waiting thirteen years to add on to the family, she was like a brand-new mother. Papa was proud about the baby, too, especially since he was a boy and would carry on the DeLony name. Papa had only one brother, Uncle Nathan, who had died in 1898, leaving just two daughters, which meant Ding was the family's last chance. It was an important thing to Papa, yet he didn't dote on the baby the way Mama did. He still sat out in the barn of an evening, daydreaming and whittling stick whistles out of hickory.

With Ding's arrival, a lot of the chores fell to Sunny. Mama kept up with the cooking, but laundry and other housekeeping became Sunny's to do after school or on Saturdays. Even though the family didn't attend a Sunday service — Papa having been raised Baptist and Mama, Church of Christ, so that they could never get settled on a church home — Mama was still adamant about no work being done on the Lord's day. Papa didn't pay much attention to her rule, but he did keep it to close-in work, tending to the animals and the farm tools or the woodworking he liked to do, things close in to the house.

Sundays were for visiting, and for big meals, and porch sitting. Mama had an old glider on the front porch where she would rock Ding on warm Sundays and wave at the neighbors passing in their buggies. Aunt Karen, who was the widow of Uncle Nathan, might stop by with Julianne and Turner. Or Papa's sister, Aunt Dellie, might show up driving her Franklin automobile.

Aunt Dellie was married to Uncle Daniel O'Barr, who was a cattle rancher with a big spread of land and a law degree from the university in Austin. They lived in a two-story house with castle peaks and stained-glass windows, big wraparound porches, and a regular cleaning woman. Uncle Daniel had bought the first automobile in McDade. He had the first inside bathroom plumbing put in, the first private telephone, even before Doc Rutherford had his line installed. But Aunt Dellie wasn't one to just sit in her big house all day admiring her pretty furnishings. She was a free-thinking woman and whenever she came by, it was usually Papa she came to see.

They talked about the war that had started up over in Europe. Their papa had fought with the Confederacy at Shiloh and Pea Ridge, and Uncle Nathan had received his eventually fatal wound roughriding with TR up San Juan Hill in Cuba. He had died before Turner, his second daughter, was even born. In Papa and Aunt Dellie's opinion, the DeLonys had given enough to war and just the chance of one involving America brought dread to them both.

"It's nothing but a family squabble over there," Papa said of the European war, meaning between the crown heads of Britain and Germany and Russia. "Not one damned bit of our business." Aunt Dellie agreed with him.

When the *Lusitania* was torpedoed and sunk in May of 1915, drowning 114 Americans, including women and children, Aunt Dellie came running over with the Bastrop newspaper clutched in her hand. "Oh Dane, this is just liable to do it," she said, almost in tears. Then she went out and joined the Women's Peace Party. She was in the delegation that marched with signs up the steps of the capitol building in Austin.

Mama thought it was a pure disgrace for a woman to make such a spectacle out of herself. But then, Aunt Dellie had been a paid lecturer for the women's suffragists for years, was said to have even done some jail time, although that was a subject of discussion Papa wouldn't allow. But being around Aunt Dellie caused Mama to act unnatural. She pretended interest in worldly topics, then gave away her ignorance by laughing at the wrong things. She put on airs, getting down the good china to serve coffee and wearing her best ruffled apron.

One summer, Mama spent a good portion of her grocery money on some thin colored paper she stuck to the front-room windows so as to make them appear like stained glass. Nobody was fooled, and practically the first thing Ding did once he learned to pull himself up was to take one of the wooden blocks Papa had made to that window. Ding scraped away the whole bottom foot of paper before Mama caught him and tanned his little behind.

As the months wore on, Sunny found herself spending more and more time out in the garden. At first it was just another chore, but gradually it became an excuse to get out of the house and off alone for a little while. There was a soothingness to garden work, a real joy in watching something she had planted with her own hands take root and sprout and come into flower.

Anyone who cared to look could see Sunny was flowering herself, maturing. On the heels of the onset of her monthly cycles came breasts that ached and got in her way, until finally one Saturday Mama took her up to Flaxman's for a first-timer's corset. "This'll keep you from fluttering up top so much," Mama said as she snugged in the lacings.

The corset made Sunny feel like she was wrapped in lumber. She couldn't bend without losing her breath or even slouch without getting a pinch in the ribs. She had to learn how to kneel to pick up Ding, to sit tall and straight in school all day, and the horrible thing itched like it was full of lice. Sometimes she couldn't resist jabbing a pencil down in there to scratch. And the pretty embroidered corset covers Mama made, with tiny sateen roses and shiny pearl buttons, didn't change Sunny's opinion either.

Becoming a woman wasn't easy. Besides having to wear hot, stiff clothes, she had to learn to twist her hair into a roll at the back of her neck. The sides Mama trimmed just below jaw length, so that when the roll was in place and pinned just right, her hair looked like a cap on her head. A psyche knot it was called in the beauty pages. It was the newest style, the same way Mama fixed her own hair in ripples and ringlets framing her face. Except that no amount of smelly waving lotion or heating rods could make Sunny's hair hold a curl for long. She hadn't inherited that thick, glossy brown Lange hair. Hers was more like Papa's hair, except lighter and redder. Strawberry blond, Papa called it. Board straight, Sunny thought. It caused Mama no end of torment. "Get that hair out of your eyes, child," she said at least a dozen times a day.

The summer of 1915, Aunt Prudie sent Calvin to help Papa on the farm. Calvin had just turned eleven, but he was small for his age, and hard to wake in the mornings. As soon as he arrived, Sunny found she still hadn't forgiven him for tattling that day after all those games of marbles. She could barely even be nice to him. She thought Papa seemed dissatisfied with him, too. But Mama enjoyed how well Calvin ate, and he did bring a new picture of Gil.

The picture wasn't of Gil only—the whole Dailey family was in the photograph. But when Sunny looked at it she didn't notice Aunt Prudie or Uncle Nolan, sitting so stiffly, or Calvin standing just behind his mother, straining to see over her fancy feathered hat. It was Gil who Sunny focused on, so grown-up and tall, looming there behind Uncle Nolan. His tie had canted a little off center and his collar appeared to be choking his neck. His hair was combed to one side, but even slicked down tight it still seemed on the verge of springing free. A faraway look was on his face and Sunny wished she knew what he'd been thinking about at that moment when the photographer clicked the camera lens.

One Sunday afternoon, while Mama sat out on the porch with

Ding and Calvin, Sunny took the photograph down from the spot where it stood on the mantelpiece and carried it into her room. She closed the door and propped the frame beneath the dresser mirror. For several minutes she studied Gil's face, comparing it to her own, back and forth, before she decided that there was no resemblance between them at all. Not a smidgen. Even if they were blood cousins, half the same inside the way Mama had said, just by looking Sunny didn't think there was a soul in the world who would ever guess.

THE WAR IN EUROPE kept raging and another one broke out down in Mexico. When the Mexican war strayed over the border into the United States, Mr. Wilson sent Black Jack Pershing to quell the trouble. Aunt Dellie's son, Gabriel, quit his college studies to join a cavalry unit of the National Guard and Aunt Dellie threw a conniption the likes of which nobody in the family had ever seen. She drove from one house to the other, in desperation, enlisting everyone's help in changing Gabriel's mind. Papa spent one long, worrisome evening over at their house, but to no avail. Gabriel went off to El Paso anyway, determined to help Pershing root out Pancho Villa.

At school, Miss Plimper began holding ten-minute sessions of "intelligent patriotism," wedged in between parsing verbs and long division. Out on the spit-and-whittle bench in front of the barbershop, toothless old men who had fought under General Lee and John Bell Hood began to argue the merits of "reasonable preparedness." Everyone had an opinion, and everyone knew where everyone else in town stood on the issue.

One side effect of all this war was an unexpected bit of prosperity. The French and British soldiers fighting in France needed meat. So did American troops in Mexico. Uncle Daniel O'Barr and other local ranchers had plenty of beef cattle to sell them. Cotton prices went soaring. Papa got the most money ever for his yam crop. Late in the spring of 1916, he decided to break out some new land he had just inherited from his old stepmother, who had died the winter before.

Even though Papa had never gotten along with the old woman, she had written a will dividing her 501 acres evenly among Papa and Aunt Dellie and Aunt Karen. Since Aunt Karen had lived with the woman and cared for her for so many years, she got the big house, too. But being a schoolteacher, Aunt Karen had no desire to run a farm, and so almost before Uncle Daniel, who'd forever been the old lady's lawyer, finished reading out the will, Aunt Karen had sold all but twenty acres of her inheritance to Papa. In one day, Papa more than tripled the size of the farm. He came home, walking proud from the buggy shed.

The Lange family had moved around too much for Mama to get in much schooling as a girl, but she could add and multiply and it didn't take her long to figure out how much, at twenty-five dollars an acre, Papa had paid to Aunt Karen—a sum of money Mama never dreamed Papa had in the first place. It was the only time Sunny could remember hearing her parents raise their voices at one another. They kept it behind their bedroom door, but she could hear them anyway, especially Mama, shrill and shrieking.

"Don't you ever think about what I might want? Don't you ever even think about me at all? Or these kids? We need us a new house, Dane DeLony, a lot more than we need that land. One that ain't about to fall down around us. With a better kitchen, and a new stove that don't smoke up everything. And I want to take a trip someplace. I need new clothes, and so do the kids. I'm tired of living like church mice. I want luxuries same as other people have got. I want an indoor bathroom like Dellie—"

"And maybe you'll be wanting yourself a new husband, too!" Papa shouted just before he slammed the door behind him, his pillow gripped under his arm, storming out to sleep in the barn loft.

Sunny lay in bed awake nearly all that night, worrying. Mama had gone too far asking for that inside bathroom. Anyone who knew Papa knew he would never agree to such a thing. He didn't believe outhouse business ought to take place inside the same walls where he ate his meals. To him it was uncivilized and unsanitary. And he'd been living one way his whole life with no intention of changing just to suit a woman's fanciful notions.

After a couple of sullen, tiptoeing days, Papa took Sunny aside and asked her to look after Ding while he carried Mama into town. He wasn't talking about McDade, either. He meant all the way to Bastrop, which Sunny well knew was where the courthouse was located. She watched them pull away from the house, their backs stiff, sitting apart, Papa whipping the lines down on the mules' backs. People whispered about divorce, the terribleness of it, how it ruined lives and disgraced families. Lovie Brast, who had run the local cathouse until it was finally shut down by the sheriff, was said to have been a divorced woman, and so was Gladys Matson. She'd had her kids all taken away from her and had to wait tables up at the depot cafe. Sunny wondered what would happen to her and Ding if Papa and Mama got divorced. About all Sunny got accomplished that day was rocking Ding down for a nap on the first try.

After sundown, Mama and Papa came back with two new, brown-wrapped floor rugs sticking out of the wagon gate. Mama said they had picked out some new furniture, too, and gone to the picture show while they were in town, a Charlie Chaplin picture. "Your papa nearly split his sides laughing," she said, glowing at him with complete adoration in her eyes. Sunny watched, mystified, as Mama went to work cooking them a big supper of fried ham and potatoes, and she didn't even fuss about Papa dumping chowchow all over his. She let Sunny, and even Ding, stay up past nine o'clock that night.

The next evening, after the new furniture had arrived, Mama sat down at her fancy mahogany ladies desk where the old wash-stand had been and wrote Aunt Prudie a letter. Papa hadn't given up his easy chair and it looked out of place amongst all the new modern things, but he sat there as usual reading his newspaper. Sunny lounged on the bright green sofa, trying to get used to the way the front room now looked. She pulled Ding up beside her and pitty-patted his little hands. It made him laugh and scream, "More. Do more." Mama seemed to be having a good time over at her desk, too, dipping her pen into the inkwell, asking Papa every now and then how to spell certain words, like *practically* and *probably* and *desperate*. Big words stumped her.

When she finished the letter, she ran the blotter over the paper, then waved it in the air for the ink to dry. She said, "Listen to this now," and waited for Papa to put down his paper before she cleared her throat. She wasn't a good reader, even when she herself had written the words. She pronounced all the *a*s and *the*s slow and clear. "Dear Prudie and all," she read. "You know I don't write letters much since my spelling is no good, but it has been a while and time for us to say howdy. We are fine. Ding is growing like a weed and talking some finally. We didn't any of us think he ever would do nothing but grunt. Sunny is about done with school for this year. You ought to see that girl's garden. She has got okry as high as a man. Dane has some new land to break, which is partly the reason for this letter.

"Prudie, we was wondering if there is any way for you and

Nolan to spare Gilbert this summer. You know I would never ask except Dane is desperate for help. It ain't that we don't want Calvin. He is always welcome in this home. But Dane says this is heavy work he has got this time, and he just feels like Gilbert is the best one for it. But you know, Prudie, I will have them both if you see fit."

As Mama read, Sunny's face slowly fell slack. And every time the word *Gilbert* came from Mama's mouth, Sunny felt herself flatten deeper into the green sofa. But her attention stayed absolutely on Mama and nowhere else.

"We will take the best care of Gilbert, see he's fed proper, and keep him out of trouble. Dane will fix him a good place to sleep out in the loft. It is empty of hay this time of year, and you know how clean Dane keeps his barn. We got no rats that I have seen. It will be like Gilbert having his own house out there practically. If you can spare him we sure could use his help, and he could probably sure use a little money in his pockets. Our love to all, Tessa." Mama looked up from the letter. "I put in that last part so she'd know we're planning to pay him."

"I wish you hadn't of invited Calvin," Papa muttered.

"Why, Dane!" Mama said, scolding but with a flirty smile on her face. "You know he's a sweet boy."

"And worthless." Papa shook out his paper. "It's a fine letter, Theresa. We'll go tomorrow after an envelope and a stamp."

Ding rested heavily against Sunny's side, almost asleep, and the only movement Sunny allowed herself was to stroke his baby hair away from his forehead, cooly, calmly. But what she needed to do was to go running around outside the house, down to the creek to splash through the water, to throw her arms up at the stars and shout thank you for finally, *finally* granting her wish.

"I don't know how she's going to feel about him sleeping out in the barn, though," Mama said, a note of doubt rising in her voice. "You just never can tell about Prudie."

A week and a half later, the following letter arrived:

May 11, 1916
Dear Tessa,

We have talked it over, and Nolan says it will be fine if Gilbert comes to spend a few weeks. Calvin will go to Walter's. I wood not do such a thing to my baby sister. You have only got Sunny and Ding. You don't know how much it takes to feed these 2 boys.

Gilbert has school till the 19th. He will come on the 25th if that is alright with you, on the 10:45 train to McDade. Tell Dane dont work him plumb to death.

Your sister,
Prudie

Chapter Two

THE FIRST FEW DAYS after Gil came, Sunny could barely think straight, let alone talk, especially not to him. As soon as he stepped down off the train, she knew everything had changed. He wore a man's vested town suit, had a shadowy stubble above his top lip. He was seventeen that summer, practically a man, and he stood taller than Papa, wasn't the least bit awkward in his body anymore. He moved along easy, almost with grace, though when Sunny thought about it later—as she couldn't help but do, since he had taken over her mind completely—*grace* seemed an odd word to use about any boy, or man.

She stayed so addled she didn't notice Mama watching her, watching Gil, too, looking for signs of any rekindling of the puppy love between them. Sunny handled the distraction of him the only way she knew—by ignoring him. It was easy enough to do during the day when he was gone with Papa over to the new land working. And at night he slept out in the loft, so it was only breakfast and supper she had to deal with, and the best way she found was to pretend he wasn't there. If Mama took this for disinterest, it was her own misjudgment.

Sometimes Gil tried to talk to Sunny. At least he would aim part of the supper conversations he had with Papa and Mama at her, but she never piped in with an opinion or even let him catch her looking in his direction. She gave her attention to Ding, helping him use his spoon properly, wiping food that spilled down his chin, serving more mashed yams onto his plate. She pretended not even to hear the talk around the table, or Gil's voice.

Disrupted. Off balance. That was how she felt. She lay in bed at night trying to fall asleep while the lantern light from the barn shone through the cracks in the walls, fell out the open doors and across the chicken yard to glow against her eyelids.

They were gone by daybreak, he and Papa, and they stayed gone all day, eating sandwiches or cold fried chicken at noon from a syrup bucket Mama packed each morning. It was nearly sundown when they came home, hot and tired and dirty, dragging over to the cistern, both of them, to wash up for the evening. Sunny was always out in the garden by then. She made it a point to be there.

Papa would bathe off neatly, bending at the waist to cup the water to his face, scrubbing away the day's grime. Then he would dry his hands and arms and hook the towel back on the nail where it stayed until wash day. But Gil, he was rangy and messy, yanking his shirt over his head, washing his armpits and neck, the water sluicing down his belly to wet the waist of his britches. Sometimes he dipped his whole head into the cistern and came up shaking off like a hound, water spraying in shimmery droplets all over everywhere, like sequins in the last bit of sunlight. Sunny couldn't pull weeds when Gil was bathing off. She couldn't pick ripe vegetables or sprinkle the plants.

After six days of this, she looked up from harvesting pole beans one evening and there he was, right in front of her, his hair still wet from the cistern. He had on his plain gray shirt, the one with the tiny snag hole on the back yoke, like a prick from barbwire, or a burn from a spark of fire. She knew that snag because she had ironed the shirt. She knew about all his shirts.

The sight of him standing there, with nobody else around, startled her so much she nearly dropped her whole apron full of beans. She probably would have, too, if she hadn't already been sitting in the dirt, gathering off the lower vines.

"You do all this by yourself?" He motioned at the garden plot.

"Papa runs the turning plow for me," she answered, proud of how fast she recovered her wits. She didn't know how he had managed to sneak up on her so quietly. "And he hung the fence, too." Which Gil was leaning on, and it was just chicken wire, not sturdy enough to hold his weight. "We had to trench it in to keep out rabbits."

He nodded, although without much interest. "Ma tries to get me to help her in her garden. But I got to say, I've just about had it with any kind of dirt work. Soon as I'm through with school, I'm packing up, heading out. Ain't ever looking back."

She folded her apron around the beans. "Where're you planning to go?"

"Someplace else." He glanced at her bare foot, which was curled in next to her. She'd left her shoes over beside the gate. She tucked both feet underneath her skirt. "I'm going to get me an automobile," he said, "and then I'm going to hit the road. Maybe go to New York City, or up to Alaska to see if I can strike gold."

She laughed out, shrilly, excessively—nerves. She pressed the back of her wrist to her mouth and looked away. His eyes lingered on her for a few seconds—she could feel them—before he stepped over the fence like it wasn't there, ignoring the gate. He mashed a squash plant with his thick-soled work boots, but she didn't say anything.

He came down through the okra and tomatoes, looking all of it over like a judge at a county fair. He snapped off a big yellow okra bloom as he passed, ruining the okra pod that would have come. He twirled the flower between his thumb and forefinger and kept coming toward her. Without the fence separating them, she had a sudden urge to jump and run.

"I'm only going to be here a month," he said. "Did you know that?" She shook her head and stared at the whirling maroon inside the okra flower. He stopped three feet in front of her. "Yeah. That's all she's going to let me stay."

Sunny knew he meant Aunt Prudie. He didn't have to say it. "No wonder Papa's slave-driving you if that's all the time you've got."

He chuckled and studied the flower twirling in his hand. "He's not exactly slave-driving me." He glanced back at the house. "I bet Aunt Tessa's standing beside one of those windows up there right now watching us."

"If she is, she can't see me." Sunny motioned at the tomato plants shielding her from the house.

His face took on a mischievous glint and he suddenly squatted down to her level. For an instant he seemed like the boy he used to be. "Now we'll see if she's been in there watching." A breeze riffled his hair; it stirred the willows down by the creek.

"Do you have a sweetheart?" she said, without even listening for the back door, or Mama.

One of his eyebrows lifted just a twitch. "Do you?"

"I asked first."

"Well, I asked second."

She laughed, feeling bashful, awkward. She shook her head.

"Nobody special." Nobody at all, but she didn't want to admit that quite yet.

"Remember how we used to be . . . friends?" He stuck the stem end of the okra flower behind her right ear. She nodded and reached to touch the flower, but he caught her hand. Dirt sifted from inside her palm.

She knew he was about to kiss her again, saw it before he leaned forward, and so she rose toward him. A few of the beans slid out of her lap. Both her arms slipped around his neck, and that might have been what surprised him, but whatever the cause, she upset his balance. As he fell forward onto his knees, his arm locked around her waist to keep her from falling, too. But she was already reaching again for his mouth, and he saw that, and all at once the whole mood between them shifted.

He grabbed her up tight—tight enough to squeeze the breath out of her—and kissed her strong, pressing her lips apart, touching his tongue to hers. It felt dangerous and daring for him to do that. The flower fell from behind her ear. Picked beans scattered all around.

Just as quickly as they had come together they broke apart. He stared at her, his cheeks red, damp brown hair everywhere. He sat back on his heels. She sat back, too, legs outstretched in front of her, hands flat in the dirt behind her, holding her upright. Her chest heaved like she'd been running. So did his. Sweat beaded in front of his ears.

"Did you hear something?" he said, huffing into his fist.

She shook her head. She saw him swallow, watched his Adam's apple move up and down his neck.

"Here." He started gathering pole beans. They were spread all over the ground. She cupped her apron like a basket and started gathering them, too. She wanted to reach over and kiss him again, to touch his hair. He caught her watching him and he dropped a handful of beans into her apron. "It's probably best we don't go inside at the same time."

She nodded, plucked up one bean from beside her knee.

"I'll go in first," he said. She nodded again and he stood up, dusting dirt off the knees of his clean britches. "I don't see why we can't talk to each other, do you?"

She looked up at him and shook her head. "I guess not."

"All right then, don't be so quiet all the time. It's suspicious."

"It is?"

"Yeah. To them." He sounded angry, but he smiled one of those slow-breaking smiles he had that made three creases in his cheeks, like ripples on a pond, one rising above the next until his whole face was lit. "If I didn't know you ..." He laughed. "If I'd never seen you in my life, I'd swear you look like somebody's been kissing you."

She chucked a bean at him, but didn't come anywhere near hitting him as he hiked himself over the fence and started for the house.

THE FIRST NIGHT HE came to her window, she nearly screamed, thinking it was a prowler in the dark. His face was crosshatched behind the wire screen, his suspenders drawn up over bare shoulders as if he had dressed quickly.

"Get your shoes on," he whispered, and she was suddenly wide awake.

He held the screen while she stepped out, one leg at a time. Every scrape and rattle seemed to echo in the June night. She gathered her nightgown to keep from tripping and ran with him, hand in hand, through the chicken yard to the lee side of the barn, out of sight of the house, and down to the creek. Moonlight glowed on his skin.

They lay down on the sand bank, flat on their backs, and looked up at the stars. When one fell, Sunny squeezed her eyes shut and made her wish. An impossible wish. The same one she'd been making all this time: that Gil Dailey might not be her cousin.

IT GOT TO BE their habit each night, him coming to pull her out of her window, going down by the creek to look at the stars. He told her stories, things he'd read, places he wanted to go, exotic, faraway places. His wanderlust was even worse than Mama's. After he read *Tarzan of the Apes* he wanted to go to Africa. But then he read *South Sea Tales* and decided he'd rather be shipwrecked on a Polynesian island. He lifted her hand up over the two of them so it was outlined against the sky, his hand underneath, longer than hers. "I'd take you with me, of course."

Some nights, though, he wasn't in the mood for telling stories. On those nights all they did was kiss, so much and for so long that their lips seemed to meld together. But when their breath started coming short and fast, he would suddenly extract himself from her arms and sit up, elbows resting hard on his knees, hands gripping his temples like a vise, staring down at the ground between his feet. If she tried to touch him then, to stroke his arm or lay her cheek against his shoulder blade, he wouldn't respond. It was as if he had turned to concrete.

In the daytime, she hardly dared glance in his direction for fear he would glance back, and those nights and those troubling kisses would be plain on their faces. Neither of them got enough sleep. Sometimes after lunch she dozed off rocking Ding, who was spoiled to rocking and wouldn't take a nap without it. How Gil made it through his days, she couldn't imagine. Grubbing new land was the hardest work there was to do on a farm. Yet every night he would slink up to her window stealthy as a cat and she'd be waiting for him.

Once they fell asleep twined together on the creek bank. Only a possum in the woodpile roused them, or roused Gil rather, and he shook the sense back into her. Over breakfast that morning, Gil looked especially worn out and Mama worried he might be trying to get sick.

"I'm all right, Aunt Tessa," he said, but Mama put her hand to his forehead anyway.

"Well, I'm going to fix you another pillow. That one you got out there is flat as a board. You can't get a good night's rest on a flat pillow."

Sunny kept her head down and stirred Ding's oatmeal like it was the most important thing in her life.

For Ding's second birthday, Mama decided to throw a big party. She baked a white cake and sprinkled colored sugar all over the top. She invited the relatives and a few close neighbors. Ding was Mama's darling and she wanted to dress him up, show him off.

The day before the party, Aunt Prudie and Uncle Nolan arrived from Burton. Mama cleared Sunny out of her bed and put her on a pallet in the front room. Ding moved in with Mama and Papa, and Aunt Prudie and Uncle Nolan took over the vacated second bedroom. Calvin shared the barn loft with Gil, and Sunny lay on the hard front-room floor, wondering if he missed her as much as she did him.

In the morning, folks began to show up early: Aunt Dellie and Uncle Daniel first; some neighbors next. Aunt Karen came, and Julianne brought her beau along—Sterling Williams, whose father owned the pottery factory where Mama had worked as a girl.

Of course, Turner came too—tall, beautiful Turner, who was smart like Aunt Karen and seventeen just like Gil.

The first thing Sunny knew, they were walking off together, the two of them, talking about some book they had both read, headed toward that special, secret place by the creek. Gil held his hand on Turner's elbow, laughing, smiling at her the way he smiled for Sunny. And while Sunny's eyes were still turned in their direction, Aunt Prudie took her by the shoulders and twisted her around like a rag doll, this way and that, as if to study her, left side then her right.

"Tessa," Aunt Prudie said, just as if she weren't frowning right into Sunny's eyes, "I believe this child got the best of you and Dane."

Mama raised her eyes from slicing Calvin a second big slab of cake, and maybe Mama saw the sulky tears brimming in Sunny, or maybe it was just a mother defending her young, but Mama answered, "She's a good girl, Prudie. Don't turn her head just 'cause she's pretty."

Aunt Prudie's fingers seemed to squeeze a little harder on Sunny's shoulders. "Pretty is as pretty does," she said, almost under her breath, before she loosened her hold.

At the end of that long lonely week, Gil left on the train with the rest of his family. He wouldn't look at Sunny when they all said good-bye. He didn't snatch even one glance after he was settled in his seat by the window. Aunt Prudie waved around him. Calvin waved, and so did Uncle Nolan. But Gil sat face forward like a statue, as if Sunny wasn't out there on the platform, as though she didn't even exist.

Chapter Three

*N*OTHING CHANGED. THE SUN still rose in the east and set in the west. Earth still rotated in its orbit. Only Sunny felt a difference, in the heaviness of the air, in the burden of waking up each morning, of trudging through each day as if she were still the same as she had been before June.

Mid-September, school started. Turner had already received two letters from Gil, which she delighted in showing to Sunny during the noon break between classes. Not that Turner was a malicious person. Gil was Sunny's cousin. Who better for Turner to share his letters with?

At least they weren't *love* letters. He didn't talk about tropical islands or darkest Africa. He wrote to Turner of practical things, everyday things: of helping Uncle Nolan forge iron for wagon bracings and axle springs; of picking cotton for his Uncle Walter in Brenham; of heading for college after his graduation in May. A&M was the college he was considering. He thought he might study civil engineering. He'd always had a head for mathematics.

"He writes the most interesting letters, doesn't he?" Turner said. "You'd think he was so much more than the son of a wainwright. Not that there's anything at all wrong with that profession." She was blushing. Her hazel eyes twinkled.

Sunny handed the letters back to Turner and concentrated on the egg sandwich Mama had made. "We just always say Uncle Nolan's a blacksmith."

"A blacksmith? Oh. Well . . ." Turner pulled the rind off her bologna, using her teeth to strip the thin skin from the red wrap. She had flat cheekbones and a small, thin nose, perfect straight teeth. Sunny wondered if Gil had kissed Turner yet. She threw the rest of her egg sandwich up under the schoolhouse for the possums to eat that night.

The Daileys came to McDade for Thanksgiving that year. They came at Christmas, too. And each time it was the same. Mama and Papa went to collect them at the station, leaving Sunny at home with Ding. She could hear the train whistle all the way out at the farm. A half hour later the wagon would rattle up into the yard and her breath would catch in her throat. Then there they would all be, filing inside, Aunt Prudie with big hugs, Calvin and his scowly smile, looking as if he'd rather be anyplace but there. Once the wagon and the mules were put away, Papa and Uncle Nolan would come to the house, and so would Gil, happy-go-lucky Gil, tossing Ding up a foot in the air, giving Sunny little ruffs on her head. He took to calling her squirt, as if he had outgrown her, as if he had forgotten about last June.

He spent his time down at Aunt Karen's house with Turner. Once Sunny walked all the way there, taking the shortcut along the creek, along the backside of the Dillons' pasture, and around Papa's new wheat field, to stand in the cedar brake outside Aunt Karen's yard. The two-story house of gray cypress looked gloomy in the winter, with all the trees bare of leaves and the grass dead brown. Their old collie dog slept on the porch and Sunny kept at a distance, for fear of waking him to bark. She watched the front windows, but nothing happened. A couple of times the dog sat up to scratch himself and shift his sleeping position. The sunlight faded. Lamplight had begun to glow in the windows before she walked back home.

THAT FEBRUARY, GERMAN U-BOATS started sinking American ships. Papa said, "That goddamned war is coming right to us," like a prophecy. But when British spies intercepted a German telegram sent to the ambassador in Mexico proposing that the two countries join together to invade Texas and New Mexico and Arizona and California, returning to Mexico lands it had lost a hundred years ago in exchange for cooperation with Germany, even Papa got angry.

On April 6, Mr. Wilson finally declared war on Germany. Papa stayed in town with Uncle Daniel and Doc Rutherford and most of the other townsmen, gathered around Mr. Felty's telegraph office at the depot, just in case some other news came over the wires. It happened so fast that for a few days everyone's head swam.

The first person Sunny knew who joined up was Sterling Williams, Julianne's fellow. He asked Julianne to wait for him, gave her a diamond engagement ring, and went off to San Antonio to train as an aviator. Next the banker's son, Pip Meyers, joined the navy; then all four of the Strong boys signed on for the regular army. Uncle Daniel lost half his cowhands inside of a month to the National Guard, including Vernon Jack, who had been the O-Bar-J horse jingler for more than twenty years. Mr. Jack was sent back home within a week, disappointed, humiliated over the recruiters refusing him. Seemed they considered an arthritic cowboy of fifty too old for soldier work.

Enlistment fever spread like a flood. By June 5, the official draft enrollment day, there were hardly any eligible men left in McDade to sign their names. Nevertheless, Mr. Lusby set up a registration table outside his hotel and several of the other townsmen, including the mayor, took turns manning it. They put out placards with the slogans GET YOUR PAL and YOUR COUNTRY NEEDS YOU. Aunt Karen helped with the colored men. Since she taught all their children at the Paint Creek school, they trusted her more than they did any other white folks around. The library ladies and the newly formed McDade Red Cross provided hot dogs and barbecue. Old Confederate soldiers donned their moth-eaten uniforms and hobbled down Main Street behind the flashy fire-brigade band.

It turned into a big holiday, with horseshoe pitching and base-ball games. Mr. Landers made a small fortune selling flagpoles. Just about everyone wanted the Stars and Stripes flying in their front yard, now that the country was at war with the evil Prussians. Atrocity stories about the Germans abounded, of burning Belgian babies, of dragging men through the streets of Brussels on the ends of chains, of boiling down the dead from the frontline trenches for gun oil.

"We're going over there to kick their ass!" Fenton Franklow shouted with a doubled-up fist as soon as he finished signing his name on the registry rolls. Nobody even scolded him for using foul language in a public street. On that day, any man between the ages of twenty-one and thirty could get away with anything short of murder. Mrs. Lusby put a paper Uncle Sam top hat on Fenton's head, gave him a hug and a kiss on the cheek, and sent him into the barbecue line.

After Black Jack Pershing gave up on catching Pancho Villa, Gabriel O'Barr came home from the border. War with the German Hun seemed so much more important than chasing after a small-time Mexican bandit. No one even mentioned the border skirmishes, let alone suggested that Pershing had failed. Gabriel came home a sergeant, with a chestful of ribbons and thirty days' leave before he had to muster at Camp Bowie, the brand-new army camp they were building fast up at Fort Worth.

Sunny never had been close to Gabriel. He'd always been too busy on the ranch working with Uncle Daniel. He was the quiet sort—at family gatherings he tended to keep to himself. Military life hadn't changed his personality much, so far as Sunny could tell. He was twenty that year, underage even for the draft, but in his uniform he looked and acted twice his age. He had a girl sweet on him, Catherine Shanklin from across the Middle Yegua, over in Lee County. She didn't mind telling anyone who would listen that she intended to marry Gabe O'Barr just as soon as he won the war. In July, the Friday before he was scheduled to leave for Camp Bowie, Uncle Daniel threw Gabriel a big party.

As it happened, Gil was in town for the party. He'd come to help Papa harvest corn and to court Turner some more. The evening of the party, he drove Aunt Karen's Oldsmobile right up into the farmhouse yard and blew the horn. That blasting *oogha!* sent the chickens into a panic. One hen dropped an egg and it cracked in two.

Gil wanted everyone to pile into the Oldsmobile despite the fact that the car was crowded enough with him and Turner and Aunt Karen and Julianne taking up the seats. "Come on, Aunt Tessa," he urged. "There's still room."

Mama laughed and held on to Ding's hand. She was already dressed for the party. "You can take Sunny. I'll stay and ride with Dane in the wagon like sensible folk."

"No, I want to stay and go with you and Papa." Sunny tried to hang back, but Aunt Karen and Julianne both reached out for her. Together they dragged her into the car and wedged her between them.

Ding started waving. "Bye-bye, Sunny."

Mama said, "Have fun."

"See? There's plenty of room," Aunt Karen said, but there wasn't. The three of them had to sit sideways and up on their hipbones to keep from getting smushed.

Sunny hated how schoolgirlish her pale blue, sashed-in-at-the-waist dress looked beside Aunt Karen's bold patterned skirt and Julianne's bright pink crepe silk. She didn't even want to go to this party, except that Mama kept saying it would be rude not to. In the front seat, Turner looked pretty, too, dressed in a peach organdy, drop-waisted party frock. And Gil was all suited up in a coat and tie. They laughed and leaned toward one another all the way there. It seemed like the motorcar hit every hole and wagon rut in the road.

When they got to Aunt Dellie's house, Sunny fled up the stairs and found an empty room where she could hide. She lay down on the hard bed and thought that this might just be where she would spend the rest of the party. There wasn't anyone she wanted to see down there. She didn't care to watch all the lovebirds, one pair in particular. She knew she was letting Gil Dailey ruin her life, but she didn't seem to be able to stop. It wasn't in her nature to turn her feelings off and on like a well spigot, or to pretend last June hadn't happened when it had.

For a full hour she lay up in that room watching the sunlight fade, listening to the downstairs noise increase as more and more people arrived. "The Four-Leaf Clover" was playing on the gramophone when Mama found her.

"Sunny! I declare, I've been looking all over ever place for you."

Sunny felt as if she might have dozed for a minute. She raised herself. The back of Mama's hand touched her forehead.

"Are you feeling poor?"

"I'm just not in a party mood."

Mama sat down on the bed next to Sunny. "Did you get your curse today?"

"Lord, Mama, no! That's not it." Sunny glanced toward the window. The first stars were peeping out. Maybe she did feel tearful enough for it to be the curse. "I just can't see celebrating over sending a soldier off to war, that's all. I think we all ought to be crying about it instead of dancing. There's men getting their heads blown off over there."

The room got quiet. Downstairs someone changed the record to a warbling Caruso, but that didn't last but five seconds before someone else changed it again. "Let Me Call You Sweetheart" came filtering up through the floor.

"Sunny. Sunny, look at me," Mama said, but Sunny couldn't see her too well in the darkening room. Her voice sounded low and lecturing. "He is your cousin," she said, and Sunny's heart jumped into her throat. Was she that transparent? Her misery so obvious? "You have got to put your feelings aside. We all want him to know we're proud of him for serving his country and send him off in a fine fashion."

Realizing Mama meant Gabriel and not Gil Dailey, Sunny almost laughed. "Oh, Mama . . ."

"You've been paying too much attention to all your papa's talk. And Dellie is just as bad. Do you know she's got that beautiful piano down there covered with a black shroud? Just on account of it's some brand made in Germany. She said she don't want anybody playing it. Folks have gone too far with all this. They're getting mixed up over things. It's our boys. That's the only thing that matters right now. We have got to support our boys."

Sunny stood up, smoothed the skirt of her blue dress. "You're right. I'm going down there right now."

Mama stood up then, too, confused by the sudden agreeable change in Sunny. Except that Mama never let confusion stay around her for long. It made her feel inadequate and stupid, so she just ignored any attack of confusion that flared up. She felt she'd won an argument and went to talking about something else entirely, who was here already and who wasn't. What the help had set out for snacks. They descended the stairs into a din of people talking and the racket of the gramophone.

Sunny helped with the food table, making sure the silver cookie trays stayed full. It passed the time and prevented her from watching Gil and Turner try to dance. Of course, he was no dancer, but it wasn't his fault. Aunt Prudie didn't allow it, her being such a steadfast Campbellite. Gil had never had a chance to learn. But he had figured out how to hold Turner the right way, and that was mostly what they did.

There were too many people squeezed together for proper dancing anyway. The furniture in the front parlor had been shoved aside to make room, but it still wasn't enough. Doors and windows were thrown open to let in the night breeze and some of the couples had overflowed onto the front porch. The black-shrouded piano became a catchall for hats and purses and drink glasses and napkins. Sunny kept meaning to make her way over there and gather up the empties for the hired girls in the kitchen to wash, but that was the side of the room Gil and Turner tended to occupy, so she stayed away.

On one of her passes through with fresh cookies, she glanced over there and didn't see them, and was just about to have a look out one of the windows when someone took hold of her elbow. She jerked around fast and looked right into the smiling face of Jesse James Peeler—J.J. to anyone who knew him well enough.

He lifted the tray out of her hands and practically tossed it at the table. "I've been waiting all night for you to stop fidgeting long enough to take a whirl with me." His arm circled her waist. Before she could refuse he had already danced her out into the crowd.

She was acquainted with J.J., of course. Until last year he'd gone to school with her. He'd had to drop out when his papa died, to go to work with his two older brothers up at Mr. Seawell's sawmill. She tried to remember if he was one year older than she was or one year younger. Whichever, he certainly had changed since the last time she'd paid attention. He had to bend low to get his arm around her. Part of it was on account of the high-heeled leather boots he wore, but the other part was that he was just flat tall, pine-tree tall. A few inches taller than Gil Dailey.

"My papa won't like me hug-dancing," she said, finally getting her sense back.

"I bet he won't notice." J.J. nodded off in one direction and when Sunny looked she saw with amazement that Papa had Mama up dancing, except Papa wasn't holding Mama nearly so tight as J.J. had hold of Sunny.

She raised her face to peek up at her partner and he peered down at her. He had light blond hair, blue-green eyes, and a deep, dark tan that made his teeth show up. He seemed to like smiling a lot. And he had good rhythm, knew the cowboy schottische and the hesitation waltz. Once he got her dancing, he didn't seem of a mind to give her up to anyone else. Jim Buck Murphy tried to cut in, and Jim Buck was well known to be J.J. Peeler's best friend.

"Nope." J.J. shook his head. "You go find yourself your own gal. I got dibs on this one here."

When old Early Horner showed up with his fiddle and his son-in-law, who played a washtub bass, the older folks started taking over the floor. They knew all the old round dances and the younger couples were left to watch. Mama and Papa were right in there, Mama's face as pretty and flushed as a girl's.

After a while of this, J.J. leaned down to ask Sunny if she wanted to go outside and cool off. She nodded and he led the way through the mob of people standing around.

As soon as they stepped outside, the night air struck Sunny. Some of her hair had come loose from its knot and rested against her neck. She lifted it so the sweat there would dry and let J.J. guide her down the front steps into the yard. They walked right past where Gil and Turner were standing under an oak tree, and despite herself, Sunny stiffened as they went by and felt self-conscious for a minute, like she could feel their eyes following her. J.J. kept his hand at her elbow. Once they were out of the crowd, he slowed down to a stroll. He didn't seem to be headed anywhere in particular. His attention was all on her, and it felt nice to have it so. She wasn't used to it, and she wasn't sure what she ought to say, so she let him do all the talking.

"I'm fixing to go to work for your uncle," he told her. "Me and Jim Buck have both hired on. Mr. O'Barr said we could move into the bunkhouse if it suited us."

"Are you going to do it?"

"Might." He kept his hand firmly on her elbow. "Always wanted to do that kind of work. Rastling steers. Cowboying. You want to go down to the pen and look at the horses?"

She didn't have anything better to do, although it seemed to her that there were plenty of horses to look at lined up outside the house, still hitched to wagons some of them, or buggies. Mules, too. From the looks of the lane in front of the house, it appeared

that half the county had come to the party. She spotted Papa's
mules tied together to a sycamore tree.

"There's my brothers over there." J.J. pointed. He evidently believed that the group of men alongside the hitch fence was what
Sunny had been noticing. "You want to go over and say hidy to
them?"

She saw that the men were passing a crock jug amongst themselves and she knew she probably shouldn't go any farther, but J.J.
had already taken her hand and was leading her toward the
group.

The Peeler family was not considered to be of the highest station around town. Royce and Finis Peeler were always getting
into brawls somewhere, and there was one sister with a baby and
no husband who still lived at home. But J.J. was the first person
her age who had been nice to her all evening, so she went along
with him.

"What you got there, boy?" Royce Peeler said when they
walked up. His tone of voice was low and friendly. He didn't
sound drunk, but he had that jug in his hand. He was almost as
good-looking as J.J., and so was Finis, but then all the Peelers
were good-looking, even if they were just a little bit trashy. Jim
Buck Murphy was standing with them, and so were some other
fellows Sunny recognized: Ben Millage and Corker McCarty. All
of them loafing, waiting for the draft board to call them up.

"Y'all all know Sunny DeLony, don't you?" J.J. sounded proud
of himself, like she was a real prize. "Pass me that jug, Royce."

"Listen at him." Royce laughed, and so did Finis. "Sounds just
like he knows what the hell he's doing, don't he? Your little lady
want a taste, too?" Royce said, and Sunny was about to answer no
and to correct him about being J.J.'s lady, but J.J. spoke first.

"She wouldn't mind it," he said.

"That so?" Royce came down from his perch on the rail fence. Either Ben Millage or Finis handed forward a tin cup and Royce poured it full from the jug. He offered it to Sunny, sloshing some out onto his wrist, which he loudly sucked off. "Here. Have a drink on me, sugar."

J.J. intercepted the cup. "Thanks," he said, and then he turned Sunny away from the group spraddling the fence. One of them made a few protesting remarks about the two of them leaving so soon, but J.J. guided her away.

He put his hand on her shoulder, and it felt awkward to her resting up there. Unnatural, and maybe a little too fast. She tried to shrug away from him, but he kept his hand tight as he walked her down past the carriage shed where Uncle Daniel's Franklin automobile was parked and around back to the horse lot. The bunkhouse was a black blur just over the rise.

"You ever had a drink of whiskey?" J.J. held out the cup. When she shook her head, he said, "It ain't going to hurt you none."

She took the cup and dipped her upper lip into the liquor, and even that small amount burned her throat going down. She coughed. He laughed, fetched the cup back from her and took a big swig, swished it around in his mouth, showing off.

"Now, that'll clear you out good," he said, grinning.

A horse moseyed over to investigate them and that took J.J.'s attention. He extended his arm over the rail fence and talked low and coaxing to the animal until it came over for a pet on its nose. In a couple more minutes, two other horses had come over wanting their rubs.

"Mr. O'Barr's going to give me and Jim Buck our own string to ride," he said. "Wonder if one of these here'll be in it."

He gave Sunny the tin cup to hold, and since she had it she

went ahead and took another swallow. It felt like fire all the way into her stomach. J.J. got so caught up talking with the horses that her interest wandered. She took to gazing around and thought she saw somebody inside the car shed inspecting Uncle Daniel's Franklin. Curious, she took a couple of steps in that direction. She sipped at the liquor in the cup.

"Sure am glad you come out here with me, Sunny," J.J. said, and she turned back toward him. The horses bobbed their heads over the fence rail. One of them snorted. "Get back there, you old coot." He laughed and it had a nice sound. "I've been wanting you to get to know me better for a long time."

She didn't know what to say to that. She just leaned against the fence down a piece from him and the horses, except the darkest one decided to come over to her for a smell. She stepped back, but J.J. stuck his hand out to scratch the creature between the ears.

"Most folks when they get to know me like me pretty good," he said. "I reckon I grow on them." He knuckled the horse's foretop and the animal reared back his head. J.J. glanced at Sunny. "I forgot how you ain't a chatterbox. Most gals you can't get to shut up."

He stepped away from the fence, took the cup from her, lingering a little bit too long on her hand. He drank the remains of the cup in one big swallow, turned it upside down to shake out the last drops.

"How 'bout you, Sunny? You like me all right?"

She opened her mouth, then looked at him, tall and straight as a tree, blond hair like cotton floss. He was sure handsome, but she didn't know what else she thought about him yet. She shrugged. "I like you."

"Always did? Or you're just starting to?"

She heard something over by the car shed again and glanced that way. "Oh, always, I guess."

"Glad to hear that. I always thought you was the cutest thing around here. Smart, too. I remember you was real smart in school."

She kept looking off at the shed. "I'm not that smart, J.J."

"I like how you say my name." He had a grin in his voice. She turned to him. "I wasn't even sure you'd remember who I was a while ago."

"Course I remembered you."

Voices came from the car shed, voices she recognized, and she knew at that instant who was over there. On an impulse, she threw her arms up around J.J. Peeler's neck. He chunked the tin cup down into the weeds and grabbed her up closer than she expected. He laid such a big kiss on her that she started to struggle against him, but he had his arms gripped tight around her. She had to shove hard to push him off. "Stop that!" she said.

"Sunny?" It was Gil's voice, coming from the car shed. He appeared in the clearing holding Turner by the hand. "Is that you? Are you all right over here?"

"We've got this spot," she said, and snuggled up to J.J. again. She reached on tiptoe to kiss him that second time, wrapped her arms so quick around his neck he didn't know what to do. And she hoped—God, she prayed—that Gil Dailey saw it all.

Chapter Four

JULY 12 WAS THE day the man from Austin rode into town driving a brand-new Model T Ford. He came through fast, running Ambrose Dillon's cow off the road and into the yard at the feed store, which was where she had been headed anyway, the smell of those grain elevators strong in her nose. The Model T got the attention of others in town, too, most especially the two old codgers riding the bench outside the barbershop.

The man who got out of the Model T was dressed in olive drab, with a campaign hat on his head and gaiters on his legs. He was on his way to Bastrop and he needed directions. The man and the Model T were scheduled to participate in a parade there, which was the reason for what he called the bunting on his car, the tiny flags, one American and one Texan, attached to the front fenders of the automobile. On the side door hung a banner with some writing that said TEXAS SECOND REGIMENT OF THE NATIONAL GUARD.

Mr. Crager and old Mr. Candlish tottered over to give the man directions, but they couldn't agree on the best route to Bastrop, whether he should go by way of Lottman Hill or along the Alum

Creek road. While they were arguing, several little boys quit their game of tiddlywinks to come over and admire the Ford automobile. A few older boys came as well, and one of these happened to be Gil Dailey, who seemed to have more in mind than admiration for the Ford car. He wanted a look at the motor and he folded back the hood for an inspection.

It was just about the hottest day Sunny thought she had ever lived through and she was doing her best to stay cool, standing in the cross-breeze between the two windows in Mr. Harvey's store. Mama was shopping for new undergarments for Ding. The past few weeks had seen Ding begin to spurt up, and since he was three and completely housebroken now, Mama had decided it was time for some big-boy drawers. Papa had wireworms threatening his yam crop, so he was over at the feed store buying poison. And Gil was supposed to have been down at the post office mailing a letter home to Burton, but Sunny had been watching and he hadn't made it down there yet. It didn't look as if he were going to anytime soon, either. He had started up a nice long chat with the man in the uniform.

She watched him scratch at his neck like he was thinking about something and then point off southward as if he were giving that man directions. Gil wasn't even from McDade, and she didn't think he ought to be pretending to know the best route to Bastrop. The man said something that caused Gil to laugh. She could hear his laughter, but Mr. Crager and Mr. Candlish had returned to their bench and they were making too much noise bickering at each other for her to hear any of the conversation out by the Model T, where Gil now leaned. He held his bill-cap wadded up in one hand and had the other buried to the elbow inside the hood of the car. He and the man kept talking, nodding, smiling.

Papa was always bragging about how Gil could fix anything of a mechanical nature. The week before, he had put new gears on Papa's hay kicker, and before that he had fixed the McCormick reaper that Papa had bought secondhand last winter. Gil's fixing ability was one of the reasons Papa was always eager for him to come to the farm. The other reason was that they got along well. So well that it sometimes felt to Sunny as if Gil had taken Papa away from her. It felt like he wanted to take away everything that was hers.

"Sunny! Come over here and tend Ding while I settle with Mr. Harvey," Mama said, but Sunny didn't move. She couldn't. The man in the uniform had gathered some papers out of his briefcase and handed them to Gil. Gil read them with an intensity that kept her at the window. "Sunny!" Mama said, firmer. "Quit day-dreaming and get over here!"

Gil took the ink pen the man offered. As Gil bent to write, using the car hood like a desk, Sunny said, "No," and bolted through Mr. Harvey's door out onto the sidewalk. "Gil!" She dodged around little Mittie McCarty, who skipped by with a friend. "Gil! Wait a minute, Gil!"

He looked up and she saw it on his face—that mixture of self-pride and wonder, a smile breaking over him—and she knew what he had done.

"No. You can't do that." She snatched the pen from his hand and gave it back to the man. "He's not but eighteen. He can't serve. He's too young."

Gil grabbed her by the arm. "Sunny."

Her eyes lit right on him and she jerked her arm away. "Well, it's the truth. You're underage."

"He knows that, Sunny. Shut up." Gil was nearly gritting his teeth.

"You're absolutely right, young lady. We do require parental signature for anyone under twenty." The man slapped Gil on his shoulder. "I'll be back for that paper tomorrow, son."

"Yessir." Gil folded the paper. "I'll have it ready for you."

"Listen, Gil," Sunny said. "Mr. Wilson has said it in all the papers that he's going to call out the National Guard—"

"We've been called already." The man smiled and she felt the urge to knock his teeth in.

"My cousin." Gil shrugged in explanation. Then his eyes riveted on her like pins. "It's the Austin Motor Truck Company, Sunny. They need drivers—"

"They don't need you."

He ignored that. "And mechanics, and he thinks I can measure up."

"So do I," Mama said from behind them. She was standing on the walkway, holding Ding's hand, but she let him go long enough to come down into the street. She gave Gil a big, joyous hug. "Oh, I am so proud of you."

"I just hope Ma will be, too," he said, and hugged Mama back.

"She will be. I know my sister, and she will be. But you've got to go and send her a wire right now, Gilbert." Mama looped her arm through his and squeezed his wrist with her other hand. She patted his cheek.

The whole scene disgusted Sunny. Even Papa came grinning out of Franklow's to shake Gil's hand. She couldn't believe they were all acting this way, as if Gil's doing something as idiotic as joining the National Guard in the middle of a war, when he didn't even have to, was such a fine and noble thing. She almost threw rocks at the man in the Model T as he drove off out of town.

At home, as soon as all the store goods were unloaded from the wagon, she went off down to the garden, and though it was as hot as blazes, she stayed out there pulling weeds, wiping sweat off her face with the back of her hand. She didn't want to be around any of them, and she was glad when she saw Gil walk off down the road, headed for Aunt Karen's to tell Turner.

By the time J.J. Peeler came by, Sunny was muddy head to toe. He stayed to supper, and he was a big eater, which pleased Mama. She was giddy that night anyway, babbling on and on about Gil joining up, and about Aunt Prudie and Uncle Nolan coming in tomorrow, speculating on whether or not Gil would give Turner an engagement ring before he left for training camp the way Sterling Williams had Julianne. Even with Gil gone off to supper at Aunt Karen's, he still dominated the conversation. Not that Sunny could have eaten anyway, what with Papa giving J.J. dagger glares from the head of the table.

"Do you have to make him feel so unwelcome, Papa?" she said after J.J. had gone. Papa frowned hard and shook out his newspaper, but for some reason he didn't snap back at her. Mama, though, excused Sunny from the kitchen work to get Ding bathed and off to bed. Mama hated a row unless it was one of her own making.

Ding wasn't in the mood for a bath, or to go to bed either. Sunny wiped him with a wet rag and wrestled him into his nightshirt. But when she tried to tuck him in, he clamped his arms tight around her neck. "Tell me a story, Sunny," he begged.

"I don't feel like it tonight, Ding. Go to sleep."

But he wouldn't quit begging, so she ended up scooting him over and lying down beside him. She told him a pirate story, and then one about a boy lost in the jungle and raised by apes. She sang "The Glowworm," which Ding liked to sing along with her: "Glow, little glowworm, glimmer, glimmer . . ."

She stopped singing when she heard Gil tromp in the back

door, listened to him talk for a little while with Mama about what all Aunt Karen had fed him for supper. Mama always had to have specific details: if there were onions in the soup; if the snap beans were tender.

"Sing me, Sunny." Ding pushed at her side, yawned. So she sang "Li'l Liza Jane," but softly so she could hear anything else going on in the kitchen. Before she got to the last chorus, Gil had gone out to the barn and Ding was breathing heavy against her arm.

She blew out his candle and crept to her side of the room. She pulled the folding screen across to partition off her bed and bent to peer out the window. The lantern glowed out in the loft. She wondered what would happen if she just went out there and gave Gil a piece of her mind, told him what a fool she thought he was for joining up. But she couldn't do it, of course. Because now Gil knew—she'd already given herself away that afternoon—how important he still was to her.

IT WAS PAST MIDNIGHT when he woke her, whispering outside her window. He tapped on the frame to rouse her. He was out there fidgeting, leaning backward to glance toward Mama and Papa's window. She rolled her fists against her eyes to get the sleep out, and to make sure she wasn't seeing things.

"Open the latch," he whispered again.

She was still trying to clear her head, trying to decide what she should do. It felt like a recurring dream to her, seeing him on the other side of that screen. "What do you want?" she whispered back at him.

"For you to come out here."

"What for?"

"Just do it, Sunny."

Slowly, hesitating, she reached her first finger down and punched the hook out of the eyebolt. The window screen popped loose and he caught hold of the sash to swing it up and out of her way. She sat still, uncertain.

"Come on." He waved her out.

"I don't have my shoes. I got them muddy in the garden today."

"Well, where are they?"

"By the kitchen door."

He glanced away again, along the backside of the house. "I'll carry you. Come on."

She stepped through the window. The night was humid and it didn't take but him trotting through the chicken yard with her piggyback to work up enough sweat to dampen his undershirt. She held tight to his shoulders. He didn't settle her down until they were on the other side of the barn.

"I don't think there's any stickers right here," he said, searching the spot.

She watched him, almost incandescent in the darkness, and a longing swelled in her chest.

"I should've thought to bring something out here for you to sit on," he said.

"I don't need to sit down."

But he wasn't listening to her. He disappeared around the end of the barn.

While he was gone, she looked up at the sky and took a deep breath. There were so many stars she couldn't make out the constellations. She shivered but she wasn't cold. A kind of heat mist rose up off the creek waters. And bullfrogs chirruped loud and deafening. There must have been hundreds to make such a racket.

In a few seconds he came back with a tow sack, the corners

curled from having been stashed in one of Papa's barrels. Since Gil had gone to the trouble of getting the sack for her, she went ahead and sat on it. He kept standing for a moment, looking down on her. He paced in a circle away from her, like a hound tamping out a place to lie, before he sat on the bare ground beside her.

"Twenty-one spots is all he had to fill. Twenty-one brings the company up to war strength, and he'd already got four recruits in Elgin. No telling how many more he got in Bastrop, with them having a parade today and everything. I had to sign up. I might've missed my chance if I didn't. Driving a truck, Sunny. You know that's right up my alley."

She glanced at him and felt she should be back in her room, in her bed, where things were simple. "You don't have to talk me into it. You've already made up your mind."

"But I don't want you against me."

"Why does it matter?"

"Because you're the only one who is."

"So what."

He chunked a stick in an arc toward the creek. It plinked off the ledge of the old smokehouse. He stretched back, propped on his elbows. She caught his smile, but she didn't feel like smiling back.

"Well?" he said. "Are you going to write to me at least?"

She hugged her knees into her chest, aware all of the sudden that she was in her nightgown only, no corset, no underslips, barefooted. "I hadn't given it any thought." She kept her gown tight around her legs and rested her cheekbone against her kneecap. Her eyes traced his profile. "Are you going to marry Turner?"

He laughed and reached to pinch the skin behind her elbow, a teasing pinch, but it felt more like a caress. "Who said that?"

"Mama. Other people, too, probably."

"I don't want to talk about Turner." He sat up as if he had something important to say. She raised her head off her knees in anticipation, but he didn't speak again. Bullfrogs filled the silence.

Then he leaned toward her and touched her bottom lip with his finger, sweet and light. He pressed his forehead to hers, and it caused the old thrill to surge through her. She flung her arms around his neck and kissed him hard. If it surprised him at all, he didn't show it. He hugged her up, too, and it didn't take but a couple of seconds for the breathlessness of last year's June to overtake them both.

Chills rose on her as his kisses traveled to her neck. She closed her eyes tight and he moved her hair aside to make room for more kisses. He tried to push her nightgown out of his way, too. She felt his fingers on the drawstring but didn't think to stop him. All she could feel was his breath on her skin, his hair in her hands.

The nightgown was more or less a big sack that she stepped into and drew up over herself. So when he untied the knot, the gown didn't just loosen to bare her neck, it fell all the way down to her waist. When it did, a gasp came out of her. He startled, too. Nobody in the world besides Mama had ever laid eyes on Sunny's naked breasts before, and she struggled to pull the gown back up. She got it over one shoulder before he came back to life and bore her down onto the scratchy feed sack. He cushioned her head with one hand, took her breast in the other, and he kissed her there. His mouth caused a peculiar feeling to sweep over her. He seemed overcome, too, like he might stop breathing.

She plucked at his suspenders, peeled them down his arms. He raised long enough to grapple his undershirt over his head and fling it away, and then they were flesh to flesh, pressing, fevered lips and hands. His heart hammered against hers. He let out a soft moan. She kissed his jaw, found his mouth. He gave it to her and his hand slipped under her hip. He lifted her against him and she felt the pressure of him. She hooked her foot behind his knee and their kisses turned to all air.

"Christ, Sunny," he said, rising suddenly away from her. "Jesus Christ!"

She clung to him. "What's the matter? What is it?"

He pushed free of her and grabbed for his undershirt. He raked the shirt on over his head. "You'd just let me do whatever I want to, wouldn't you? Dammit, Sunny . . ." He wiped his face with both his hands, then looked at her. "Hadn't Aunt Tessa ever told you nothing?"

"Why're you mad?" She reached again for him, but he arched away.

"Christ! Don't touch me! Put your gown back on. Here." He grabbed up the drawstring and tied a quick knot underneath her chin. "I swore this wouldn't happen again. Dammit, I swore. Uncle Dane ought to horsewhip me."

"I love you, Gil. I tried not to, but I can't help it."

"Stop thinking about me. Just stop. There's that new fella coming around here. Think about him."

"But I don't care about him."

"Sunny, listen to me—" He took her by both shoulders and kind of shook her, except his desire seemed to come back, and she thought for a second he would kiss her again. Instead, he let go of her as quickly as he had snatched her up. "I'm going to be long gone pretty soon anyway. You'll forget about me then."

"No I won't. I'll write to you every day, Gil, I promise."

"That isn't a good idea. You concentrate on this new fella—"

"But you *said*—" She heard the whine come in her voice. "A minute ago you were *begging* for me to write to you."

"Well, now I'm saying it's not a good idea."

Something in his tone hardened her, some condemning something. The warmth left her face and she stood up, dusted her gown. "It's not my fault, Gil. I didn't even want to come out here with you in the first place."

He stood up, too, shrugged on his suspenders. "Did I say I blamed you for anything?"

"You do, though. I can tell. You always do. Like I tempt you. Like I'm wicked Eve with the apple." She stiffened her chin. "How come you picked Turner anyway? Aren't there any girls for you to go with in Burton? Or do you just like flaunting her in front of me?"

In the darkness, and with the distance between them, he was nothing but a shadowy outline in front of her. When he didn't move and didn't answer her, she felt she had hit on the truth.

She wrapped her gown close to her body and started toward the house. He didn't come after her, or offer to carry her piggyback to her window, not that she would have let him anyhow. She didn't step on any sticker-burs either. She knew her way just fine. Once inside, lying in her bed, she resolved to do exactly what he had said to do. From now on she would spend all her concentration on J.J. Peeler. At least he treated her nice, and looked at her with love-eyes. She would forget Gil Dailey. She would cut him right out of her heart.

*F*ROM INSIDE THE KITCHEN Aunt Prudie yelled, "I send him up here in your keep, Tessa, and look what happens!"

Papa said, "Now, you wait just a minute."

Gil shouted, "Whether you like it or not, Ma, I'm going!"

Sunny wound her arms around Ding and hugged him tight. She tickled his ribs. He laughed and grabbed hold of her hands.

One of the hens came right to the porch steps to peck a seed off Sunny's shoelace. Ding kicked out at the bird. Smells left from dinner drifted through the screen door—steak and onions, and candied yams.

"You ought to be proud of him, Prudie," Mama said. As usual she was trying to soothe everyone. "The boy just wants to serve his country."

"I'm not a boy anymore!" Gil's vocal cords sounded ready to snap. "That's what none of you can see!"

Aunt Prudie said, "Well, I hope you don't think you're a grown man!"

"How about it, Pop? Are you going to sign this paper for me?"

Ding looked backward over his shoulder at Sunny. "How come they's all hollering so loud?"

Sunny rubbed the inside of his hand, rolling up dirt from the creases. He needed a real good soak-bath. "Because Gil's going off to be a soldier."

Ding slapped the rolls of dirt from his hand. "Where is he going to?"

"Across the ocean, I guess. To where the war's at."

Aunt Prudie came slamming out the back door in such a hurry she nearly stumbled over Ding and Sunny sitting there. Sunny jerked Ding aside and Mama came out the back door, too.

"Prudie, wait!" Mama chased her sister off around toward the front of the house. Sunny watched them disappear and thought how odd it felt to finally agree with Aunt Prudie about something.

Ding poked his finger at three freckles on Sunny's arm. "Can Gil swim good?"

"What?" She leaned around to look at Ding's face. He was so serious, and all at once she understood the question. She chuckled. "They'll take him on a big boat, Ding. A ship."

She swept his fine hair up into her hand. He needed it cut, but Mama was so partial to it Sunny figured she would probably have to be the one to get the scissors. She wound a lock of it around her middle finger, making a topknot.

From inside, Gil's voice came full and heavy. "Thanks, Pop."

The soft thud of backslapping sounded. Uncle Nolan never spoke a word. He was the emotional sort and probably worried that he would choke up.

Papa said, "We better get a move on if we want to catch that fella up town this evening."

Sunny blinked out toward the garden. She had squash that needed gathering, both pattypan and crookneck. She took Ding's hand. "Come on with me." She didn't care to be sitting there eavesdropping when they all walked outside.

Halfway to the garden the back screen slapped. She turned in time to see them—Papa, Gil, and Uncle Nolan—trooping down the steps in a line. Gil kept his head bent, eyes fastened on his feet.

Aunt Prudie came running around the end of the house and right into Gil's arms. He leaned down to take her, pressing her between her shoulder blades. She wept loud and mournful. He rocked her a little, side to side, patting on her back. One of the leghorn hens squawked and the rest went scattering across the yard.

Sunny pulled Ding on toward the garden. At the fence she stepped out of her shoes. The ground seemed wavery underneath her feet. She went in through the gate to pick her squash.

Chapter Five

GIL LOST HIS VIRGINITY in Lunéville, and it was a huge relief to him to have it done with. He was nineteen already, a month past his birthday, much later than most of the guys claimed they had lost theirs.

Romeo McKeller found the whorehouse. Rome could find out about anything. They had barely drawn the truck into line at the plaza, barely made it with their bags into billets, before Rome was pulling out a business card decorated with one long red rose that read CAVE ABRIS. He winked. "We got a short leave. Time to see the sights. Time to take the bloom off your lily."

Back at Camp Mills on Long Island, before they had ever set sail for France, Gil made the mistake of confessing one night to Rome the status of his sexual experience, and since then it had become Rome's mission to get Gil laid. Rome claimed the words *soldier* and *virgin* didn't mix. By Lunéville, Gil was tired of thinking about it, tired of talking about it, tired of Rome pushing him headlong into strange girls they passed on the street—"There's you one!"

Rome McKeller was a crude fellow from Lockhart, twenty-two, with big galoof feet and ears that stuck out from his head. He was red complexioned, so he seemed like he was forever blushing over something, though the truth was, he was the most uninhibited fellow Gil had ever met. He drank and swore, told latrine jokes, and bragged about all the women he'd screwed, the kind of guy Ma would hate. Gil liked him immensely.

Rome had been with the Texas Supply Train since the border skirmishes with Pancho Villa, and so being a border rat, he had just made corporal. Gil was Rome's assistant driver. There was another pair of drivers in Rome's squad, Van Winslow and Derek Hardesty, and the four of them had named themselves the Toot Sweets. Gil was the youngest, the dumbest, the most gullible of the group, and these three older Texas boys had taken him under their wing.

He'd never before had friends of his own choosing. Fellows he'd grown up with had all come from church or they had been kin to him in some way, fellows Ma approved of, who wouldn't taint his soul or lead him to the devil. There had never been the opportunity to meet a wild bunch like these Toot Sweets. And even as a soldier, a slick-sleeved buck private, told where to go and what to do, when to eat, sleep, brush his teeth, or visit the privy, Gil still had more freedom than he'd ever had at home.

Red, strap-hinged shutters hung on the front windows of the Cave Abris. The establishment claimed to have only fresh young ladies. Gil let Rome and Hardesty pick out his girl for him. He gave some money to Van Winslow, who spoke the best French and knew how to order wine. They shared the bottle with the girls. They bought another bottle and shared again.

Hélène, she said her name was, a little bitty thing. She sat right down on Gil's lap. He couldn't tell how fresh she was, but she surely wasn't young—probably as old as thirty. No lady either, from places she touched him right in front of everybody. She had pretty hair, though, like a black river down her back. She wore it tied in a purple ribbon, not too much makeup on her face like the other whore, the one Rome went off with.

As soon as the second bottle was empty, Hélène took Gil up four flights of narrow stairs to a cluttered little room above the bar. She wore black garters with tiny American flags stuck inside a satin flower. There was more wine in the room and she poured it, held the glass to his mouth for a sip. He was pretty sure he was already drunk. Some of the wine sloshed down his chin. She laughed, purred, *"Sept francs, m'sieur, s'il vous plaît."* She had to repeat it three times before he understood she wanted her money first.

$\mathcal{R}$OME AND HARDESTY WERE waiting for him out on the street. They had a bottle of Mirabelle cognac, one-third gone. They handed it to Gil for a swig. Rome snapped the black American-flag garter around Gil's wrist.

"Well? How was it?" Rome's cheeks were sharp red points.

Gil shrugged, but he felt fine, elated, like he'd passed a kind of test. He wanted to tell them about her rouged nipples, but he couldn't bring himself to say the words out loud. The three of them looked at each other and they broke into fits of laughter, punching at one another, ducking half-thrown fists, proud of their victory, even with bought-and-paid-for whores. They sang: "Where do we go from here, boys?! Where do we go from here?!" Their voices echoed up and down the cobbles, off the old stone buildings. The moon came down cold and wet through the dark haze of clouds.

Across the street, a Frenchman, his chest full of medals, watched everything they did. He flopped along on crutches, one leg missing. *"Salut!"* Hardesty said, raising the cognac in the old soldier's direction. They shared a round with the fellow, spilled a little more, lit cigarettes. Van came out of the Cave Abris pulling on his greatcoat. They all walked off arm in arm down the street. "Where do we go from here, boys?! Where do we go from here?!" They kept an eye out for any stray MPs, steered clear of the big château where the officers were headquartered. Their hobnails clomped in time.

"Hélène," Gil said during a silence, and they all burst into new laughter. They stopped to pass the bottle of cognac. Gil's feet kept getting in his way and his tongue tangled on words.

They ran into a couple of Tennessee boys from the Third Ambulance Company, and then three from the Missouri Signal Battalion joined them. All Rainbows. All drunk or drinking. All walking with purpose.

"Where do we go from here, boys?! Where do we go from here?!"

They visited one bar and then the next. Gil ran out of money, but somehow wine kept flowing. He lost track of where they'd been, how much they had swallowed, how far from their billets they had wandered.

Cigar and cigarette smoke billowed from a house with an arching doorway. The Tennessee boys led the way inside. Low, dark ceilings. A dog barking somewhere in back. A long-jawed woman as big as a wrestler, with ham arms and broken English, showed them past other soldiers milling—French soldiers, Algerians wearing turbans, Scotsmen with their bare knees shining from underneath their kilts. It felt like a dream. Gil rubbed his eyes.

"C'mere. C'mere, Daily."

Rome was waving Gil across the smoky room. Gil didn't think he could make it, but he wove his way through the crowd and they sat him down. He felt so sleepy he almost couldn't sit up straight. He thought he saw Hélène, and she could speak English now, and she was telling him how much she liked him, how he had pleased her, and in the middle of her telling him all of this he became vaguely aware that his arm was on fire.

"Ne vous énervez pas," the hammy woman said. She continued to prick his skin with a needle. He blinked, came wide awake all at once.

"Relax, pal." Rome stood in front of Gil. "We're all getting them. Didn't think you'd want to be left out."

"Fucking Christ!" Hardesty said from another chair. He was pale in the face, grinding his teeth, looking faint.

Gil watched the fat fingers of the woman pull at his right bicep. A little blood ran out from under her needle. A rainbow, half a black rainbow, reached across his arm, and a pot of gold, and a Texas Lone Star, 117th. She daubed the blood away. She looked at him and smiled. She had some teeth missing. He smiled back.

"Ça vous plaît?" she said.

"Oui, oui. Merci beaucoup." He was speaking French.

SEVEN MONTHS BEFORE, BACK in August, right after Gil was inducted into the National Guard, the Texas Second Regiment had been absorbed into the army. The Texas Supply Train had become part of the Forty-second Division, called the Rainbow Division since it encompassed twenty-six National Guard units from across America, including five hundred Texans, the 117th Supply Train. They drove five-ton Pierce-Arrow trucks, steering wheel on the right side, two men to the cab, open to the weather, the dust, the mud, hard rubber tires. It took muscle to drive those trucks.

Nothing the recruiter who had come through McDade told Gil had turned out to be true. He'd been promised no training camp, but he had spent three months drilling and marching, stabbing sacks of hay with a bayonet and crawling on his belly through fake barbed-wire entanglements. Skipper said they were all soldiers first, no matter what their jobs ended up being once they got to France.

The Rainbows were one of the first divisions to go. Twenty-six thousand men marched up the gangways at Hoboken, four thousand to a ship, packed in like sardines, nothing to do all day but play rummy and puke into the little boxes dangling from the end of each bunk. They had arrived in France the first week in November — cold, shivering wet. They marched halfway across the country, then caught the little forty-and-eight cars and trained it the rest of the way. It was snowing. Gil's feet stayed soaked, even with two pairs of woolen socks.

At Vaucouleurs, he and the other Toot Sweets drew lots and won a hayloft in some farmer's barn. It was frigid, dirty and lice ridden, nothing like Uncle Dane's snug loft back in Texas. No food to eat but corn willy. No fires allowed, no smoking, a habit he had taken up in New York at Camp Mills.

There was said to have been a fellow who, at the camp in Vaucouleurs, had lit a cigarette and been shot dead by a German machine gunner. Gil and Hardesty spent one whole night on guard duty lighting matches and tossing them into the road where this shooting supposedly happened. Nothing. No sign of the enemy. "It's all a bunch of hoi," Hardesty said.

But when they climbed the hill behind their billets they could see, way off on the horizon, right at the edge where the earth curved, a red glow like the coke fire in Pop's forge. When the wind breezed just right they could hear the big guns, faintly, like thunder rolling in the distance. They imagined that the ground underneath them shook. That first time struck a little awe in both of them. Hardesty said, "I think they moved us up too damned close, Dailey."

There was a captain in the French army who drilled them on gas alerts. This captain had been in the war since the first year of hostilities, had been at the Marne when the French drove the Germans back from Paris. Captain Delaveau loved his pinot and he was good to share when the American officers weren't looking. He would take a drink himself, hand the jug to the nearest soldier, then turn to write the name of some gas chemical on a chalkboard. While he was writing and rattling at them in English so broken nobody could understand a thing he said, the jug of wine would make its way around the room until it was empty, at which point Delaveau would send someone sneaking out to the barrel for a refill. The jug would make another round during his demonstration of the gas mask, and another just before class was dismissed. Captain Delaveau was a great favorite around the truck pool. Whenever one of his drills was scheduled, the word spread quickly. He always had a full house.

There were classes in French, too, put on at the YMCA hut. Gil made it a point to go to these as well. He didn't like not being able to speak the language, and he learned fast. In letters home, he referred to the supply trucks as *camions,* the railheads as *la gare.* The base camp became, with tongue in his cheek, *le château,* and among the guys *merde*—shit—was for meals.

At Lunéville, they carried small-arms ammunition, the three-inch shells for the Stokes trench mortar, rolls of barbed wire, heavy marching shoes. The first time German avions flew over, the distinctive iron cross on the underside of the wings, they all climbed down from their trucks to watch the planes dive in the sky. They called out, waved their arms and battle caps.

"You goddamned fools!" Skipper ran around hollering. "That's the enemy! You fools!"

The boys all jumped back into their trucks just as the bombs started hitting the ground. French soldiers, hardened by years of war, raced out to fire at the aeroplanes with their rifles just before the anti-aircraft took over.

Lunéville was considered a quiet sector. It was frozen. Ice covered the trees and shone like diamonds. Gil and Rome drove blankets down to the boys in the Alabama infantry. They went right down into the trenches, which smelled like a cesspool from all the sour humanity, and from the rain that wouldn't quit falling. Resupplying took place at night. Big searchlights swept the heavens through the mist. They heard the guns boom, felt it in their bones. Shells screeched overhead through sparkling clouds of shrapnel. It would have been almost pretty if it hadn't been so deadly. The tired Frenchmen didn't even duck. The raw Alabama boys hit the dirt. A star shell lit the trenches like daylight and Gil saw his first dead body, a fellow with half his face gone, slumped over in the corner of one of the zigzags they came around. He'd been hit by shrapnel during a morning barrage. A quiet sector, but men were still dying.

You had to put it out of your mind, the thought that death was right in front of you. You had to make your short hauls from Lunéville up to the front and hope the engineers had found any mines that might be lurking in your path. You had to think about other things. Gil and Rome talked about women. They complained about the miserable weather and the never-ending slumgullion the cooks served up. They laughed at the latest Kaiser Bill jokes and raced like demons through a barrage of hot fire. They laughed at that, too. You had to laugh to hide the cowardly fear that gripped your bowels and robbed your dignity. And you laughed for your buddy's sake, to keep his fear down, too.

The tattoo on Gil's right arm scabbed over and peeled. It itched like the dickens. The Skipper found out about the tattoos and threatened to bust Rome's stripes. Didn't they know it was against army regulations? Didn't they know tattooing was illegal in France? "I ought to put the lot of you on report," he said, but instead he gave them all freight detail, two days of unloading railcars at the supply dump, hand-bruising, shoulder-aching work.

The Rainbow Division stayed in Lunéville for a month. Gil visited Hélène a couple more times, once with the Toot Sweets and once sneaking off from billets by himself, going AWOL. Breaking laws seemed to come easier each time.

"Poor, poor *soldat,*" said the woman who answered the door. She clucked her tongue at him. "He need *beaucoup* nooky."

He looked at his battle cap, which he held between his sinful hands, and wished he could evaporate back through the door. But then Hélène came down the stairs with her velvet hair and her silky little girl's voice. She called him honey in pretty good English and led him up to her room, and he felt all right again.

GIL AND ROME WENT to the picture show behind the Y canteen hut, a Tom Mix picture with lots of horses and shootouts and Indians. Even without a piano player to provide music, the picture made them homesick. They found a cake stand kept by a little old Frenchwoman. They pooled their money and bought something chocolate. They didn't have enough for any other pleasures. The paymaster hadn't found them in weeks.

The night was as cold as the devil, and damp, but they sat atop a caved-in stone wall, huddled inside their greatcoats, smoked Lucky Strikes, and ate their cake. Gil told Rome about Sunny. He hadn't planned to—the subject of her just came out of the blue.

He hadn't planned to write to her either, but he'd been doing that as well. Back at Camp Mills he'd sent her a couple of picture postcards, one of the Woolworth Tower and another of the tent city at Camp Mills itself. Once they got to France, he'd sent her a Christmas card, and another card on New Year's Day, for her birthday. He'd put a photograph of himself in his uniform into the birthday card, and he'd asked for her to send him a picture, too. But he had yet to get one, or any answer from her at all. He figured she had taken him seriously that night behind the barn when he told her she'd better not write to him. He hadn't realized then that she would be the one he missed the most.

"She's the most kissable girl I ever knew," he said to Rome as they ate their cake. "Soon as I see her it's always the first thing I want to do."

"I knew a girl like that once," Rome said. "But it wasn't the first thing I wanted to do to *her*." He growled and raised his hips an inch off the wall.

"Christ, McKeller. I'm trying to tell you something here."

Rome took another chomping bite of the cake, swept crumbs from his coat. He pulled a straight face. "This the girl that sends all them sweet-smelling letters?"

"No." Gil shook his head. That was Turner. He sometimes got nine, ten letters at a time from Turner. It was almost a joke among the Toot Sweets.

"Ah." Rome grinned. "The one that *doesn't* write."

Gil laughed at how stupid it sounded and felt his ears get hot. He wished he had a big glass of milk to go with the cake. After all the weeks and months in a foreign country, a thing as simple as a glass of sweet milk seemed a distant memory.

"She's my cousin," he said, sounding more melancholy than he intended.

"Kissing cousins," Rome said around a wad of cake.

"Hell, I know it's wrong. I know it." Gil picked a crumb from the corner of his piece. He stuck that bit into his mouth. The cake was surprisingly tasteless.

Rome scooped up a fingerful of the dark frosting, put the whole finger into his mouth and drew it out with a healthy smack. "What's wrong about it, Dailey? She married or something?"

"No, she's . . ." Gil glanced sideways at Rome. "Well . . . you know, she's my cousin. Her ma and mine are sisters."

"Yeah?" Rome shrugged, frowned. "And?"

All of a sudden Gil felt apprehensive talking about this. He'd never mentioned Sunny to anybody before, at least not in the way he'd just done, like he might be stuck on her or something. He didn't want to cause any shock or, God forbid, revulsion. He felt like he'd walked naked through church.

"Yeah . . . well . . . ," he breathed, gathering the courage to tell about Ma slapping the snot out of him all those years ago, right in front of Sunny and everybody. He could still feel the sting and humiliation, how Ma had dragged him out to Pop's shed. The worst part was Gil knew he could've stopped her. He'd been strong enough to, even at fourteen. He could've just slung her off, shoved her away from him. He was too old for her to whip like that. Nights he used to dream about what he would do if he could take back that day.

"See that cloud over there?" Rome pointed. "That's gonna splatter us all to hell. We better get back."

Rome stuffed the rest of his cake into his mouth and jumped down from the wall. He trotted off, leaving Gil staring after him. A dozen yards away Rome stopped to look back.

"Hey, Dailey," he hollered. "You staying out here in the wet, or what?"

Gil shook his head and shoved himself down from the wall to follow.

Chapter Six

IN BACCARAT, THEY WERE billeted inside the *cristallerie*. The factory had shut down with the war and its buildings made into barracks. Almost as soon as the Rainbows arrived, measles broke out. The boys from the Nebraska Field Hospital came around with quinine and aspirin and hot toddies.

Gil came down with the measles right after Rome did. Both of them lay in their bunks sweating like horses. Van and Hardesty brought Camels and chocolate they had procured from somewhere. Van was particularly adept at bartering: a Victrola and several chipped Victor records for a case of field rations; two bottles of Moët champagne for a pair of rubber boots. They drank the champagne with a box of tea cakes Aunt Tessa had sent. The cookies were crushed, but Gil passed the box around and they gorged, drinking the crumbs out of their cupped hands like peanuts.

"Nothing from your cousin, Dailey?" Rome said later, when they were recovering from the champagne binge.

Gil just shook his head and tried to concentrate on Ma's latest. She seemed to think he liked hearing what all she had fixed for supper that night—a pork roast, smothered carrots, and corn bread without wheat flour. She said wheat was being conserved for the troops in France, but Gil couldn't recall them getting any of it. Ma's letter was already four weeks old.

"What color hair does she have, Dailey?" Rome said out of the silence.

By instinct, Gil knew Rome meant Sunny. She had become a regular topic of conversation. Especially on mail day. Rome was getting a little blue, missing home and American girls.

Gil closed his eyes and pictured Sunny's smile in his mind— pretty and fresh, rosy cheeked. "It's red. Light red. Kind of blond *and* red. Her eyes are green."

A silence came while Rome fixed this information in his brain. "She got freckles? Lot of times redheaded girls have got freckles."

"They look good on her. She's real little and cute."

Silence again except for the sound of the war, way off in the distance, sounds they'd grown accustomed to. The few panes left in the boarded-up windows rattled.

"What about her tits?" Rome said. "They little too?"

"Jesus, McKeller," Gil said, yet the thought of that night behind the barn slipped into his mind. Her gown falling down around her elbows. Breasts round and high. How good she felt, and how badly he wanted her. But he could never get Ma's voice out of his head: *Act decent, Gilbert. Don't be vulgar.* How he regretted pushing Sunny away that night, like a perfect damned, straitlaced fool.

He rolled to his side, concealing an erection. "She's gorgeous all over."

Over on his cot, Rome made a groaning noise. "Keep her away from me, Dailey. Once we're back home, you'd best keep her away, or I'll swipe her from you."

Gil smiled, laughed, and shut his eyes to daydream some more.

    A few of the fellows discovered that the metal in the ten-franc piece was so soft it could be bored through the center and wrought into finger rings. Gil watched one of the other guys in sick bay, one of the Ohio boys, work over one of the coins, and he knew he could do a better job. He'd been shaping metal all his life. All he needed was a drift punch, a hammer, and a file. These things he borrowed from the sergeant mechanic in Company C.

    All one afternoon he worked on the ring. He declined the Toot Sweets' invitation to get out on the town for a while. The division band was giving a concert and there was a traveling troupe of thespians performing *Oui, Oui, Marie.* But he stayed in billets, wondering just how small Sunny's finger was. He would send her the ring as a souvenir and write her another letter, a real letter, one like she had never gotten from him before, one she would have to answer. He planned to cast aside the brainwashing from Ma, the shame she had planted in him, and tell Sunny his honest feelings.

    It felt like a big weight lifting to admit he loved Sunny. And he couldn't get his mind off the matter until it was done, declared. First he would finish the ring and then write the letter. He repeated this to himself while he hammered and smoothed. He wouldn't leave one tiny burr to cut her skin. The ring had to be glassy and flawless, the words "Liberté, Égalité, Fraternité" showing upright across the top band. He imagined her delicate, little finger sliding into the ring, the light that would come into her eyes, the same light he could put there when he kissed her, the light that made him feel brilliant and special.

    The letter was more difficult than the ring, putting his feelings down plain and true. He'd spent such a long time hiding them that it almost seemed sacrificial letting them come out. Fleetingly

he thought about Ma, but he'd already broken all her other rules
—swearing, drinking, sleeping with whores—and God hadn't
yet struck him dead.

After a couple of poetic false starts, he wrote what was in his
heart, and once he got started, it seemed to just come spewing out.

1918 May 20
Dear Sunny,

I have been thinking a lot about you and those things
you said to me that last night we were together, those
things about Turner and why I had picked her, and I want
to tell you why. I've only just figured it out myself. It never
was to flaunt her in front of you, or because there weren't
any girls to pick from in Burton either, there were plenty. It
was a whole lot more simple than that. Turner lived at
McDade, and so did you, which meant if I went with her I
would have an excuse to be around you without making
Ma or your folks or anybody suspicious. I thought it would
be enough just to get to see you, but it wasn't, and all the
time I spent down there with Turner I never could wait to
get back to watch you across the supper table, or while you
held Ding, him about as big as you are, or out on the porch
of an evening fanning your face with a page of Uncle
Dane's newspaper. Did you know you turn pink when you
get hot? Well, you do. The prettiest shade of pink all over
your skin.

I've got this buddy here named Rome McKeller. I have
been telling him about you, and I have come to realize
some things. One of them is that I'm nuts about you, and I
don't care anymore who knows it or what they think of it.
If it's one thing I've learned from being over here in this

war, with people getting killed as easy as that, and seeing everything bombed to smithereens, it is that there isn't time for pining and yearning or for beating the devil about the bush. God isn't up there worrying about the small stuff, little man-made sins like who ought to be with who and who is forbidden to who. There's too much big sin keeping him occupied. Besides all that, I believe he wants us together, Sunny. I think we're supposed to be or else it wouldn't have happened like it did. Just look at some people who go their whole life and never find the person that's right for them. You and me found each other early, that's all. I think I knew it clear back to when you were about six and I was eight, and I stobbed my toe on Uncle Dane's old oil can that time. Do you remember that? How my toe turned black and you rubbed it for me. Well, I already loved you then, and I still do.

When I get back home again, Sunny, everything is going to be different. I know I've hurt you before with stupid things I've done. I've hurt myself, too, but I've changed. I wish more than anything that I could see you right now, and hold you and kiss you. I miss you so much it's almost making me crazy. When I get home let's make plans to be together. Hell, let's get married. Why not? I know we're cousins, I haven't forgotten that, how could I? But so what? Nobody gives a damn about it over here, I can tell you that. All these kings and queens marry their cousins all the time, and they don't think there's anything wrong with it. I love you, Sunny. That's what counts. Write to me, please, and tell me you love me too.

I'm yours,
Gil

"Damn, Dailey," Rome said when Gil showed him the letter. "This just about makes me want to bawl." He pretended to wipe his eyes, but when Gil didn't respond, Rome folded the letter and tucked it into the envelope. He scratched one finger on his newly shaven head. Barbers had been on cootie patrol. Everybody in the company was shorn clean. "I'll take this to Sarge myself. I'll say I already checked it."

Gil nodded. It was what he'd been hoping for, the whole reason he'd shown Rome the letter in the first place. Rome sometimes did mail detail. Censoring is what it really was, but nobody called it that.

A couple of days later, a whole batch of soldiers made private first class for no apparent reason, and Gil was one of them. Rome helped sew the patches on Gil's sleeves and took pictures of the event with the Brownie camera he'd smuggled from home. Afterward, they found a French canteen, where they drank their share of the strong-tasting, potent wine sold there.

The boys in the supply train kept up with their small part of the war, running supplies back and forth from the dumps to the front, occasionally carrying soldiers who were hitching rides one way or the other, or transporting wounded when the ambulance corps' GMC trucks, with their fancy pneumatic tires, went on the blink. There was one wounded fellow in particular who haunted Gil, an Alabaman with raw meat and blood where his right arm and shoulder should have been. No matter how steadily Gil tried to lift the stretcher, the fellow moaned, a moan from deep, deep down. One of the ambulance drivers rode in the back and Gil was never so glad to be up in the cab again, away from that moaning. The time they hauled fresh caskets, Rome cursed the war all the way to the front lines.

They were starting to get tired of it. They ran their loads out, came back in, checked over their trucks, ate the god-awful slum, and went to bed. If the roads were torn to hell by the shelling, and no one could go across, they stayed in billets, played poker, peeled potatoes for the cooks, complained about the paymaster, wrote letters home. One day the sun broke through for a while—a cause for celebration—and they were able to wash their clothes. They burned cooties in candle flames, picking them off one another like apes in the African jungle.

The supply train moved into billets closer to the front. The Heinie bastards started sending over a lot of gas shells, so Skipper ran them all through the drills again, herding them into a room filled with a thick, grayish vapor. They all looked like gargoyles standing around in their masks. They missed Captain Delaveau back at Lunéville, and his jug of pinot. Some days the gas Klaxon seemed to sound every twenty minutes, false alarms mostly, but enough to shake up everyone's nerves.

Hardesty got it first, on a short haul with burnishing oil and rifle ammunition. His truck went off into a big new mud hole and got stuck, badly bending the front axle. He'd gone out alone since Van was recovering from a bout with tonsillitis. He was down on the ground, stretched underneath the truck checking the damage, when the gas shells started falling. He'd left his mask in the cab just a few feet away, but before he could squirm out from under the truck, he knew he was done for. Medics took him to the hospital in Vittel, and Rome and Gil visited him there.

Against the white bed linen, Hardesty's skin looked slime green, and his eyes were muggy, oozing, swollen nearly shut. The nurses gave him dry-vapor inhalations twice a day, but he didn't seem any better for it. "I went blind for a while," he said in a flat, dejected voice. "Water flowed out so fast, I thought my eyeballs would wash away. I puke up everything they give me to eat."

"They'll get you all fixed up in no time," Rome said. "Find yourself a pretty nurse to pass the days."

"Ain't seen no pretty ones." Hardesty reached up to swipe at his runny cheek.

Rome said, "Well hell, Hardesty, you'll get yourself a wound stripe for this. Soon as you do we'll all go out and find some whores. They really take to a guy with one of them wound stripes."

But the next they heard Hardesty had been transferred to another hospital, farther back, at Allerey. Later still they heard he was at Tours guarding German prisoners. Wherever he was, they never saw him again. A million Doughboys had landed in France by then. It was easy to lose track of one guy.

The squad got a new driver named Barfield who wasn't even a Texan at all, but came from Detroit. He had a pointy beak nose, eyes so close set they looked crossed, and he talked funny, almost like a colored boy. He complained that he'd joined up to get in some real soldiering. He wanted to jump into it bait, hook, and sinker, except he made the mistake of mentioning that he'd worked at the Chevrolet plant back home, and the next thing he knew they'd assigned him to the 117th. Gil learned an awful lot from Barfield about mechanics.

Mail finally managed to find Company B around the middle of June, and with no excuses for the delay. There were letters and cards from Turner, of course. She was working at the Red Cross hospital in Bastrop now, excited about moving to that town with her sister, Julianne. She sent a picture of herself in her Red Cross uniform, which Rome snatched up and passed around to the other fellows for a look. It was an unspoken pact they had all made. Any pictures from home were to be shared, especially pictures of girls. One fellow from Temple had a whole packet full of smutty photographs, one especially dandy one inside a tiny kaleidoscope. When you cranked the tube, the naked girl belly danced.

Gil was disappointed that no letter came from Sunny, even though she hadn't yet had time to get his. Mail took four weeks or more to make it back to the States, and only two had passed since he gave the letter to Rome. There was a card from Uncle Walt and Aunt Jo in Brenham with a drawing of a Doughboy stomping the butt of a Prussian general.

He saved the letter from Ma for last. She wrote to him every Saturday whether she had any news or not. And she always included some bit of Scripture he was supposed to feel grateful for, like he had time for such things, or cared anymore. He liked hearing news of the family, what Calvin was up to, and Pop. He'd learned to skim through the sermons and get to the interesting parts. This letter was dated April 16. It said:

Dearest Son,
   It is so good to hear from you and know you are well. We got your letter about the villages. Calvin liked hearing about those people in their wooden shoes, and about their fat cows, but Gilbert you stay away from those French girls now.
   I just think it is horrid that the army wont let you tell us where they have got you. Your father beleives he knows, and he keeps a map out in the shop where he keeps track of the Rainbows. I tell him that don't mean nothing about you, being as your driving that truck all over God's creation. You dont know how I worry and pray for you. I just have the worst nightmares about you. I never did think they wood put you in a advanced section as you call it. I

wood have put my foot down harder if I had known such a thing could happen.

Everybody here is just fine. We hear from Turner now and again. She is such a sweet girl to write us. I know she writes you, too. She is doing that Red Cross work over in Bastrop now. Of course, we get news from Tessa. She says she sends you sweets and that you always write back to say thank you so I reckon you must know all about Sunny and her young man.

I cant say as I am the least bit surprised, tho this boy is nearly a hole year younger than she is. Its to his credit that he faced up to Dane DeLony, saying there weren't no need for breaking out his shotgun that he had every wish to marry Sunny and make her honest. Knowing Dane and how he dotes on that girl it is a wonder the boy is still alive. But Tessa says Dane and the boy are getting along fine now. He helps around the farm and they are building on a new room at the side of the porch. According to Tessa this boys family is nothing but white trash so Dane wood never allow Sunny to move in over there. If you ask me that is Sunnys big problem. Her pa has always been bad to coddle her, and Tessa tho she is my dear sister never has taught Sunny right from wrong which I do beleive is how come her to find herself in this pickle now. No telling what will become of the poor baby when it arrives with no more for parents than its going to have.

Well, thats enough of that mess. I was telling Brother Thurston just yesterday . . .

Gil put the letter down and stared at it like it was poison. Then he picked it up and reread the part about Sunny to make sure he understood it. A lump he couldn't swallow formed in his throat. He felt gut-sick and grasped his forehead in his hands. He tried to recall how many times he had spilled out his love for her in that letter he'd given to Rome. Three? Four times? Five? He felt like an emotional fool.

"What's up, Dailey?" Rome was lounging on the next cot over, studying Gil's expression.

Gil said, "How the hell am I going to get that letter back?"

"Which letter?"

"That one I gave you to slip past Skipper."

"*That* letter," Rome said, but it was clear he hadn't forgotten about it at all. "I reckon it's crossing the Atlantic by now. Why?"

Gil held out Ma's letter between two fingers and Rome rose up from his cot to take it. Once he'd read it through, he let out a sigh and glanced up at Gil. "Your ma don't like Sunny a damn bit, does she?"

Gil shook his head and took the letter back.

Rome reached into his pocket for his Camels. He leaned across and stuck one into Gil's mouth. He struck a match. "Fucking women," Rome said, cupping the flame to the end of Gil's cigarette. "You can't trust a one of them."

Gil drew a deep lungful of smoke, blew it out through his nose, and sank back on his cot. He crooked his arm over his head. "Least I never mailed her that ring. Never could find a box for it."

Rome lit himself a cigarette and waved out the match. "Sell it to me." He sat back on his cot. "I saw what a good job you did on it. So sell it to me."

"For what? Who're you going to give it to?"

Rome grinned. "I'll send it to my kid sister."

"I'll bet. You'll give it to some whore."

"What, me? Dailey, you know me better than that. I never mess with whores."

Gil sold him the ring for a hundred cigarettes, but Rome never found a box to mail it home in, either. He wore the ring on his pinkie finger and insisted he was still searching. And he went with a lot of whores, but the ring didn't disappear.

ORDERS CAME TO MOVE. Nobody knew to where. The line of trucks snaked its way over the French hills, going north, then east. Gears clashed. The big Pierce-Arrows swayed to the left, then to the right, like clumsy boats on a sea. They straddled holes, lumbered down into others, sank into mine craters and climbed out on the other side. Each one labored along behind the truck ahead, which tried to draw away and vanish in the misty night.

Rome passed Gil a canteen filled with Mirabelle. Gil took a big swig and passed it back. The cognac flowed down hot enough to take away his breath, but it numbed everything, too. Rome huddled in the corner, tucked behind one of the tent halves they had tacked up over the doorways to block out the wet, but since there were no windshields, they didn't help much. No headlights either. They were moving under blackness of night.

Rain continued to slap at the roof of the cab. The tailgate of the truck ahead came up, faded away, came back again. As the hard rubber tires hit another deep shell hole, the steering wheel jolted out of Gil's hands and the truck veered for the ditch. He came awake with a jerk, unaware till that second that he'd gone to sleep for a moment. He wrestled the truck back into line. Over in the corner, sheltered under the tent half, Rome snored softly.

The truck ahead faded in, faded out. Came. Went. Gil started singing, "I've been working on the railroad, all the livelong day . . . ," to try to keep himself awake. He'd taken over from Rome just after midnight. Dawn was near. It had to be. It felt like two weeks had passed since nightfall.

The convoy moved through what had once been a quiet village but was now nothing but black rubble, not one stone left atop another. Two hundred trucks, all in a line, moved up a long hill with a sweeping curve in the macadam road. To the north the flashes of war became visible. The crump of distant guns grew louder. The Rainbow Division was moving into the sector to relieve the weary men in the front line.

Open portions of the road were draped with camouflage net strung from fifteen-foot poles. Troops tromped past on foot, on horseback, on bicycles, in caissons, and in two-wheel mule carts carrying ammunition for the machine guns. The Pierce-Arrows clambered past ammo dumps with acres of shells stacked up like cordwood in small separate piles. They passed a damaged tank discarded by the road, a crooked graveyard with hasty white crosses scattered around. They passed men coming away from the front with eyes that seemed to glow red in their blackened faces.

"*Vive l'Amérique!*" a group of them shouted, with fists raised and voices loud enough to roust Rome from his slumber.

Rome scratched his eyes, sat up to stare. For a moment he seemed numbed by all that was around them. A pile of dead horses had been shoved off into a ditch. A group of French refugees straggled by, bundles on their backs, stooped old men driving nags, an old woman walking with a cane.

"God, Dailey," Rome mumbled. "This sure ain't no quiet sector this time. They've done sent us to hell."

Gil peered at the gathering light on the horizon. He glanced at the leaping flashes of war, the sounds of high explosives whistling from the valley. The whole world seemed colored in shades of red, orange, and brown. It was mesmerizing, but he forced his eyes to stay on the truck ahead, moving up, falling back. He felt as if a blanket had been thrown over his soul.

Chapter Seven

$\mathcal{T}$HE LETTER FROM GIL came the first part of August. For weeks afterward, Sunny stayed in a dither. She couldn't sleep, barely ate. She drooped around on the verge of tears, the least thing rending her nerves. Mama blamed it on the coming baby. She said, "Don't you remember how I bawled the whole time I carried Ding?" Sunny didn't remember, but it was handy to have an excuse.

Of course, Mama knew Sunny had gotten the letter. Papa probably knew, too, but it was Mama who had brought it in from the mailbox. "Here's another one for you." She had pitched the envelope into Sunny's lap. "I really wish you would write back to that poor boy, Sunny. Prudie says he just loves getting mail." And Sunny remembered thinking how odd it was, with Gil gone off to war and with her safely married now, that everyone wanted them friendly all of a sudden.

She slipped her thumbnail under the flap, pulled out the letter with the red YMCA triangle and ON SERVICE WITH THE AMERICAN EXPEDITIONARY FORCE in bold print at the top, and began to read, expecting more details of army life, more observations on France and the French people, more of the same things he'd written to her in other letters. Letters she didn't seem able to respond to. Instead, halfway through the first sentence, her body became heavy, and the further she read, the heavier she felt. Before she even reached the end she had to tuck the letter into the pocket of her apron and go outside, into the crushing August heat, for air. She finished the letter in the garden, kneeling beside the bell-pepper plants, numb in the shoulders and arms, numb all over.

She folded the pages back along the same seams his own hands had creased. She stared at the envelope, thumbed at a smear of ink beside her name. Such words. Such beautiful words. Why had he chosen now to say them? When it was already too late?

Mama wasn't the only one who noticed Sunny's sudden dreariness. Papa made her a present—a little box he'd sanded and polished till it glowed. He told her, "I was just piddling around the other day," when he handed it to her, as close as he would come to saying he'd made the box especially for her. They had been fragile with each other, she and Papa, since the wedding. For a whole month he had barely spoken to her, but he had finally come to tolerate J.J., and the jewelry box felt like a peace offering, as if Papa thought his own moodiness might have caused hers.

Ding said, "Papa, it ain't Sunny's birthday," laughing his deep little boy's laugh at how silly it was, Papa giving Sunny the box for no reason. Ding had just turned four; birthdays and presents were fresh on his mind.

"I put a locking gadget on it there." Papa showed her the latch on the side where the lid fit flush. "So you can store your valuables in it if you want to."

"What valuables, Papa? What valuables do I have?" She tried to laugh as she held up her left hand. Even the ring J.J. had given her had already turned green on her finger. Everything she owned was worthless.

Since the box had a key, she went ahead and put Gil's letter inside, along with the photograph of him in his uniform that he had sent on her birthday. She put in her last report card from school, too, feeling a little wistful as she did. Well, she had made it through ten grades anyway. Mama said ten was all she would need. J.J. thought she was silly to mourn for something like school. "Hell, Sunny, ain't nobody in my family ever went past the eighth grade," he told her, and he sounded proud.

From the start she had known he was no Thomas Edison. And at first she had even enjoyed that she was smarter than him. She imagined herself teaching him things, showing him the right way to live, culturing him, changing him. She explained to him that it was good and healthy to wash every day. He'd never even owned a toothbrush, and furthermore, she came to realize, he didn't care either. He had bad table manners, would swear in front of anybody, like he didn't understand it to be impolite behavior. One day Papa finally came down on J.J. for talking about "the crapper" right in front of Ding and Mama, and doing it at the supper table. While Papa was certainly no church deacon, he would draw the line at crudity. J.J.'s feelings got hurt and he sulked all the rest of that night.

Yet even as mindless as J.J. could sometimes be, even he noticed something amiss with Sunny.

"What's the matter with you, babydoll?" he said, a few weeks after Gil's letter had come, whispering right up next to her ear in the dark room that still smelled of fresh lumber and new paint. "Don't seem like you want me touching you no more." He put his lips against her neck and she shrank from him.

"Stop it, J.J. You're making me hot."

"Well, that's kind of what I was hoping for." He pressed against her.

She turned over and shoved her pillow between them. "We don't have to every single night, do we?"

"You used to like it," he said, and she could hear he was pouting. "What's got into you?"

She didn't answer him. There was no simple answer she could give. She lay still, thinking about their first time up in that old abandoned line shack on the Knobs. He was wrong. She hadn't liked it much even then.

The shack where they went was left over from the days before fences, when open-range grazing was still the way of ranchmen in the area. J.J. had hauled a plank up there and made them a bed, planned it all out beforehand, even took a blanket since it was winter. He brought a jar of whiskey, too, and gave her some to warm her up, then kissed the taste of it off her lips.

"I ain't gonna hurt you," he whispered. But it did hurt, and it surprised her, too—that he could even fit inside her, at how quickly it was over, and at the mess he left behind. She hadn't expected the mess. No one had ever warned her about it. "You're mine now, Sunny," he murmured when it was over, cuddling her. J.J. tended to cuddle. "You're my sweet darlin. My sugar pie. My honey dove."

She wanted to laugh at him talking so stupidly, at him thinking such love words meant anything to her at all. Even though she tried, she just couldn't seem to forgive him for not being like Gil. But she kept on going up to that line shack anyway, and lying down underneath him. It seemed that she just blinked and he was slipping that cheap ring on her finger. She had peered up into his blue-green eyes that day standing in church and felt as cold as death.

In the dark lumber-and-paint smell of the new room, he poked at the pillow wedged between them, punched at it with stiff fingers, flopped backward and sighed loudly. "I can't believe I got me a wife that's already gone frigid," he grumbled.

 *F*OR A WHOLE MONTH she attempted to write an answer to Gil's letter. She sat out on the porch. She tried it at Mama's desk. She even went down by the creek where they had spent so many late summer nights. She made several starts.

Dear Gil,
 You addressed your last letter to Sunny DeLony. I thought I had better tell you my name is Sunny Peeler now.

She used up page after page of paper, wasted it, wadded it up or tore it into little pieces to burn in the trash bin when no one was watching her. The right words wouldn't come, things she wanted to say. She wasn't even sure what they were.

Dear Gil,
 I'm surprised you have not heard already that I am a married woman now. Turner came to the wedding, and I would've thought at least she would tell you.

She couldn't seem to keep from sounding too lighthearted or else too angry and disappointed. There was no way to put into words what all she felt. No way to acknowledge the emptiness that had come to her since his letter, as if she had won the grand prize but missed the deadline to claim it.

In the end, she decided against answering him at all. She figured that once he finally came home, enough time would've passed, and time had a way of fixing things. She thought she could pretend she'd never gotten a passionate, confessing letter from him. She could even picture herself looking him in the eyes and saying, "Letter? No, there never was any letter." It would be the easiest way. And maybe, yes, the cowardly way, too. But she had stood up in a church and said some words before God and a preacher and all of the family. And they were supposed to be sacred words, and solemn, not something you could take back.

"Good Lord," Mama said one evening, rummaging through her desk. "What in the world's happened to all my writing paper?"

Sunny put on her most innocent face, shrugged, then went outside to sit on the porch to wait. She didn't know what she waited for—night to fall, and then morning to come. Then night again. And morning.

Her belly heaved to one side with the movement from within. She put her hand there and looked out toward the road. Papa and J.J. would be coming in from the Kennedy fields any minute. She wondered if this was going to be her life forever.

SEVERAL WEEKS LATER, CLOSE to noon, a telegram came. Mama had gone off to Aunt Karen's weekly Red Cross meeting, to sew bandages and leggins and shoulder wraps for the boys overseas. Papa and J.J. were out in the fields, getting ready to plant red wheat. Mama had sent them off that morning with sandwiches, which they would eat under a shade tree somewhere. They wouldn't be back till supper.

Eldie Birdwell's bicycle was leaning against the yard gate. Sunny signed her name to his receipt pad and he stood there a few seconds longer, waiting on his tip. But Sunny had never signed for a telegram before and she didn't know that a tip was expected.

"Should I open it?" she asked him. Mama's name was the only one that showed through the window on the envelope.

"I would, ma'am. Ain't usually good news in them." He waggled a finger playfully at Ding, who was peeping around the doorway. Eldie was about fifteen, had a mama with sick blood he took care of at home.

Sunny ripped open the flap of the yellow envelope.

Western Union
Telegram

BURTON TEX 950A 1918 SEP 23 AM10 14

TESSA DELONY

MCDADE TEX

=GIL WOUNDED. FEW DETAILS. PRUDIE SICK. CAN YOU COME=

NOLAN DAILEY

"Oh . . . no, Ding. No . . ." Sunny took her brother by both his shoulders and looked into his little face, but she wasn't seeing anything. It was as if her brain were suddenly encased in fog.

"Can I get you something, ma'am?" Eldie said, holding the screen door open. "A drink of water or something?"

She blinked at him, but she didn't really see him, either. She had to get to Mama. "Oh, Eldie. I need to borrow your bicycle."

His shoulders stiffened. "Well now, I don't know about that."

"I won't be but a few minutes. I need to—oh . . ." She dropped the telegram. She put her hands to her face, then bent to pick it up. Her bulging belly got in the way, so Eldie stooped for the paper. She said, "I'll be back in just . . . I've got to go get Mama." And she pushed right past him, walking toward his bicycle. "Stay with Ding."

Eldie raced after her. "Maybe I better be the one to go. Where's she at?"

"No. No. I'm all right."

Sunny got up on the bicycle, and after a wobbly start she went off down the road, not even thinking about what a sight she must have made with her ripe belly poking out, no hat on her head, no gloves, heading off down the road, trying to stay out of the ruts. Gil was wounded. *Oh God, he was wounded.* She had to find out what that meant.

"I ain't supposed to be lending my bike to nobody!" Eldie hollered after her. He'd come out the gate and was standing in the middle of the road. "You're going to have to give me a tip for this!"

Chapter Eight

*I*T SEEMED ODD TO Gil that it should be on the ship, tossing against the Atlantic waves, that some of the strength returned to his left leg. Halfway across he found he didn't need to lean so heavily on the crutches. Two-thirds of the way over he swapped the crutches for a cane. He missed out on the seasickness this time, too. The doctors in Nevers had sent him off with a bottle of pills, something for the muscle spasms, and he thought it must be those pills that kept his stomach settled. That and being able to go up on deck to smoke. Things were better on deck than down below. The sailors were all friendly, patient with his hobbling along, slowly and carefully, down the quarterdeck rail to keep his leg from stiffening up.

Most everybody was in a good humor since the armistice, and he needed to be among good-humored souls, not down below with those others. Men with half their faces gone or their limbs shot away, or the man without a voice because of the shrapnel that had splattered his throat, or the blind one whose look of accusation Gil couldn't bear. He could read their minds, some of them, wondering why he was on board the ship going home, why he wasn't back with the rest of the AEF, the newly renamed Army of Occupation, pushing to the Rhine.

He hadn't asked to be invalided home. It wasn't his idea. The doctor had done it, a captain from Pennsylvania. "Orders are Rainbow wounded get to go home for Christmas. Don't complain, Private. We're sending you back to God's country."

All the church bells in Nevers rang that day. People outside shouted, danced in the street. A brass band played "The Marseillaise." One of the Sisters of Mercy brought in a bottle of champagne to the convalescent ward. *"La guerre est finie!"* she said as she poured two drops into each patient's water cup. *"C'est la victoire!"* But none of that was the same as being there, at the front, hearing the guns go quiet. The Eleventh hour of the Eleventh day of the Eleventh month. To him it didn't feel finished.

The Statue of Liberty, when it came into view, shrouded in a misty gray rain in the middle of the harbor, right where he had left it over a year ago, didn't seem real either. Nothing did. He had hoped for sunshine in God's country. It was thirteen weeks to the day since that Austrian whizbang had blown him into the mud off the Jaulny-Thiaucourt crossroad.

At the dock in Hoboken, two medics grabbed him by both arms. They escorted him so rapidly down the gangway, he lost his footing. It made him angry and he slung them away from him. *"Va-t'en!"* he said, the words coming in French out of habit. He could walk on his own.

At the bottom of the plank they let go of him, and as he stepped onto land, he staggered and had to grab on to a lamppost. Sea legs. That was all his good balance had been—sea legs. He'd found them on board the ship, and now they were lost. He felt heavy and stiff again, old and bruised, and strangely indifferent to the other walking cases who fell to their knees and kissed the ground.

Some were loaded onto ferries, others onto streetcars, and sent off in different directions. Gil went on the ferry across the Hudson River and then on to Camp Mills, right back where he had started. They gave him an envelope with all his uncollected wages plus sixty dollars in separation pay and a ribbon, which a major pinned to the breast of his uniform. The major returned Gil's salute and said, "Welcome home, soldier." And that was that. He was out of the army, on his own. An unyoked mule.

At the train station on Long Island, a whore approached him. She had black eyes and hair, looked Italian, could've been French. It sounded wrong to him when she spoke in American English. "When does your train leave, soldier boy?"

The station teemed with noise, the clang of the streetcars, foghorns from the harbor, laughter close by, a panhandler shouting about hot dogs.

"In an hour."

The whore's red lips parted in a smile. "Then you got time. Got ten bucks on you?"

"Ten?" Mentally he converted that into francs. He knew only what French whores cost. He had to compare the price.

"Eight?" she said.

He laughed. "No."

"How about six?"

He followed her to the flophouse across the street. The sheets smelled rancid. Creatures ran in the walls. He didn't know why he went with her. Later, aboard the train, he thought maybe he had just needed to see if there was a difference. There wasn't. A whore was a whore, American or French. He worried that she had given him a dose. Worried how he would feel seeing Ma and Pop again, if he could be normal, smile, laugh at jokes, step one foot in front of the other through each day.

He thought of Rome's girl in Neufchâteau, the one Rome had fallen for on a two-day pass. By then Rome had had his fill of the war. After Champagne and the Marne they'd all had their fill. There were too many killed, too many wounded, too many goddamned Heinie prisoners to herd. It had actually felt good to be back in Lorraine, and Rome had been ripe for a little love. He had said he aimed to marry the girl, take her home with him back to Lockhart. He had sounded serious about it. Gil couldn't even remember her name. Probably Marie. They were all Marie. She'd had light eyes and brown hair.

He didn't want to spring for a sleeper car, so he dozed sitting up in his seat. After all those months in the cab of the truck, he could sleep anywhere, a heavy, dreamless sleep, rocking with the train, probably snoring, too. The rales in his chest caused that. From the White Cross. Or maybe it was Green Cross. They both smelled like silage. Both were heavier than air and sank into shell craters. And both were used by the retreating Germans in the St. Mihiel salient.

One minute Rome was laughing, talking about his Marie, smoking cigarettes. The next he was gone. Nothing. An arm and a hand with fingers, that godforsaken pinkie ring down in the shell hole with the mud and the blood. And Gil could still hear his voice from an instant before. . . .

WHEN GIL STEPPED OFF the platform at Burton, the sun was blaring. A bright, warm December day in Texas. A dream. He'd been able to walk in the moving train, too, easier than on stable land, and he didn't understand that. It didn't make sense. He spotted Mr. Eberhardt coming toward him and he steeled himself. A familiar face. The first one.

"Gil Dailey," Mr. Eberhardt said, in a German-thick voice. Gil had never thought of the stationmaster as a Hun before. Never considered it. "Your mama know you're home today?"

"No sir." Gil shook Mr. Eberhardt's hand, allowed the man to slap him on the shoulder.

"I will telephone to your papa then." Mr. Eberhardt started toward the ticket office.

Gil followed. "Pop's got a phone?"

"Oh yeah. Good for business. Anybody can call and see if he's too busy."

"Don't." Gil's voice stopped the old man. "Don't call him. I'll walk. I want to surprise him." He couldn't bear the thought of a big welcome, not even with just ten minutes' preparation. What he wanted was just to evaporate back into his old life, no fanfare.

Mr. Eberhardt eyed the cane in Gil's hand, looked toward town. "It's a steep hill there."

"That's OK. I'll walk."

Before Gil got to the top of that hill, though, he was having second thoughts about that telephone call. Even in December he began to sweat. His breath shortened. He tried to concentrate on the birds that flittered in the pecan trees along the way, and not on his throbbing hip, or the pins and needles in his thigh. He needed to build some muscle, that was all. He needed to walk up this hill.

At the top he shook out his handkerchief, mopped his forehead. He took off his greatcoat and slung it over his shoulder. The house was just up the road. He could see the flagpole rising above the blacksmith. He'd forgotten about that pole, put up just before he left. The Stars and Stripes flapped in the breeze.

Mrs. Silsby was out in her yard clippering the last of the season's roses. "I swan . . . Gilbert Dailey? Is that you?" she said out from under her sunbonnet. She straightened from her rosebush. "We heard you might be coming home."

He managed a smile. "Yes ma'am, it's me." He walked on by.

The house loomed ahead, drew into closer focus. Ma still had flowers in the yard, some kind of leafy blue flower she had let go to mostly all stem. His leg felt like a log he was dragging. The hill had been too much. He shouldn't have tried it yet.

At the yard gate, he stopped, held on to the fence and gazed up at the house, an in-service flag in the window, blue star on a field of white, to tell the world they had a son over there. For a second, he wanted to turn around and head back down the hill to the station. Go anywhere. Just away. From the shop came the strimmering ring of a hammer on iron and he glanced that way. He'd sooner face Pop first than Ma.

He hobbled on, grimacing with each step. He noticed the big red-and-black Texaco sign out in front of Mr. Honeywell's filling-up station across the street. Long ago, Gil had tried to talk Pop into putting in some gasoline pumps, too. Mr. Honeywell had a booming garage business going, automobiles parked all over his lot.

Out of breath, Gil reached the open doors to the blacksmith, and there was Pop inside, fullering an iron rod. The smell of the forge, of burnt horn and the anvil, the black walls—painted black on purpose, to better read the colors of a heat—all of it came at him where he stood, resting heavily on the cane, holding to one of the doors. The map Ma had mentioned in her letter, the map of the western front, hung on the near wall. A calendar with the date from two days ago hung there, too—December 15, 1918.

He waited to get his breath and until the hammer blows quieted before he said, "Hey, Pop."

The hammer fell from Pop's hand, and he had never been clumsy. The rod he'd been working slipped into the slake, then onto the floor. "Good Lord Almighty," he said, and turned. He came forward. "It's my boy."

He clamped his arms around Gil and hugged him almost violently. Pop was a strong man, had broad back muscles and shoulders, and Gil felt every one of them squeezing him, vise tight. "Thank you, dear Lord," Pop said, whispering, burrowing his head near Gil's ear.

EVERYBODY ACTED HAPPY TO see him. Ma had a good cry, then she went out, just as Gil had expected, gathering neighbors, laughing, hollering over fences, "Our Gilbert's come home!" Making a big fuss. Calvin seemed especially interested in Gil, and that was something new.

Calvin was fourteen, smart as blazes, plowing through school without any trouble, had in fact skipped a grade last summer. He'd thinned down, turned leggy, still had that sun-freckled nose, and he'd gotten control of his stutter. It only showed up a little when he talked too fast. He asked a hundred questions, about France, about the army, the ship going and coming back. He wanted to know what the patches on Gil's uniform stood for, the winged helmet in a wheel for Motor Transport; the circle and Lorraine cross for Advanced Section, Service of Supply. *Goddamned slacker bastards in the SOS.*

"You kill anybody?" Calvin's voice was serious. "Germans?"

Gil broke out in laughter, thought of Rome, and the laughter faded. "I drove a truck, Cal. That's all."

"But you saw a lot of dead people." Calvin's face radiated. "You must've. We've been hearing that they're lying all over the place."

Gil stared into his brother's eyes and didn't feel inclined to answer. He patted his pockets for some cigarettes, remembered he had run out on the train, and then Ma was bringing in the Baggetts from over the hill, followed by the Parkersons from church, and Brother Thurston.

A steady flow of people came and went all afternoon to make over Gil and wish him welcome home. He heard "Good job" and "We're so proud of you" until he wanted to puke. Proud of what? He wondered if they even knew. The women wanted hugs and kisses, the men, handshakes and claps on the back. One or two asked if he'd gotten his German with just the same gleeful look that had been on Calvin's face. They wanted him to tell them about the war, how he had suffered. They wanted misery and glory.

He escaped to his old room, made an excuse about finding some other clothes to wear. He hadn't even had a chance to wash his face of train dust. He closed the door, and the air felt instantly lighter. His eyes passed around the room, lingering here and there, on the old kite tail still strung over the bureau mirror, the shelf of yellowing books above his bed, the quilt across the mattress, a pattern of houses, a crazy quilt, all colors. Had he lived here?

He sat down on the bed, leaned his cane against the side table, unbuttoned his tunic and tossed it on the floor. He tugged his shirt out of his pants, took it off, too, fished the wallet from his pants pocket, pulled the dog tags over his head. They had been there for so long he felt naked without them around his neck.

Voices came from the front rooms, muted by the walls in between. He lifted the window, let the cool twilight inside, and he lay back on the bed, his bed, on his pillow. *God, it still smelled the same.* And he thought maybe this was the comfort he'd come home for after all: this bed, this pillow and quilt, a fresh Texas breeze purring in through the window, skimming his skin. Darkness fell. The muscles up his spine began to relax. His forehead smoothed. France, Rome McKeller, the war, felt like a long-ago dream he'd had.

"SON? GILBERT?"

Ma's hand on his shoulder woke him from a sound sleep. He opened his eyes. Daylight streamed in the window, heating up the pillow.

"You slept all the way through," she said, her voice laden with concern. "Since six o'clock yesterday. Your pa said to leave you alone, but I thought you might need a little something to eat. Are you hungry? Maybe some biscuits and gravy. I've got pork sausage."

He rolled over on his back, blinked up at her face. She smiled sadly, tilted her head to one side. She reached her fingers into his hair, fluffed at him. Tears filled her eyes. "My poor boy."

"Ma!" He angled away from her hand. "Don't do that, Ma."

She pulled back. "I was just—"

"I don't want you babying me." He sat up, put both feet on the floor. He hadn't even taken off his shoes or untucked the covers, but somebody had let down the window. *Welcome to another day.* He wiped his face in both his hands. "Does Mr. Honeywell sell anything else over there besides gasoline?"

"Gilbert?" Her mouth pursed like she'd just eaten something salty. "Is that a tattoo on your arm?"

He glanced down his shoulder, lifted his arm to better see the rainbow and the pot of gold, the Texas star, the 117th. It was a stupid question for her to ask. What else did it look like? "Cigarettes, for instance? Does Mr. Honeywell sell those, too?"

"You took up smoking?"

"Yeah, Ma. I pretty much took up everything." He lifted his eyes to her face, and her eyes moved away.

MR. HONEYWELL HAD A car for sale sitting outside his station—a closed-car Hudson, big enough for two families.

After all the mud and cold in France, those pull-up windows interested Gil. So did the hot-air floor heater that funneled warmth from the radiator. The car was the devil to look at on the outside, needed a paint job, had those old-time, 1915 coach-style parking lanterns, big boxy top, but it had a six-cylinder engine, and it ran like a top once it got started, which took a little coaxing.

A man from Wharton had left the car off with Mr. Honeywell for some tuning work and never came back to claim it. Almost a year passed before Mr. Honeywell put the for-sale sign on the windshield. He was asking a hundred dollars for it, all he claimed he had in it. Gil figured he would take fifty.

Gil bought a pack of Chesterfields and smoked them in his room, with the door shut and the window open. The first one made him light-headed it had been so long, but he got over that soon enough. He practiced walking without the cane, but found himself holding on to the furniture instead. He cursed himself and tried again, taking more care, going slower. The surgeons had carved so much of his thigh out, he hardly had any meat left. And the bone had been broken, a multiple fracture from hitting the ground after the concussion lofted him skyward. That was something a high-explosive shell could do: kick you in the air and slam you back down again.

They hadn't been able to plaster his leg at first because of the shrapnel, but once the open wounds healed, they'd cast his leg and put him in traction. *"J'en suis très désolée,"* the sister had whispered in apology each time she adjusted the weights. But the morphine had kept him from the pain; then later caused it.

While he'd been across at Honeywell's, Ma had brought a basin of water into his room. He swallowed one of the doctor's pills. He didn't know what was in them. They were sweet enough to be candy. He took off his tunic and his undershirt, soaped his hands, scrubbed his face and armpits. Time for civilian clothes. He wasn't a soldier boy anymore.

In the bottom drawer of the bureau he found a pair of jeans britches, but when he tried them on they were too loose in the waist and came too high up his ankles. Same thing with the other two pairs of pants in the drawer. He had to put the uniform pants back on, and they were beginning to smell pretty ripe.

The shirt situation wasn't much better. His old ones fit in the girth just fine but not in the sleeves. The cuffs stopped two inches above his wrists. Those he could wear rolled up, though. He reached into the top drawer for an undershirt and his hand brushed something that shouldn't have been in there. He pulled the drawer out farther to have a look and discovered an envelope, blank on the outside, sealed with old red wax he recognized from Pop's desk out in the blacksmith.

He backed up to the bed and sat down, curiously turned the envelope over in his hand. He couldn't think of a reason why there would be an envelope in his underwear drawer. The sealing wax crumbled easily, and inside, folded into a slip, two inches by three, were two sheets of paper from Pop's shop, lined for billing.

In Account With

N. E. DAILEY

BLACKSMITH AND WHEELWRIGHT

Horseshoeing A Specialty

Unwrapping the folds was like reaching down into the toe of a Christmas stocking.

Dear Gil—

I hope you get to read this letter because that will mean you are back home and all right. Everyone here is worried sick about you. Aunt Prudie does nothing but bawl herself silly and can't be consoled, not even by Mama. She holds Uncle Nolan to blame for signing you up, so he stays out of her way in the blacksmith all day long. I go out there some, too. He's got a map out there and he showed me every place where you had been. Poor Calvin wanders around lost, one minute out there helping Uncle Nolan, the next in here trying to soothe Aunt Prudie. He has grown up so much I bet you won't hardly recognize him.

On the train ride coming here we saw some soldiers in uniform already home. One had an empty sleeve and Mama asked him did he know you. I told her there are three million men in our army now, but she just kept on at him, describing you and what outfit you are with and everything. He had heard of the Rainbow Division. I guess everybody has, but it made me embarrassed how she wouldn't shut up about it. Probably she was just nervous on account of his arm being gone. Gil, if you come back like that, with missing parts, it won't matter a bit to any of us.

I'm sleeping here in your room with Ding. I had to beg Mama to let me come, and to promise I would keep Ding out of her hair, so that's what I am doing. We all hope to hear from you soon, but it takes so long for letters to get back and forth, that it's just no telling when we'll know more about what all has happened to you. I hope you aren't in terrible pain.

Gil, I am a married woman now, about to be a mother, and I know I shouldn't, but I still think about you a great deal. Not only because of you being off in the war, though knowing that doesn't help much either. I could say I feel by you like a brother, but I've got Ding so I know it isn't exactly the same as that. So much has changed since you've been gone, and I have come to see that you were right about a lot of things. But you are and always will be my dear cousin, and my friend too. I pray that you come home safe and sound, and I swear to God if he'll answer me just this once, I will never ask him for another thing.

Yours,
Sunny

He sat there holding the letter, pondering on what it said, which was a whole lot of nothing. Why had she even bothered to write it? In answer to that love letter he'd sent last May? But she hadn't mentioned that letter at all, and she would have, wouldn't she? Unless she never got it. Could he be so lucky? There was a mail call once when a whole bunch of the boys received nothing but empty, ragged envelopes with LOST AT SEA stamped on the outside—the result, everybody assumed, of a torpedo attack. Might that letter he had written to her, that mushy-soft, stupid letter, have been blown to kingdom come?

He reached for his pillow, lifted it to his nose, thinking maybe Sunny was what he had smelled there yesterday evening. He breathed in deeply, just as Calvin came clomping down the hallway. Gil dropped the pillow, folded the letter, and shoved it under the quilt. He surprised himself how quickly he made it to the door, jerking it open just as Calvin was about to step into his own room.

Gil grabbed Calvin by the arm. "Come in here."

"What for? *Hey*—" Calvin let Gil drag him into the room.

Gil shut the door. "When was Sunny here?"

Calvin shrugged. "I don't know. After we heard about you." He pointed at Gil's rib cage. "What's that?"

Gil glanced down at the shrapnel scar there. It was puckered and still pink, but it had only been superficial, a graze. "So . . . that was in September?"

"I think so. Does that hurt?"

Gil gave an impatient shake of his head. "Has she had her baby?"

"She hadn't had it then." Calvin lowered his voice in warning. "She's married, you know."

"What do you think, I'm that big a bonehead? I know she's married." But maybe he was a bonehead. He had written that stupid letter. He tugged an old soft work shirt over his head, buttoned it up the front, started rolling the sleeves. The grin on Calvin's face bunched up the freckles on his nose. Gil said, "What?"

"You grew." Calvin laughed.

"I don't have a goddamn thing here that fits me." Gil tucked in the shirt.

"Show me your leg wound."

"Hell no. Get out of here." Gil clapped his hand on top of Calvin's head, throttled him back and forth, and gave him a playful shove toward the door. He and Calvin had never gotten along too well, yet Gil sensed a strange new closeness, and it made him feel generous. "You want to go with me to McDade?"

A frown twitched Calvin's brow. "When?"

"Couple of days."

"What for?"

Gil buttoned the fly to his pants. "See everybody. I'm going to buy that Hudson off Mr. Honeywell."

Calvin's face brightened. "You are? That'll be slick."

"Think Ma'll let you go with me?"

"I'll tell her she's got to."

Gil reached for the Chesterfields on the bedside table, stuck the cigarettes in his shirt pocket. "Somehow I don't remember that ever working with Ma."

Chapter Nine

THE ROAD BETWEEN BURTON and Giddings was so bad Gil could almost have mistaken it for one in France right after a shelling. What should have taken no more than an hour took three. In Giddings they stopped for lunch, cold fried pork chops Ma had sent with them, and two pieces of corn bread apiece. She hadn't been happy about them setting off by themselves, but she wouldn't let them go hungry. And she and Pop would be following on the train in a couple of days.

Gil and Calvin leaned against the Hudson and cleaned the bones. It tasted like sirloin steak to Gil. For the last two days he had been eating everything in sight, as if he had a pit in his stomach he couldn't fill up fast enough. While he stuffed himself, Calvin jabbered about school. He had a girl he was sweet on, Willidean Greer from over at Sandtown, and Calvin's stutter showed up every time he said her name. Gil had gone to school with her oldest sister, but he couldn't recall Willidean.

"She like you, too?" Gil said, smiling to himself.

Calvin nodded, his cheeks full of blood. "That's what I wanted to ask you about. I mean, how do you know if a girl wants you to kiss her or not?"

Gil took time to lick the grease off his fingers. "You can ask her, or just grab her and do it."

"What if she slaps you?"

"Then you'll know, won't you?"

Calvin looked openmouthed at Gil and nodded.

Outside of Giddings, Gil offered to let Calvin drive, and even though it would mean losing some time, the thrill on Calvin's face was worth the loss. He showed him how to work the clutch and the gas, to shift gears, and told him what all the gauges on the dashboard meant.

"Are you sure I can do this?" Calvin eyed the steering wheel.

"You don't think so?"

"Yeah." Calvin grinned.

The automobile handled nicely, hit on all six cylinders once it got running. Wheel wasn't too tight, cornered easy. A baby could have driven it. There was that cold-to-start problem, and when they stopped for gas at Hill's Prairie, it reared up again.

Calvin about broke his thumb cranking the handle. "Something with the carburetor," Gil muttered to himself, but he couldn't find anything wrong. He sent Calvin into the store with a nickel for a bottle of Coca-Cola. They both shared a swig and then Gil used some to boil corrosion off the battery poles. He took out the spark plugs one by one. After an hour of tinkering like that, the engine finally turned over and stayed there.

"Next time we stop we'll just leave the damned thing running," Gil said.

Night fell and they drove by headlamp, but that wasn't any great marvel for Gil after all those kilometers in France under blackout conditions. He even had a remembrance of going up to the St. Mihiel front, the all-new First American Army, slogging through the rain. The roads turned to slick mud half a foot deep, frog-swallowing mud that no truck could get through.

Calvin said, "If you need me to, I can drive again, Gil," but that only fit right in with the memories. Gil could hear himself, sounding just like Calvin, pleading with Rome to give up the wheel—*Sure enough, now. Slide over here and let me drive awhile.* And like Rome, Gil declined the offer. In another few miles Calvin was sound asleep anyway.

The smoky blue dawn had begun to glow in the sky when Gil went through McDade. Hard-packed wagon ruts on the Knobs Springs road jarred the Hudson, so he slowed down, and then he could hear mourning dove and bobwhite calling. The fresh smell of dew filled him. Everything looked exactly the same—the curves in the road, trees growing along fence lines. Almost as if he'd never left.

When he drew the Hudson up to the gate at the farm, he noticed the room that had been added on to the front porch. It appeared odd there, throwing the house out of symmetry, and with two front doors to confuse everybody. It was the room for Sunny and her husband. He knew that, and he knew she'd had a baby girl. He had managed to get that much out of Ma. Born November 8, just three days before the armistice. It wasn't hard for him to imagine Sunny as a mother. She had been mothering Ding for four years.

Gil reached across and thumped Calvin on the chest. "Get out and open the gate."

Calvin blinked for a couple of seconds, groping his way back from sleep. He rubbed at his eyes. "Think anybody's up?"

"Are you fooling? Uncle Dane?"

"Oh yeah." Calvin popped the door on his side of the car. He had some trouble untangling the tie rope around the gate, but finally managed it, and Gil drove the car through. Calvin hopped onto the running board. "Blow the horn, Gil."

But it was too early for that, and just the sound of the motor was enough to bring Uncle Dane and Aunt Tessa out onto the front porch. Calvin went running around the head of the car, shouting something that got buried underneath the loud engine noise. Gil pulled on up in the yard, shut off the headlamps, and also, but with reluctance, the car.

And then Aunt Tessa was on him. "Oh for Pete's sake, Gil," she said. She practically dragged him off the seat and hugged him so tight he thought he'd lose his breath. Uncle Dane reached around to pump Gil's hand. Aunt Tessa said, "Gilbert, I declare—" She pinched both his cheeks. "Look at how tall you are."

"He grew two inches while he was gone," Calvin said, and Aunt Tessa jerked him up for a hug, too, pounding the life out of his back. It was a family joke, how hard Aunt Tessa could love you. Calvin's voice rattled. "Ma and Pop'll be here by Christmas."

Ding had come outside, too, and he tugged at his mother's apron. He said, "Who's this man, Mama?" Gil hadn't even noticed him there until that instant. And it was Ding who had grown a mile, had two big front teeth, ten freckles across his nose, shiny dark shoe-button eyes.

"I'm not a man. I'm Gil. You forgot me?" He bent to lift Ding like he used to do, but the scar on his leg pulled so hard he thought better of it. The pain could still surprise him. He reached for the cane lying on the front seat of the car, and it seemed that for just a beat after he brought it out, everything got quiet. A rooster crowed from somewhere behind the house and broke the silence.

All at once they started in talking again. Aunt Tessa explained to Ding how Gil was kin. Uncle Dane asked when Gil had gotten home. Calvin bragged about driving the car from Giddings to Hill's Prairie all by himself. Aunt Tessa opened the rusty yard gate, held her arm out for Gil to follow her through. He lifted his head and there was Sunny, up on the front porch, right in front of him, standing still, in a plain yellow house wrapper. The instant his eyes landed on her, he remembered how much he still loved her.

She looked away from him, watched her feet—little feet scampering down the four porch steps—as she came on the run, infecting him with her smile. A sad, relieved, terrified smile. She collided with him and threw her arms around him so fully that for a moment he just stared down at the top of her head, stunned, before he touched the inside of his palm against her hair. It *was* red. *And* it was blond. Just as silken as he remembered. He folded her against him and she felt so perfect there, exactly what he had longed for all these months. The desire to kiss her almost overcame him—*just grab her and do it*. He might well have if Ding hadn't spoken when he did. "This is Cousin Gil."

That caused Sunny to break away, laughing, catching a tear on her first finger. "I know who it is, Ding." She rounded her eyes at Gil. They were as clear and green as salt water. "Good Lord, Gil," she said, stepping back. "You're as thin as paper."

The door to the new added-on room opened and a lanky, blond, bowlegged fellow stepped out onto the porch. "Sunny, are you gonna come in here and tend to this baby?"

Little mewing cries came through the open door and Sunny rushed to the steps, flinging a backward look. "J.J., you remember Gil Dailey, don't you?"

"Sure do," J.J. answered, but he didn't smile. He thumped down the porch steps to squeeze the hell out of Gil's hand and Gil squeezed back. J.J. had the leavings of a black eye, and faded yellow bruises along his nose. Sunny went into the room her husband had just come from, and with her gone, J.J. dropped Gil's hand. "Well . . ." He looked at Aunt Tessa. "Reckon I'll see you folks after while," he said, and he headed up the yard path.

Aunt Tessa watched after him. "He's got to go to work. Saturday's the busiest day they got down there at the mill."

Ding called out, "Bye-bye, J.J." And J.J. gave a backhanded wave.

"He doesn't work here at the farm?" Gil asked, and Uncle Dane made a sound like *sheew* under his breath.

"He don't work period," Uncle Dane grumbled as he went in the front door. Ding and Calvin followed him.

"*Dane,*" Aunt Tessa scolded, then linked her hand inside Gil's arm, forced a smile. "Once his brother came home from the army, J.J. went back to work up at the sawmill. Now, you get on inside there and let me make you some breakfast."

Gil turned as J.J. sauntered out through the farm gate and onto the road. "I ought to give him a lift to town."

"No . . . no, he's used to walking. You just come on inside here."

She steered him for the door, and he let her. He wouldn't have given odds on the Hudson starting up anyway.

"*I*'VE GOT A JOB I've been saving for you," Uncle Dane said to Gil over breakfast. "A plow point that needs drawing out, if you're up to it."

Gil glanced around at the closed door to Sunny's room. "It's been a long time since I did any metalwork."

"It'll come back to you."

"Dane DeLony, this boy has been driving all night." Aunt Tessa piled another biscuit and more eggs onto Gil's plate. Then she leaned to hug her arms around his neck. "We've missed you so much. You're just going to have to bear with us till we get used to looking at you again."

Across the table, Calvin motioned with his fork at something behind Gil, and thinking it was Sunny finally coming out, Gil jerked around. His quick movement startled Aunt Tessa. She let his neck go, backing away. The door to Sunny's room stayed shut.

"I was trying to get him to look at all those pictures up there," Calvin said, coloring up, stuttering a bit, aware that he'd caused an uncomfortable moment.

Aunt Tessa's expression eased. She moved across the room. "Oh, these . . ."

On the mantel Gil saw the array of photographs Calvin meant —recent ones and old, yellowed ones—and he realized he was the subject in all of them. It was like a shrine somebody might put up to the dead.

"I found some of these in my album and decided we'd just set them out," Aunt Tessa was saying. "I've been telling folks, 'That's my nephew in France, and these are staying up here till he gets home again.'"

She lifted one of the frames from out of the group, brought it over to the table, and set the picture in front of Gil. He'd seen it before, of him when he was about a year old, wearing coveralls, a corncob pipe stuck upside down in the corner of his mouth.

"I know you don't remember, but I took you to have this one made. That was back when I used to watch you for Prudie. Back before I married this scoundrel." She was acting flighty, almost self-conscious.

Ding leaned over Gil's arm to get a better look at the photo and Gil gave it to him. Ding's bacon fingers smeared the glass.

Since none of Gil's old clothes fit him, he'd been forced to wear his uniform, or parts of it anyway: the pants, but without the hated puttees; the tunic, open like a suit jacket over an old shirt from home; the hobnailed shoes. Ding pointed his greasy finger at the brass collar pins on Gil's tunic. "What's that say?"

Aunt Tessa was back at the mantel picking out another photo, droning on about when it was taken, too, as if Gil cared in the least. She meant well, he knew that she did, but all the sudden it started getting hard for him to breathe.

He unfastened the ornaments from his collar. "It says *U-S*. That means us." He pinned them both, the brass US and the Forty-second Division pin, to Ding's nightshirt.

Roses bloomed in Ding's cheeks. The kid sat back against his chair, pinching out his shirt for a closer inspection. When Gil looked up he saw Calvin's face had gone dark, and Gil realized right away he'd just made a big mistake giving Ding those pins.

Uncle Dane said, "You ready to get after that plow point?" and Gil was so grateful for the diversion he practically leaped up from the chair.

As soon as they were out in the barn where it smelled of the animals and manure, a loft full of sweet-grass hay, things got easy again. The cow stable was right where it had always been. There was Uncle Dane's workbench, too, and his little Sears, Roebuck forge and bellows. Toys, Pop used to call them.

While Uncle Dane set about getting a fire started, Gil smoked a cigarette. On a whim, he leaned his cane against the wall and walked all the way across to the corncrib. Then he walked all the way back. His leg and hip hurt like the devil, but he made it on just his own two legs—a damned baby taking its first toddling steps. That cane was a weakness. And so was the limp. A giving in to the pain, and he decided right then that he wasn't going to give in to it anymore. He didn't like people treating him differently—like Ma, like Aunt Tessa—as if he were an invalid, throwing him pitiful looks. But he didn't want to be treated like a hero either. It was complicated and impossible for even him to understand. He kept walking, gingerly, across the barn.

Uncle Dane said, "You're moving around pretty fair. Don't hardly need that swagger stick, do you?" He poked at the fire, banked the coals. "They tell you how long it's going to be before you're a hundred percent?"

Gil laughed, wiped some of the barn dust from his eyes. He took off the tunic and hung it on a nail. "This *is* a hundred percent."

Uncle Dane glanced again and nodded. "Well, I reckon you'll make do."

Gil felt a rush of love come over him. He'd always had a particular affection for Uncle Dane, liked his gruff ways, and his big, stout heart. You didn't have to talk around him the way you had to with other people. He was comfortable with silence, and made you feel comfortable with it, too.

Once the fire was forging hot, they got busy on the plow point. They had always worked easily together, anticipated each other like a well-matched team in harness. Gil found he could still use a hammer. It even felt good to be applying some muscle again, striking that iron, thinning it down. It wasn't as smooth a job as Pop would've done, but it wasn't terrible, and Uncle Dane seemed grateful. He always needed help with something, which made Gil curious again about Sunny's husband.

While Gil was fastening the plow point back onto the moldboard, Uncle Dane brought out a pint of brandy he had hidden behind his bench. He pulled the cork and grinned. "Just between us," he said, and took a swig. He let out a long *ahhhh* to cool his mouth, then he passed the flask to Gil. "I reckon you're man enough now."

"I heard Texas had gone bone dry. That's the word we got over there."

Uncle Dane snorted. "They wanted to make sure you boys coming home ain't corrupted."

Gil could have laughed at that thought if it hadn't been so absurd. He remembered what a schoolboy he'd been when he'd left for France, and compared that to how old he felt now. In seven weeks he would turn twenty.

He took a long, soothing pull from the pint of brandy. The brassy taste of it reminded him of France and his canteen, the cold wet mud, and Rome McKeller. He handed the pint back to Uncle Dane, who took another swig himself.

"When you get ready, I've got a little proposition to make you," he said. He held the flask out as if to admire its pewter shape.

"Proposition?"

Uncle Dane's eyes shone bright and big through his heavy spectacles. "I've decided to rent out some of my land. With both the Kennedy fields, I've got more than I can farm, and it's just sitting there idle. I figured if you was interested, I could help get you set up."

Gil didn't know what to say. It was a generous offer, one that had probably taken Uncle Dane a long while to mull over. He wasn't the kind to part with his land easily, even on a rent-share basis, or to admit that he had more acreage than he could handle. But Gil didn't want to be a farmer any more than he wanted to be a blacksmith. It just wasn't in him, that love of the land, that need to feel the dirt between his toes. Before he could form a proper answer, though, they heard somebody coming. Uncle Dane hurried to hide away the brandy.

Sunny stepped into the doorway of the barn. She had her baby in her arms, and if Gil had been a better person than he was, the baby would have been the first thing he noticed, instead of the fact that the sun coming at her back made her dress almost transparent. He could see the outline of her thighs, the whole curve of her from the waist down. Half an erection had already begun before he thought to turn away from her to light a cigarette. He concentrated on the match flame, on leaning against the workbench just so, even crossing his left leg over his right, nonchalantly, disregarding the ache that particular stance brought to his hip.

When he looked again, she was out of the sunlight, had come on into the barn, and was saying to Uncle Dane, "I thought Gil might like to see Isabel," as if she had to explain her interruption. She smiled at Gil. He picked loose tobacco off his tongue and tried to keep his affliction from returning.

She came nearer. "Since when do you smoke?"

He shook his head. He was speechless with looking at her, or else that big swig of brandy had made him dopey. He'd been awake for more than twenty-four hours, but he was used to going without sleep. He was finally beginning to feel like he'd come home and he didn't want to miss a minute of it. He let himself smile.

"Well, show him the little dickens," Uncle Dane said with impatience.

"Isabel Marie," Sunny said. "I'm not letting Papa make her a nickname, and it's about to kill him."

She unwrapped the blanket from the baby's head. A little swirl of white hair peeped out. Gil leaned forward, away from the workbench, and Sunny tucked the blanket under the baby's chin so he could see her face. She was a tiny thing, big dark blue eyes, that one white curl atop her head. A doubled fist flailed out and she yawned, which made them both laugh.

"Can I hold her?" he said, and Sunny lit up like a diamond.

"I guess so. If you want to."

He crushed the cigarette in a nail can and wiped his hands on his britches. Sunny set the baby carefully into his arms. He tried to copy how she had held Isabel, easing the baby up against his shoulder. She was warm, almost hot. You couldn't help but kiss her head. "She's soft, isn't she?"

"She's going to be in a Christmas pageant up at the church tomorrow night. They asked could she be in the manger scene, and I said I didn't see what it could hurt. It's the church the Peelers go to."

"They already got her acting in plays," Uncle Dane said. He was busy squirting oil in all the joints on the plow.

"She's not going to be acting, Papa, she's just going to be lying there." Sunny made a face for Gil's benefit, pretending exasperation. He noticed she had put on some face powder, added a little peach color to her lips. She smelled like gardenias or lavender, something from a bottle.

Holding tight to the baby, he strolled toward the door. At least he believed he was strolling, though in reality he moved more like a hound with a thorn in its paw. It wasn't that simple to walk steady with a baby in his arms. And yet Isabel was good bait. Just like he figured, she lured her mama right outside the barn after them.

"Do you want me to take her now?" Sunny said, following.

"I think she's happy enough," he said. The baby *was* quiet, about the quietest baby he thought he'd ever seen.

He started around the east end of the barn, heading down the garden path, and Sunny kept on following, just like he was the pied piper. He'd been wondering how he was going to get her alone while he was here. He didn't figure knocking at her bedroom window come midnight would go over too well with her husband. When he spied Calvin piddling around down by the creek, skipping rocks, he halted just outside the garden fence.

"I'm real glad you can walk, Gil," Sunny said, and he turned to her. "We didn't know what to expect."

He thought he could stand there staring at her for the next four or five hours and still not have gotten his fill. There was something especially pleasing about the way she had rounded out. A few tendrils fell loose from her hair knot and whispered against her neck. Her skin looked almost buttery. He smooched the baby again, his eyes fixed on her mama.

"Did you see the Eiffel Tower?" Sunny shaded her face with her hand, little hand, fingers as delicate as birds' wings. He thought about that pinkie ring and willed the thought away.

"I never did get to Paris." Isabel squirmed a little, wobbled her head. He patted her back. She was catnapping; eyelids twitched. "I saw the Statue of Liberty, though. Twice. It's just like in pictures, out there guiding in all the ships."

Sunny seemed to search his face. "Well, you always did want to go places."

"I was an ignorant kid. About a whole lot of things."

Isabel squirmed a second time and Sunny drew the blanket over the baby's head. "Look at those weeds and vines taking over my garden," she said. "I haven't had time for it since Isabel got here. Every day I say I'm going to get out there, but . . ."

She fussed with the baby's blanket some more, and as she did her fingertips grazed Gil's shoulder. She smiled at him. He smiled back. The feel of her fingertips stayed there on his shoulder and he wondered if she had touched him on purpose.

His lips went dry, heart pulsed in his eardrums. "I wrote a letter to you, Sunny, that I'm wondering if you got."

She blinked. "A letter?" Blinked again. "I got several letters from you, Gil."

"I believe this particular one you'd remember."

Her smile faded a little, turned almost wooden as if she were thinking hard. "I don't guess it came then, Gil." She shook her head. "No..."

The tiniest whimper rose from Isabel and Sunny rushed to take her. She moved so quickly, practically snatching the baby right out of his hands, that he didn't have any choice but to give her up.

"It's too bright for her out here. Her little skin'll just bake. I better take her in the house now." Sunny shielded Isabel against her shoulder and moved up the path almost as if she couldn't wait to get away from him, like he had something contagious. He hadn't touched her. He'd hardly had a chance to say anything to her at all, yet already she was walking off from him.

Disappointed, gloomy, he watched her all the way up the path and through the chicken yard to the kitchen door. He waited to see if she would look back, but she didn't. Not even a glance or the least hesitation before she disappeared inside the house.

From the creek bank, Calvin called, "There's a school of big ol' carp in here, Gil." Calvin had his shoes off, his pants rolled to his calves. "They're so slow, I bet I can catch one with my bare hands."

Gil eased down past the garden to the creek bank, wishing now that he had the cane. His leg ached unbearably. A heavy tiredness seeped into him. He sat on a stump while Calvin waded out into the water.

Chapter Ten

J.J. DIDN'T COME HOME for supper. He wasn't home by bedtime either. Of all the days for him to pick to go out tomcatting, this day—what with Gil Dailey showing up without any warning—had to be the worst. Not that it was anything new for J.J. to stay out on a Saturday night after he'd collected his weekly wages. He had been doing it regularly ever since his brother came home late in September. It was something Sunny hadn't realized about J.J.—that whatever Royce Peeler did, J.J. was bound to copy.

Royce had been off in the army for a year and during that time J.J. had tried to be a good husband. He hadn't much liked working on the farm, but he'd done it anyway, as a sort of repayment to Papa for letting them live there. But just when J.J. was winning everyone over, just when Papa had almost stopped criticizing and frowning all the time, Royce Peeler got kicked out of the army and J.J. started running downhill.

There didn't seem to be anything much Sunny could do about it. Nagging only made him stay gone more and scolding riled his anger, so she tried not to do either one. Sometimes she couldn't stop herself, though, when she was so tired out from wrestling with the baby all day long, nursing every thirty or forty-five minutes trying to get little Isabel full. Sunny could count on one hand the number of times she'd gotten more than two hours of unbroken sleep in the six weeks since the baby came. And J.J. was no help at all. If he wasn't in town at his mama's house doing something, then he was out brawling around with Royce. He hadn't even been home for the birth of his own daughter, or for the long, hard labor that came before. The baby was already seven hours old by the time he shuffled in from wherever he'd been, smelling of cheap whiskey and even cheaper perfume.

Sunny knew he was unhappy. It didn't take a soothsayer to see that much. He could barely stand it around the farm. Most days he ate dinner at Mrs. Peeler's house in town, had breakfast there, too. Evenings he suffered through the suppers Mama cooked, hardly saying a word. And if someone tried to talk to him his answers were short, barely uttered monosyllables, after which his sulking silence continued.

He'd had to give up his cowboy work for Uncle Daniel, and she knew he blamed her for that. She knew he wanted a horse, but he lost or spent all the money he earned. He wanted to ride in a rodeo show, or go down to Houston and work in the oil fields. He wanted to do anything that got him the hell away from Mc-Dade and from "everybody in your whole damned family watching me all the time." So she realized he wasn't happy, but his behavior had become hard for her to defend.

And right in the middle of all this, here came Gil Dailey to cause more complications. She hated that all it took was one glimpse through the hazy window screen that morning, of Gil stepping from that ugly black car of his, and she was consumed again, full of sick longing for him. He was still her torment. She didn't know how she was going to make it all the way through Christmas with him there when after just a few hours of him she was already a nervous wreck. She wondered why she couldn't just shake him off, like a dog with a case of fleas.

At three o'clock in the morning, J.J. fumbled in, drunk and stinking, crashing into the granny rocker Mama had bought off Georgia Speck for two dollars. He disturbed the whole house. She imagined Gil in Ding's room, pictured him sitting up, listening to the bed creak after J.J. climbed on top of her. There wasn't any tenderness in it. He was like a cur dog marking his territory. And he woke the baby.

THE CHURCH PAGEANT TOOK place at seven o'clock on that Sunday night, two days before Christmas. The preacher was a visitor, Reverend Halbreath, from a Georgetown church in neighboring Williamson County. He said a long, long prayer, thanking God for the end of the horrible war and asking Him to help those in need, in particular the ones struck down by the flu terror raging over the land. After he finally said "Amen," mumbling whispers broke out amongst those present, everyone discussing in worried tones the latest sickness report they each had heard. Georgia Speck said everyone should say an extra prayer in their hearts for the Dillon family, which had just received word that young Thomas, Jr., had been killed up in the Argonne. It wasn't long before the extra prayer turned into plans for a dish supper to be made by all the women and carried out to the Dillons' farm the next evening.

During this discussion, Sunny had to take Isabel into the preacher's office to nurse. Mama brought in the swaddling the baby was to wear for the manger scene. Mama had Ding to get ready, too. He was playing one of the wise men, along with Rocky

McCarty and the youngest Murphy boy. The boy who was playing Joseph wasn't from McDade. He was a nephew to Ike Landers, just in town for the holidays, and Mama had taken charge of him as well. She rushed out of the office as quickly as she had rushed in.

J.J.'s little sister, Ivy, was Mother Mary, and it was the perfect part for her. Ivy was eleven and just crazy about Isabel. She came out to the farmhouse sometimes to hold the baby. She said she wished she could have a baby all her own to hold and kiss. Sunny thought Ivy was a little bit slow. But then the whole Peeler family seemed slow to Sunny. They didn't even understand about court-martials and dishonorable discharges. Mrs. Peeler had actually thrown a party for Royce when he came home after spending six months in the stockade for striking an officer. He'd never made it to France.

The door to the office opened again and it was J.J. this time. He had been helping to put up the walls to the manger and he had someone with him, someone Sunny couldn't see because he shoved the person back from the doorway as he came inside.

"For God's sake, Sunny, cover up your tit. You look like a fucking milk cow."

She glared at him. "You're not afraid somebody'll hear you cussing? Right here in church?"

He made a grunt and moved his eyes off her. He was wearing his Sunday suit, hair all combed neat. He looked downright pretty, but she wouldn't have admitted it right then, not even if someone had held a match flame to her feet. She hadn't yet forgiven him for his rough handling of her in the middle of the night.

Over breakfast, she had imagined everyone looking at her funny. Except Gil. He hadn't looked at her at all, and that had been a switch from the day before, when he'd been unable to take his eyes off her. She didn't know which way was worse. All afternoon he had stayed outside working on his automobile while she helped Mama make Christmas stockings for the mantel.

"How much longer are you gonna be in here?" J.J. said. "Me and Royce needs this room."

"For what?" The baby was already asleep at the breast, but Sunny wasn't about to let on.

"Just hurry up." He turned and left the room.

The church had put up a tree in the front hall, with little boxes tied to the limbs for all the children. Papa hadn't let Mama put up a Christmas tree. He said it was a tradition of German origin. To have been so opposed to war at the beginning, he'd become almost a fanatic by the end of it. Sunny just hoped there was a little box on the church tree for Ding.

She took Isabel, all swaddled head to toe and asleep, to the rough cradle the men had placed inside the manger. There was hay straw in the cradle, and someone had spread a flannel blanket over the straw. Lying there so sound asleep, Isabel looked like a little angel, if not the baby Jesus himself. Sunny stayed over to the east side of the church, just in case Isabel woke up and cried for her.

In marched Ivy and the Landers boy, and Georgia Speck took her place at the pulpit to read the Christmas story. Mama had Ding over at the west side with the other two wise men, awaiting their cue. Ding's head was turbaned in Mama's old paisley shawl, and he held a loaf tin Mama had painted gold. He was the wise man bringing myrrh. Sunny wondered just what myrrh was anyway.

"It's a resin," a voice said near her ear. She turned and Gil was standing right behind her.

"What?" she said. She hadn't even known Gil had come to the pageant. Last time she'd seen him, he'd been on his back underneath his car. Now he had on a stiff linen collar and a red tie with white polka dots.

"Myrrh. It's a gum resin from a thorny little tree in Africa. They used it for making medicine." He smiled and there was that chipped front tooth. "And some other things, too. Like perfume."

"Oh . . ."

In confusion, she turned back around to face the manger scene. Had he just read her mind? She would have sworn she hadn't spoken a word out loud.

All the sudden, and out of nowhere, a bad case of the giggles came over her. She pivoted her head toward the wall and covered her mouth, trying to stifle the sound and concentrate on the passages Georgia Speck was reading.

Gil leaned in close to her ear again. She could feel him like electricity. "If you can't straighten up we'll have to kick you out of here."

She twisted around until she could see his face. His smile had turned teasing. She smiled, too, but the truth was she just almost couldn't stand how gaunt and pale he looked, with those big, sad raccoon circles under his eyes. It made her want to rush him across the hall to where the ladies had their cakes and pies piled on a table and spoon-feed something into him.

"Where did you get that suit?" she said.

"How do you like it?" He held open the jacket to show her the vest and corded britches, neither of which fit him quite right. The toes of his army shoes peeked out from under his pants hems. He didn't have his cane with him, and she thought he probably should have. She wondered about his leg. It must be pretty bad for them to send him home so early. None of the other soldiers were due back for several more months.

"It hangs on you," she said, and laughed.

The woman in the end pew closest to where they were standing cleared her throat and gave them both a glaring look. "Sshh," the woman said. It was Priscilla Bright, the harness maker's wife. Sunny turned to the wall to laugh again. She didn't know why she was acting so giddy. She tried to stifle it.

Gil tapped her shoulder and nodded toward the manger. Ding was coming forward with his tin cake box, bashful, dipping his head. At the foot of the cradle where Isabel slept, he bowed low, so low he almost lost his balance. The collar pins from Gil's uniform glinted on the paisley turban Ding wore. He wouldn't part with those pins, not even to sleep. The kimono that was supposed to be his robe belonged to Aunt Dellie, who sat out in the church with Papa and Uncle Daniel and Calvin. They were all of them out there smiling. Over on the other side of the church, Mama was so delighted with her darling she looked ready to cry.

The rest of the pageant went along fine until Mr. Horner's goat kicked over the east wall of the manger. People in the church burst into laughter, but Sunny didn't join them. In her mind she saw that wall toppling right onto little Isabel in the cradle. Thankfully the Landers boy caught it in time. Ivy helped him lay it down flat on the floor. That ended the play, and Ed Speck came running up to take pictures before the players left the manger scene.

The flash of the camera startled Isabel awake and Sunny lifted her from her hay-stuffed cradle. Mrs. Peeler was right there and she took the baby from Sunny's arms to show her off to members of the church, and to brag about how little Isabel favored her daddy. Papa liked to say that Mrs. Peeler could talk the legs off a brass bed.

Folks herded toward the rear of the hall where the food was piled up on tables. Sunny saw J.J. and Royce sneak out of the preacher's office. She was pretty sure she caught the flicker of a silver whiskey flask, too, sliding into Royce Peeler's breast pocket. She marched right over to J.J. and she could smell the liquor six feet away.

"Too bad you missed the whole thing," she said.

"I seen enough," J.J. said.

Royce grinned at her. "You're looking mighty pretty in that dress."

She almost said thank you, that was how uneasy Royce Peeler made her. But she realized in time that he was probably just making fun, since she hadn't lost all her baby weight yet. The dress, one of Mama's with a flouncy collar and a kick hem, fit too tight across the bosom. It wasn't stylish, and it was out of season being made of jersey cloth with silk wisteria blooms tacked at the waist. Sunny was glad when Ding came running up to hug her, so she could turn away from Royce Peeler's grinning face.

"Did you see me up there?" Ding said, breathless and blazing hot. She wiped off some of his sweat.

"You did just fine," she said, and then looked around for Isabel.

Ivy had the baby now, and some of the women were still making over her. Papa stood with Uncle Daniel. Papa always enjoyed Uncle Daniel's company, and Mama was with a group of ladies by the food table having a good time, shining. She looked pretty and young beside most of the others. Calvin was out by the Christmas tree with the Landers boy and some of the Petersons close to his age. Gil had vanished.

J.J.'s buddy, Jim Buck Murphy, had shown up and he stood

over across the room with J.J. and Royce, ogling Anita Harvey and her friend from Cedar Creek. Royce still had on his flirting face and he said something to the girls. Sunny was too far away to hear what, but J.J. laughed at it and then he said something, too. And the Cedar Creek girl reached up to stuff a cookie between J.J.'s lips.

Anger surged through Sunny. Not on account of jealousy really; she was used to having girls and women admire J.J.'s good looks. But it proved how little he thought of her anymore, that he would cavort like that right in front of her. In front of everybody else, too. When Aunt Dellie came up to chat, Sunny stood there like a statue, smiling, forcing herself to focus on Aunt Dellie's mouth moving and not on J.J. across the room dallying with those girls.

Aunt Dellie told Sunny about the letter that had just come from Gabriel, how he was fine, though sorry the war was over without his unit ever having gotten into action. "All this time I've been worried half to death about him and he was still at a training camp in Brittany." She sighed, laughed. Sunny laughed, too, as she cast another glance about the room. J.J. was gone from where he'd been standing. Jim Buck and Royce were gone, too. She couldn't spot the Cedar Creek girl or Anita Harvey either. Aunt Dellie continued: "Hard as he has tried, Gabriel has managed to miss out on two wars now, so I'm hoping when he comes home he'll get himself back into college."

"Oh, sure he will," Sunny said vacantly. Mama had the baby right then, so Sunny kissed Aunt Dellie's cheek and made for the side door that went out to the churchyard.

As she stepped outside, she was almost swept away by the norther that had come in unexpectedly. The wind blew fierce and stinging. It took an effort just to get the door shut again. She hadn't brought a coat or even a shawl, and so she just hugged her arms against the change in temperature.

Out in the yard, J.J. and Jim Buck were passing a crock jug back and forth, upending it like it was nearly empty already. Both of them leaned against the cistern stand. Even with the brake on the windmill and the sails curbed, the vane rattled up a storm. Over by the fence arbor, Royce had his arm around the Cedar Creek girl's neck. Sunny heard Anita Harvey say, "Let's go back inside, Eunice. I'm freezing to death out here."

Sunny started for J.J. and Jim Buck said, "Uh-oh, here she comes."

J.J. twisted around toward Sunny, the leavings of laughter on his face. A frown moved in quickly. He stood and put his hands on his hips. "What the hell are you doing out here?" He was so loud, even the girls over by Royce stared. "You get back inside there with the baby."

"You come back inside then too, J.J." Sunny shivered. The wind seemed to blast right through her.

Jim Buck made a clucking noise, then a squawk like a hen laying an egg. J.J. cracked a grin back at him, but he wasn't grinning at all when he started in Sunny's direction. Royce ducked the Cedar Creek girl under the fence arbor and Anita Harvey followed.

"Don't you stay out here drinking liquor again tonight." Sunny lowered her voice as he drew nearer.

"I thought I told you to get back inside." He took her by her shoulders and turned her around, pointed her toward the side door of the church. She wrenched free.

"Stop it, J.J."

From the cistern, Jim Buck let go with some more chicken noises, softer, in between swigs from the jug. J.J. glanced again, and she could tell those henpecked sounds were nagging at him. She wanted to saunter over there and slap the jug right out of Jim Buck Murphy's hands.

She said to J.J., "Next you'll be running off with your trifling friend, and with your damned brother and his damned floozies—"

"Stop that cussing. I won't have a woman of mine cussing me." J.J. stretched his neck at her and drew up his hand, threatening, all of it just show for Jim Buck's sake.

"Don't raise your hand at me, J.J." She glared into his eyes, and they stayed that way for a couple of seconds before he lowered his hand.

"Why don't you go back in there with your war hero? Yeah, go find gimp-leg and let him keep you company."

"That's not funny, J.J."

"Who's laughing?" His lip curled into a mean smile. "I seen the two of you groping each other out there, giggling in front of everybody in church. Don't think I missed that, Sunny girl."

"You don't know what you're talking about." A knot of guilt formed in her throat. She'd thought J.J. had been in the preacher's office drinking with Royce. "Good Lord, J.J., he's my cousin."

The smile slid sideways, became mocking. "That how come you to put on that face paint and tart your hair all up? 'Cause he's your goddamned cousin?" He plucked at the cloisonné hair clip she had borrowed from Mama.

"Quit it!" She deflected his hand.

"You think I'm blind? Or that I can't smell the toilet water you got splashed all over you like a two-bit whore? Hell, Sunny, this is your lucky day. I'm giving you permission." He turned her around and pushed her toward the door. "Now you get back in there like I told you to."

Her neck burned hot, followed close by a chill that kept her from saying anything in reply. When she whirled around, he was already walking away—that cocky, bouncing walk, full of himself.

Without thinking straight, she went at him. She hurled herself at his back and shoved him with both her hands on his spine. He came near to losing his feet but didn't quite. He turned and latched on to her left wrist with a bruising grip, but that didn't stop her. She swung at him with her other fist. She was fed up with his loose ways and at how he thought he could say any horrible thing to her he wanted. She hit him on his shoulder, his chest. Her heart pounded, and she socked him right in the face, a blow so hard it tingled all the way up her arm.

A delicious, gratifying shock came into his eyes. He backed up, dumbfounded for a second, but then his hand swooped down, clawlike, and caught her right wrist too, pinned it together with her left, and his strength astonished her, that he could so easily immobilize her that way, with one hand wrapped tightly around two of hers. Before she could shrink away, his eyes went as brittle as a cock rooster's and he gave her an open-palmed wallop across her face. Bells rang in her ears. Real bells. Real stars, too, circled in her vision, just like in a silly picture show. Her sense hadn't yet returned when his hand landed with a smack from the other direction, the backside of his knuckles connecting with her cheekbone. She flopped to the ground in a crumpled heap, legs tangling beneath her. As if from inside a well she heard Jim Buck's voice —"That's enough, J.J.!"

Hands reached for her, clutched at her. She blinked and J.J. was bent over her, his face all screwed up and regretful. "Shit, Sunny! Why'd you hit me? Why'd you do that, sugar?"

Jim Buck hovered behind J.J., both of them peering worried at her. Jim Buck had his hat on, two toothpicks stuck down in the band. "She's all right," he said.

J.J. kept grabbing at her. "You shouldn't of swung at me, dar-lin. You shouldn't of done that. Did I hurt you, baby? Did I?"

She battled at his hands and kicked her feet, crabbing back from him. "Get away! Just get away from me!" Her voice seemed to disappear in the wind, but he heard her well enough. Her tone straightened him upright.

"See?" Jim Buck said. "I told you she's all right. Now let's go. Royce's leaving without us."

She pushed herself to a sitting position and J.J. raked at his hair. "Goddammit, Sunny—"

"Go on. Get out of here," she said, and she watched as Jim Buck prodded J.J. toward the fence. J.J. hung back for another second before Jim Buck dragged him through the arbor. J.J.'s voice, high-pitched and whining, said something that she couldn't make out. But she didn't care to hear. Except for precious Isabel, she wished she had never laid eyes on him.

Once they were gone, she dabbed at her jaw, her nose, mouth, checking for blood. There wasn't any, but her whole head and face throbbed. She got to her knees, felt wobbly. One side of Mama's dress was filthy and had two snagging rips in the seam. She brushed at the skirt, tried to scrape the dirt off with her fingernails, but it did no good. The wind blew at her again, cold, stirring dust into her eyes.

"Sunny? Is that you out here?"

She raised her face and saw Gil coming around the far side of the church building. An egg-shaped moon had risen, so she could see well enough to recognize his limp. He needed that cane. He hobbled into the beam falling from the gas lamp along the side door to the church.

She sighed. She pushed at her hair, which was a solid mess. "Go away, Gil."

"I thought I heard something." He kept on coming forward and glanced off in the direction J.J. and Jim Buck had gone. "I was out front smoking a cigarette . . . What's the matter?"

Now she was going to cry and get emotional. *Now,* with Gil there to see for himself how miserable her life had become. She shook her head and bit back tears, but her resolve didn't last past the first touch of his hand.

He helped her to her feet and she buried her face in the lapel of his jacket. She could feel his ribs and smell the wool in the suit, cigarette smoke in the fibers. More tears got past her, and she knew if she didn't stop she would make his shirt soggy. But he hugged her hard, and when she felt his lips press her hair it came to her that it had been inevitable from the second he drove his motorcar into the yard yesterday that she would end up right where she was. She wondered at how little control she seemed to have over her own destiny.

"Take me home." She pulled away from him. "Will you please just take me home?"

"Tell me what's the matter." He lifted her chin and reached with his thumb to wipe away a tear. As he did, he touched the tender place along her cheekbone where the back of J.J.'s hand had already brought on a swelling. She flinched.

"I need to go get the baby," she said quickly, drawing out of his reach.

But he had seen that flinch, and he held fast to her elbow. He tilted her around so she was positioned fully in the light. His mouth tightened. "Where'd he go?"

"It doesn't matter."

He turned as if to head for the fence arbor, but he couldn't move fast enough, and she caught up with him easily. She clutched his arm.

"What do you think you're doing, Gil? Please . . . just take me home."

"He's got no right to beat you, Sunny."

"He didn't *beat* me. I hit him first. I started it." She forced herself to smile, but even as she did, she felt the soreness on her face.

"Somebody needs to teach him a lesson."

"But not you." The bothersome tears came gushing back again. She yanked hard on his arm and he stopped moving to look at her. "Please . . . I just want to go home, all right? Will you take me home?"

He glanced again toward the fence arbor, frowned, though maybe with less hostility. Then he shrugged off his jacket and wrapped it around her shoulders. She clutched the coat closer. It was warm from his body and it stopped her quivering.

"I'll go get the baby," he said. "You wait in the car. If he comes back—"

"He won't come back. He'll be out raising hell till morning at least." She laughed, trying to get a smile out of Gil. He kept his frown.

After lingering for another moment, he aimed for the door. She watched him struggle with the three steps and go inside.

Footsteps and giggling voices came from the direction of the arbor. She wiped at her face, sniffled to clear her nose. In another second Anita Harvey and her friend from Cedar Creek bobbed through the fence. Their cheeks shone with the cold; hair windblown. They hurried past the cistern and the rattly windmill, hugging their arms around each other. "Why didn't you say you were married to one of them?" the Cedar Creek girl said as they rushed by Sunny and up the steps to the church.

Chapter Eleven

SUNNY WAS RIGHT WHERE Gil had left her, nose red from the cold, eyes red, too, but she wasn't crying anymore. He was glad of that much. But the swollen place on her cheekbone made him want to hunt down that bastard husband of hers and gut him like a fish. The suit coat belonged to Gabe O'Barr, lent to Gil by Gabe's mother, and the sleeves hung so long on Sunny she looked like her hands were missing. It brought an image to Gil's mind of some of those boys on the ship coming back. Her fingertips emerged when she lifted her arms to take the baby against her and the image receded.

"Thank you," she murmured, and folded a flap of the coat around Isabel's little head.

Even after all the work he'd put in on the Hudson that afternoon, the damned thing wouldn't start. He'd spent three hours at Uncle Dane's workbench cleaning the carburetor with spirit oil, taking it apart, putting it back together again, but the choke still wouldn't close right. He got out in the stinging wind and shut it manually, and when the car still wouldn't start, he let loose with a string of swearwords before he remembered Sunny sitting beside him.

"Well," she said. "I guess they taught you how to cuss over there."

"Sorry."

She shrugged and turned her attention back on the baby, patting her to sleep.

The car finally fired up on the tenth try and held. He pumped the accelerator to prime the carburetor. He checked to see if the air register beneath Sunny's feet was open to let in the heat funneled back from the radiator. "It'll warm up in here in a minute," he said, holding his hand flat toward the floor, but he might as well have been talking to himself. She was staring off out her window. He shifted into gear and moved the car from the church lot.

In the dim glow from the dashboard, he could see that her jaw had also swollen out of shape. That place on her cheekbone was high enough to creep into a shiner. Everybody would know then that her pissant husband had smacked her. He didn't think Uncle Dane would tolerate a shiner on her, no more than Gil himself planned to. Uncle Dane kept a shotgun in his barn, a heavy-bore, single-barrel shotgun that would even up the odds if that little bastard's brother or his buddy tried to involve themselves.

The wind was vicious and it took both hands to hold the car on the road. He tried to keep an eye out for ruts, but it was hard with Sunny tugging at his concentration. The tires hit a few.

The silence between them seemed to gather its own momentum, and he knew if he didn't speak soon the opportunity would be lost. He said, "Is it because of how he looks? Blond hair and blue eyes?"

She turned her face toward him, coming out of whatever trance she'd been in. "What?"

"He treats you like dirt. And if he's got any brains, he doesn't show it. So I figure it must be his looks." Gil almost missed a curve watching for her answer. He had to oversteer to keep the car on the road. "So tell me what you see in him. Give me something to go on."

She bent toward the baby in her lap. "He never lifted a hand to me before."

"Well, now he has. And that'll make it easier for him next time. And before you know it, he'll be slapping you around whenever he feels like it. Any time you don't answer him quick enough, or he doesn't like what you have to say."

They came up on the last turn to the farm and he wasn't ready to be there yet. He still had things to say, questions to ask her, answers to hear. And he knew once they got there she'd go running off into her room, avoiding him like she'd been doing since he arrived. So he pulled the car over to the side of the road. The headlamps caught tufts of muley grass lying supine in the fierce wind.

He took the car out of gear and let up on the clutch. He couldn't stand too much of that clutch. He massaged his left thigh, kept his right foot on the brake. "Grab yourself some sense, Sunny, and quit him. Do it right now."

She patted her baby's back, but it had become more like a nervous tic than necessary. Isabel was fast asleep, and Sunny's eyes were fastened on him. "It's none of your business, Gil."

"Well, maybe I'll make it my business. Uncle Dane offered to lease me a piece of the Kennedy tract. Maybe I'll just take him up on it."

"What? Why would you do that? You hate farming."

"Yeah, that was my first thought, too. But now I don't know. Maybe it's not such a bad idea. Got no other prospects looming on my horizon. And it seems like you need somebody around here looking out for you."

She stared at him, then she tucked Isabel against her shoulder and reached for the door lever. "Thanks for bringing me home. I can walk from here."

He grabbed her before she could get the door open. "Dammit, Sunny, stop acting like you don't know me."

"Quit trying to butt in, Gil!"

The baby went to fussing at the loud talk and at getting jostled around. Sunny took up her patting again, faster and harder, but at least she settled back from the door. He left his arm resting on the seat behind her, watched her calm Isabel down again. He quelled the urge to apologize.

"I don't know what you expect of me," he said, speaking quieter. "When I think about you going around with a guy like that—"

"I'm not going around with him. He's my husband."

"You know what I mean." He let his hand touch her shoulder. He could feel her bones, small and fragile, through the thick wool of the jacket. "You were supposed to wait for me."

"You told me to forget you."

"No, I did not say that."

"To stop thinking about you, then. It's the same thing." She dropped her head back against the seat of the car and his arm, as if she were too tired to use her neck anymore. Little Isabel had gone back to sleep, and a tear glittered down Sunny's face.

A sharp gust rocked the car, whistled around the windows. He reached across and gentled his thumb along the curve of her throat. She didn't move. "So did you?" he said. "Stop thinking about me?"

She kept on staring at the roof of the car, her neck ivory white and smooth. She swallowed and turned her face toward him. Later he would try to remember if he kissed her first or if she kissed him, but whichever the case, passion took control of it. He remembered the taste of her lips, the desire she roused in him. He pulled her closer and he never even felt his foot leave the brake pedal.

The road at that particular spot was fairly level, but with a subtle slope to the ditch for drainage. Gil had stopped the car a little to the right of the center, so there was a slight incline, just enough to start the rotation of the wheels. That afternoon he had set the idle higher to compensate for the temperamental choke, and without his foot on the brake to hold the car back, they went bouncing out into the ditch, up onto the other side, and smacked into a barbed-wire fence. Luckily it didn't take but a second or two for Gil's reflexes to recover. Any longer and they might have plowed right through that fence and into Ezra Hennesey's cow pasture.

"Are you OK?" he said, after he had bucked the car to a halt. Sunny had a tight hold on little Isabel, but the baby didn't appear to have even awakened. A feisty Boston terrier–type dog came woofing out onto the road at them.

Sunny laughed, a releasing kind of laugh, the same way she had laughed at his teasing her during the pageant. The sound of it sent his heart beating again. He almost forgot that the car was spraddling the ditch and reached to pull her back in his arms. Out on the road, the terrier kept raising hell.

"Mr. Hennesey'll be coming out any minute." She sounded gleeful and mischievous. She tugged away. "Can you get us out of here?"

He touched her hair, kissed her baby's head, and shifted the Hudson into reverse. The wheels spun dust for a second before they caught hold. The barbed wire scraped a long, screaming gash down the side, but the car needed a new paint job anyway. He shifted gears again and pulled out onto the road.

In another hundred yards, they came to the farm gate. He was about to set the brake and get out to open it when she said, "Why don't you just keep on going," in a steady voice. A smile crawled up his cheeks. He felt it there and didn't know what to do with it except leave it alone. She didn't want to go home any more than he wanted to take her there.

He continued on down the road, past Karen DeLony's darkened house, past the county-line marker. Another half mile and Sunny said, "Turn here," which he did. She showed him when to turn again.

The final road they took was the poorest yet, hardly more than a game trail, and little used. In places, grass almost obliterated the two tracks. When the car pulled out of the last cedar brake, Gil saw that they were at the top of one of the Knobs. The moon rose high and bright in a sky shot with stars. Wind lashed the cedars like scarecrows. A crumbling-down shack stood weathered and sun bleached, reflecting the moon and flickering tree shadows.

"It's an old line shack," she said, and Gil didn't ask her any more questions. He didn't think he would care for the answers. His imagination saw her coming up here with J.J. Peeler, that little bastard, but he didn't want to know for certain.

He set the hand brake this time, switched off the lights, but he didn't shut down the motor. Didn't want to get stranded. He reached for her and she came without any reluctance. The long drive had only increased the anticipation and he kissed her with the same passion that had come so quickly down on the road. But it was awkward, holding her, kissing her the way he wanted to with the baby in her arms. They made Isabel a little nest on the floorboard out of the baby blanket and Gil's suit jacket, and Isabel snuggled in like it was a feather bed.

"She'll be just fine down there," he said as Sunny sank back into his arms. "She'll be warm as toast."

They were no longer two kids playing at lovemaking. He wanted her, had hungered for her, and with no guilt or shame he meant finally to have her. He tasted the inside of her mouth, removed the cloisonné clip from her hair so it fell in a tangle around her shoulders. That night behind the barn had deviled his dreams for too long. He ached to look at her again, to press her naked breasts against him. His fingers found the tiny buttons at the back of her neck.

"Not with the baby . . ." She dragged herself out from under him, combing at her hair.

"I'm crazy about you, Sunny. In case you doubt it."

She looked at him, came against him again. He opened his door and pulled her out after him.

The wind was raw and shivery. He wrapped his arms around her and nodded in the direction of the shack. "Is it safe to go in there?" Her eyes were big, shining bright, and he saw her waver. He kissed her.

It was nearly as cold inside the shack. The wind swooshed in the chinks and cracks. Moonlight flooded from the high-set windows. Broken glass and bottles from somebody's drinking spree glinted on the dirt floor. A long plank lay among the debris, but he knew he would never make it down there. Not with his leg.

Her underwear was made of cotton, elastic at the waist. He helped her peel them down. She helped him with the buttons on the pants he wore. He shouldered off his suspenders on his own. By the time he wound his hands under her thighs and lifted her around him, they were both short of breath.

It was not the way he had imagined, or how he would have chosen. He would have preferred a snug bed with her naked, stretched out beneath him where he could feel her body all along his own. But since the shack with its glass-littered floor and the blowing cold was his only choice, he took it.

She clung to his neck and he pushed into her, and in, and she opened like a rose. He half expected lightning to strike them both dead, or for the ground to split and them to fall into hell together. They kissed and broke away gasping, found each other's mouth again, both of them in a kind of rapture.

He'd had his half dozen whores. Copulated; fornicated, as Ma would say. But he had never made love and at the same time *been* in love, and the difference overwhelmed him. He heard the surprised moan escape his throat—too quickly—felt the kisses she planted all over his face. In another second, he was too weak to hold her or himself upright. He stumbled, his left leg sliding out from under him. She went down, too, but she scrambled quickly to her knees.

"Gil, my God. Are you hurt? Are you all right?" She touched his shoulder, his face.

He reached for her and gathered her onto his lap. His heart still raced, but he squeezed her against him. He kissed her wherever his lips landed, and she curled her arms around him. "Christ, Sunny," he whispered, all he could think of to say.

Wind sang in rafters and the cold slunk back in. He felt a shiver go through her and he tried to bundle her closer, but she was as close as she could get. He kissed her forehead and the bruise on her cheekbone. Making love to her had soothed his soul. He felt like anything was possible—a feeling he thought he'd left in France. She raised her face, and with the moonlight sifting down and her hair everywhere, she looked like something wild he had caught. "You're a knockout."

"I don't love him, Gil. I never did love him."

"I know." He backed her hair from her face. A tear slipped silvery from her eye. "Don't cry, Sunny, for God's sake. We'll go away someplace. I've got a little money. Enough to last till I can find a job." He kissed her brow. He couldn't seem to stop kissing her. "We'll get married. You want to do that? You want to marry me?"

She laughed and another tear slid out. She wiped it away. She laughed again, childlike and shy. "Someplace where?"

"Anywhere you want to."

She hugged him, rested her chin on his shoulder. "I always thought I'd like to see Galveston."

"All right. We'll get us a room at the Tremont, live in the lap of luxury. Why not?" He laid her back on his arm and ignored the ache of his leg underneath him. He kissed her and pushed her dress off one shoulder, kissed her there, too. He wanted to make love to her again. "Let's go right now. I want to sleep with you beside me, and every time I roll over I want you there where I can reach you."

She lifted his hand from her breast and kissed between his thumb and first knuckle. "What in the world would they all think?" She said it in a lazy voice. "Aunt Prudie would die. But I wonder about Mama. She loves you dearly. So does Papa." She touched his forehead like she was tracing some new lines she'd found there. "She told me one time ... she said, 'Half the blood in Gil is the same as in you.' She said we couldn't love each other. She called it incest."

The word jarred him. Not that he'd never heard it before. Ma had told him the same thing. Except she had used a lot of other words, too: Blood cousins. Sin and immorality. Satan's work. He pushed himself upright. "That's a bunch of crap, Sunny. See what they've done to us? Telling us a damned thing like that? They've kept us apart when all this time we should've been together."

She sat up too. "Then you don't believe it?"

"Hell, no. I'm not your brother. *That's* incest." He tugged his suspenders on over his arms. "How close do you think either of them ever read the Bible? Not too damned close, because right off there's Jacob, marrying *two* of his first cousins. Right in Genesis. If it's such a big sin then why did God bless it and give them all those kids together? A whole damn flock of kids. Enough to make the people of Israel."

"Is that the truth?"

He looked at her and his anger ebbed. "All you got to do is just read it."

She hugged her arms. He reached for her and she cuddled against him, kissed his neck. He rubbed her hands, stirring up warmth.

"I love you, Sunny, and I'm not apologizing. It's not a sin. But you know what, I don't care either way. If we have to we'll go to France to get married."

"France?" she said, as if it were a place she'd never heard of. "You just got back from there."

"Yeah, and I'll tell you something I found out. Texas isn't the only place in the world to live."

"It's not?" She pressed their noses together, grinned.

He kissed her, and kissed her again. And they kept on kissing and snuggling for another minute or two, until she was trembling with the cold. They had to go back. Neither of them wanted to. That shack, that hill, had become like a haven, the place where they'd found each other again. It would have been much easier to just stay there forever than to go down and face the rest of the world. Because the truth was, they had denied themselves to each other for so long, it was hard for them to imagine it could be any other way.

Sunny helped Gil to his feet, and he needed her to help. His leg and hip had stiffened up, ached deep down from the cold and from sliding to the ground so hard. They righted their own clothes and each other's, and Gil could feel her already losing her nerve even before she said, "What if he's already there? J.J. Waiting on us?"

"I hope he is, the damn fool. Thinking he could steal you from me."

Her hand caught his arm at the crook of his elbow. "It's no telling what he might do, Gil."

He held her cold face in both his hands. "He doesn't scare me."

Steam from the running engine puffed out around the car in a cloud. They went arm in arm and he opened the passenger door for her, helped her in onto the seat. He leaned in, too. The wind came wailing up over the hilltop, but inside the car was warm.

"A vacation on Galveston Beach sure does sound good right now, doesn't it?" he said.

She nodded, but her smile was worried. She was trying not to let him see it, and he let her think he hadn't. He whistled around the front of the car, but his leg hurt so much he had to brace himself on the hood. When he got in, he yanked that leg in after him like it was a ball and chain. He hoped he could work the clutch, but in any case, he wasn't going to let a little pain spoil his jubilation. She was still his. He hadn't lost her.

"If this flivver won't make it, we'll ditch it and catch a train," he said. Sunny lifted the baby off the floorboard. Little Isabel still slept sound and quiet. "When we get down there, Sunny, you just go inside and start packing what all you need for you and the baby. Let me do the talking."

"You mean for us to go tonight?" She pushed the blanket out of Isabel's face.

"Isn't that what we said? I'm going to tell them you're leaving him and coming with me. I'll tell *him* if he's there. There's not a damn thing any of them can do to stop us."

He let off the hand brake. Without wincing too much, he managed the clutch and levered the gears into reverse. He reached his arm across the seat, turned to look backward, and a cry rose from Sunny. A cry so eerie and out of place it stood the hair on his neck. His foot slammed the brake pedal.

"What?! What is it?!"

She raised her head and he watched her face cave in. She shoved the bundled baby at him and threw herself against her door. "Oh God! Oh God . . ."

Something inside him blanked and he was back in that shell hole off the Jaulny-Thiaucourt crossroad, wallowing in mud, gas closing around him, smelling the rotten tomato smell of his wounds. Scrabbling for his mask . . .

Where is it? Wedged under you, stupid. Hold your breath, just hold it. Eyes, watery eyes. Itching throat. Burning. Closing up. Jesus! I'm not going to make it! Yank harder . . . put it on. That's it. Breathe. Just breathe. You're OK, you're OK. Now reach up. Reach. Try . . . if you could just reach . . . that tree root. No! A dead thing. An oozing, blown-apart dead thing . . . a hand. A hand! Somebody's hand! . . . Let it go! Let it go, let it go . . .

He jerked back, gasping, fear thickening his blood. He didn't know how long he'd been sitting there, staring, blank. The passenger door stood open. Cold air swirled in. Sunny was out on the ground—"oh God oh God oh God"—rolling in the dirt like a mad dog, and he didn't think he could take this. Not this. Not yet.

The baby was in his arms, already cold, stiff and heavy, but he tucked the blanket around it anyway. He put it over in the backseat, then took the jacket and wrapped that around it, too. Decided to cover up its head so Sunny wouldn't have to see it again. To him, the baby was already an it. Easier that way. Easier than with a real person. He'd learned that in France, too. Shove it away, hold it back. Go numb.

Crazy Barfield, driving through the battleground, busting open Germans' heads like cantaloupe under the wheels. Pop! Pop! Pop!

Sunny was doubled over, arms across her belly, forehead down, rocking and moaning like an Indian squaw. He had to stop her. He went out there to try to pick her up. She wrenched her shoulders and threw off his hands.

"Let me get you in the car," he said. She allowed his arms to slide under her. His good leg wobbled with the extra weight it had to bear, but he gathered her up, gathered himself up, too. He had to pause and get his breath. "I've got you," he said to reassure himself.

As soon as he settled her inside the car, nausea swept over him with such force he had to lean against the door. He didn't try to talk to her. The bundle in the backseat leaped at him. He blocked his face with his arm. What had they done? His palms were sweaty.

Sunny turned to him, her cheeks soaked, eyes strange. Grief in there. Guilt, too. She gave the guilt to him, passed it on like a disease with that one look. "Where's my baby? Where is she?"

"In the back. She's OK."

Her hand clamped his forearm, fingernails dug in. "No, she's not! She's not OK!"

"Sunny . . . Sunny, I didn't mean . . ."

He tried to pull her against him but she wouldn't come. She scratched him away and scrambled over into the backseat. She started unwrapping the bundle. He couldn't watch. His chest was so burning heavy it was all he could do just to breathe. Breathe and drive. An eternity down from that hill.

Part Two

To Walk in Thy Ways

Chapter Twelve

THE GARDEN CORN GREW to such a height that year, a silver variety, the seed for which Sunny got from old Ambrose Dillon when he came to collect the raw milk she couldn't use. Both cows were giving, having just been freshened, but she didn't have time for separating and churning, so she took what she could get for the milk raw. The corn made good tassel, better than the dent corn Papa usually planted every spring for the animals. That year he didn't have the strength for it, and the hired man Uncle Daniel sent over couldn't be expected to tend to everything. The man had already harvested the wheat and delivered it to the thresher, took care of all that while Papa lay flat on his back in bed sweating through the convulsive fevers of the flu.

Some folks believed the Reverend Halbreath brought the sickness over from Georgetown. Or maybe it was Ike Landers's nephew, who had played Joseph in the Christmas pageant. Others said it was the Germans who had planted the germs. Still others blamed sin. But however it arrived, it took folks down like dominoes.

Annie Belle Speck went first. The Peelers lost little Ivy, and another sister, Louann. Lukas Strong made it back from the war but couldn't beat the flu. And Mama, she didn't last but thirty-six hours. Shockingly quick. And Sunny barely got the sheets wound around Mama before Papa went down.

As long as she had been alive, he had never been sick a day, and she aimed to bring him back before he joined Mama in the graveyard. She did everything the doctor said to do. She wore the germ mask and fed Papa liquids, piled on mustard poultices, nursed him night and day while he lay like a stone. Aunt Dellie took Ding off to their house and sent Aunt Karen to help with Papa, but Sunny couldn't sleep with him lying there so still. Sometimes she had to lean down close to hear him breathing.

"He's very sick, Sunny," old Doc Rutherford said, as if he were trying to prepare her for the worst. But how could anyone prepare for losing both parents within a week?

A lump of fear plugged Sunny's throat. "Yessir" was all she could think to say.

She didn't know why she was one of those not to be struck by the flu. Nobody could put reason to it. The strongest seemed to go first. Down at the lumberyard they ran out of wood for caskets.

When Papa's fever finally broke, Sunny sat on the trunk at the foot of his bed and let herself cry two tears. No more. If she allowed herself any more she was afraid she would never quit.

In March, Gabriel arrived home with a French bride and he came out to the farm with three colored men to get the yams planted. The activity coaxed Papa out of bed, but just barely. He leaned his weight on the windowsill and watched out toward the fields.

"Gabe's home?" he said, sounding stiff and tired.

"And with a French bride that can barely speak English."

"Gabe talks French?" Papa seemed to have turned old overnight, but his color had started to come back.

"Aunt Dellie says no, but I guess they make out all right." Sunny used the opportunity to strip the bed and fluff up the pillows. The room smelled sharply of sickness and she cracked open the window. "Anyway, he came home married."

Papa just leaned there, staring off at the men working. "For crying out loud."

They never spoke of Mama. It was as if neither of them could digest her passing well enough to even grieve for it.

By June, days were easier to tolerate. The garden came in lush. There'd been good rains. And Papa felt well enough to take the buggy out to look at the fields, but he was so changed. Like a broken tree. Aunt Dellie still kept Ding. None of them could ever get set on a day for him to come home. And little by little, half his things got moved over to the big house with the stained-glass windows. There were lots of things to keep a little boy occupied there: dogs, a barn cat with a new litter of kittens, saddle horses, and six thousand acres in which to play. Nobody seemed in a big hurry to put things back to normal.

Sunny had forgotten how normal went. She cooked meals, something she had never done much of and was no good at. She cleaned house, did laundry, fed the animals. When she found a little free time, she worked the garden, turning in manure, thinning sprouts, sowing seed saved from last year.

The cool of morning was her favorite time to escape out there, after Papa had gone off in the buggy and breakfast was laid away. She used a hand spade to dig out weeds. She preferred to work on her knees, where she could smell the dirt and crush the soft clods in her palm.

"Sunny? You in there, girl?"

The voice disturbed her solitude. She parted the cornstalks and Royce Peeler stood there, hatless, hair the color of pecans left out in the sun. A hank of it fell across his forehead.

"I come to see if you needed more wood chopped," he said.

"I think there's plenty for now."

"All right." He wobbled one of the fence posts surrounding the garden. "I called at the front-porch door so I reckoned you was around back." He glanced toward the creek and then back at her. A smile tried to crack his lips. "That cukes you got growing there?"

"Pickling." She peered up from the row of new vines. "No word from J.J.?"

"No." He shook his head and looked thoughtful. "Hadn't seen you in a few weeks," he said. "Thought I'd check how you was doing. Where's your pa at?"

"The Kennedy fields."

"He's feeling peart then?"

"He's fine, thank you."

Royce nodded, then gestured at the bucket of weeds on the ground beside her. "You gonna throw them weeds to the chickens?"

Milkwort and chickweed spilled over the sides of the bucket. She lifted her head. "In a minute."

"Well, hand them over and I'll do it for you."

She rose with the bucket and stepped her way through the corn to the fence. He took the bucket from her and at the same time grabbed her hand. He looked at her mouth.

"Why don't you come out of there for a little bit?" he said.

She stared at his eyes. They were blue like J.J.'s, but flame blue where J.J.'s had been a greenish blue. She took the straw hat off her head and hung it on the post. She went down the fence to the gate.

He was there to open it for her. They went toward the house. He left the bucket of weeds on the bottom porch step. The hens came right up to inspect it as Sunny wiped her feet at the back door.

Royce didn't touch her until they were in the bedroom—Ding's room. She never used that front bedroom anymore. It had become a storage room for unwanted things. Royce's hands gripped her around the waist, slipped up behind her neck. She opened her mouth for his kiss. He untied her apron, worked through the buttons down her spine. As the dress came off her shoulders, she reached up automatically to clamp it there. He raised his face away from her, lips moist and shining. A rough finger traced along her jawbone.

"Just let it go, sugar," he whispered, so close she felt his breath.

Her grip eased and the dress caught on her hips for a second before it fell down around her bare feet.

She had no illusions about Royce Peeler. She knew exactly what he was, but it didn't matter. It was all instinct, animal, earthy, two bodies locked together, taking. It had nothing to do with emotion. She didn't feel anything besides his hands on her, didn't wish or regret or mourn. She was a husk, a figure in a newspaper cartoon, nothing inside the lines but emptiness.

When Papa was deathly sick, Royce had come the first time. After Mama's quiet funeral, after the Peelers had lost little Ivy and Louann, he brought a cauldron of cabbage stew from his mother. He stayed and chopped wood for two hours. The next day, he came back and chopped some more. He didn't run from the quarantine flag the way everyone else did.

When the Peeler family got a first letter from J.J., Royce brought her the news. J.J. was roughnecking down near Beaumont. Had no plans to come back. He was making good money and happy to be doing something important with himself. On

Royce's next visit, he brought two photographs taken with Ed Speck's camera—little Isabel in the manger, the other, in Sunny's arms. She'd looked at those pictures and been barely able to talk. She'd had to sit down on the porch glider.

"I didn't mean to cause you to bawl," he said, sitting down beside her.

"I'm sorry." She let his arm go around behind her. She couldn't look away from those two pictures.

"Don't need to be sorry, just give me a grin. Can you do that?" He tipped up her chin so she was facing him and he smiled wide. She smiled back, from embarrassment and because he had always made her feel jittery. "That's right." He gave her forehead a smooch, then kissed the tear streak on her cheek. She saw his tongue come out to taste it. "Pretty thing like you. My brother's a damned jackass," he said, just before he kissed her mouth.

There was never any lingering afterward, no lazy talk in bed. He would get up and matter-of-factly put back on his clothes. She did the same. Once he said to her, "Don't feel bad, sugar. You can bet J.J. ain't doing without."

Occasionally she saw Royce up town and they would barely acknowledge each other. He was usually with Lula Mae Alsbury anyway, a young widow who owned a boardinghouse out the Sayersville road. Some said she ran more than a boardinghouse out there and that Royce Peeler helped her with her business. Nothing about Royce would've surprised Sunny. She knew he was bad, probably dangerous. She told herself it was part of her flaw, letting a man like Royce Peeler touch her when she didn't care for him at all; something lacking in her that she couldn't say no. She was cheap. And unfit. And everyone in town knew it. She saw the looks they gave her, how talk stopped when she appeared. There was a stain of bad blood running through the family and it had shown itself in her. It seemed like not even Papa could look her full in the eye anymore.

Papa knew nothing about Royce's visits, and Sunny didn't intend for him to ever know. Each time Royce left the farm she vowed it would be the last time she'd allow him to set foot inside the house. Yet somehow when that next time came around, she never found the strength of will. He was big and strong, and he was easy with her. His arms around her gave her some comfort she didn't understand. She thought she should probably go away, maybe try out one of those business colleges that were popping up in every city. Learn about office systems and how to typewrite letters. Since the war, women were doing that sort of work, and she knew she had to do something to stop these downward steps.

Leaving became her obsession. Secretly she took to looking through Papa's newspapers at all the ads before she threw them out in the burning bin. As she busied herself with chores, she made her plans. She needed to look forward, not back. Start anew. Go someplace where she could hold her head up again. Get a job and pay her way through one of those business schools. Come January, she decided, on her nineteenth birthday, if Papa was feeling all right, that was when she would tell him.

"I think I'm going to divorce J.J.," she said one evening in late summer.

She had been thinking about it as she cooked supper and an impulse made her spill it out. She thought she might as well start to prepare Papa for changes that were fixing to come. But Papa barely raised his eyes from his plate of salt jowl and beans.

"I've decided he's not ever coming back, so I'm going to go ahead and divorce him." She took a bite, chewed, and waited for Papa to give his opinion. He just scooped more beans onto his fork. "I figure since Uncle Daniel's a lawyer," she went on, "I'll get him to do it for me. I don't know how much it'll cost, but if you can loan it to me, I'll pay you back someday."

Papa shoveled up more food. "You got to have grounds." He stuffed his mouth full. "You can't just decide to get divorced."

"Well, evidently he doesn't want to be married to me anymore either. I don't see him lurking around here, do you?"

Papa broke off a hunk of corn bread. "I'm just saying you got to have grounds." He swabbed the bread around on his plate. "And then you got to live with it."

She leaned back from the table and sighed, shoved her plate away and sighed harder. She was already living with it. And sometimes she felt like she had too much built up inside her.

Washing dishes later, she thought about J.J., remembered clearly that last time she saw him, storming out of the barn after having beat Gil Dailey nearly to a pulp. J.J. had guessed correctly what had happened up on the Knobs, guessed it right off—"You fucked him, didn't you? Your own fucking cousin"—and she had felt so vile and filthy she couldn't even protest his language.

She had underestimated J.J. Maybe some had believed Mama's sweetened story: "Poor Sunny. J.J. lost his temper and knocked her to the ground outside the church house. And Gil was only there getting her away, trying to console her. And the baby, dear lamb, she had been weak right from the start . . . not thriving . . . never smiled . . . never cooed . . . ," as if Isabel had only her little self to blame for dying. But J.J. had never been fooled. All he had to hear was the word *Knobs,* just that one word, and he figured out the truth. And during all those months of marriage, Sunny had been thinking he was stupid.

"*I* KNEW THERE WASN'T nothing but grief going to come from you marrying that boy," Papa said the day she was set to go to court. She was dressed in Mama's dark green suit with the white embroidered collar, and Papa was agitated, watching out the window for Uncle Daniel's new gray Cadillac to come around the bend in the road. "No DeLony has ever got divorced," he said quietly.

She clutched her purse in both hands and watched out the window, too. "I'm sorry to disappoint you, Papa."

He paced away from her. He wasn't going along to the court in Bastrop. He was dressed for the fields, he just hadn't made his way out there yet. He said, "I admit I don't understand this new generation."

"I'll leave, Papa," she said, her voice struggling. "As soon as it's all over, I'll leave. I don't want to be your disgrace."

His boots stopped thudding across the floor behind her. "I didn't say nothing about disgrace. Anyway, it ain't me I'm thinking about." She turned to look and he had his spectacles off, cleaning them with his pocket-handkerchief. His eyes looked small and sunken without the glasses. "It's going to be hard on you. Folks have a certain way they feel about a divorced woman. And you ain't but a girl yet. It's just a dirty shame, that's all."

"Does that mean you think I'm doing the right thing?"

He curled his specs back around his ears. "I swear, I don't know."

Uncle Daniel was smooth with his lawyering. And J.J. didn't show up for the hearing. The judge granted Sunny the divorce on grounds of cruelty. She felt just a twinge hateful calling J.J. cruel when that really wasn't it at all. Disinterested would be more correct. She figured she had probably hurt him more than he had her. But she could get on with her life now, like he was getting on with his.

• • •

IT WOKE HER UP—the knowing. The dead certainty of it. Her eyes popped open, blinked a few times at the ceiling, clearing away the film of sleep. A dark horror spread through her like sand in her veins. She sat up and threw back the covers, still staring, almost hobbled by the black feeling.

The morning chill drew around her. The bed creaked with the release of her weight. She went to the mirror as if she thought she could see it, this thing inside her, but she saw only her own reflection and felt she didn't even know that person. She turned away quickly, almost frightened, and put her head in her hands.

Royce Peeler. Oh God, what had possessed her? Her hand crept down to rest on her belly, which seemed harder than usual. Quickened. His seed had taken root. She knew it had. She imagined she could feel it growing in there, like a parasite.

She would have it taken out. Right away before the idea attached itself to her mind. She didn't want another baby. She wanted her Isabel back, not *this* baby. She wouldn't love it. In fact, she would hate it because of how it had come to be. She had to get it out of her body.

There were people who did that sort of thing. She'd heard of it, but she didn't know who they were. She wondered how she could find out. She thought of Aunt Karen, who worked down at Paint Creek among the colored folks and might know of someone. She thought of Lula Mae Alsbury and the floozies living at her boardinghouse. Surely one of them would know of someone. But Sunny couldn't bear the thought of having to admit to Aunt Karen, or to anyone, that she had made such a shameful mistake. It was Mama she needed. Mama, who could somehow always make the best of things.

A rap came at her door, and Papa's voice. "You getting up in there? Or am I going to have to go off without my coffee this morning?"

She smoothed her forehead, pulled in a deep breath. "I'm coming."

He was standing right outside her door. She almost ran into him going through, and it startled her. He said, "You sick?"

"No sir, it's just—I almost knocked you over." She went around him to the stove. Ash still smoldered from supper.

"It's ten of seven," Papa said. "Are you becoming a slugabed now?"

"No, Papa . . ." She reached into the kindling box and when her hand went down inside, a mouse jumped out, went two feet in the air as if it were aiming for her face, and she screamed. Kindling sticks flew everywhere and the mouse landed, skittering up behind the stove. Papa chased it out with the broom and it went darting into the pantry. By then Sunny was in tears at the table, head on her arm, sobbing her heart out.

"It wasn't nothing but a little old mouse," Papa said, coming out of the pantry. "It got away."

Sunny felt she was strangling on tears. Her face was like someone had splashed a bowl of water at her.

Papa said in bewilderment, "We'll set a trap before bedtime."

She didn't answer, couldn't stop long enough. It had taken over her body, the gasping, racking shakes. Like she had fallen into the horrible rhythm of it and couldn't seem to take back control.

Papa said, "Girl, what the devil's gotten into you?" and his hand came down on her upper arm, rubbed. His voice went gentler. "Hear me, Sunny?"

Her head felt like a boulder, but she raised it, mouth open, cheeks slack. She was like a drunkard, in a stupor. His face blurred in and out, but she saw enough of it—the earnest concern. She nodded, grasped hold of his hand and squeezed. "Papa. I've got to —I need to . . ." She shook her head, unable to go on. She melted back down onto her arms.

He scooted a chair up beside her. She heard him sit down. Then his hand began to pet her hair, the same way he petted his stock animals, fingers close together, pressure firm. But he hadn't touched her with such tenderness in so long, not since she was a child, and it made her want to crawl over in his lap.

She swiped her face dry, gathered in a breath. "I think, Papa— I believe I'm going to have a baby . . ."

His spectacles already magnified his eyes, but they widened a little bigger. "You said J.J. hadn't been back around here."

"He hasn't." She looked his face over and his frown deepened with understanding. Their eyes met for just the briefest second.

"Has somebody hurt you?"

She shook her head. "No, Papa. Nothing like that."

She could see how painful it was for him to talk about this. It was too personal, and despite everything, she knew he still found it difficult to think of her as a grown woman. She kept holding his hand, but it had gone limp.

"Gil?" he said.

"No!" An angry flush swept over her. She jumped up from the table and started feeding kindling to the stove, stuffing it in, pressing her mouth. Her face felt tight and dry. "I need to go away, Papa. But I don't have any money, so I'll have to borrow some more from you."

"Go where?"

"I don't know. Maybe to Austin. Or over to San Antonio."

"You think a big city's the answer?" He shook his head. "No. I can't turn you loose like that. I've got money I'll give you, but let me think on it some. I've still got a sister up in the Panhandle. Let me write and see what help she can give us."

Sunny felt her tears wanting to well again. She bit down on her bottom lip and nodded, grateful, relieved to have it out of her hands. She shut the firebox on the stove and in a few minutes the coffee was brewing.

Chapter Thirteen

*I*N HIS DREAM, GIL flew in the air, straight up, turning over once before he came down. He landed flat, and like a drop of water slipped over the rim of the shell hole, slithered to the bottom. It was always the same: turning over once in the air, seeing all that concrete sky flash past, sliding through the slick-as-owl's-shit mud into the depths of that hole. By then, he'd be quaking, struggling for his breath, bolting up from the pillows before the dream could take hold. But it was always there anyway, lurking around the bend, chasing him in his sleep, ready to pounce on him. The same dream. He couldn't get away from it.

He raised himself on the bed, looked across the dark ward and wondered if he had made any noises, cried out or moaned. Sometimes he did. Not that the others in here would notice. They all had their nightmares, too.

Fred Boedeker in the bed next to him had lost his left arm at Champagne and wore a patch over his eye. He had headaches so bad he groaned in pain while he slept. That dull, at-the-bone pain that he could live with in the daylight snuck out at night to rob him. The nurses gave him lots of morphia tablets, and some kind of treatment with a light, but nothing seemed to help Boedeker, the poor bastard. Shrapnel in the head. No telling what his dreams were like.

And O'Donnell in the bed to Gil's right, laughing, teasing, joking O'Donnell, who claimed he'd put the war behind him, said he wouldn't even be here at all if it wasn't for the neuralgia left from a facial wound he received when a percussive shell knocked him from his dispatch motorbike into a ditch full of riprap. O'Donnell sometimes cried in his sleep, sobbed like a baby for his mama, who came up every Sunday from Angleton to sit by his bed and crochet doilies.

For Gil, the best way to avoid his dreams was to stay awake, till he was walleyed if he had to. And this particular night would soon be over. He could already see the gloomy light edging through the window blinds. Not even a real glow yet, just a shadow of light in between the slats.

He lay there, arms behind his neck, and did the same thing he always did during sleeplessness: he wrote a letter to Sunny in his head. He didn't bother with paper and pen because he knew he would never mail it to her even if he had really written it down. She'd made it clear she was finished with him, standing beside that old Hudson, barely back from the cemetery. The funeral of a baby had to be the worst.

"Just go away, Gil. I don't want you here. I don't need you."

He'd stared in her face, at J.J. Peeler's fist marks there, feeling the nearly identical marks on his own face, though his were fresher, earned, unretaliated. "I know you blame me," he said. "And I take the blame. I blame myself—"

"Oh, don't be so tragic," she'd said, cutting him off, slicing down to the bone, before she went inside the house without him. And since then he thought of her almost constantly, like an obsession.

In the letter he wrote in his mind, he told her about his latest operation. The third one in seven months. This time they thought they really had gotten out all the shrapnel. Anyway, the bone fragments were gone, and that had been what was giving him the most trouble. The scar was bigger, but the pus and oozing had stopped. It looked like he was going to get to keep his leg. Again. Of course, in reality, at least so far as he knew, she was unaware that he'd ever been in danger of losing it. She was unaware he'd been in the hospital the first time, let alone all the other times.

In his memory, 1919 would become the year of the hospitals. It was where he'd been when they buried Aunt Tessa. It was where he had been when the boys of the 117th Supply Train came home to parade in Fort Worth. It was where he had spent most of the summer, and half the fall. He'd run the gamut, from fluid on the lungs to a synovitis knee, probably caused, the doctor said, from the way he had to walk with all that infection crippling him. But he was doing better. Getting by OK.

Down the hall, one of the other patients in the ward coughed, waking. The room was nearly bright enough to read. Gil had a newspaper wedged between the mattress and bed rail, one of dozens of papers that floated around the ward unclaimed. He reached for it and unfolded it to the page he'd been studying just before lights-out. The print was too small for the morning gloom, but he already had the item that interested him memorized. It said WORK IN FRANCE, and it said WAR REPARATIONS. An engineering firm in Houston—Ingram and Overlook—was advertising for skilled labor willing to go overseas. With care, he tore around the advertisement, leaving a hole in the middle of the page. He leaned half out of his bed for the cigar box on the floor underneath.

A nurse came down the row between the two lines of beds,

checking the names on the boards at each one. The head scarf wrapped around her hair made her look like one of the Sisters of Mercy at the hospital in Nevers. She stopped at the foot of his bed.

"Mr. Dailey?" she said, reading his name written in chalk above his head. He struggled to push himself back upright. "I don't believe crawling around under the bed is on your prescribed list of activities just yet. Call a nurse if you need something."

He gazed at her, stupidly. She leafed to a page on her clipboard. "Have you voided this morning?" she said in her starched voice.

Voided? Peed. Pissed. No, he had not pissed this morning. He had only just opened his eyes, but he shook his head, feeling the need come over him fast, almost uncontrollably. She reached for the duck under the bed with the cigar box and laid it on his belly.

"Use the urinal, please. Hang it on the hook above you when you're through. We're getting you out of bed today."

He watched her go, her backside bobbling like a tow sack full of jelly. He pulled the covers off his chest, put the duck down where it needed to be, waited. His bladder was so full it felt ready to explode. He waited. "Come on, come on," he muttered through his teeth, disgusted, hurting now . . . waiting. He tried to relax. He thought of waterfalls. He thought of babbling brooks. He quietly whistled one line of "Wait Til the Sun Shines, Nelly." He shut his eyes and bore down. Nothing. Not a drop. Not a bead. He wondered how far it could back up before it hit his brain.

"Still can't piss, Dailey?" O'Donnell said from under his pillow. His head came up. He had a deep scar from temple to jaw. "They'll tube you if they find out."

"Then stuff it, O'Donnell," Gil said.

Everyone in the ward was awake now, watching. Boedeker said, "Pitch me the goddamned duck. I'll fill it up."

So Gil did, and Boedeker had no trouble. A few drops spilled when he pitched it back. He'd been a lefty before the war. Now he didn't have that option. Gil hung the duck on the hook on the bedstead and lay there with his aching bladder till the nurse came back.

"How'd we do?" she said, and inspected the volume in the urinal, pencil poised over her clipboard.

O'Donnell said, "*We* did just fine," and muffled his laughter.

IT SURPRISED THE HELL out of Gil when Turner came to the hospital to visit him. He crutched into the solarium and she was sitting there. She had on a plaid suit, a navy blue sailor cap over her brownish blond hair. She looked smart and womanly as she stood up to greet him. He'd forgotten how pretty she was, bright golden eyes and good skin.

"Good that you're walking," she said.

He took her hand. "How did you know I was here?"

"I stopped by to see your mother. I was coming back from a visit home. You know I'm at John Sealy in Galveston, studying nursing."

"No, I didn't." He smiled, and she did, too.

"Houston's right on my way, so I thought I'd—well. Here I am." She hesitated a minute, then pivoted toward the chair she'd just left. "I brought along my chessboard just in case. We play in the dormitory some, and I remembered that you used to like it. I don't have to be back until"—she checked her wristwatch—"well, later. Do you still like to play?"

"I don't think I have since I played with you the last time." He laughed. "When was that?"

"Before you joined the army." She settled herself. "Do you need some help?"

"No." He had to laugh again as he sat himself down, stacking the crutches together and laying them aside. He couldn't get over the surprise, or stop staring at her. He hadn't thought of Turner DeLony in months and months, and here she was, pretty, friendly, wanting a little game of chess. "So you're a nurse."

"Not yet. I've got another year."

"The nurses around here sure don't look like you," he said, and she smiled again.

As they played, the game began to come back to him. Turner had been the person who taught him in the first place. He remembered that she was a good player, and she beat him quickly and soundly. She didn't wait for him to ask for a rematch. She set up another game and he smoked a cigarette.

She asked about his leg and he gave her the details of the various surgical operations he'd undergone. He could see that she understood more about it all than he did. She explained to him why he had to keep off the leg as much as possible for a while. The muscle needed to strengthen. The cartilage and tendon were delicate. She urged him to listen to the doctors and do as they told him. She sounded suspiciously like Ma and he suspected a conspiracy cooked up between them. And right in the middle of this she said, "Why haven't you kept in touch?"

She caught him so off his guard he didn't have an answer.

"I sent you all those letters while you were in France. Did you think I was just being a good Samaritan? Keeping up a soldier's spirits and all that?" She smiled. "Well, I wasn't. I thought you were the nicest boy I had ever met. And you never even bothered to write back to me." She reached for his cigarettes. "Mind?"

He fumbled for the matches, struck one on the underside of the table. He reached with the flame to give her a light. "I thought I did write to you."

"A postcard." She tipped back her head and exhaled smoke. "It said, 'This is what it looks like here. Love Gil.'"

That would've been at Camp Mills. He'd sent one like that to everybody. He smiled, embarrassed. "They didn't give us much time for letters."

"I had thought we might get serious once you got back. Well, I thought it was possible. Don't laugh."

"I'm not laughing." But he was and he couldn't seem to stop it. And she was kind of laughing about it all herself. He'd never had a woman who wasn't a whore be quite so forward with him. It felt all right, flattering even. She moved a pawn to take one of the knights he'd left out in the open. "I ought to be keeping my head in the game," he said.

"And then, once you got home, you didn't even bother to let me know." She flicked the cigarette ash, scrutinized the board. "You broke my heart." She said it flippantly and he looked to see if she was serious. He couldn't read her expression. She lifted her eyes. "Don't worry. I'm over it. Didn't last too long. It's your move."

He pulled his mind back to the game and moved a bishop. As soon as he did, her knight came out of nowhere to take it. He grabbed her hand and shook it, trying to get back his bishop. "You're cheating," he said over her laughter. The other people in the solarium turned to stare at them as he peeled the bishop free from her fingers. She kept laughing until he said, more earnestly, "What if . . . when I get out of here . . . what if I wanted to see you again?"

"Don't go making tall promises."

He let go of her wrist. "No, I'm not. I just wondered if you would even consider it."

She shrugged. "It depends."

"On what?"

She smoked the cigarette, then stubbed it out, looked at him. "Julianne told me I'm crazy to come here like this. She said you'd get the wrong idea, and that I would be opening myself up for it." She kept her gaze steady, a little smile. "I didn't come to get you interested in me again. Or maybe you never were in the first place, I don't know. You can't imagine things I've thought about, reasons I've come up with for why you, well, dropped me." She was angry. He could hear it, despite the little smile she kept flashing. That touch of anger made him feel awkward. He'd never considered that he might have hurt her, too. "After all those letters, I think I deserve to know, don't you? I've heard the rumors. Some are far-fetched. Others . . ." She shrugged.

He took his eyes off her and leaned back, consciously aware of the other people in the room: a mother with her son, a husband and wife or a pair of lovers, murmuring low to each other. A nurse peeped in the doorway, then went on by. He straightened his leg out into the room. "What've you heard?"

"That you and Sunny were . . . mixed up together, of course. That's the rumor." She sat still a second, and then she started gathering up the game pieces. "You know what, Julianne's right. I shouldn't have come here. It was silly of me."

He reached out and stopped her hands. "No, it's all right. I don't like talking about it, is all. It's not a good memory for me. And it's still just a little bit . . ." What? What was it?

"Do you remember when I spoke to you that day? What I said? At the funeral for Sunny's baby?"

His hand tightened on hers involuntarily. "You were there?"

She nodded. "I knew you didn't remember. I asked what had happened to your face. Your nose looked like it was broken, and your right eye was bruised red."

"J.J. Peeler," he said.

"I found that out later."

"I deserved it."

"Oh. Well, I guess that answers it." She gave him a wry, close-mouthed smile. "You know she divorced him, don't you? No, I can see you don't. Well, she did, and now she's gone up to North Texas somewhere."

"Divorced?"

Turner's eyes felt like bullets on him. "Yes. Divorced. That marriage was pretty much doomed from the start, don't you think?"

"Why did she run off to North Texas?"

"I didn't say she ran off. She went to work for a railroad man up there."

"A railroad man?" he said, muddled. "Did you say *man?* Not railroad *company?* The KATY or the Southern Pacific?"

"All I know is he's a railroad man." She shrugged, tilted her head. "I guess you're still in love with her."

He blinked. "No," he said, reacting. "No, I . . . no." He rubbed at his thigh. "She's . . . no, Sunny's—" He fell silent, contemplated the game board and the scattered chess pieces for a while before he moved his eyes back on Turner. She was watching him. "I'm not sure how I feel about anything these days."

"I understand." It came out gently, and she looked suddenly soft to him, fragile almost.

"I don't see how you possibly could. I don't, and it's me."

She relaxed back and folded her arms for a few more seconds. Then she dug in her pocketbook for a pencil. She reached across for his packet of cigarettes, licked the lead of the pencil, and wrote down something on the wrapper. She slid the pack back across the table.

"The number to my dormitory," she said. "In case you're ever in Galveston."

16 December 1919
Dear Uncle Dane,

I have wanted to write to you for a long time and am just now getting around to it. Things have been unsettled this year. I hate it that I wasn't able to make it to Aunt Tessa's funeral. I know you miss her. Ma misses her. We all do. She was like a second mother to me. At least she didn't suffer long.

Your niece Turner DeLony came to see me recently. I was at the Red Cross Hospital at Camp Logan in Houston. Since that's so close to John Sealy where she's practicing to be a nurse, she paid me an unexpected, though pleasant visit, and caught me up on all the happenings in McDade. She told me that you had been sick, too, but that somehow Ding and Sunny kept well. I hope you're back to full speed by now. If I know you, then no doubt you are.

Speaking of Sunny, Turner mentioned she had a job up in North Texas now, working for a railroad man, or something along that line. I hope that's going OK for her. Does she have an address up there?

I have been keeping busy since I got out of the hospital. Somehow word has spread that I know a little bit about cars. Don't know how long it will last, though. Soon as folks find out I'm not a real grease monkey they'll likely start driving the twelve miles into Brenham to have their work done. I have managed to put together enough to buy a good used Ford, though, and I'm planning a trip your way soon. Had to get rid of that Hudson. It never did run right.

Well, Uncle, I can hear the postman's buggy coming up the hill, so I better close for now and get this in the mail. Merry Christmas to everybody.

Your nephew,
Gil

Dec. 22nd, Instanter

Dear Nephew—

I have never been one for letter writing. Theresa took care of it. But you asked after Sunny and I thought you ought to get an answer. Yes, she is living up in North Texas, working for a family who lost their mother and eldest sister to flu. The father is a conductor for the T&P and so is gone from home regular. There are three children left to look after, and this is the job Sunny has taken on. She is doing fine up there, and it would be for the best if you didn't do anything to upset the applecart. I reckon you might not like me saying that, but we have always spoken straight with each other. A visit from you here though would be welcome. Come any time. I could use the company. Mighty quiet some days.

Good to hear you are done with hospitals and doctors. My experience is they are worthless for anything but grubbing money from your pockets. Say hello to the family.

Dane DeLony

Chapter Fourteen

*I*F 1919 WAS FOR Gil the year of the hospitals, then 1920 was the year of the jobs, a succession of them lined up in a row. He tried to work with Pop, to get interested in the family business, but he just couldn't make a go of it. Mr. Honeywell gave him a job for a while patching up tin lizzies for a few bucks a week. But Honeywell didn't really have enough garage business for a full-time employee and Gil felt like a charity case. For a couple of weeks that spring, he worked for Uncle Walt and Aunt Jo getting their crops planted. Then he found a room in Brenham and applied for a job at the Ford dealership there.

They put him in the back down in the grease pit until he fought his way up front into sales. He could turn on the charm with the best of them, run that line of bullshit like those other guys, except he didn't have to make up things to sell cars. He knew what was underneath the hood, understood how a farmer could hook a belt to the driveshaft and run his binder or his cornhusker. Sometimes he would even go out to their place, roll up his sleeves, and show them the way it was done. He became the number-one salesman, until he got tangled up with the boss's wife.

It was a foolish thing for him to do. He knew it even while it was happening. Her name was Lucille Heartson and she claimed she was in love when really it was more like in heat. And he guessed he was just killing time. But he was forced to move back home again, and that was the worst part about losing the job.

Ma told people he got fired for having to go back into the hospital, which was completely false. Since the last operation in November, his leg had felt so good he almost missed the pain. But Ma could tell a lie so well, she could convince herself along with everybody else. As if by repeating something often enough she could make it so. The way she had done with Baby Isabel, using the flu as the excuse for what had happened that night on the hill above McDade.

But it didn't work for him. He couldn't explain away his actions so easily. Not even on his steadiest days. He knew what had happened to Sunny's baby. He remembered things he'd heard, read about in the army, how the lyddite and melinite from the big guns at the front left a poison behind in the trenches, a deadly poison you couldn't see or smell but that could kill—the same poison produced in the exhaust of an internal combustion engine. He had killed Baby Isabel by leaving that damned Hudson running just as surely as he had killed Rome McKeller by asking him to stop the truck in the middle of the Jaulny-Thiaucourt crossroad. And now Rome was in a grave in eastern France and Sunny was up in North Texas living with some family she didn't belong to. He wished like hell he could take back those two days. Just those two, to do over again. They had become like one in his mind.

In July, he counted up the last of the money he had and bought a train ticket to Lockhart. He didn't tell anybody he was going; he just went. When he got there, he stopped at the blacksmith to ask directions. The town smithy always knew everybody, and this one was no exception.

The house was on a side street, lined up with all the other houses, appearing just as the smithy had described: green roof, wide front porch, brick tie-up at the end of the walk, big live oak in the yard with a round bench circling its trunk. He took off his hat and combed his hair with his fingers, wiped his face with his handkerchief. The weight of the heavy air bore down on his neck.

"Just do it," he said through gritted teeth. "Just go up there and knock, you goddamned coward."

Voices came through the open windows. Female voices. An embroidered curtain fluttered. He imagined Rome going up that walk, sitting on that porch, parting back that curtain. Birds twittered around a laurel, already hunting for a night roost. He raised his face at them, and for that second he was back over there, watching the magpies or swallows or whatever the hell French birds those had been settling down on a busted stick of a tree right above his shell hole.

This is it. This is your blighty, old son. The medic had talked to him like there were years between their ages instead of maybe months. There wasn't even any peach fuzz on his face. *The show's almost over here anyway. We got them fucking Kraut bastards on the run now.* The jolting bed of the mule cart. The medic's voice. The low, mud gray sky bumping past, broken shoots of trees, a soft rain sifting onto his face.

Gil folded his arms over his chest the way he would when the memories caught up with him again, hands wedged under his armpits. He didn't know what had made him imagine that he would get a big welcome from these people. So he had known their son; so they had been buddies; so what? They would probably hate him for being the lucky one. He'd been kidding himself, nobly saying to himself that his visit would bring some comfort to them, when all along it was his own comfort he was seeking. He felt if he could just have a look at them all, maybe that would be enough, if he could find Rome's face in any of theirs. But as he lurked outside their house, he knew suddenly that he wasn't ready to confront them. For just as soon as they understood who he was, they would want details about that day in the mud, details he couldn't give them. Better that they believe the official letter from the government saying how Rome had died bravely in service to his country. Anything would be better than them knowing about that shell hole and that hand and that pinkie ring. So he turned and walked away from it. All of it.

On the train ride home, a thunderstorm broke. Fantastic lightning flashed in the deep black night. He stared out the window, transfixed by the sight, fearful of being swept off the tracks, loathing his own yellow spine.

At Giddings he got off the train and walked through the downpour to a place he knew, knocked the knock—*a shave and a haircut*. Wrong night, wrong place. He got busted with the rest of them in there, a wild man that night, full of whiskey and war songs with other wild men around the tables. They kept on singing, even down at the clink. A couple of the cops had been over there and they joined in on the songs. "If He Can Fight Like He Can Love, Then Good-by, Germany," and "Mademoiselle from Armentières," with all those bawdy verses going on and on. They had a grand time, everyone of them. Including the policemen.

At dawn the next morning, Gil was released with the rest of them. He never told anybody he'd spent the night in jail. He wondered what story Ma would have made up to explain away that mistake.

"MY PRECIOUS LORD IN heaven, we were ready to send the rangers out after you. You want to scare me to death, don't you? You're trying to put me in the grave, aren't you? Gilbert? You better talk to me. You better tell me where you went off to without a word." Ma followed him all the way to the door of his room.

"I'm tired, Ma," he said, and closed it in her face.

"Gilbert!" She banged with her fist. "I don't want to have to barge in there—"

"Then don't." He leaned there listening, waiting for her to either move away or try to force herself inside. He imagined he could hear her breathing through the door. "I'll be out later."

"And we'll talk then? Promise me we'll talk later."

"I'm tired, Ma."

"You've got to learn how to be happy, son. You just can't let this black spirit take hold of you. You got to beat it back."

"Don't preach at me, Ma."

"I'm trying to help you, Gilbert. You've got to give your heart to the Lord—"

"Nobody wants to hear that, all right? I'm tired. I'm going to rest now."

There came a silence. "All right then." She sounded resigned, worried. "You lay down awhile."

When her footsteps moved away, he let down, too. It was like all his energy left him. He took a deep breath, sprawled back across the bed. He lit a cigarette and shoved up the window so he wouldn't need an ashtray, inhaled hard enough that he made himself cough. Damned Chesterfields, all he could get at the train station. They fell apart in your mouth and had no taste.

He pulled out his billfold, found the newspaper clipping: WORK IN FRANCE. WAR REPARATIONS. He didn't know why he didn't just go ahead and pack it back over there. Get in on the work. There was plenty of it. He'd seen for himself how blown apart the whole country was. And the franc was down to almost nothing. He could live cheap there. But he needed some money to start with and he had exactly zero. He folded the clipping back into his billfold and lay on his side blowing smoke out through the window.

TWO THINGS HAPPENED NEAR the end of that year that made a big change for him. The first was the Firestone Tire Company hired him as a territorial salesman, gave him a car allowance and a draw against commission, his freedom; and the second was Turner DeLony. She was just there one day, sitting in the kitchen with Ma. When he walked in, he did a double take, exactly like in a Buster Keaton picture.

She smiled. She'd bobbed her hair, wore it side-parted, had put in a wave since he'd seen her at the Houston hospital.

Ma said, "Look at who's here, Gilbert. She's gone to work at the Brenham hospital. A full-fledged, genuine nurse now."

"That's so?" He stepped on in through the door.

"Take off your hat when you enter a room," Ma said. "What has happened to your manners?"

He fumbled off his hat, clutched the hand Turner held out for him to shake. It was soft like a nurse's hand. He didn't know it yet, but she slathered her hands in lotion and slept with gloves on at night to preserve that softness.

"What's it going to take to get you to answer my letters?" She squeezed his fingers, said it like a joke. He'd been meaning to get in touch with her all year. He really had. Just one thing and another had kept him from it.

She seemed so clear and levelheaded, seemed to know just what she wanted, and for whatever reason, that was him. He never found out if it had been a scheme or not, her landing that job in Brenham. But what the hell. She was a good kid, persistent, and she could put up with Ma. In early December, he went ahead and married her. Time to knuckle down, give in, give up, get married, shut Ma up. And he figured he owed a debt of a sort to Turner.

Ma was ecstatic, didn't cry a drop like a mother is supposed to at her son's wedding. She left the tears to Pop, who saturated his pocket-handkerchief. Calvin came home from A&M College, where he was a freshman, to be Gil's best man, and Gil needed Calvin there, standing at the altar with him.

As he watched Turner come toward him, her on Daniel O'Barr's arm, doing that fancy one-step, a wreath of flowers round her head like a Grecian goddess, a tulle veil covering her face, Gil wondered what in the world he thought doing this would fix. He tried to smile around the growing panic, the smothering collar on the suit he wore, the cutaway and cummerbund that Ma had wasted twenty dollars on. He felt himself begin to sweat, and then to sway, and if not for Calvin's steadying hand at his back he might have pitched forward in a dead faint. Or turned to run from the church.

"Who gives this woman?" the preacher said, and Daniel O'Barr answered clearly, formally, "I do."

Turner's hand was cold, almost icy, inside Gil's clammy one. He repeated the words, his voice a choking whisper, like an actor in a play, going through the motions. The ring nearly slipped out of his sweaty hands as he slid it onto her cool finger. And all the while he kept thinking, *Cold hands, warm heart.*

His fingernail snagged on her veil, so she lifted it for him. And there was her face, skin glowing, yellow-brown eyes full of light. His heart settled down. *All that other mess is behind you now,* Ma's voice said inside his brain. A tender, uncertain smile creased Turner's lips, and as he leaned forward to kiss her, he thought he smelled vanilla. Man and wife. It was done.

He got drunk at the reception, some gin concoction of Gabe O'Barr's, and missed his own honeymoon night. He knew it was a poor start.

Chapter Fifteen

IN FEBRUARY HE TURNED twenty-two. The married man, the wage earner, the traveling salesman. He had dealerships from Brenham to Austin, San Marcos to Temple, and every little hamlet in between. He had the Ford dealers, except for the one in Brenham that Heartson managed. That one Gil gave to the Houston salesman. He still had the cab companies, service stations, city municipalities. He had Camp Mabry in Austin, where his old Captain Tolbert was a colonel now, the camp commandant. He was away from home an average of nineteen days a month, and made enough money to buy the red brick house on Main Street that Turner picked out, plus start a savings account, plus exercise his stock options in the company, which were deducted from his quarterly commission checks. He bought a new car, a Templar roadster with a European flair, and he gave the secondhand Ford to Turner to use for going back and forth to the hospital. He outfitted himself in the new two-piece business suits, bright-colored ties, linen shirts, hats, wing tips, a silver cigarette case, a hip flask. He wore his hair slick, a pencil-thin mustache above his lip, and he became a man of the future. On good days.

Bad days were when the old bleakness would descend, when he would wake up strangling from the pointlessness, the mediocrity, feeling like a guest in his own life. Those were the days when he dug out the faded yellow newspaper ad from the depths of his billfold to study it and contemplate the possibilities—WORK IN FRANCE. WAR REPARATIONS. Packing up. Leaving. He even had a passport, which he had applied for through the mail. Turner would never agree to go, of course, but he didn't think he would want her to anyway.

She was always working, or else talking about work, patients she was fond of, doctors she hated or admired. He tried to listen. He kept waiting for devotion to set in, but the truth was, after the first few weeks, she bored him. And he thought he must bore her, too. When you got down to it, they didn't have much in common. But then they never really had. Nothing beyond Sunny, and that subject was off limits. He couldn't even mention Uncle Dane without getting one of her odd, shaming glances. Sometimes he felt as if by marrying her, his kinship had to defer to hers.

"I always forget that he's your uncle, too," she said with that smug little smile she could put on her face.

"Just as much mine as yours."

"Well . . . actually, no. He isn't. My father was his *brother*. Whereas he's only kin to you through marriage."

Things like that began to annoy him, little stupid things she did to nearly drive him over the edge. Like eating bacon with a fork. Like putting throw rugs all over the floor so he wouldn't track in his filth. He wondered what she meant by that word *filth,* if she was implying something deeper. Even things he had appreciated about her at first started to gnaw at him—the way she downplayed his service in the army. "Gil only drove a supply truck. He didn't really see action." As if she knew what he had and hadn't seen. And about his wound. "Oh, he's completely over that. You'd never even know it." Except he had a scar the size of Chile down his thigh. Sort of shaped like Chile, too, including the craggy mountains and valley gorges.

Married sex turned out to be a disappointment, too, something you couldn't foresee before the vows were spoken. Turner liked things pretty and soft-focused. To her the sex act was dirty. As modern as she looked and pretended to be, in her heart she was as old-fashioned and closed-minded as Ma.

"Do I touch you enough?" he asked her once, trying to break through the shell. But her answer had come quickly, in an almost angry tone.

"I don't want to talk about *that*, Gil. I really don't." She was prone to sick headaches anyway—another thing about her he didn't know until after the vows. But he soon noticed how frequently they seemed to arrive right at bedtime.

Their marriage was eleven months old the first time he strayed. He expected to be eaten alive with guilt. The jubilation worried him. The release, the renewed energy. The woman wasn't a whore, but a girl who worked in a diner he visited. A hostess, she called herself. She had a sweet face and a ten-year-old kid, and a husband who had bought one up in the Argonne, along with the seventy-five thousand other Doughboys who'd gone west in that campaign. Her taste for gin surprised Gil, also that Kosse would have its own speakeasy just outside the town limits.

He spent the entire night in her bed and left her house early the next morning, before her boy got up for school. She came all the way outside behind him to wave good-bye. "You look in on me again now. Next time you're in town, hear?"—like he was some long-lost relative. He drove off with a smile busting out on his face.

It wasn't that he was proud of his philandering. He didn't brag to other salesmen he ran across the way some did. But he found the only time he felt completely at ease was toiling inside some woman's body, smoking in her bed afterward, telling lies about himself and listening to her lies.

Sometimes the lies felt truer than the truth. He could fix things with lies, do his life over how it should've been instead of the way it was. Little lies. Nothing that mattered: He'd gotten that scar in a car wreck, not the war. Never even went over there at all. Too young to enlist, and it was all over before they could draft him anyhow. Or maybe he *had* gone off to war, and had left his one and only love in France, a girl who had disappeared but who both governments were trying hard to locate. Women loved the romance in that story, and he could speak a little French to convince them. It was like having a light shine on him, feeling in control of his life.

He caught a dose from a girl in San Marcos. He knew the one. Funny bones. Little twinkle toes. He'd gone a whole year in France and then snagged the clap right here in the good old U.S.A.—God's country. For God and country. A doctor in Marlin fixed him up. He knew he was slipping down, knew it without Ma having to tell him.

"You've got the world by the tail, Gilbert. I don't know why you can't be happy."

"Who says I'm not happy, Ma?" He held his hangover, swallowed a big gulp of coffee.

"You make too much money, that's what your problem is."

He laughed, shook his head at her. She was hopeless. He didn't even know why he bothered to stop and see her. Habit, he guessed. He was always planning to visit with Pop, but then Ma would dominate.

She said, "Turner needs to stay at home and take better care of you."

"She'd love to hear that."

"You look worn out. Both of you do. It's nothing but fast living. Give her a baby, son. Something besides that hospital she can sink her teeth into."

He smiled at the image that conjured, even though it was a sorry one. He wanted to blurt out that in order for there to be a baby there had to be some hanky-panky going on, and that every time he touched his wife she cringed from him. Oh, it wasn't always as blatant as that. Occasionally Turner would roll over and lie still for him. But where was the joy in that?

"Ma says you need to be taking better care of me," he said one morning over breakfast.

"She means well." Turner poured him a cup of coffee and sat down across from him. "Maybe you do look a little sickly."

He laughed. "So nurse me."

"You wouldn't like it." She started buttering her toast. "If I stayed at home and tended to you, you wouldn't like it."

"Of course I wouldn't. I'd feel guilty." He watched her salt and pepper her egg. "Do you want us to have a baby?"

Her eyes raised, locked with his. "Do you?"

"I want whatever you want."

"That's sweet." She smiled and forked a piece of bacon into her mouth. She chewed and gave him a pleasant look. "See? That's the reason I married you. Because you're so sweet to me."

He didn't flinch. He willed himself not to. She forked another piece of bacon into her mouth, and that was the end of the baby conversation. It never came up again.

• • •

Now and then at family gatherings, somebody would slip up and say something about Sunny in front of him, always with a regretful glance afterward, as if there were some family plot not to give him any information. It made him feel peculiar, and like he wasn't free to ask questions about her either. Sometimes he wanted to wring Uncle Dane by the neck until he coughed out her address.

She was married again, to her railroad conductor, a man much older than her, a man named Goodner. Gil didn't know when it had happened, only that it had, and he guessed he was glad for her. He couldn't shake the feeling, though, that she had run away from him. And he thought that by knowing her last name and that her husband worked for the T&P Railroad somewhere in North Texas he ought to be able to track her down if he wanted to, if he tried hard enough. He wondered what she would do if he suddenly knocked on her door one day.

But thoughts of her didn't consume him anymore. Not like they had that first year. He had his job, the road, to occupy him. And sometimes he would get in a soft mood about Turner, think to himself what a lucky fellow he was to have such a girl for his wife, pretty and smart. Sometimes he could almost convince himself.

Shortly after his twenty-third birthday, Turner's sister, Julianne, delivered twin girls. Turner wanted to go with her mother and her Aunt Dellie to San Antonio to see the babies. Julianne's aviator husband, Sterling Williams, had made major and was stationed at Kelly Field there. Gil drove Turner to McDade, where she joined her family. He promised Dellie that he would take Ding to Uncle Dane's while they were gone, and he helped Ding pack up a suitcase.

The kid was like a nomad, living here, there, and the other. He was a few months from his eighth birthday, rangy and sun-dark, a miniature version of Uncle Dane with overserious eyes. He seemed used to being shuffled around, and he piled into the Templar with Gil for the short drive to the farm.

When they got there, Uncle Dane wasn't anywhere in sight. He didn't come out of the barn at the sound of the car either, so Gil figured he must be gone off someplace. Gil parked the car in the yard and went inside to help Ding get settled in his old room. Halfway through unpacking the suitcase, Ding handed Gil a letter, opened but still inside the envelope.

"I can't read real writing yet," Ding said.

Gil turned the envelope over and there it was, the forbidden address in Weatherford, Texas. Sunny's loop-the-loop handwriting spelling out Master Lange DeLony. A buzz started in Gil's head. He cleared his throat. "You go by Lange now?" he said, the letter like a slab of gold bullion in his hand.

Ding shook his head. "Only at school."

"Well, evidently Sunny thinks you do."

"Read me what she wrote."

So Gil read every word on the outside of the envelope, pulled the letter out and read that, too. It was written on lined foolscap, and in pencil like a grade-schooler. It said:

Jan. 10, 1922
Dear Ding,
    You need to go back home and live with Papa.—Aunt Dellie, if you are reading this to him, I'm sorry to say it in such a blunt way, and I don't mean anything against you.— Papa needs you, Ding. He's got that big farm, and you're old enough to help him with it now. He's getting on in years and decrepit and as much as I would like to I can't

come down there and tend to him. You have to do it, Ding.
Papa won't ask but I know he would like to have you back
home.

—Aunt Dellie, thank you for writing down letters to
me for Ding. It means so much to me to hear from my
family.

Lots of love,
Sunny

P.S. Nina says hello to her big Uncle Ding. XXOO

Ding scratched at his head and took the letter from Gil's hands.
"What does *decrepit* mean?"

"Wore out."

Ding folded the paper back into the envelope. "You reckon I
ought to come home for good like she says?"

"I don't know, Ding. Maybe so." Gil sat down, staring at the
envelope in Ding's hands. He had the urge to snatch it back to
reread it and hear Sunny's voice speaking the words.

"Aunt Dellie won't want me to."

"You're not her kid, though."

"I know it, but Papa won't let me have a dog here. He says it'll
run the chickens. But I can train it not to, I know I can." Ding
looked dejectedly at the floor. "I just think I ought to have a dog. I
never did have one of my very own before, and everybody else
does."

Gil reached out and muffed the kid's head. "Oh hell, Ding, do
whatever you want to do." He watched as Ding tucked the envelope into the mirror frame on his dresser. Gil eyed it there.
"Nina's the name of Sunny's baby?"

"You want to see a picture of her? We got one at Christmas."

Gil straightened as Ding ran off into the other room. He followed and stopped a couple of steps through the door. Ding was reaching on tiptoe for a frame on the mantelpiece. The picture was of a little girl with fat cheeks and light hair, dressed in white lace, dark stockings, and shoes, standing up with her doll and a parasol, and staring straight out of the photograph.

Ding handed over the picture frame. "She looks like Sunny. That's what Papa says."

Gil's eyes moved over the image of the little girl, her face and hair, little arms already thinning of baby fat. The little girl did look like Sunny, exactly like her, but she didn't look like much of a baby either. "How old is Nina in this picture, Ding?"

Ding shrugged, snicked a finger at his nose, then crawled up on the arm of Uncle Dane's chair. He pointed over Gil's wrist. "Looks like her dolly only has one eye. See it?"

"You better get down off that furniture, boy." Uncle Dane had come in through the back door, and his voice jarred Gil. He raised his face and saw Uncle Dane glimpse the picture frame. "Well, will you look at what the cat drug up," Uncle Dane said by way of a greeting. "Appreciate you bringing Ding over."

"Reckon I'm staying this time, Papa." Ding dusted at the arm of the chair where he had been perched.

"You are?" Uncle Dane hung his hat on the backside of the door. He wore a pair of denim overalls with a bibbed front and loops for hammers and things. One shoulder strap had a broken latchet. "What does your aunt have to say about it?"

"Ain't told her yet."

"Might better before you decide for sure. Women sometimes cry and carry on about a thing like that. Am I right, Gil?"

Gil smiled. "Yes sir." He eased over to the mantelpiece to set the photograph back in its place.

Ding shook his head. "Sunny says you need me most. She wrote a letter, and Gil read it to me while ago."

Uncle Dane's knowing eyes shifted to meet Gil's, then went back over to Ding. "That's one woman against another, son. I'd be mighty careful. Sounds like big trouble to me."

Gil chuckled. He let his gaze run down the line of photographs along the mantel in an effort not to seem to focus on the one that interested him the most. Ding and Uncle Dane kept up their conversation, one serious, the other teasing. Gil stayed to the background, waiting for a good place to break in and take his leave. Uncle Dane must've seen that moment coming before it got there, because he suddenly switched off of Ding and said, "Stay to supper, Gil." It sounded more like an order than an invitation.

The supper wasn't much—fried pork ribs and mashed, half cooked yams. There was some bought bread, apple jelly for dessert. The whole house felt different without Aunt Tessa or Sunny, empty and cheerless. There wasn't much said while they ate, and once they were through and had the dishes piled on the drain board, Gil thought he could go in grace. But Uncle Dane said, "Smoke your cigarette inside the house. There's a can you can use over there for your ashes."

He pointed toward the easy chair and the sofa. So Gil sat for a while longer, all of them reading the same newspaper, swapping pages around. Even Ding pretended to read. Nothing of much interest. Eleven million in war debt was still owed the United States. They were still counting the bodies after an airship explosion in Virginia. Uncle Dane chuckled over the antics of Mr. Jiggs in the funnies. Eventually Ding fell asleep at the other end of the sofa and Gil smoked up most of his cigarettes.

"I'm afraid she's in trouble up there," Uncle Dane said from behind the page he was reading. Gil raised his attention, realizing they were finally getting to what Uncle Dane had been stalling to discuss. "Been thinking about going up there and getting her."

"What kind of trouble?"

"Not sure. It's just a gut feeling." The newspaper rustled down into Uncle Dane's lap. "You know, he's a man of forty-four."

"That old . . ." Gil's mind did the arithmetic. That made the railroad man twenty-three years older than Sunny. Old enough to be her father.

"Now I realize Theresa wasn't but a young girl herself, and I should've known better, but I wasn't no goddamned forty-four." Uncle Dane spit tobacco into his juice can and set it back on the floor beside his chair. "He got her in the family way, and it wasn't supposed to be that kind of union. She wrote me herself she was planning to be a mother to his children, and in exchange he was going to adopt her baby as his own. It was supposed to be an arrangement, but . . . well . . ." He folded the newspaper, then folded it again. "Course, I knew better than that."

Gil's neck felt prickly hearing this, and hearing it all at once after such a long drought on the subject. For it to come from Uncle Dane, of all people, was the most surprising part. There wasn't much Gil could say. Sunny had always been too trusting. "So she's going to have another baby? Besides that one up there?" He nodded at the photograph on the mantel.

Uncle Dane glanced at Ding and, lowering his voice, said, "Already did. It was stillborn."

Gil stared into the vacant fireplace and felt a pang of new guilt, as if this latest loss of Sunny's was somehow his fault, too. "I could drive up there and get her. Bring her back down here —"

"No. No, thank you."

"If I drove all night it probably wouldn't take but a couple of days."

"No. I shouldn't have told you none of this. Getting as bad as a woman about flapping my jaws." Uncle Dane studied Gil for a second. "When do you stop butting into your grown children's life? That's what I'd like to know."

"Ask Ma," Gil said, but didn't laugh. Uncle Dane spit another wad. "What if your gut feeling's right, though?" Gil asked. "What if Sunny *is* in trouble? She might be wishing for somebody to come up there and get her."

"If she needs me, she'll let me know. She always has before. I shouldn't have said nothing to you about it."

But there was still a kind of desperation in his voice and Gil wasn't sure what caused it, if Uncle Dane was saying one thing and meaning another or if he really was sorry to have spilled it all out. Gil sat still awhile longer staring at the charred brick inside the fireplace, smoking his last cigarette, before he got up to go.

"No need to hurry off, is there?" Uncle Dane said, rising. "I got a spare room you can use."

Gil knew which room that was, too. It probably still smelled like Sunny in there. Confused, distracted, he sat back down. His eyes wandered up to the picture of that little girl with her doll, those big round eyes, pressed-down mouth forcing a smile for the camera, a little doll herself. Could it be—was it possible that he and Sunny had made a baby at the same time they were losing one, in that broken-down line shack up on the Knobs?

Chapter Sixteen

*I*T TOOK LONGER THAN Gil had figured, even driving twenty-four-hour stretches. He had his Blue Book along to guide him, and the Templar came loaded with a compass. Even so, he still made a couple of dead-end turns, and the roads slowed him down. Only a few of them were gravel. Most were dirt, and narrow. He had three spare tires piled in the back like cordwood, but he had four flats, so he had to stop once at a garage for patch repair.

He hadn't felt the need to let anybody know where he was headed. He'd beaten Uncle Dane out of bed, had hardly slept a wink anyway, and so he took off before dawn. Turner was busy with her sister, but she would just assume he was working anyway. Besides, this was between him and fate, something he had to find out on his own. The picture of that little girl haunted him. If there was the least chance that child was his, then he couldn't rest until he knew, no matter what Sunny felt or didn't feel about him now.

The weather was mild as he drove into Weatherford his third day out. He stopped at a gasoline station and used their back faucet to wash the road dirt off his face. He had his safety razor and he water-shaved, wet his hair and smoothed it flat, swished his mouth, rinsing out the grit. He considered checking into the hotel he passed downtown and having himself a real bath before he went to find her. But he decided that since he might not be here long, a hotel room would be impractical. He felt as jittery as a snake and wished he had thought to bring a little bottle of something to nerve himself.

The streets and houses were all well marked and it amazed him how easily he found the Goodners' address, almost like God was with him for a change. It was a corner house and he pulled the Templar along the side street, turned the engine off. He stared up at the second-story windows. It was a plain, square house, not many trees, no bushes, a wire fence all the way around it. He stepped out of the car, stretched to release some of the tension. He smoothed the lapel on his jacket, wiped at his hair again. A cigarette might calm him, and he thought about getting back in the car to smoke one and drive around town a little while. He could come back later, once he'd gotten better hold of himself. A face peeped through one of the upstairs windows.

The yard gate gave a rusty creak as he swung it open. It was chain-weighted with an old plow bit so it closed on its own, with a sharp, metallic clang. He glanced at the house. The front door was shut, even with this mild weather. He stepped onto the porch and then stalled there, straining to hear any sounds from inside. Nothing. What if she took one look at who had come and slammed the door in his face?

"Well, if that happens then you'll know," he mumbled, made a fist of his right hand, and knocked. The screen door shimmied in its frame. He waited. Sweat rolled under his shirt. Still no sound came from inside. He raised his fist to repeat the knock and the inside door clicked, swung open. The stuffy smell of a closed-up house came through the screen.

"Hello?" he said, leaning to see. Then the latch gave and a little girl's face was looking up at him. Not the little girl in the picture on Uncle Dane's mantel. This girl was darker, seemed a bit older, had her hair in a braid like a headband. She stared at him with big brown eyes. She waited for him to say something. He waited for her.

"We don't need anything," she finally said in a timid voice.

"Is this the house where the Goodner family lives?"

"Yes, but we don't need anything. Good-bye." She started to shut the door.

"Wait. I'm looking for Sunny DeLo—for Mrs. Goodner."

"We don't need any," the little girl said again, something she had apparently been taught to say and had practiced. The inside door shut on him. He heard talking on the other side, then a squalling fit.

Instinct took hold of him and he yanked back the screen door, pushed open the heavy inner door, and stepped through. The little girl with the braid was struggling with a smaller girl who was flopped down on the floor, yelling and kicking. The older girl had hold of the younger one's arm, dragging her back from the doorway.

"Hold up there," Gil said, bending to lift the fit-thrower.

"Me see!" the little one in his grasp said. She stuck her tongue out at the other one and spat. It blew all over his arm. He wiped it off on his pants leg.

Her hair was as red as blanketflower and he knew in an instant that he had hold of Nina. She didn't seem the least bit scared of him, but the other girl was backing off warily.

"I'm not going to hurt you," he said quickly to her. "I know you

don't know me, but I know Nina. She's my—" Nina threw up
her bright blue eyes at him when he said her name. "I'm her
cousin." Which was true in any case. "I'm Sunny's cousin, too, and
I came to see her. Is she here?"

The little girl with the braid nodded. Nina started pushing on
his hands to let her loose. When he did, she went running, sailing
past the other girl, disappearing round a corner. He heard her
call, "Mama! Mama!"

Gil stood up. "What's your name?"

"Ruthie Mae Goodner," the little girl said breathlessly, running
all the names together like one. She seemed ready to dart off any
second.

"Can you show me to Sunny, Ruthie Mae?"

"I'm not supposed to let anybody in while she's sleeping."

"It'll be all right, Ruthie Mae. I promise."

He'd either convinced her or she'd caved in, because she led
him down the dark hallway. Family photographs lined the walls,
but his concentration was on Sunny. Dread had hold of him. If
she was all right she'd have been out already, either with a greeting or to send him away.

Ruthie Mae stopped at a partly opened door. Gil sidestepped
her and palmed the door back on its hinges. Inside the room,
heavy curtains blocked out most of the daylight. Sunny sat
slumped on the edge of an iron bed. She wore a rumpled cotton
nightgown. The bed was rumpled, too. Nina lay up on the pillows, her thumb in her mouth. When the door opened, Sunny
turned her face toward him and his heart stopped dead. She
looked at him with eyes old and bleary, like somebody starving, a
ghost of a girl staring at him.

"Gil," she said in a whisper, but with no trace of surprise in her
tone, as if it had been only yesterday since the last time she'd seen

him. She pushed a scraggle of hair off her forehead. Her wrists were like twigs.

"I'm here to take you home," he said, choked.

"Oh?" She gave a wobbly glance over her shoulder. "I don't have anything packed."

"That doesn't matter." He strode into the room, jerked open the wardrobe. He pulled out some clothes and dropped them on the bed beside her. "Where's a suitcase?"

She had summoned Ruthie Mae to her and she held the little girl's face in both her hands. "Honey, I want you to go down to Mrs. Greathouse, all right? Tell her I need her to watch you this afternoon."

"Where are *you* going?" Ruthie Mae said. A fat tear squeezed out of her eye.

"Just go on down there, all right? And take your sweater in case it's cold."

When the girl left the room, Nina sat straight up from the pillows, popped her thumb out of her mouth, and hollered, "Bye, Ru-mae."

SUNNY WAS IN A half stupor for the first ninety miles. Gil had done all the packing, found a cardboard suitcase in a hall closet and thrown some stuff in, some solid stuff and some frilly stuff. He didn't know what all he had. Whatever was missing could be replaced. She'd grabbed a yellow bottle of some kind of medicine. Besides Nina, that medicine had seemed the only thing Sunny had an interest in bringing along. He hadn't yet had a chance to study the bottle, but he would bet that whatever was in it was the thing making her dull and thickheaded. He let Nina sit on his lap and pretend to drive until she fell asleep against his chest.

North of Hillsboro he rented a little roadside cabin. The owner had only one left, but it had three cots inside. Gil carried Nina to the middle one and laid her down. Her thumb stayed plugged in her mouth. She didn't wake up.

Sunny wandered in behind them. She looked around the cabin, then said, "Why are we stopping here?"

"I've got to get some sleep. I've been up for three days." A kerosene heater stood in the corner. He bent to light the wick, waved out the match just before it burned his fingers. "You hungry?"

She shook her head no, but he went out after food anyway. He found a grocery a block away and bought some bread, a hunk of cheese, and a loop of dried sausage.

When he got back to the cabin, Sunny was sitting on one of the cots staring at he didn't know what. Daylight had left and the room was dark. He lit the lantern hanging by the single window. A three-legged table stood propped in the corner and he set the food down there. He used his pocketknife on the cheese and to cut the sausage into coin-sized rings. He stacked some on a piece of bread and took it over to her.

"No plates," he said.

She raised her face at him. "Did Papa send you?"

"No. Not exactly. Here. Take this."

He put the food in her hand and went back to the table to cut some for himself. When he glanced back at her, she was eating, slowly, but eating.

The sausage was greasy and full of salt, but the cheese wasn't bad, and the bread was fresh. They needed something to drink. He hadn't thought of that. He kept a tin coffee cup in the car and he went for it, washed it off under the well spigot outside. With night, the temperature had dropped. He got the lap blanket out of the car and he brought that inside, too, but the kerosene heater was doing a fair job at keeping the cabin warm. He shrugged out of his jacket.

He handed Sunny the cup full of water, which she drank half of and handed back. He said, "We'll save some for Nina," and set the cup on the floor between the cots. He opened the lap blanket over Nina where she was curled up on the middle cot and tucked it around her.

Sunny was watching him. "You married Turner."

He nodded. "A year and a half ago." So she had been keeping up with him, too. He turned back toward her. Her eyes were black sinkholes. "You look like hell, Sunny."

"I lost another baby." Her mouth grabbed in a grimace. "Right after Christmas."

She reached for the suitcase standing between the cots. She knocked over the half cup of water and it went flowing under Nina's cot. He knelt to retrieve the cup, then watched her dig through the clothes he'd packed. He spotted the yellow bottle of medicine she was after before she did and he snatched it up.

"Don't take any more of this, Sunny," he said. "It makes you drunk."

"No, it doesn't." She reached for the bottle. "It puts me to sleep, that's all."

He stepped away from her, took the medicine into the lantern light to read the label. "I bet it's nothing but pure alcohol. Or something worse." All the label said was A RELIABLE REMEDY FOR SLEEPLESSNESS. He set the bottle on the corner table. "Stay awake and talk to me."

"I don't want to talk. I'll just bawl." She shook her head. "Ira says get over it."

"Well, I'm not going to say that."

She faced toward the wall away from him, her shoulders slumped. She looked so miserable and he couldn't just stand there and watch her. He went to the cot and sat down beside her. His hand touched her back. "Hey . . .," he said, and that was enough.

She turned like she was startled, then reached for him. She pressed her face into his shirt and his arms went around her. She was nothing but a bag of bones. He pulled her closer.

She let him hold her like that, quietly, until it began to last longer than was natural, went beyond a comforting hug. Increasingly he became aware of all the different parts of her pressing against him. He thought he could even feel her heart, her lungs filling up, then settling back. The longer the embrace lasted, the more noticeable and awkward it became, a thing with a will all its own.

Finally she raised her head. Her eyes were bone dry. She touched his face, traced half of the line of his mustache. Then she kissed him, a long, real kiss, as if to acknowledge the need he was feeling. He wondered if she felt the same need. Her lips were warm and solid. Inside of one second he was lost, pulling her tighter, lengthening the kiss. It was still there, whatever it was. That magnetic something between them.

She broke away, looked him clear in the eye and he looked back at her, studying each other close up in the lantern light. She lay down on the cot and pulled him down with her. The cot groaned with the weight of both of them.

"Don't try to make love to me," she whispered.

"I won't," he said, his heart thick in his chest.

"Pull the covers up."

He reached to the foot of the cot, drew the blanket up around them. Her arms never let him go. He still had his shoes on, and so did she, but she burrowed her face against his neck. A quiet settled over him. He felt her eyelashes rake his jaw a few times before she fell asleep in his arms. As tired as he was, he wasn't long to follow. In another hour or so, the fuel in the lantern burned out.

Chapter Seventeen

$\mathcal{D}$AYLIGHT STREAMED IN THROUGH the window. It opened Sunny's eyes. They fixed first on the knotty pine boards above her as she got her bearings. From habit, she glanced across at Nina, still sleeping, worn out from yesterday. The breath in her rose and fell steadily.

Sunny moved the limp hand—Gil's hand—that rested on her breast, eased it down to her ribs and left it there. She felt dry mouthed, loggy headed, stiff from having Gil Dailey wrapped tightly around her. He was asleep, eyelids shut, hair rucking out in crazy curls, mouth relaxed. His head smelled of Wild Root Hair Oil, a little broom straw underneath. He'd caused her a restless night, while he had slept as soundly as Nina. He shifted against her. His hand pulled back up to hold her breast.

It was the thing that had caused her—more than any other one thing—to come to loathe Ira, the way he was always at her with his groping hands, his body rubbing up against hers. She had wanted to scream when he crawled into the bed with her each night. Sometimes he would take her even when she said no, almost cruelly. She had thought long and hard about running away, even before she lost the baby—tiny, blue, mangled Richard

—just as soon as she had learned she was pregnant again by another man she didn't love. Now here she had done it, flown the coop, right in the middle of the day, and he wouldn't have a clue where to find her.

Except that they had come off so fast, she had left the valuables box Papa had made for her. It had been so sudden, and she hadn't been thinking straight. That box was still sitting on the shelf in the little pantry off the kitchen. She hated that she'd left it, with both those pictures of Isabel inside, other treasures—Gil's army photograph, that love letter.

She became extra-aware of his hand resting on her breast. She started to move it away again, but before she could, he did, gliding around to press near her spine. He snuggled up closer. She didn't know what had made her invite him in with her last night—a weak moment, gratitude, a feeling that he could protect her, all those things. For so long she had felt too tired, too spiritless to get through an entire day. She had resigned herself to becoming one of those closed-up, broken women, too sad to tend to a family, and then Gil walked into that hated bedroom. She had wanted to ask what had taken him so long.

A gray shame settled on her as she thought about leaving Ruthie Mae behind. She didn't feel the same guilt about the other two children, Cloyde and Mitch. They would be all right. They were old enough, nearly, to take care of themselves, and they had resented her anyway for not being their real mother. But Ruthie Mae would feel abandoned again, become withdrawn the way she'd been when Sunny first arrived, their mother's death still fresh and raw inside the house. That house, which had at first been a sanctuary to Sunny, had begun to feel like her prison. And she could stake no claim on Ruthie Mae. Taking her would have brought certain revenge from Ira.

She extracted herself from Gil's embrace, slid slowly downward, squeezed herself free. He collapsed into the empty space that she left and she crawled out to the floor. The room was icy. She went to check the heater and he came pushing upright. He yawned, stretched, unaware that her exit had awakened him.

"Did we run out of kerosene?" he said, his voice sleepy, and so much softer than she remembered it.

She nodded. She hoped he wouldn't mention last night's kisses.

His clothes were a wrinkled jumble on him, his hair too. Whiskers shadowed his chin and cheeks. She remembered the feeling she used to get just admiring his face, the texture of his skin, those beautiful clear eyes. She lifted the bottle of medicine, looked at the label, and set it down again.

Sugar ants had found the bread. Sugar ants in winter—that surely meant something ominous. A line of them trailed across the table, down one of the three legs to the floor, disappearing behind a baseboard. The cheese had gone transparent and rubbery. The sausage had left a spot of grease on the wood. Not even the ants would touch that sausage.

"We'll find some breakfast somewhere," Gil said as Nina began to stir.

She came up fussy, red hair sticking out all over her head. She was a big frowsy mess of a thing, with a booming set of lungs and a quick, happy grin, which she gave to Gil as soon as he said hello to her. She had deep dimples in her cheeks, those flame blue, Royce Peeler eyes. Sunny never got over her awe that such a child could have come from such a cold, unliving part of herself.

It was warmer outside the cabin, so Sunny went out to rinse her mouth under the spigot. The medicine always left a bad taste. She tried scrubbing her face with just her hands. Nina wouldn't hold still for a wash of any kind at all. She screamed and kicked until a pair of gray tabby kittens came up snooping. They distracted Nina's attention.

"Mina want these!" she said, and yanked after the kittens.

Gil was loading Sunny's suitcase into the car, in the space behind the front and only seat. It was a sporty automobile, but not made for more than two people. He went hurrying after Nina, scooped her up, and Sunny noticed how much improved his leg was since she'd seen him last. You would have to have known him before to detect any difference at all in his gait. He did or said something that caused Nina to squeal out a laugh. They were already great friends.

Back on the road, Gil and Sunny talked a little, careful to keep on the surface of things. He told her about Ding moving back home, the solemn way this decision had been announced. He told her about his job with Firestone, which she already knew about from Aunt Dellie's letters. He said he liked it all right, at least he wasn't wearing out a desk in an office somewhere. She could see he was making plenty of money, by the car and the clothes he wore. Wrinkled as he was, she could tell his suit was tailor-made.

He drove carelessly, the way a person used to spending long hours behind the wheel will do, managing all the sticks and levers with ease. She tried to forget about his hands that morning, seeking her breast. Remembering it made an odd feeling start in the pit of her stomach.

In a cafe, over bowls of eggs and plates of biscuits and ham, she said, "I don't want to go home." She broke a biscuit in half for Nina. "You can drop me off in Austin."

Gil stopped eating. "Drop you off?"

"Yes." She ignored his stare. "There's a business college there that I was going to go to once. I think I might try it now."

"Business college."

"Where they teach you to typewrite, and file by the alphabet, and make—"

"I know what it is." He dipped a little honey onto his plate, mixed in some butter. "I'm just surprised—"

"At what?" she interrupted. "Me having ambitions?"

"No. That's not what I meant." His fork stirred the honey into the butter until it was smooth. "You'll need money."

She had money, stashed in a jelly jar in the cupboard, but it wasn't doing her any good now. "I'll get a job somewhere. Cleaning houses if I have to."

"And go to school at night?"

"Yes. If I have to." She didn't like him questioning her. "I want to *do* something with myself. *Be* something."

He picked up a biscuit half and dolloped on the honey butter. He took a devouring bite, licked honey off one finger. "What'll you do about Nina?" he said.

Sunny followed his eyes down to her side where Nina was squishing scrambled egg in her fist. "Oh for gosh sakes, Nina. Stop playing in your food." She snatched up a napkin to wipe Nina's hands and the discussion of her future ended there. Much to Sunny's relief. She didn't have all the answers yet.

Gil left a generous tip on the table. She had to resist the impulse to gather up some of it and shove it down in her pocket. She yearned for that jelly jar.

On the way out of the cafe, he bought some cigarettes for himself, and for Nina a scribble book with a nubby pencil so she'd have something to do in the car. Once they were settled in, he dropped a pack of Juicy Fruit in Sunny's lap. "I thought you might like some chewing gum." He pulled the car out onto the road.

Sunny stared at the thin yellow package nestled in the folds of her skirt. She picked it up and rubbed her thumb over the shiny wrapping. She wanted to weep suddenly for no reason. She peeled open a stick of the gum and stuck it into her mouth. Liquid sweet slathered her tongue. She swallowed and chewed and let the wind grab at her hair.

"Thank you," she said when her breath came back.

He glanced, gave a little shrug. "It's just a pack of gum."

"No. I mean—" She smoothed her hand over Nina's busy head. "You saved us. *Me*. You saved *me*." She laughed to keep from sounding too dramatic, but she meant it. She felt saved.

"Will he come after you, you think?" Gil said, as if it were something he had been pondering

"I doubt it. He's probably glad to be rid of me." But she didn't really know what to expect from Ira Goodner. After a year of marriage he was still a mystery.

At first glance, Ira had seemed like a clean, simple, if gloomy man, but there was more to him than that. He was passionate about his religion, went to church every time the doors opened. In a year, Sunny had learned more about the Bible and Jesus than she had ever known was possible. And he was loyal to the railroad, disagreed with the union, had stayed on the hall telephone continuously through the last strike trying to help work things through. He was strict about games the children could play—no cards, no dice, no marbles—yet lenient about their bedtimes. He made weekly treks to the cemetery to lay flowers on the graves of his wife and daughter. And he always insisted that Sunny join him on his knees for nightly prayer, right before he took her onto the bed to satisfy his sexual appetite.

It had surprised her that first time, two days after their courthouse wedding. It wasn't supposed to be that kind of union. He came to her little room off the kitchen that night, to move her into his big bedroom. "I've cleared a drawer for you," he said, "and made space in the wardrobe."

She'd blinked at him, holding her nightgown closed at the neck so as not to reveal any part of her body, although later she thought how stupid and blind she had been. "Nina's too little to leave alone in here," she said, and it was true. Nina hadn't been but a few months old then.

"You'll hear her if she cries." He took Sunny by the arm.

The drawer he'd cleared out was a bottom one, and the space in the wardrobe amounted to two double hooks. He peeled back the bedcovers. She hadn't known if she should help him or start moving her things into his room right then. He answered the question when he shut the door.

"Will you pray with me?" he said, and she had stood there half stupefied until he jerked her to the floor.

IN AUSTIN, GIL DROVE straight to a rooming house he knew of—Mrs. Redmond's. He stayed there a lot, he said, whenever he came to town. "She cooks good," he added with a smile before he went inside the house.

Sunny waited in the car, Nina asleep across her lap. It was dark already, had been for a good while, and she felt like she could collapse into sleep herself. It was cool out, but not so cold as in North Texas. The sounds of people in the neighboring houses came: a woman shouting at unruly children, some laughter, a trombone bleating out scales. Cooking smells seeped out at her.

In a while, Gil came back. "OK. You're all set for one night. Let me take Nina. I'll come back out for the suitcase."

"I can carry the suitcase," she said, handing Nina over to him.

An elderly man sat with a game of checkers in the front room, playing himself. He didn't look up when they passed. They didn't see anyone else and Gil led the way up a long staircase that turned twice before it broke out onto a wide circular landing. Numbered rooms opened on all sides. Gil had the key for number four.

"She doesn't usually allow kids," he whispered, juggling Nina to free his hand.

"Here." Sunny took the key from him. "What's that smell?"

"Roast beef, I think." He grinned. "I'll go try to charm us up a couple of plates."

There was an electric overhead light and Sunny found the button on the wall. The light was yellow and put a brassy sheen on the room. A bed, a chair, a sink, a dressing table, a locker against one wall. It was stuffy and she opened the window as Gil plunked Nina into the middle of the made-up bed. He went right back out after some food and Sunny took a horrified look at herself in the mirror.

Her hair was wind-tangled, face shiny, eyes dark underneath. She unbuckled the suitcase and found a brush inside and started giving her hair quick strokes. Mama had always believed in a hundred, but Sunny stopped at seventeen to rummage through the things Gil had packed. There wasn't much—a long flannel nightgown too warm for such a mild night, a gray skirt, lots of underwear, a thin corset she couldn't use anymore. No blouses. She would have to wear the same one she had on.

She changed into the nightgown, smelled the blouse. It seemed all right. She draped it over the back of the chair beside the window in hopes the nighttime air would take out some of the wrinkles. She turned on the faucets at the washbowl, scrubbed her face with the soap and water, and used the roller towel. By the time Gil came back balancing a tray of food, she felt better—cleaner anyway.

"What did you bring us?" she said eagerly, and took the tray from his hands.

It looked like a vegetable stew, with corn bread and buttermilk on the side. She couldn't remember when her stomach had felt so empty. She set the tray on the table and started buttering the bread.

"Come on and get some of this," she said, glancing up. She caught his eyes raking over the length of her body. He knew he'd been caught. He looked away quickly, hung back at the door.

"Save it for Nina," he said.

"There's plenty here, Gil."

"You eat." He reached behind him for the doorknob. "I'll be by to get you tomorrow. We'll go find that business college."

She stopped buttering the bread. "You're leaving?"

"There's another place down the street. I've stayed there before."

She took a couple of halting steps in his direction. "You can't stay here?"

"No. She's only got this one room."

She remembered the cot last night, and his hands, and she knew he was remembering it, too. She couldn't help the glance she gave toward the bed. Nina was sprawled there asleep.

"If you need anything," he said, "just ask Mrs. Redmond. She'll take care of you. And I'll be back first thing in the morning."

His hand twisted the doorknob and she rushed forward, in a sudden panic, as if she might never see him again if she let him walk through that door. "No, Gil, don't go." She threaded her arms through his. She didn't mean to reach inside his jacket, but that was where her arms ended up. She could feel the heat and the realness of him. "I'm not used to it here. I won't sleep a wink with you gone." She felt his mouth press her head.

"I already told Mrs. Redmond the room's for you. My cousin. How would it look, Sunny, if I stayed?" He moved her away. His hands silked down both her arms. "I'll be back bright and early, I promise."

She grabbed his face, brought his mouth down to hers, and kissed him. She didn't think before she did it, or question herself once it was done. She was tired of thinking and trying to figure things out. She wanted him to stay, and she felt desperate enough to do anything to keep from being left alone. And he needed the kiss, she could tell by how he clutched hold of her. She moved his hand over her breast and pressed it there.

His lips hardened on hers and his hand gripped her. For a moment she felt the heat in him swell. But he broke their lips apart, leaned his forehead against hers, breathing through his mouth, and his hand moved off her breast. He touched her jaw, rested his eyes on hers as he let her go. And then, as if to keep from changing his mind, he pulled open the door and left.

As soon as he was gone, she felt sick to her stomach, whorish at trying to lure him with the promise of sex, to manipulate him that way when she didn't mean it, or even want it—she didn't think. His hand still burned like a brand on her breast. And his eyes— the way he had looked at her, as if he'd seen through to her core of cheapness. She almost threw open the door and raced after him, to tell him it was a joke, an accident. She wasn't like that, he had misunderstood. But he hadn't, so she kept still, listening for the sound of his automobile driving away.

Chapter Eighteen

WHEN GIL DIDN'T COME as bright and early as he had said he would, Sunny began to worry that she really had disgusted him with her behavior. The minute Nina woke up she started in asking for Ruthie Mae, which gave Sunny something else to worry over. She fought Nina into her clothes, got dressed herself, and they went downstairs. All through breakfast, Sunny kept hoping Gil would show up, but he didn't.

Mrs. Redmond had a bird in a cage and she whistled to it as she brought out platters of food. The other boarders were all men, most being regulars who knew each other. They talked cheerily amongst themselves, stirring their coffee, passing and grabbing bowls of grits and gravy, platters of batter bread, bacon, eggs fried crispy around the edges. One man was a clock salesman. Another sold books. Their plates disappeared beneath the piles of food.

To Sunny, it all tasted like ash in her throat. She felt out of place and worried about the reason Gil wasn't there. Just as soon as he came—if he came—she would apologize for last night. She pushed the food around with her fork and tried to remain as inconspicuous as possible. But Nina didn't understand the meaning of the word *inconspicuous*.

Halfway through the meal, she dunked over a full glass of milk, spilling it all over herself and the table. Some sloshed onto the book salesman's plate and slopped into the clock salesman's lap. The rest poured off onto the floor and rolled into a puddle under the sideboard. Sunny mopped with a napkin until it was saturated, then used the hem of her one clean skirt. Nina, knowing she'd caused trouble, dissolved into a fit of temperamental tears, and her screaming continued even after Sunny carried her back upstairs to change clothes.

It was nearly noon when Gil finally arrived. He walked in smoking a cigarette, dressed in a blue pinstripe, shirt of pale ivory, with a zigzag tie of red and dark blue. He was clean shaven, hair knife-parted and as slick and shiny as patent leather. His smile lit up and Sunny couldn't keep from hurling herself across the front parlor where she'd been waiting. She threw herself into his arms and he folded her up tightly. Like a lover, not a cousin.

"I didn't think you were coming," she whispered.

Mrs. Redmond was standing there. "Mr. Dailey? You want to step in my office a minute to settle your bill?"

"I got busy," he said to Sunny. He smoothed back her hair and let her go. He followed Mrs. Redmond and dropped his cigarette into a spittoon on the way, tweaked Nina's topknot as he passed her. They disappeared into the depths of the house.

Sunny breathed in deeply, gathered up the suitcase, took Nina's hand, and went out to wait in the car. While she sat there it dawned on her that he was probably anxious to get her and Nina set somewhere so he could go home to Turner, get back to his own life. She realized she hadn't been thinking of Turner, or anyone besides herself.

In a few minutes, he came smiling out of the house, moved the hat he'd left lying on the driver's seat, and climbed in behind the wheel. She said, "Any place like this one'll do fine for us, Gil. As long as they take kids."

He gave her a slight frown and palmed the hat onto his head. He seemed older with that hat on. Even Nina stared at him. He reached into the breast pocket of his suit coat and brought out some folded papers. "They said you can bring in your address to them later," he said as he handed her the papers.

One was a brochure that said WALDEN'S COLLEGE OF BUSINESS. It had a pencil drawing of a building on the outside, and sketched inside was a line of ladies sitting at typewriting machines. There was a list of requirements and a carbon copy of an enrollment form, already filled in. She squinted at him. Nina took the brochure out of Sunny's hand.

"You already signed me up?"

"I thought it would save time." The car revved and they jolted away from the curb. "They start a new session next week. You said it's what you wanted to do."

She studied the carbon-paper enrollment form. He'd put her name down as Sunny DeLony. She wondered if that was deliberate or absentminded. Her date of birth was correct—January 1, 1901.

He drove without talking much. There was a lot of street traffic, as many mules and wagons as automobiles. At one place he overshot his turn and had to back up half a block. He cussed a man who blew his car horn at nothing. By the time he got them where he'd been taking them, he seemed edgy, irritable.

It was on a steep hill, so when he parked the car, he racked the wheels against the curb and set the hand brake. Sunny gazed around at the row of houses on either side of the street, gas lamps at the corners. She hadn't finished looking before he came to help her out of the car.

"Who lives here?" she said, taking in the blue house where they'd stopped. It had white shutters on the two front windows. One shutter was missing a couple of slats, but the paint was all fresh. A big oak tree grew in the side yard.

"Nobody. Come on. I want to show you."

There were eight steps to the front porch. He carried Nina on his hip. She pointed at the birds chattering in the top of the tree. He wedged himself inside the screen door and worked a key into the lock, then pushed the door open for Sunny to go in first. She ducked under his arm.

The curtains over the windows made the room dim. Gil set Nina down and she raced off. "Electricity's not on. But the landlady said they could hook it up with a day's notice." He pulled a cord to part the curtains.

There was a humpback sofa in the front room, a chintz chair, a long table, and a hat tree. A fall of maroon drapes separated that room from the dining room. Four chairs, a square table, a breakfront china cabinet, empty and with a chipped corner, but so big it took up one whole wall.

Gil hung his hat on the tree. "She might be willing to look after Nina while you're at your business college. The landlady. At least, she didn't say no when I brought it up. She lives right down the street."

Nina had crawled under the dining table. She peeped out at them and laughed.

"There's another table in the kitchen," Gil said, coming up behind Sunny. "You could set up one as your desk to do your studies."

She turned around. "I can't afford a place like this, Gil. No matter how good a job I find."

"Here. Let me show you something else." He put his hand on her elbow and guided her into another room that opened from the dining room. A bedroom, with a mattress that needed new ticking, a dressing table angled in a corner, a window seat. "Take a look at this view."

"What's the rent, Gil?"

"Come on, Sunny. Daydream a little." He positioned her in front of the window, left his hands on her shoulders. "Now, look at that."

They were higher up than she would've imagined, standing at the back of the house. The view overlooked the city. Treetops and the roofs of houses. The capitol dome shown coppery in the sunlight. Cars moved silently on the streets. A trolley snailed along.

"Don't you bet it's grand at night when the lights are all turned on?" he said.

"What's the rent?"

"Paid. It's all paid."

From behind, his arms slipped around her. His breath touched her neck, then his lips. His mouth opened on her skin, and for a moment she wanted to melt into him. She almost did, almost gave in to it. But she caught herself in time and she turned to tell him that she couldn't take the house, not from him, it was too much. Except before she got out the first word, he hugged her tight and kissed her with such strength and fire, it overwhelmed her. She felt small and weak, and that night in the line shack up on the Knobs came back to her, how he had overwhelmed her then, too, and what the consequences had been for it.

She yanked away from him and bolted out of his reach. She swiped at her mouth. "All this kissing has got to stop, Gil," she said. "You can't just grab me up like that."

He gave his hair a dazed rake of his hand. "You mean, you can, but I can't? Don't play with me, Sunny. If you knew how much I want you . . ."

"Oh, don't start saying things, Gil. Just stop it right now." She pressed the back of her hand to her face, still feeling the kiss. "So you've got a lot of money. That's wonderful. I'm happy for you. And don't think I'm not grateful, I am. But this—" She waved her hand at the room. "This is too much. Everything. It's just way too—"

"I don't want you grateful to me. You think *that's* what I want? Jesus Christ, Sunny."

"I don't know what you want. Or why you came to get me." She sat down on the bed and a dusty smell rose up from the mattress. "Or what you think you're doing now."

"Doing? It's not me. One minute you're begging me to stay the night with you, and the next you're—"

"I shouldn't have done that. I was just—I don't know why I did it. It was wrong of me."

He shoved his hands down in the pockets of his pants, looked at the floor, then up at her. She could see his confusion and felt sorry for causing it.

"Let me help you, Sunny. I want to. I need to, all right?"

"You've done enough."

"No, I haven't, OK? I haven't." He dragged his hands to his hips, rested them there like fists. Then he turned to peer out the window. "Look. For three years I didn't know where you'd gone. And nobody was telling me a damned thing. All I wanted was just to know how you were. If you'd forgiven me yet, or if you still hated me."

"I could never hate you, Gil."

He turned from the window and came over to squat in front of her. His eyes looked like brown bottle glass. "Listen to me, Sunny." He put one knee on the floor and took her hand.

"No. I don't want to." She turned her face and looked off from him, afraid he was about to bring up Isabel, and that was a subject she wasn't ready to approach with him. She didn't know if she'd ever be ready. "There's no use in doing all this talking. You can't change anything."

Slowly he kissed the knuckles on her hand. She went stiff and kept her eyes away, even when his head dropped onto her lap and his arms laced around her hips. But then his shoulders began to shake and her eyes moved onto the back of his head.

He wasn't weeping. No, she wouldn't let him do that. Men weren't made for bawling and sniveling. They didn't do it well. And anyway, *she* was the weak one. She shoved at him. "Stop it, Gil."

But he clung to her tighter, buried his face against her lap. The shaking got worse. He felt steamy hot, a sweaty little boy. He pressed his face to her belly and then she heard him. A strangled and inhuman sound.

"Stop, Gil." She tugged at his shoulders. "I mean it." But he wouldn't budge. Uncle Nolan had always been as easy to cry as he was to laugh. Papa called him chickenhearted. But Gil had never before shown signs he'd inherited that trait.

"Please . . ." She didn't know what to do with him. She lay back on the ticking and pulled him with her. He held her tight and hid his face from her. "Hush, now." She cradled his head to her breasts, wiped sweat from his temple. "Sshh." She kissed the pulse there, stroked his hair.

Gradually the tension in him relaxed until he got heavy on the arm she had wedged underneath him. She patted him and soothed him, as if he were a child who had a skinned knee. He lay for a time as quiet as a grave before he turned his face. His eyes were horrible, bloodshot things, and she touched her thumb underneath the right one, unmatting the lashes. She bent to kiss his other eye, tasted the saltiness, and he reached for her mouth, sliding his hand behind her neck, transforming back into a man again as quick as that. She took the kiss he gave her, and it felt like something broke inside her, something that wasn't even fixed yet.

They lay there side by side. She traced the circle of his ear and allowed herself to love him again, but in a different way, with more comfort in it. It made strange sense to her, this new love she felt as she traced the lines of his face. They shared the same memories, and miseries. And even though another person could never know exactly the sorrow in her heart, how the shine had gone out of everything when Isabel died, more than anyone else she guessed that Gil understood it the best.

"You shouldn't wear all this goop on your hair," she said, plucking at him, rubbing her fingers together. "And this mustache . . . it isn't you either."

He smooched at her, all smiles, feeling better. "I haven't been me for a long time."

Nina's little pittering feet came running and Sunny strained up from his arms, realizing right then that Nina had slipped completely from her mind.

"Mina found dis." She crawled up on the bed, prying herself between them.

She had a fistful of playing cards from a deck she'd found somewhere in the house, and black grease on her face and arms. She'd been off playing quietly, probably getting into things she shouldn't.

Sunny sat up and Gil pulled Nina against his shoulder. He

started reading the cards out loud to her. "Three of clubs. Six of diamonds."

Watching, Sunny thought how he could still do it to her. Take her over. Absorb her like a huge sponge until nothing else in the world mattered but him. She knew it was something she would have to guard against, to toughen up that part of herself. She reached out and touched his cuff link and he smiled at her, eyes bright. He continued flipping through the cards. "Nine of spades. Two of hearts. Jack of clubs."

So THEY BECAME LOVERS again. It wasn't something they discussed, yet when Gil took them into town later that afternoon for housekeeping necessities, it was assumed by them both that they were shopping for the three of them. They spent four hours buying things, like a couple of dewy-eyed newlyweds: groceries and cooking pots, dishes and tableware. The house needed everything: linens, and bar soap, a little pint-sized rocker for Nina because she looked like a doll sitting in it, a framed print of the Eiffel Tower because Gil wanted it to hang above the sofa. He took them for hamburgers and Cokes at a soda fountain, and later for a walk in a small downtown park to feed the pigeons Nina's leftover bun. He showed Sunny the Littlefield Building and pointed out the fifth-floor windows where Walden's College of Business was located. The trolley stand was right outside the front doors, and the line ran all the way out to the end of the street of the blue house with white shutters.

They slept together that night on sheets, new and scratchy, Nina in the bed in the other room, on her own set of new and scratchy sheets. Gil didn't touch Sunny except to hold her, as if he somehow sensed her reluctance. She knew he wanted her. She felt the pressure of his erection against her thigh, but she thought he was as scared of it as she was, and so neither of them made the first move. They lay in each other's arms, a repeat of the night in the cabin outside Hillsboro, till sleep finally overcame them.

For Sunny, it was a fitful sleep; for Gil, a sleep interrupted by a nightmare. He came bolting up, jarring her awake too, clawing out for a firm hold, as if he thought he was falling. His shoulders heaved for air and she sat up with him.

Murky night light came from the window. He wore only the bottom half of his combinations and his body was smooth and hairless. She touched his back. "Are you all right?"

He nodded, pulled up his knees and rested there, collecting himself. His breath slowed to normal, then deepened.

She rubbed her finger around the tattoo high up his arm. Chills rose on his skin. "You want to tell me what it was about?"

"It won't sound like much."

"You could try me."

He stayed still for a moment longer, then he turned and gathered her to him. He reached to peel off her gown and she didn't try to stop him. She raised her hips to let it pass beneath her. He kissed her and she helped him push off his underwear. When they were both naked, he laid her down on her back. Her hands slipped down to his rump. She folded her legs around him and pulled him inside her.

Later, when he was asleep again, the foreboding crept in, like a shadow over her heart. She eased out of the bed, tried to keep it from bouncing him awake, and as he reached out, she moved a pillow over to replace her. She found her nightgown on the floor, shrugged it on over her head.

Across the dining room, the door to Nina's room stood six inches ajar just as Sunny had left it. She stopped outside it thinking how quiet Nina was in there. Too quiet. She pushed into the room, left the door wide, and went around the bed to peer into Nina's face. She dropped to her knees, held her hand close to Nina's mouth. Light, even breath hit the back of Sunny's knuckles. She lay her forehead on the mattress, feeling foolish. A quick tear spilled down her nose.

Chapter Nineteen

On Friday morning, Gil got up intending to get dressed, and since he was in Austin, put in at least one day of work that week. But it was raining out, a real downpour, so he thought what the hell and crawled back in bed with Sunny. Rain pelted the window. A little thunder rumbled. She had that sweet morning smell about her. He took his time waking her up, went slow, relishing the velvety feel of her naked skin. She blinked at him, her eyes sleepy, emerald green.

For the past two days, he had pretty much kept her in bed. He hated to be a greedy pig about it, but making love to her was all he could think about. It was like sitting at a meal and never filling up. He would watch her doing the most ordinary things—fixing coffee or washing her hands—and his desire would nearly overcome him. But it was more than just a physical desire that she provoked in him. It was also a desire to be known—to know and be known by her completely.

She was almost back to sleep, cradled against him as limp as a rag, when he heard Nina up and playing, crooning a strange monotone sound from the other room. He moved Sunny over onto the pillows. "Stay in bed," he said, kissing her head. He got up, smiling, tucking the sheet around her, then hunted down the pants and undershirt he'd worn yesterday.

He found Nina on the floor beside her bed, in her little nightie. She showed him her doll, gritted one of her dimpling smiles at him. She put her finger to her lips—"Ssshh"—and hugged the doll to her shoulder. She started rocking to and fro and he recognized then the sound she had been making before he walked in. It was a song. She was singing. He picked her up, swung her into his arms, and danced her a little bit.

He sang, "Casey would waltz with a strawberry blond, and the band played on . . ." She watched his mouth, and laughed, and threw back her head so far he had to brace her between the shoulder blades to keep from dropping her.

The wet weather had his leg a little crampy, but the dancing helped it, and they sang till his stomach started to grumble. He carried her into the kitchen, sat her on the table. They needed ice for the box, so there was no food that required refrigeration. No milk. No bacon. He drew them tap water to drink and fed her soda crackers with sardines for breakfast. She liked it well enough, especially if he put each bite into her mouth himself, like feeding a hungry new bird.

"Where did you come from, little girl?" he asked, talking mainly to himself. She babbled back something completely incoherent to him, as if they were having a real conversation. Sunny could understand her just fine, but he was having a hard time getting used to the way she talked.

He had already figured it out that she wasn't his. She wasn't quite old enough, wouldn't be but two at the end of next month. Well, this month. February had turned into March when he wasn't watching. Every day felt like a new ending to an old dream of his. He kept a bad case of the grins.

Nina took a piece of cracker out of her mouth and held it on the tip-end of her finger. He wasn't sure if she was just showing it to him or if he was supposed to take it away.

"Can you say Daddy Gil?" He wiped off her finger. "Dad-dee-Gil." He slapped his chest. "Me. Daddy Gil." He sounded like a Comanche. She laughed at him. He tried a few more times to get her to say it. She just kept laughing at his efforts.

A knock came at the front door and a voice called, "Yoo-hoo! Anybody home?"

Gil went to see who was there and Nina followed. It was Mrs. Dentler, the landlady. He opened the door for her. "Get in out of the rain."

"Oh, it's stopped raining." She stepped inside. She was dressed like for church, hat and jewelry, smelled of pressed powder. She had an umbrella, but it was dry. He glanced out the door. All the dark clouds had left.

She said she'd walked down to meet Sunny, called her Mrs. Dailey. Gil had lied and told Mrs. Dentler they were married. He'd wanted the house for Sunny, and he could tell by looking that Mrs. Dentler wasn't the type to have rented to a divorced woman, or a runaway wife. She was too much like Ma. So he had just acted as if he and Sunny were married. And all along he had intended to be around often enough to make that lie believable.

Mrs. Dentler had brought a coffee cake, which she deposited on the sofa table. The cake took Nina's attention right away. Those bright blue eyes widened.

"What a sweet child," Mrs. Dentler said, and Gil smiled, watching Nina, hair uncombed, little nightie dragging the ground. He liked having the landlady think that Nina belonged to him.

"Nina, can you say hello to the lady?" He caught a glimpse at the pendant watch pinned to Mrs. Dentler's bodice. It was nearly noon and Nina was still in her nightie. She poked her finger into the side of the cake.

"Why, I'd be proud to have her stay with me whenever you and Miz Dailey are out. If you'd trust me with her," Mrs. Dentler said, reaching to pat Nina's tangled hair.

As if she'd heard her cue, Sunny came stumbling out of the back room. She was wearing a dress she'd just thrown on with nothing underneath, which was plain from things that jiggled under the light cotton fabric. She was barefoot, her hair more disheveled even than Nina's. She looked like she'd been making love all morning. He figured he must look the same way.

"Sunny," he said, smiling, "this is our landlady, Mrs. Dentler."

Sunny's face turned ten colors when she saw they had company. She grabbed her arms around herself.

Mrs. Dentler held out her hand and took a step in Sunny's direction. "So pleased to know you, Miz Dailey."

Sunny shook the lady's hand, then refolded her arms. Gil barely held in his laughter. Sunny gave him a dark glance.

"So sorry to barge in on you," Mrs. Dentler said. "I know you all must be busy getting yourselves settled."

Sunny answered, "Oh no, please, come in and sit for a while."

Gil made his exit, taking the coffee cake to the kitchen, where he went to his haunches with suppressed laughter. Nina followed him. She watched him laugh, then patted his cheeks in both her chubby hands and laughed with him. He circled her with his arms.

"You want cake?" he said, wiping his tears. She nodded. "All right, sweetheart. Daddy Gil will get you some cake."

"You TOLD HER I was your wife?" Sunny said, after the landlady had gone.

"I wish you could've seen your face."

She broke off a chunk of the coffee cake. "It didn't strike me that funny."

"Well, but she agreed to watch Nina, didn't she?" He saw her face stay serious and he reached out to cover her hand. "Ah, Sunny, who does it hurt?"

She pulled her hand out from under his and leaned her elbows on the kitchen table. "Turner for one. I'm sure she wouldn't like it a bit."

"She's not a factor."

Nina wandered over to pat his leg and blabber something at him. She had his silver cigarette case, which she had emptied, and she showed it to him. He strained to understand what she said.

"Don't make light of it, Gil," Sunny said, bringing his attention back to their conversation. "You married her."

"I'm not making light," he said. Sunny frowned and bit at her bottom lip. She reminded him of Aunt Tessa when she did that. His hand moved out to her elbow. "Listen. I don't want to start already talking about Turner. I don't want to think about that yet. Let's just be together."

She straightened her arm on the table and he rubbed the inside of her elbow. "I was in there while ago," she said, "after you got up this morning . . . thinking about everything—"

"That's a bad habit. It's detrimental to good health."

She shook her head to tell him she wasn't listening to his poor joke. "All this time, these years, I pictured you and her as happy together. I never dreamed that the first minute I saw you again I'd . . . " She stared at his hand rubbing her arm.

"That you'd what? Want to be with me?"

She nodded. Her eyes flicked at him. "Well . . . or just—" She looked across toward the sink and the stove. "Maybe this is all too crazy, Gil. You being here, and me, too. I don't know, like we're playing house. I need to feel that I'm in charge of things I'm doing. I don't want us making crazy decisions."

He folded their fingers together. His throat lumped up. "Don't leave me, Sunny. I just got you back. Don't think about leaving."

"I didn't say that. I'm figuring things out, that's all."

"Good. That's fine. We'll take turns figuring them out. Just say you won't leave me, all right? Say *Gil, I will never leave you again*."

She smiled at him and her eyes filled up. She added her other hand to the knot of their hands already on the table. "I won't leave you."

He squeezed her fingers, raised them to his lips to kiss, and then Nina was there, tapping at his leg again. "Here Dattagu. Mina bring dis." She had a fistful of broken cigarettes, which she gave to him. She dusted the tobacco off her hands.

"Sweet thing," he said, trying to count how many he could salvage.

"What did she just call you?"

Gil looked at Sunny and grinned.

ALL DAY SATURDAY SUNNY spent with a packet of his Firestone stationery writing letters at the dining room table. Letters to her husband, to Ruthie Mae, to Uncle Dane, and she didn't finish a single one. Wadded balls of paper littered the floor and Nina lined them up like white tumbleweeds underneath the table. Gil kept walking behind Sunny's chair, trying to read what she wrote. Each time she blocked the letter with her body or covered it with her hand. He didn't insist; he was trying to give her control of her own self.

"What if they're looking for us," she said on Sunday morning before they were even out of bed.

"You're letting yourself get all worked up—"

"No, I'm not. I'm trying to be clearheaded. We've got to do this the right way."

"There's a right way?" He laced his hands behind his head and watched the shadows drift across the ceiling.

"You've got to go home, Gil."

"I am home. I recently moved."

"Do you always have to make jokes?"

"Yes. As long as you're going to be so serious."

"Well, this is serious. She's my cousin, not some stranger I've never seen. Even Papa might turn against me over this."

"Dammit, Sunny." He got out of the bed. "I'm sick of making sacrifices. I've tried living like other people want me to. And none of it matters. You don't get happy."

"That's how life is. You're not supposed to get what you want."

"That's bullshit." He snatched his pants off the closet hook.

"Just because you want it. That's not how it goes."

"You don't really believe that." He stared at her. "These past days . . . it's been heaven, hasn't it?"

She rose on her knees, winding the sheet around her. "So what do you say we do? Just tell everybody else to go to hell?"

He smiled at her cussing and worked through his shirt buttons. "Yeah. That sounds pretty good. If they can't take us." He shouldered on his suspenders. "Or we could just stay lost for a little while. I don't know why we can't do that. But you don't think we can, so . . ." He sat down for his socks.

She peered over the end of the bedstead, watching him. "Where're you going?"

"To get this over with so you'll be happy." He stepped down into his shoes.

"Get what over with?"

He tied the laces. "I figure I'll stop in McDade first and see Uncle Dane. Then I'll head on to Ma and Pop's—"

"Oh God," she murmured.

"Then to Brenham to talk to Turner."

"Gil—" Sunny rose out of the bed, keeping the sheet wound around her.

"You write that letter to your husband. Tell him you want a divorce." He stepped to the mirror to tie on his necktie and saw her reflection, stricken, behind him. He turned and gathered her firmly against him. She was naked under that sheet. "It's going to be OK, Sunny." He kissed her just above her ear and she clutched him tight.

"I'm scared."

"Look at me." He raised her head. Her eyes were wide and glassy. "It's going to be OK."

She nodded slowly and he kissed her quick on the mouth. He got his hat off the rack by the front door. She followed him. She stayed inside the screen as he went down the outside steps headed for the car. And he thought he would keep that image in his mind, of her standing there naked except for that sheet, her hand up, fingers waving. It was an image he thought could get him through anything.

Chapter Twenty

"*I* TOLD YOU NOT to go up there. I knew you wasn't going to listen to me, though. You went to bed looking like a sick calf."

Gil sat on the apple box in the barn while Uncle Dane planed a door for the new workshop he was building onto the carriage shed. So far Gil had taken only one swig from the pint of brandy Uncle Dane had put into his hand. He didn't think he should be drunk through this. In his other hand he held a burning cigarette and a yellow telegram from Ira Goodner.

"I don't know why he would think she was in danger," Gil said, reading the message for the sixth time. "I told his little girl who I was."

"But he don't know you from squat. You're lucky he hasn't sicced the law out after you." Uncle Dane ran his hand over the spot he'd just planed and went at it again with more muscle, but it was just busywork, something to keep his hands occupied while they talked. Gil could see the worried set of his mouth.

"I didn't kidnap her," Gil said. "She wanted to leave, so I took her."

Uncle Dane stood up, pressed a hand to his lower back, and

stretched. "I hope you hadn't got yourself into a whole lot of trouble here. I'll have to share the blame, since I as much as gave you the idea."

"She looked real bad. I think she had a case of nervous fatigue or something. He's bound to know I didn't kidnap her."

Uncle Dane came over for the pint of brandy. He sipped at the lip of the bottle. He frowned in thought and scratched one finger up under the edge of his hat. Uncle Dane wore straw, summer and winter. "What's in Austin anyway?"

"A business school she wants to go to. To learn to be a secretary. I signed her up for it." Gil felt his breath get a little short. "And I rented her a house."

"You did?" Uncle Dane recapped the bottle. "Well, I'll pay you back whatever you're out for that."

Gil shook his head. "No." He wet his mouth. "I'm taking care of her now."

Uncle Dane had been about to stick the brandy bottle back up on its ledge. Halfway there, he stopped and reconnected his eyes with Gil's. "Does your wife know about this?"

"I'm headed to tell her now."

The energy seemed to go out of Uncle Dane. He pulled off his glasses and wiped out the lenses. "You two never have used good judgment about each other."

"It's important to Sunny what you think."

Ding's black pup came bounding into the barn, all legs, snarling at the milk cow that had wandered in for a nip of grain. The dog jumped around Uncle Dane's knees, then dashed head down at Gil. She jumped on him, leaving a set of paw prints on his suit pants. The dog had a black tail like a fan that swished dust up into Gil's eyes. He grabbed her by the ruff of her neck and scratched her absently.

"That thing's got marbles in its brains." Uncle Dane put the brandy bottle on the ledge. "Y'all are fixing to tear up this family. But I reckon you already know that."

Beside the workbench was a straight chair with the ladder back broken off, and Uncle Dane sat down heavily. The dog went over to lean against his leg, hassling like it had been running in mid-August, tongue strung out like pink taffy.

"I'm gonna say something." Then Uncle Dane seemed to reconsider, or to measure out his words. And it all suddenly seemed harder than Gil had thought it should be. He wished he'd tried harder to talk Sunny into just running off somewhere, avoiding all this.

When Uncle Dane raised his eyes, he looked old and weary. "I'm gonna shoot straight from the shoulder now, Gil." His finger pointed down at the ground and the pup whimpering between his feet. "Theresa — and me, both — always thought the sun rose and set in you, but Sunny's my daughter. And if she wants you, then I can't argue with that. But I'm telling you right now, you had better treat her right. You understand me? Or else you're going to have me to deal with."

Gil's scalp tingled. "I'd never do anything to harm her."

"I don't believe you'd mean to."

Gil let go of a laugh that had no mirth in it and shook his head. He clenched his jaw. There was a silence that only added to the lousy feeling left from those words of threat. He hated that Uncle Dane had even thought a threat necessary.

The dog chased the Templar out of the yard, tried to bite a tire before Gil got through the gate, then she stood in the center of the road barking. Gil gunned the engine and left McDade in a cloud of grit. His chest felt like a pile of bricks.

• • •

By the time he got to Burton it was late evening. He was having second thoughts about this whole trip, spreading the word, making the big confession to them all. It wasn't anybody's business but his and Sunny's. He didn't care who they were, he didn't need to be belittled and made to feel bad about himself and what they were doing.

He decided not to stop and see the folks. They'd be at church on Sunday night anyway. He blew right through Burton. Brenham wasn't but twelve more miles. If Turner was there, fine, he'd tell her it was over between them. If she wasn't, well, he'd pack his things and go, maybe leave her a note and his house key— *Dear Turner, I won't be back. We can stop lying to each other now. We're neither one of us too good at it* . . . He started hoping she wouldn't be home, maybe working the night shift at the hospital or something.

Big improvements had been made on the Brenham road thanks to all the money coming into the state since the Highway Act and he made that last twelve miles in record time. The Ford sat in the driveway. When he saw it there, he realized he had really been counting on leaving that note.

He found Turner lying in the dark bedroom with a cold wet rag resting on her forehead. She was having one of her headaches. He asked if he could freshen the rag and she said, "Would you?" clumping the clammy thing into his hand. Just that. No hello. No hugs or kisses, or even words of greeting after eleven days apart.

At the kitchen sink, he tried to focus his mind on Sunny standing behind that screen door, uplifted hand, alabaster shoulders. She was worth whatever happened. The feelings they had for each other had always been too private for others to understand. But he wished he had stayed in Austin long enough to get a phone line installed so he could've telephoned her right then. He needed her voice to give him courage. He wrung out the rag and went back into the dark cave of a bedroom.

Turner's hand clamped his wrist, feeling for the rag. She took it, arranged it. She murmured, "Thank you."

"How long has this one been going on?" he said.

"Three days. I haven't been able to move since I got back from Aunt Dellie's." Her voice was thin. "Your mother's been a dear, though. She brought over some food yesterday. Did you find it?"

"I didn't look. I'll get some later."

He gazed down at the dark figure of her on the bed. He would gladly take the blame for their failure. All of it. He'd known a month into the marriage that he'd made a mistake, played a big joke on himself, thinking he could settle for this nothing kind of life.

"You want an aspirin or something?" he offered.

"They upset my stomach too much. How was your trip?"

The drive to Weatherford flashed through his mind, sleeping with Sunny on that cot, dancing little Nina around her room. He had to hold on to all of that. "Fine," he mumbled. "But I'm just here for a minute, Turner. I . . . I came to get some clothes and some other things, and then I'm going."

"Lots of big sales, huh?"

"You just . . ." He had the sudden urge to bend down and hug her. He didn't know where the urge came from or what the point of it would be, so he just gave her shoulder a two-fingered pat. "Get some rest."

He left the dark room, squinted at the electric light in the hall. He lit a shaky cigarette and went to fix himself a sandwich. He recognized Ma's baked ham. He looked in the cabinet where he kept the liquor and poured himself a Dewar's, splashed in a little tap water. He carried the drink and the sandwich into the spare room.

Right after they moved into this house, Turner had bequeathed the closet and highboy in the spare room to him. He dragged a suitcase out from under the bed and started throwing in things, haphazardly, distractedly. Sunny had said there was a right way to do this. He wondered what her ideas had been on that. He should've asked. He felt sleazy, as unlovable as a snake.

There was a box at the top of the closet and he hauled it down. The box held, among other mementos, his army uniform folded up neatly in tissue, the Rainbow shoulder patch that had come in the mail, the flashlight he'd been issued and somehow managed to keep. He remembered the night on watch in Vaucouleurs when he'd scratched *G. M. Dailey 117th* on the housing. There was the photo of him and Rome posing beside the truck, Gil showing off the brand-new PFC patch on his arm. Rome was mugging cross-eyed for the camera. Van Winslow had shot the picture.

"Why are you taking all *that* stuff?"

Turner leaned in the doorway. She wore a faded, rose-colored robe, in need of laundering. Two brown coffee stains blemished the skirt. She was never sloppy until these headaches struck her. Then everything went to pieces. Her hair hung in uncombed strands, eyes circled under like she'd been days out of the sunshine. She picked up his glass and took a sip, made a sour face.

"I don't see how you can drink this."

"Might cure your headache." He resumed his packing.

She watched him. "You should see Julianne's twins. They're adorable."

"Are they?"

"Yes. They made me want to think about starting a family."

He raised his face at her, made no comment.

"She's got her hands full, though." She bit a nail and spit it out, reached for his cigarette burning in an ashtray. "Something's wrong with the hot water again. I've had to take cold baths for the last three days."

"Well, call somebody. There's money in the bank for that."

"*You* could probably fix it, I bet. If you'd take a look at it before you go." She massaged her temple with her fingertips. "I don't know a thing about that sort of stuff."

She sat on the end of the bed and he kept gathering up his clothes. She took a draw on the cigarette and reached for the stack of shirts inside the suitcase, flipping through them like pages in a book. "How long are you planning to be gone? You look like you're packing for months."

He straightened and stared into the open suitcase. "Turner . . . we need to talk about something."

A thump of ashes dropped onto the bed from the cigarette in her hand. Automatically he scooped them up, and since the ashtray was across the room, he slapped the ashes into the thigh of his pants and rubbed them in.

"Don't do that," she said. "That suit's alpaca. I can't wash it."

He dusted at the gray smudge. Ding's dog's muddy paw prints were still there, too.

"So talk," she said. She shrugged. "Well, what? Are you in some kind of trouble? Is that why you're packing for such a long trip?"

"I'm not coming back."

"It can't be that bad, can it?" Her smile lessened. "Is someone pregnant?"

He couldn't hide his surprise. He thought he had been careful with his little infidelities. He sank down on the bed across from her, staring.

"Oh . . . you didn't think I knew." She pulled in smoke, let it out with a sharp exhale. "Don't all traveling salesmen do it?" She sounded almost airy.

His ears burned. This wasn't going at all the way he had planned. He'd meant for it to stay simple: in, pack, and out. "Nobody's pregnant. Jesus Christ." He didn't mean to growl. "Look. Turner . . ." He forgot what he had been about to say. He couldn't get past the shock of her words. "Why the hell have you put up with it?"

"Did I have a choice?" she said, but he saw her flinch, watched the disappointment spread on her face. She'd been bluffing, fishing. She hadn't known anything for sure, and he'd just given himself away.

He struggled to pull his thoughts back in order. She had derailed him. "I haven't been much of a husband," he said.

"Oh, you've been all right." She gave a weak smile.

He looked across at her and at that smile, and all the sudden he really hated what he was about to do to her. He got sick-feeling, light-headed, winded. "You deserved a lot better, Turner. Don't think I'm not going to be fair with you. Anything you need . . ."

She pushed herself to her feet, still staring at the suitcase. "Julianne always said you would leave me. She didn't think you'd last this long."

"It's not meant to hurt you."

"Nevertheless." She took up the glass of Dewar's and slung back a good belt. She made no sour face that time. Smoke circled her head.

He knew he had to tell her, had to make himself say the words. She would only hear it from somebody else if he didn't. He groped for that image by the door this morning, that waving hand, alabaster shoulders. "It's Sunny." He almost choked on it, but he kept his eyes steady. "I thought I should—"

"You're lying." The cigarette in her hand twitched. "She's in North Texas."

"No. She's not. Not anymore."

The hurt left her face. She laughed, a laugh thin with anger. "Well, congratulations. Does she know you can't stay faithful?"

He wished he could start the whole conversation over, plan ahead, soften it. "Turner . . . I had hopes for us. I did—"

"Oh just shut up and get out!"

She burst for the door and he started to go after her, to explain things, to somehow make it all seem less rotten. But before he could even rise off the bed, she turned back and hurled the lit cigarette at his lap. She had good aim, and he was too busy bobbling it, burning his hands and a hole in his shirt, to even notice when she left the room.

Chapter Twenty-one

March 7, 1922
Dear Ira,

   I hope that I have not caused you any worry or alarm.
As you well know, I have been very blue of late. The day
my cousin came I was so low that he offered to bring me
down here for a rest. Nina is with me and we are both fine.
I know I should probably have phoned you before I left, or
at least wrote you a note, but I was feeling, as I said, blue
enough I wasn't clear in my thoughts. I only knew that I
didn't want to give you a chance to talk me out of it, which
I thought you might do. I knew you would find Ruthie
Mae safe with Mrs. Greathouse, as I trust that you did. It
would be a nice thing if we could say what the future
holds. I can almost hear you telling me that the Bible has
all the answers, but that is like a cold wind through me,
Ira. It doesn't help the emptiness. You must let me alone to
make myself right again, otherwise I will be a lost cause. I
have regrets about our marriage as I'm sure you must, too.

I hope the children will not suffer over this. I think of them each day with love.

Sunny

WHEN GIL DIDN'T GET back to Austin on Monday like Sunny expected, she told herself not to worry. He had probably just had car trouble, or run into some of the road construction going on everywhere. Anyway, she knew how to hail a trolley and take it down to the corner of Sixth and Congress, and Mrs. Dentler was watching Nina. Everything was taken care of.

Tuesday when he didn't turn up, a tight lump formed in her throat and stayed there. She couldn't get rid of it no matter how hard she swallowed. And it stayed in place all through Wednesday's classes, too. They were learning to file by the alphabet. She had her own little index box with lettered tabs and cards with names typed in. She stumbled when she got to the *Mc* names, couldn't concentrate at all. She kept having visions of him killed in a car wreck, or lying in a hospital bed unconscious. She tried not to think it could be that he had just changed his mind, decided to patch things up with Turner and forget about the past week in Austin.

It scared her to realize how much he still mattered to her. Even after everything. For three years she had tried not to think of him, although there had been times when she wondered how she would feel if she ever saw him again. Well, now she knew. He renewed something in her that she thought was lost. Just sharing the same pot of coffee, the same breathing air, gave her hope. With him gone, she switched to his side of the bed, snuggling down where he had lain, as if the smell of him in the sheets and on the pillow could keep away the fear and doubt, the loneliness.

By Thursday she was frantic. She got off the trolley at the end of the street, uncertain whether to go on waiting or somehow try to find him. It was not as if he had never wavered in his feelings for her, or had doubts himself. Doubt was as mixed into their past as moments of happiness and sorrow. But this time it had felt so real to her. So possible. It would be hard for her to give up on that now.

These were the thoughts spinning in her mind as she trudged up the hill to the house. The study book in her arms felt like a slab of stone. The weather had turned to soup, gray and heavy, as if it might pour rain any second. She crested the hill and there was the Templar parked out on the street. A half second later she spotted him.

He was sitting on the top step of the porch, no hat, sleeves rolled to his elbows, tie undone and dangling loose around his neck. She had to control herself to keep from running, but she did quicken her pace. As she got closer, he stood. Her heart felt like a ball bouncing in her chest.

"What happened to you?" she said.

He looked hollow eyed, like he hadn't slept since he left, but his gaze was soft on her. He lumped down the steps to the sidewalk, and when she got even with him, he grabbed her up. She smelled the starch in his shirt, the cigarettes, the indescribable something that was just Gil. She felt like she might cry with relief.

"Are you all right?" she said.

"Where's Nina?" He pulled the study book from her hands.

"At Mrs. Dentler's. I'm headed there now."

"Let's leave her a little while longer."

They climbed the steps arm in arm. When they stepped in the door, she glimpsed the suitcase and the box beside the hat rack one second before he swooped her up and carried her to the bedroom. They made hungry love, and afterward as they languished in the bed, she wondered why she didn't feel ashamed for finding such pleasure at the expense of so many others.

She rubbed the loopy dark hair on his wrist and down the back of his hand. The wedding ring was missing from his finger. "I wasn't sure you were coming back," she said.

He tucked her head between his shoulder and chin. "I drove around for a couple of days. Just trying to get so I could stand myself, I guess. And then this morning it hit me. You were here waiting for me, and you're the whole point. So whatever hell is in store for me, I still come out the winner."

Sunny raised onto her elbows so she could see him. "Was it that terrible?"

He fingered a strand of her hair out of her eyes. "Undoing is going to be the hard part. Undoing all the mistakes we've made."

For the next few days things stayed quiet. So quiet it was almost possible for Sunny to pretend that they were the only three people in the world, her and Nina and Gil. They made love every night and it became her favorite time of the day. A new fierce desire came alive within her, and she allowed it, acknowledged that it was there. He had sure hands and seemed to understand places on her body she hadn't known existed. Sometimes she awoke in the dark with him sharing her pillow, his arm locked around her, and almost in wonder she would explore him then, her fingers glinting along his skin, over the line of his shoulder, finding the fuzz around his navel, the two indentations below his rib cage, and the scar embedded deep in his hip. In his sleep, he might move her hand onto his erection or she might boldly put it there herself, until he drowsily pulled her astraddle him, only to awaken a moment later, surprised to find their bodies locked together. It became a kind of craving she had, always there beneath the surface.

They took Nina to the park for picnics and to the lake to stick their feet in the water and skip rocks. Gil made a kite for Nina out of sticks and newspaper, old knotted-together rags for a tail. Sunny had to run it up. The weather had been rainy one day, clear and shiny the next, bothering the rheumatism in Gil's leg. Nina jumped up and down and begged to hold the kite string, which didn't last but a couple of minutes before she forgot and let it go. The kite went diving down, wrapped around a tree limb, and that was the end of it.

Twilights started to get longer, and going home that day, Gil began to pester Sunny about learning to drive. She tried to discourage the idea, but he swore he could teach her, so she got behind the wheel. She felt clumsy and insecure there. She couldn't remember to use the brake and ended up putting the Templar into a muddy cornfield. A helpful man with a delivery truck and a come-along happened by and towed the car out. For a few days after that, Gil took to calling her his Little Miss Barney Oldfield, after the famous speedster, but he didn't try to get her to drive again.

Schoolwork kept her busy. There was so much to learn, and she fretted about mastering all of it in just six months. Gil rented a typewriter for her to practice on and had a telephone put in. They turned the dining room table into a great big desk they shared. He used the phone to call his customers and got her to type out orders he took, which she did slowly with two fingers. She kept his ledger book, too, and it made her feel useful and like a real secretary to him.

Then he went to see a lawyer, someone who had been recommended to him by an old army buddy he ran into. He brought the buddy home after visiting the lawyer, so Sunny didn't have an opportunity to ask any questions. They were already half skunked by the time they arrived anyway, holding on to each other's shoulders, singing war songs and telling tales.

His name was Van Winslow. He had bright little hard eyes and even though he was well dressed in a tweedy vested suit with a handkerchief folded into two neat points, there was something about him that struck Sunny as shifty. He had been in the same unit with Gil and ever since the war he had been living and working right in Austin. When he walked in the door, he took Sunny by her shoulders, looked square in her face, and said, "So this is the real, live Sunny." And he kissed her on the mouth, which Gil didn't even seem to mind.

They chain-smoked cigarettes until the front room was in a haze and drank bootleg whiskey that had come from somewhere — she didn't ask. They got into the box Gil had brought from Brenham and went through all the memories there. They included her, but in an ignoring sort of way. And Nina got overexcited by the company and the activity. Sunny had a hard time getting her to go to bed that night, had to lie down with her, listening through the walls to the racket of those two drunken men, both of them seeming on the edge of something, trying too hard to be gay and carefree. When Nina finally dropped off to sleep, Sunny went back out there into the smoke and whiskey and Gil looked up at her with a stranger's eyes.

21 March 1922
Dear Turner,

I have had some time to think of the next logical step for us, in view of my intentions and the mood I left you in. My lawyer says you must make the first move. You have the grounds. Your uncle should be able to handle the necessary papers. Of course, I'll pay for everything. My money is your money, as it always has been.

With regrets,
Gil

March 27th

Gil—

I have no desire to become a divorcée. What would be the benefit for me? Meanwhile, you are openly committing adultery. Legally, I can have you arrested, and sue your whore for alienation of affections. You see, I have an attorney, too, one whom I chose for myself. His name is Wallace Lester. You will find his bill enclosed.

Turner

"Does she mean *me?*" Sunny said. "Is that *me* she's calling a whore?"

Gil snatched the letter from Sunny's hands. "Don't read that." Stunned, she watched him hide the letter under a stack of Firestone papers. "She's just trying to make me sweat. She's not—" He took Sunny's arms. "Look. Don't get upset, OK? Just let me handle it."

She grabbed at him as he started away. "She's right, Gil. Who benefits? I mean, even if you do get divorced, I'm still married."

"We'll take care of that, too."

He swooped Nina up by her waist. She had been begging him to take her outside to the tire he'd hung from the oak tree for a swing. Sunny waited until they went out the door before she fished Turner's letter out of the pile. The viciousness of it alarmed Sunny. Turner had always been so proper and ladylike. It was hard to feature her showing such teeth.

That evening while Sunny fixed supper, she heard Gil place a long-distance phone call. He acted later like everything was normal, cutting Nina's meat for her, coaxing her to eat her greens. But when the phone rang again, he jumped after it, and Sunny knew by instinct that it was the long-distance operator giving him his connection.

She put a spoon of pudding on Nina's plate and crept to the end of the short hallway from the kitchen, stopped there just out of sight where she could hear. His voice sounded stiff: "It doesn't make sense for you to fight it. Don't you want to be rid of me? Wouldn't that make life easier for you? . . . No, I didn't say that . . . I did not say that." His tone sharpened and got louder. Although they had a single-line phone, Sunny thought of the ten-party line Turner was on and what good gossip they were giving folks in Brenham.

"I don't care, Turner. Do whatever you want to . . . I said I don't care . . . don't make threats . . . listen to me—will you listen, goddammit . . . wait . . . no wait, Turner! Sonofa—" The phone went slamming against the wall and Sunny stepped out. He looked up and she could see the anger swimming in his face. "She hung up on me," Gil said as he bent to pick up the phone. Sunny bent to help him.

Nina came on the run, egg pudding all over her face and hands. "Mama! What dat sound I hear?"

Gil gave Sunny a false, heartsick smile. "She'll let me go. I know she will. I don't make that much difference to her. She just needs to punish me a little bit."

But right after that phone call, things began to deteriorate. First, Turner closed Gil's account at the Brenham bank and some checks he wrote—one to Mrs. Dentler—came back unpaid. Next, Turner called the Firestone office in Akron, Ohio, and tried to get her hands on some stock he had bought. Sometimes when Sunny came home from classes, she could tell Gil hadn't left the whole day. He'd still be in an undershirt, barefoot, a day's worth of whiskers studding his chin. There would be a pile of ash and butts in a saucer, doodled scraps of paper beside the telephone. He looked so miserable and tired, Sunny wanted to say, "Just go on back to her," except she was too selfish to, and it had all gone too far anyway.

On April Fools' Day, a Saturday that year, Aunt Prudie and Uncle Nolan knocked on the front door. The only way they could've found out the address of the house was from Turner. Sunny saw them through the kitchen window and her first urge was to run into the pantry until they went away. But the knocking came again, and Aunt Prudie's voice called through the screen door, "Gilbert! I know you're there. I see your motorcar out here."

By the time Sunny crept into the front room, Gil was already at the door. He kept the screen between them. "I'm not letting you in, Ma, unless you're here with your blessings."

Aunt Prudie grabbed the door handle. "Don't you keep your mother standing out on this porch." She whipped open the screen and barreled her way into the house. She wore a cloche hat with a geometric design and held a black lace handkerchief wadded in her hand.

"Morning, son." Uncle Nolan took off his Stetson as he came inside. He had on an old-fashioned, four-in-hand tie and striped trousers.

Gil said, "Pop, I'm asking you to help me with her."

Aunt Prudie's eyes fixed on Sunny standing just inside the red drapes that separated the two front rooms. "Land's." Aunt Prudie's hand with the lace handkerchief went to her heart as if the sight of Sunny were too great to bear. "I tremble to think what your poor mama would have to say about you right now—"

"Ma! Don't start with that—" Gil stepped toward Aunt Prudie. He threw a helpless look back at Uncle Nolan. "Pop? Are you going to help me or not?"

Uncle Nolan stood there holding his hat in both his hands. "Well, Gil, it sure does seem like you would've let us know what's going on. I hate we had to hear this from somebody else." That somebody else had to be Turner.

Aunt Prudie moved closer and Sunny felt herself wither under her bitter glare. "And what if you find yourself in the family way? Have you thought of it? Living in sin and incest with Gilbert."

"Ma!" Gil reached to grab Aunt Prudie's arm, but she sidestepped him. She kept talking at Sunny.

"It would be the devil's child. No telling what all manner of deformities—"

"Pop, will you get her out of here?" Gil's face was blood red.

Aunt Prudie put out a pleading hand. "You are on the road to perdition, son. Go back to your wife!" Then she pivoted to point at Sunny. "Give him up, Satan! Break your spell on him!"

Gil grabbed Aunt Prudie's arm and manhandled her away from Sunny. "Goddammit, Ma, lay off her, do you hear me? I won't have you speaking to her that way!"

"Easy, son." Uncle Nolan reached to steady Aunt Prudie and she lurched for him, tears streaming down her face.

"Did you hear him cuss me, Nolan? Oh Lord, where did I go wrong?"

"Can't you let me live, Ma? Can't you just learn to let me live my way?" Gil's yelling made Nina bawl. And Sunny hadn't even realized Nina was in the room until then. She bent to hug her quiet. Gil shouted, "What did you think you could do coming here like this? You won't stop us."

Aunt Prudie moaned and leaned on Uncle Nolan's shoulder. He looked at Gil, too. "The right thing to do is go home to your wife, son."

"Well, this is where I'm staying, Pop. Right here with Sunny."

Aunt Prudie broke away from Uncle Nolan. "God won't forgive you."

"Then to hell with God," Gil said. "And to hell with you, too."

With all her strength, and with her face gnarled in fury, Aunt Prudie reared back and slapped Gil across his face, exactly the same way she had all those years ago. Sunny jumped at the sound.

"Oh Aunt Prudie! Please, don't do that. Please."

Gil's arm flew out to stop Sunny. His eyes were stones as he walked across to hold the door open. He didn't say a word, didn't ask them to leave or anything. He didn't have to. It was plain on his face. And he stood with the door in his hand, just watched Aunt Prudie and Uncle Nolan walk out together. When they had passed, he slammed the door shut and threw the bolt. He was breathing hard, sweat staining his shirt. The screen door slapped back against the outside frame.

Sunny collapsed on the sofa and drew Nina onto her lap. She rocked against the cushions and Nina sucked hard on her thumb. Sunny felt her own strength dissolve. She huffed to get control and hold back tears.

When Gil finally turned from the door, his forehead was pinched up tight. Sunny wiped at her cheek and smiled at him, a strained, inappropriate smile that he didn't return.

"The Lord hath said honor thy father and mother." He aimed for the sofa. "But He didn't have my mother." He dropped beside them and Nina immediately reached out. He took her onto his lap and she curled her head against his shoulder. "Did Daddy Gil scare his girl and make her cry?" She nodded and put her thumb back in her mouth.

He lifted his gaze on Sunny. An angry purple mark stained his cheek. She reached out to touch it, and it seemed that their whole lives had come back around to square one.

"We're supposed to be together, Sunny," he said, like he read her mind. "It's not a sin for us to be happy."

Water blinked from her eye, tickled down her face. She scratched at it. "Is this happy?"

The thought that she could be pregnant or might get that way began to haunt Sunny. So did Aunt Prudie's words—*devil's child, deformities.* Sunny had heard all the horror stories of children born to parents of close blood. Babies with twenty fingers and their organs growing on the outside. There had been a woman in McDade—Mrs. Previne—who was raped as a girl by her own brother. The brother hung himself from the barn rafters afterward, but the child conceived of that rape—old Lucien—became the town idiot. Everyone liked old Lucien just fine, gave him rides in their buggies and bought him peppermint drops from the store. But nobody liked him well enough to tend to him once his mama passed on. And eventually he died all alone, in a home for simpletons somewhere down around Wharton.

It was old Lucien that occupied Sunny's mind as she figured the days from the last of February, when Gil had rescued her from Weatherford. Seven weeks had passed without nature once interfering in their lovemaking. But since delivering little still-born Richard back before Christmas, her system had never really regulated itself, so the hope stayed with her that she might yet be safe. She started watching for the blood, wishing for it.

She didn't know how to broach the subject with Gil—either of her fears or of the need for taking some kind of precautions. His spirits had sunk so low. At night he hardly slept more than an hour at a stretch. He had such terrible dreams, dreams that would bring him jerking up in a sweat. If he knew he had awakened her, too, he would pat her like a child and whisper, "Go back to sleep." As she drifted off again, she would hear him thudding around the house, or creaking out to the front porch for a smoke. He smoked way too much, had a hacky morning cough from it that Nina liked to mimic.

Papa came up on the next Saturday, surprising Sunny when he called from the train station, yelling in her ear the way he always did whenever he had to use a telephone. He'd brought Ding with him. They weren't planning to stay but a couple of hours. He claimed he'd come to town to look at a new planter.

"I guess the whole damned family'll be trooping through here to gawk at us," Gil said before he motored off to pick them up.

Sunny flitted around like a nervous bird, trying to set the house to rights, figuring out a good meal to fix for five people from what she had on hand. Nina toddled behind, underfoot, singing the little French song Gil had been teaching her—"Frera jocka, frera jocka . . ."—over and over until Sunny finally screamed at her to hush. That was a mistake. Gil had spoiled Nina rotten and she decided to start throwing a fit right then. Once it began it didn't let up for the rest of the day. She wouldn't have anything to do with Papa, wouldn't even look at Ding, who had grown so big Sunny hardly knew him.

Gil acted tense and fidgety, filling up all the ashtrays, bringing out the bottle of cognac he kept in the kitchen. Papa wouldn't share it. The only thing that interested Papa was pecking on the typewriter keys and squinting over the platen at the letters he made on a page of Gil's Firestone stationery. Ding kept running off to the bathroom to marvel over the drain tub and to flush the commode. He finally broke the pull chain.

"Where does all the water go to?" he asked when Sunny went in there to try to piece the chain back together. It seemed too complicated right then to explain about sewers and water lines.

She burned the dinner. They ate it anyway, Nina grumpy, sitting in Gil's lap, Papa's face grim. Ding talked away, though—bless him—blabbed on and on about his dog and the farm and school. When Gil took them back to the train station, it was a pleasure to have the house back to normal.

"At least he came, though. Papa," Sunny said to Gil as he helped her clean up the kitchen. "He came. That's the main thing."

"And didn't say two words to me. Did you notice that?" Gil was finishing off the cognac. He offered her a sip. She took it, but it tasted so bad she wanted to spit. He laughed and gave her a kiss on top of her head.

She said, "He was letting us know he's OK with it—us. That he's not going to judge us."

"Oh hell, Sunny, he was checking up on me. Making sure I'm doing right by his little daughter."

"You know he's not like that."

Gil chuckled and shook the last drops of the cognac into his glass. "That's what you think." He tossed the empty bottle into the garbage bin and strolled out to sit on the porch.

After she made sure that Nina was well asleep, Sunny followed him out there. The week before he had brought home a bench he'd rescued from a customer's garbage heap. It had an Ever-Ready Razor advertisement peeling off the back. She sat down there beside him and he laced their fingers together.

The night smelled of clover. Clouds drowned out the moon.

She thought about the baby she might be carrying and wondered if she should bring up the subject. It was a nice quiet time to. But the quiet was what stopped her. It seemed a shame to interrupt it. They had so few quiet moments. So she just sat there staring out at the street lamps, holding on to his hand, listening to him smoke his cigarette, until the urge to talk went past.

Chapter Twenty-two

GIL COULDN'T SHAKE THE feeling he had of being watched and followed. An uneasy enough feeling to cause him to look behind himself and study his surroundings for suspicious characters whenever he left the house. When he was driving, he would check his mirror, knowing for dead certain he had a tail behind him. A different tail every time: a Ford or an Olds, and once a Gardner Light Four, but never with a driver that he could identify. His work had begun to suffer. He was late for appointments because of having to circle down backstreets and alleyways. Sometimes he lay in bed at night sure he was going crazy, imagining all of it.

It was Turner; she was up to something, he just didn't know what. She'd been too quiet. Zeke Corothers had sent her new papers to sign, making a more generous offer, agreeing to give her everything Gil could spare: the house, her car, the savings account. But that was weeks ago and her lawyer had yet to respond.

Gil thought about her threat to have him arrested for adultery. Corothers said she could do it, especially if all she was after was revenge. He'd suggested Gil might want to move to a boardinghouse for a while, advice Gil immediately rejected. If he did that then none of it made any sense. The whole point of leaving Turner was to be with Sunny.

Of course, he didn't tell Sunny any of this. Since Ma and Pop's destructive visit, her nerves had been ragged enough. And she was trying her best with her school, to learn a skill and better her mind. She'd gotten married too young, started having babies when she wasn't but a baby herself, and now that she'd found something and was moving toward a goal, he'd be damned if he'd do anything to upset her.

He knew he needed to force his mind back on his own work, too. Firestone had just announced a big rim sale on their retractables, bonus incentives included, and God knew he could use the money with Turner trying to bleed him white. But he had a dread of taking back to the road. He didn't think he could stand going off and leaving Sunny and Nina for even a single night. They had a telephone now, so he could call her, but that wouldn't be the same as having her share his bed, or riding Nina around on his shoulders when the day was through. Lately he'd started thinking about a desk job, a nice quiet eight-to-five someplace close to home.

"You've got to do your job, Gil," Sunny finally said, urging him. "Me and Nina will be just fine. You go ahead and go."

He pulled her onto his lap. "You won't get scared here by yourself?"

"I've gotten over that." She smiled and kissed him, and so he kissed her back, which started a lot more kissing. That was the way it usually went with them. He didn't know how he'd done without her for so long. He felt changed.

He decided on a quick trip up to Temple, calling on all those small country dealers along the way. The little accounts added up.

In Round Rock, he helped string a Firestone sales banner that needed to go across a front window. He took an order for a dozen square treads in Georgetown. At Belton, he pulled off his suit jacket, rolled up his sleeves, took a broom, and swept out the showroom for the manager there, who was shorthanded that day. It felt good to be out and seeing people again, but he missed Sunny.

From a drugstore in Temple he phoned her. It took forty-five minutes and three Cokes for the operator to get the connection through. The soda jerk had already started casting him impatient looks when the telephone in the booth rang.

Sunny was in hysterics. He couldn't make out a single word she said. "Talk slower, Sunny," he told her. "What's happened?" But she fell into incoherent sobs. And on top of it all, the connection was bad. Crackling and popping and electric fuzz filled up his ear. "Sunny . . . I can't hear you," he said, getting a little desperate. "Stop crying, Sunny, and tell me what's the matter."

A couple more buzzes and clicks sounded in his ear, then the connection cut out and he was left tapping the hook, trying to get the operator back on the line. Except he didn't want to wait another forty-five minutes, so he hung up. He threw some coins down on the counter and hurried out to the car.

All the way back to Austin, he thought about those cars that had been following him. They had waited until he left town to strike. Like they saw him to the city limits before they turned back to do their dirty deed. He felt like Turner had reached down his throat and torn out his heart. "Goddamn her!" he muttered to himself. He made it back to Austin in four hours.

Sunny was in a state of collapse when he got there, shaking like an epileptic while the story spilled from her. She'd come home from school, fetched Nina from Mrs. Dentler's, and right afterward three men had barged into the house. It had taken two of them to hold back Sunny, and Nina had screamed and fought all the way out the door. The details made him sick to hear. He could imagine the goons. If he'd been home it wouldn't have happened. They'd gone driving off in a black car. A Gardner Light Four—he would bet money. They'd left a paper, which Sunny had dropped in a wad on the floor. She pointed at it like it was a live bomb or a grenade. Gil picked it up and as he read everything began to crystallize.

It was a legal copy of a court order issued and stamped in Parker County, signed by the Honorable Stanford E. Stroud. There had been a hearing held to have Nina Goodner removed from the care of her mother, Florida Faye Goodner. She had been charged with adultery and failure to provide a proper home. Her emotional state was called into question. In short, the court had deemed her unfit. The three men had been constables, not goons. Gil had been so preoccupied with Turner, trying to second-guess her next move, that he had forgotten all about Ira Goodner.

The rest of that night, Gil held Sunny in his arms, too bleak-hearted and stunned to say much past "We'll get her back." Except he had no idea how that could be done.

ZEKE COROTHERS SAID IT was going to be a long court battle to get Nina back, cost lots of money and time. He telegrammed Judge Stroud in Weatherford protesting the manner in which the court order had been served and carried out. A feeble protest that did nothing.

Goodner had filed for a divorce. On his own, without being asked to. But Sunny was too torn up to even hear that one slight bit of good news. She wouldn't go to class, barely got out of bed. She wept and moped, wouldn't speak. She had no interest in the little garden plot he'd helped her dig a couple of weeks before. Weeds started choking out the seedlings.

A daily numbness attached itself to them both. Gil felt guilty and helpless, the same way he had after Isabel. Maybe their love *was* too costly. Maybe the price they'd paid was already too high for them ever to be happy together. Yet he couldn't bring himself to say this to Sunny for fear she'd agree and want to leave him. He couldn't face the thought of that, returning to a life without her. But one thing was for certain—other people weren't going to leave them in peace.

Five sleepless nights later, he dug up the old, faded newspaper clipping that advertised work in France. It had gone brittle around the edges. He smoothed it flat on the kitchen table and for an hour he stared at it, contemplated it, before he took it into the bedroom where she lay, a huddled lump in the center of the bed.

"Sunny." He sat down on the mattress. Immediately she turned over and sat up, too. She hadn't been asleep either. The light from the other part of the house fell into the room. "We're going to go get her. We'll pack the car and just go up there and take her."

She stayed silent for a moment. "You mean kidnap her?"

"It's what they did. To hell with the courts."

"They'll come and arrest us."

"Not if they can't find us." He switched on the bedside lamp and she squinted. He handed her the yellowed clipping. She wiped at her cheeks and took it. "I've never shown this to a soul," he said, watching her read. "We could get lost over there. Use different names. It'll take some planning. I'd need to get my hands on that stock, for one thing, before Turner beats me to it."

She raised her eyes and searched his face. "You'd give up everything? Just like that?" He nodded. She said, "She's not even yours."

"She's as much mine as she is Goodner's. More mine than J.J. Peeler's. I don't want to lose her. Or you."

She turned her head and stared blankly toward the window. "I'd never see Papa or Ding again, would I?"

"It's a big decision. I know. I spent three years trying to make it."

"When would we go?"

"Soon. A few days."

She reached for him then and hugged him around his neck. And it was the first time since Nina had been gone that Sunny's eyes were dry.

Later he lay in bed thinking things over, planning, pondering train fares and ship schedules, passports and money. The jobs in the newspaper clipping were more than likely long gone, but he didn't worry about finding work. There was plenty of it over there. He remembered the devastation. He thought about driving up to Weatherford, what he would do with the Templar afterward. He wondered if he ought to buy a gun.

Long after he had believed her asleep, Sunny said, "She's not J.J.'s either." She rolled toward him in the dark. "I thought you must think—since you said his name—that he's Nina's father. Well, you probably need to know, it isn't him."

This confession dazed him, coming out of nowhere, interrupting his mental plans for their leave-taking, and it took him a minute to register what she was saying. He focused on the ceiling, the streak of light fanning out from the window. "I figured he must've come back."

"No. He never did. Last time I heard, he was down in the oil patch somewhere around Beaumont."

Gil lay still and waited for her to go on, but she didn't. She settled onto her back, where he could see her profile outlined in the dark. He watched the steady rhythm of her chest rise and fall and wished he could get his mind back onto planning. He wished that everything she had just said didn't matter to him. Yet it did. And it was more than thinking of her making love with some stranger, somebody besides her two husbands, which was hard enough; it was all those months after Isabel's death, those guilt-ridden months, wrestling with his own grief, suffering for Sunny, lying in one hospital after another hating himself.

"Just tell me who it is and get it over with." He spoke sharper than he intended.

"I don't want her to ever know."

"You still don't trust me."

She took in a wet breath. "All right. It was after Mama died, when Papa was so sick, and J.J. was gone and everything. Royce Peeler came to chop wood for us. I don't know why he did it. They'd just lost little Ivy and—"

"Don't tell me any more."

"You wanted to know."

"Well, now I don't."

He rose to his feet, groped on the lamp table for his cigarettes, found them, and went through the house out to the porch to smoke. The wind took the first match. There was some kind of weather brewing. He swore and struck another, pulled in that first deep taste of tobacco, blew it at the black sky. He couldn't keep his mind from going back there to those awful days after Isabel. "Don't be so tragic," Sunny had said to him, sending him off. She wouldn't let him comfort her, but she had let Royce Peeler, of all the lousy scum.

"I shouldn't have told you." Her voice came from the other side of the screen door. She stepped outside. "I wasn't going to have her. When I found out . . . I thought I'd go to one of those abortion doctors."

"Christ, Sunny . . ." He shook his head.

"I'm just telling you things I thought about." She moved along-side him, put her hand on the porch rail. "I never did get happy about her. Not even for a while after she was born. I used to sit in that house and pray to God to make me love her. I don't think I can stand it if something happens and I never get to see her again."

He took her wrist and pulled her to him, felt her quiver, and held her tight. He'd made mistakes, too, all those girls in all those towns. Maybe he had a kid somewhere he didn't know about. It was possible. Anything was. People weren't perfect.

"You're going to see her again," he said. "We're going to go up there and get her back."

SUNNY WAS THE ONE who decided that they would go by Lange once they got to France. It was a name that belonged to them both anyway, and it would be easy to remember. Gil agreed. He planned to keep his other names the same. He'd been Gil for twenty-three years. But Sunny wanted to change all of hers. She wanted to be Sonja Josephine Lange. She said she'd never liked Florida Faye to begin with. He was just glad to have her planning for a future.

They couldn't tell anybody good-bye. They had to pretend one day was just like the next. They told Mrs. Dentler that Nina was in McDade for a visit with her grandpa. But there was one person Gil had to tell the truth to—Van Winslow.

Van had had his share of setbacks since the war, too. The girl he had come home to marry had changed her mind. And then his pop had died of a massive heart attack and left him with a frail mother to look after and a failing hardware business. Debt was piled to the ceiling. All the collateral used up. When Van took matters into his own hands and started running bootleg liquor out of the alley behind the store, he brought the business back from the brink of certain bankruptcy. He also made a lot of connections, the kind of connections Gil needed to get him and Sunny out of the country once they had Nina back.

"It won't be cheap," Van said over coffee at an apple-pie joint down the street from his hardware store.

"Nothing ever is," Gil answered.

It took three hundred dollars and five days to get their passports and the work visa he would need, even a marriage license with a notary seal that looked like the real thing. Van came through with everything, ship's passage, a letter of employment, a palm-sized British automatic. "Just in case," he said. He wouldn't take any extra money for his trouble.

"We're buddies," he said, shaking hands. "Good luck."

SUNNY COMPLAINED THAT SHE hated wasting things: half a month's rent, two-thirds of her tuition at Walden's College of Business, Gil's divorce half done. But they walked away from all of it—the rented typewriter, food in the pantry, ice in the box, clothes in drawers. He took one box and she took one plus a suitcase, and that was it. Driving away from that house, she looked so longingly backward, he thought she might cry. But before they were out of town her mood turned almost festive.

She started to sing, and he sang with her. It helped him nerve himself for what lay ahead. They sang "Love's Old Sweet Song" and "By the Light of the Silvery Moon." They tried harmonizing on "The Old Mill Stream." She cuddled up close to him, walked her fingers up the back of his neck, and that night when they stopped at a traveler's hotel, they made good love like they hadn't in a while, wrecking the rickety bed, wearing themselves out. He needed it. Her. The reassurance. All of it.

The next day and for the rest of the trip, though, she was like a different woman: quiet and touchy, snapping at him to drive slower any time the speedometer rose above forty. Once they got past Cleburne the weather went sour. The roads turned to muck, and the car slipped around.

It was a hot and humid Saturday morning when they finally drove into Weatherford. Sunny said she had hoped never to see the place again. He had the same thought. His nerves were jangling.

They drove by the house and some kids were in the yard. Big kids. Sunny slunk down in the seat. "That's Mitch and Cloyde," she said. "Keep going."

"Keep going where?"

"I don't want them to see me."

So he made the block, but just as soon as the black-and-tan house came into view, she started to shy again. "Go around again."

"Let's just stop, Sunny," he said. "We can't keep riding in circles."

She grabbed his arm. "No! Don't stop! There he is!"

Gil looked and a bony man with lots of dark hair had just stepped from the back door of the house. He walked with a deep stride toward a shed behind the house. He was a weather-beaten man who moved in that forward slouch a lanky person sometimes has. The age of Goodner startled Gil. He tried to imagine Sunny with such an old man and couldn't.

"What's he doing home on a Saturday morning?" she breathed.

"I'm stopping." Gil pulled the car to the edge of the street and shut off the engine. He reached across her and snapped open the glove box, took out the little palm pistol, Van's parting gift.

"What're you doing?" She sounded in a panic. He hadn't told her about the gun.

"I'm going to go get her. That's what we came for, isn't it?" He tucked the pistol in his pants pocket and lifted himself out of the car.

He heard her say his name as he walked away, but he kept on going toward the shed where he'd seen Goodner disappear. He let himself through the backyard gate. The laughter and play of the children came from the front of the house. He was moving on instinct, not thinking too far ahead. Just as he came to the shed, the door opened and suddenly he and Goodner were face to face.

Closer up, the man wasn't as tall as he had looked from the street. Heavy brows made a straight, solid line above his eyes, which were black and startled. They shifted from Gil to just beyond and the light in them changed. Gil looked around and saw Sunny right behind him. She had followed him from the car. She stood still and cowering under Goodner's black stare.

Without any thought other than that it seemed like the right time, and before Goodner could make a move or speak a word, Gil jerked out the little automatic and those tar black eyes widened. Sunny gasped and Gil nearly gasped himself. He'd never pointed a loaded gun at another person in his life. The pistol was so small, it looked almost harmless. But two feet was all the distance away Goodner stood, and Gil figured at two feet even a little gun could cause some damage.

Goodner held up his hands, either in surrender or defense. Gil was finding it hard to think straight. Goodner said, "Now, son . . . you're liable to hurt somebody with that thing."

"Don't call me son. You don't know me." Gil waved the gun a bit to look more threatening. "Sunny, go inside and get the baby."

"I've got it figured out who you are, though," Goodner said. "The cousin." He eased an inch closer and Gil jabbed the pistol into his rib cage. He felt a little crazy with the blood pumping hard through him.

"You stay where you are," he said to Goodner. "Sunny, go on and get Nina."

"You didn't say you brought a gun," she said.

"Just go get her. And hurry up." A sudden sweat broke over Gil. Maybe she was right. Maybe the gun was a bad idea. It could get them in even more trouble.

He was just about to put the pistol back into his pocket when Goodner looked right at Sunny and said, "Harlot." And Gil thought that was an audacious thing for a man to say with a gun poked in his ribs.

Before Gil could react, Sunny flung herself right at Goodner, knocking him into the wall of the shed. His head made a loud thud. She shoved him again and Gil had to step aside himself to keep from staggering. She reminded him of a sparrow running a hawk off from its nest. Goodner folded up his arms to ward her off and she swung out with her fist, hollered, "You think I'd let you take her! She's mine!"

"It's all right, Sunny," Gil said, trying to get her focused back on their purpose. He held the little gun pointed skyward. "Go on inside and get her now."

Sunny turned to him and her expression was wild, but she seemed to snap back when she saw him. She nodded and started up the path, and that's when Goodner made his lunge.

For an old man, he moved fast. He grabbed at Sunny's shoulder, and the gun in Gil's hand came down and cracked Goodner square on his forehead. Reflexes took over then and Gil's leg went out, his busted-up, weak-muscled left leg. He kicked Goodner's knees out from under him. When Goodner went down, Gil pounced. Elbow to throat. Jab to sternum. Camp Mills. Basic training. Hand-to-hand drill.

"Don't kill him!" Sunny tugged at the back of Gil's shirt, and the adrenaline that had risen in him subsided. He straightened up, realized he'd been kicking Goodner in the ribs. Goodner was curled up like a snail, a bright, bloody gash on his forehead. From the front of the house, laughter and kids' hollering rippled back to them. Birds whistled loud. The sky had yellowed up. Gil still held the gun in his fist, but he had lost the will to use it, or even point it at anything.

"Get Nina," he said to Sunny. "And hurry up."

As she scampered away up the path, Goodner righted himself. Blood streamed out of his forehead. It seeped through his black eyebrows and down either side of his nose. Gil stuck the gun in his pocket, reached in deeper for his handkerchief. He shook it out. It was clean, but Goodner slapped both it and Gil's hand away.

"I'm friendly with every lawman in this part of the state," Goodner said gruffly. "You're ruining yourself for that harlot. I've got the court on my side. You're just going to end up in jail."

Gil watched the blood spread along the deep creases in the man's forehead and thought about cracking him again for calling Sunny names. "She's too young for you. Didn't you know that? You ought to be ashamed, lusting that way. After a girl young enough to be your own daughter."

SUNNY COULDN'T DO ANYTHING but cry and kiss all over Nina, who had on a prim little dress that came nearly to her ankles. She seemed unfazed, like this was just another joyride with Daddy Gil and she hadn't been away for two long weeks. He was driving like hell's demon, slewing through mud holes, chopping over ruts. In his mind he kept saying, *Seventeen miles,* repeating the last road sign they'd passed. Seventeen miles and they'd be to Fort Worth. He hadn't seen anyone following them.

Inside the city limits, he dropped off on his speed. It seemed he saw motor police everywhere. No doubt Goodner had already reported what he would call a kidnapping to the authorities. Gil only hoped that they would expect him to head south.

At the train depot, he let a porter load their boxes and suitcase onto a cart. He'd hurt his leg kicking Goodner and it was trying to seize up on him. Sunny wore a smile, almost carefree. She gave Gil the little box she'd brought out of the house to carry for her, but she wouldn't give up Nina, not even after they found their seats on the train. No Pullman, no private day coaches, just headrests covered with linen towels, a watercooler at each end of the car. He thought about the fourteen hundred dollars he was leaving parked in the lot at the depot. His only regret. It would take a while before anyone realized the Templar had been abandoned. The automatic pistol was stashed inside the glove box.

At Longview, where they picked up the Great Northern—off of Goodner's T&P line—Gil relaxed a little. The conductor came down the aisle collecting tickets. He smiled at them. The happy family. The Langes.

Nina was sprawled asleep in Sunny's lap, one little leg on either side of Sunny's knees. Gil said, "Why don't you let me take her awhile."

Sunny shook her head. "She's comfortable."

He leaned back with that wooden box he'd been gripping since Fort Worth. It was pretty wood, cut on the grain and sanded to a gloss. "What've you got in here that's so important?" he said.

She focused on the box. "Papa made that for me. For my valuables." He thumbed at the latch, but it didn't open. She said, "It's locked. I guess I lost the key. I didn't have time to hunt for it." She smiled. "I had Wild Bill waiting for me."

He breathed a laugh and felt a little embarrassed. He shifted up on one hip to dig out his pocketknife. He opened the smaller blade and held it up. "You care?"

She shook her head, but that grin kept tickling her face. Or else she was flirting with him. They were both overcome with relief. He jimmied the little lock with no trouble at all.

The box was stuffed full. Nothing much of value that he could see: some empty note cards on top, Christmas cards and birthday cards next, one from him at Camp Mills, with his army picture. He glanced at her when he got to that one. A report card from school, Florida Faye DeLony written plainly at the head. He hid that away in case anybody was watching. There were pages from a New Testament Bible—the Book of John, tenth chapter—torn out and wrapped around two more photos. Blurry photos of a baby in a manger. He didn't need her to tell him who the baby was. His throat felt thick. He glanced again and Sunny was looking at everything he pulled out like it was all brand-new to her, too.

The last thing in the box was a smudged, torn envelope, postmarked in France, stamped bright red as having passed inspection, his handwriting on the outside. She met his third glance, clear-eyed. It felt odd to him pulling that letter out, unfolding it, seeing those words again, remembering where he'd been when he wrote them, how he'd labored over each one—this letter that she had claimed she never got. He leveled his gaze straight on her and he knew then that she'd been waiting for him to get down to the bottom of the box.

The train racketed along the tracks. A late breeze blew in the window. He refolded the letter and leaned over to kiss her. On the lips. He didn't care who was shocked.

"I love you," he said.

She put her hand on his cheek, looked down her nose at his mouth like she might kiss him back, then raised her face to his. "I love you, too."

Part Three

THE LANGES

Chapter Twenty-three

*I*T'S AN ODD FEELING to watch your own country move off on the horizon, with Miss Liberty holding up her torch just the way Gil had described her, not knowing if you will ever set foot on those shores again. It's scary having all that water around you, too, and wondering what you're in for in this new place you're headed to.

I held the damp railing, the salty breeze hitting my face, and let my thoughts run together—how I would miss Papa, that Ding would grow up without me knowing him, how far away Texas seemed right then. Mama, too, was mixed up in there, me remembering her desire to travel and how she'd never gotten the opportunity. And I found myself wondering suddenly if she'd been happy with her life or, if given a chance to do it over, she'd have made different choices. When I thought back, she had always seemed a little regretful, maybe even resentful, and I knew I didn't want a life like that. I'd had plenty of regret already. Enough to do me forever.

Gil came up behind me right then. He was carrying Nina in his arms. "Evening, Mrs. Lange," he said. "Fine day for sailing, wouldn't you say?"

"You can call me Sonja Jo," I said, leaning against him.

He gave me a kiss on my temple and moved off down the ship's deck. I watched as he pointed out to sea, as Nina nodded at whatever it was he whispered to her. Then he pointed behind them at various things on board. I could imagine him telling her the names for everything they passed, making up those he didn't know. Satisfied, contented. I stopped thinking backward.

It took seven days to cross the Atlantic Ocean. Even carrying a baby, which I was nearly certain I was by then, I didn't suffer a minute of seasickness. Gil had it bad enough for all of us. The third day out, Nina came down with a case of the measles, picked up from no telling where, from one of Ira's children probably, or from friends of theirs. The captain quarantined us to our cabin and it made the time creep by, being stuffed together in that tiny compartment, especially with Gil so weak in the stomach.

The boat had been an old battleship before it was stripped down and made into a cattle freighter. I never did understand exactly how we got passage on that kind of ship going over, some of Van Winslow's left-handed arrangements, I imagine. At night we could hear the cattle milling around underneath us, lowing. Sometimes the smell would reach us.

By the time we docked in Le Havre, Nina's measles were gone but I was feverish, and Gil had turned green. The man at the official's gate surveyed our passports for what I thought was too long a time. He looked at our pictures, then at us. He studied Gil's work visa. Of course, every scrap of paper was a forgery. Gil's hand stayed on my shoulder as he struggled to talk in French, and I thought he was going to shake to death waiting for the man to let us in the country.

"I'm going to have to learn a whole lot more words in a hurry," he said to me once we finally walked past.

I smiled at him. "You're doing all right so far."

And we were in France.

It was almost too much to take in all at once, being someplace besides Texas. Even the air felt different, lighter and cooler. I couldn't quit gawking. People were walking around everywhere and riding bicycles, busy going places or stopping to greet one another and laugh. Everyone everywhere seemed to be laughing. Gil said they were just so glad to finally have their country at peace.

It's true what they say about the measles going harder on an adult. Nina barely suffered, but I spent those first few days in France flat in bed in a dusty hotel, up four flights of stairs that made me dizzy before we reached the top. I was almost too weak to walk down the hallway to the bathroom we shared with everyone else on two floors.

Gil had already had his measles in the army, so he was a perfect nursemaid to me, bringing soup he got from somewhere, sitting me up by the window in a chair with blankets so I could watch the people dancing on the long porch below us. The music came from a widemouthed gramophone that a little man in knickers kept cranking back up—some kind of rag with a woman singing. The tune sounded odd coming in another language. I knocked a cobweb out of the windowsill. I was disappointed to see that there were spiders in France.

When I was well enough, we set out in a little car Gil bought. It was a funny-looking car with isinglass panels and it never did run good. He ended up spending hours working on it.

We headed east. He seemed to have a sixth sense about finding his way around places, even in a foreign country. I don't recall us ever getting lost. I had wanted to see the Eiffel Tower, but we were too played out for much sightseeing, so we skipped Paris.

Gil promised to bring me back someday. I still had a few fading measles on me, like sun freckles across my bosom and neck.

Somewhere just the other side of a town called Beauvais we started seeing evidence of the war. There were buildings still in rubble, wide stretches of land with nothing growing, only a few blackened tree trunks where whole forests had been. Spinsters and widows, with little orphans trailing behind them, seemed to be everywhere, all wearing drab clothes, mourning weeds. We saw a lot of mangled men on crutches, too, and in wheelchairs, some with empty sleeves pinned up or tucked into pockets. People without homes. The war had been over for four years, but its mark still ran deep.

At Reims, Gil put me and Nina in a hotel and then he left for a few hours. When he came back, he had a job—as easy as that—working on a road-construction crew. He'd told the foreman, a big man who could speak fair English, "I can handle anything that goes on wheels." And the foreman took him at his word.

Twenty-four hours later, we had moved to a town called Épernay and Gil was running heavy equipment, earthmovers, graders, bulldozers, coming home covered thick with dust and smiling happy. Sometimes he had to gargle with mineral water to clear his throat of all the road dust. I watched him drive off that first morning and felt so lost and alone.

Within a few weeks, you couldn't tell Gil from the natives. His hair grew out shaggy. He learned to eat with his fork upside down and in the wrong hand. He wore their clothes, smoked their cigarettes, drank their wine, and more and more spoke their language, waving his hands around the same way as they did. I would marvel over him sometimes when we went to market, how easily he got along with the shopkeepers. In the evenings, he sipped at a glass of Martell's in our front room, reading a yellow-back detective novel from Britain, just as contented as a cat that's had its milk. He didn't seem to miss anything American, or anyone. He was a natural-born expatriate.

I, on the other hand, didn't adjust so easy. Even after months went by, I would forget our name was supposed to be Lange. I didn't answer to it and couldn't remember to say it when someone asked. I gave up altogether on Sonja Josephine and went back to being just Sunny.

The language was a torment to me. I never seemed to have enough spit in my mouth to speak any French. Even Nina picked up words easier than I did. She didn't seem to even notice it was another language these people spoke. Everyone was friendly enough, but I didn't see how to be friendly back when I couldn't talk to them. I did an awful lot of smiling, probably looked like an idiot to them. Gil tried to help me. He taught me how to ask for things, bread and milk and eggs. But if the grocer had anything at all to say back to me, I panicked.

"They talk too fast," I complained. "I'll never learn."

"Yes, you will," Gil said with his new cheerful attitude. He put an arm around me and gave me a smooch on the forehead. "You learned to speak English." Making another one of his senseless jokes.

After the first few days, we rarely mentioned why we were in France. We didn't speak of Turner, or Ira, or the charge of kidnapping that had surely been filed against us. It was as if all that belonged to other people who we vaguely knew but couldn't remember. We didn't talk much about the baby that was coming either. I was nearly four months gone before I finally gave up and told him, in the broken-down peasants' shack outside the town of Épernay, rain dripping down through the thatch that was supposed to be our roof. His reaction wasn't what I expected. He just nodded and smiled, like he'd already figured it out.

At night, though, when his hand rubbed over my growing belly, I would imagine him reliving, the same way I relived it, that ugly scene in Austin with Aunt Prudie, all those hateful words she spat at me. But we never discussed it. There didn't seem to be any point, not with the new easiness between us, the peace. By then, I thought of him as my lover and my husband, and as a daddy to Nina, never as my cousin.

ON THE FOURTH OF December, 1922, just before midnight, our son was born in the hospital in Clermont-en-Argonne, in Lorraine, where the company had moved us by then. A Monday's child. Fair of face. He weighed seven and a half pounds, had ten fingers, ten toes, no organs growing on his outsides, no child of the devil. He was perfect. He had Gil's nose and chin, but the little bit of fuzz on his head had a suspicious red tinge to it, like mine.

Early the next morning, Gil drove to the town hall to register the birth in the mayor's office the way French law required a new father to do. While he was there he gave our baby a name — Peter Romeo Dailey Lange. No one there questioned a child having such a long name. Lots of French children had names even longer. It was me who was the most surprised. We had discussed Dailey as a first name. We had mulled over Gil Junior, and Theresa for a girl. But Peter Romeo was never mentioned.

"We'll call him whatever you want to," Gil said to me, and then took a long time explaining to me about how Peter had always been his favorite of the apostles, the one who asked the most questions and seemed the most human in his heart, failings and all. "I thought our son deserved something biblical."

He didn't offer a single word of explanation about the Romeo part of our son's name, but he didn't need to. By then he had told me the awful story. Getting stuck in the mud. How it rained all the time in Lorraine, which I knew firsthand. Them drinking too much cognac because the wells had been poisoned by retreating Germans. The call of nature had drawn him over to the ditch by the roadside, away from the truck, far enough away that when the high-explosive shell hit, he was spared. But his friend hadn't been so lucky. It was the thing that haunted Gil's dreams, that pulled him to do the work he did. I understood without being told that naming our baby after his friend was a kind of settling up, something too big and complicated for him to put into words.

"We'll just call him Pete," I said, and I could see that pleased Gil fine.

WHEN PETE WAS TWO months old, we made the trek to visit his namesake in the new American cemetery outside the little town of Thiaucourt. Tears sprang to my eyes to see the Stars and Stripes up there, flapping in the cold wind that jabbed at my eyes and sucked at my breath. Hundreds of graves, thousands, with snow white marble crosses that no matter which direction you looked at them stood in soldier-straight rows.

My cheeks froze as we walked along hunting the names. I kept Pete bundled against me and inside my coat, warm as coals. Gil held on to Nina's hand, talking to her in low tones. His words fogged around his head.

The caretaker, a fat little man wearing a red cap, finally came over with a map of the cemetery. He explained to us that they were still moving in caskets, had been for most of two years, and he couldn't promise anything. He worried the map awhile, studied on the rows, and then he took us right to the spot:

Romeo L. McKeller
Corp. 117th Supply Train, 42nd Div.
Texas, September 13, 1918

I watched Gil's face as he stared down at the marker and I could see that he'd gone off someplace else, away from us. His expression seemed empty.

"I'm cold, Daddy," Nina said, tugging at him to pick her up, but he didn't notice her. I squatted down to hug her inside my coat with little wiggly Pete. I kissed her cheek, pulled her wool cap down farther over her ears. She whined a little and yanked the cap back up.

The caretaker made some remark about the wintry weather and after another minute or two he drifted off, mumbling over some work he had pressing him. With the man gone, Gil stepped closer to the marker, bent down to run his fingers over the letters carved into the marble. I wanted to touch his back, to comfort him in some way, but Nina tugged at my coat and Pete squirmed and made a little fretting sound. That sound seemed to bring Gil back to us. He stood and swung Nina into his arms, kissed the tip of her pink nose. Then he looked at me and smiled that good smile of his.

"I know it's not him down there," he said. "It's just a wooden box. But I still feel like I should do something. I don't know what."

"You want to say a prayer?"

Gil laughed once and shook his head. "No. Rome believed religion is for scared people."

"Oh," I said, not knowing what would help if a prayer wouldn't. "Well, at least he's got his name here where folks can see it. And he's got the flag flying."

Gil raised his face to the American flag like it was the first time he'd seen it up there flapping on the pole. The wind fluttered the bill of his cap. Then he blinked at me. "Come on. We shouldn't have the baby out here in this cold."

We walked back to the car, the four of us bundled together. A little family. We rode the few miles into the village of Thiaucourt. Gil pointed out the cathedral in the middle of town with a spire like a shard of jagged glass. The Germans and the Americans had both used the building to sight-in their big guns. There were shell holes and craters and war scars everywhere. As bad as any we'd seen.

He wanted to find the spot where the truck had been hit, so we started at the crossroad and went backward the distance he thought it had been. But he couldn't be sure. He picked out twenty shell holes that might've been the one where he had lain wounded and then he gave up looking. Folks in the little town watched us as we drove away. I couldn't help but think, as I looked at their faces passing, how none of them had a clue about the important piece of himself Gil had left behind there with them.

Our house in Clermont-en-Argonne was perched on the side of a steep hill, in a row of other houses perched there. It was built all of a mud-colored stone with arching doorways, arching fireplaces, an arching shelf inside the front wall of the main room, cold stone floors, no electricity, just oil lamps on every table and hanging from the ceilings and walls. The windows were fitted with little square panes that didn't latch but opened outward like doors swinging on hinges. You needed a drill bit to hang a curtain and the stone dust won every war I waged with a mop and broom. There was no running water. You had to haul

water up from the town well, which Gil did every morning before he went off to work. We had one foot of ground in the door
yard, enough for a clump of flowers in the spring, or a single rosebush, or one tomato plant. I knew we were lucky to get the house,
but everything about it seemed so old, and so foreign.

That first winter I stayed as homesick as a dog. I missed being
able to go to the butcher and order a pound of sausage without
having to draw a picture. I missed being warm. I had lived without snow all my life and I found I could go on living without it. I
didn't like being weathered in. Ice shown like glass on the road
some mornings when Gil set out. I would watch him drive off,
the chains on the car wheels clanking in the stillness, and try to
quell my worry. It seemed my whole day was spent tending to the
fire, keeping the house warm enough for the little ones. And I
missed Papa. How I missed him. Even though in the past few
years I hadn't seen as much of him, I'd always known he was near
enough that I could if I wanted to. Now he was all the way across
an ocean, six thousand miles from me, and without a clue as to
where I had vanished.

"It's not safe yet to write letters, Sunny," Gil reminded me
when he saw me at the table with a pen and paper. "We still have
to be careful. For Uncle Dane's sake, too."

But I wrote to Papa anyway, letters I never even bothered
stuffing into an envelope. I filled up the bureau drawer with letters to him, telling him about this strange, old country, about the
babies, both of them growing too fast, about Gil's work and the
people around us.

Our closest neighbors, a family named Baland, spoke both
French and German but not a word of English. They walked
around in their wooden shoes, clopping like horses, the way
everyone did in Lorraine. The grandfather went out every morn-

ing at dawn with his hand trowel to clean the street gutters so that when it rained the water would flow off our hill. Sometimes he met Gil heading to work and they would chat for a while. Their family had lost four members to the war, three as soldiers and one plowing his fields two years later. The plow bit had hit an unexploded shell buried deep in the land. Mule, plow, and farmer all went up like fireworks. There were metal scavengers combing the battlefields, but sometimes they missed things.

The Balands were a big bunch, and when the weather faired off, they dragged out a fancy dining table from their house and piled up around it, laughing, jabbering, eating their meals outdoors. I couldn't understand a word they said, but the fun they seemed to have together gave me a curious longing. The old woman finally caught me eavesdropping through the stone fence around our back dooryard and she sent one of the younger members, a boy of about fourteen with bad skin and tense eyes, over to fetch me and the children back with him. I was embarrassed and didn't know what to expect when I got to their yard. They chattered at me and about me, took Pete from me and passed him around. They kissed his little fat cheeks and touched Nina's red hair. I smiled and smiled and nodded like I understood everything they said. Guinea hens roamed around underfoot.

"They want us to eat," Nina told me, already acting as my interpreter, a thing she would do a lot of through the years. She was three, big and beautiful, friendly. She played dolls with a little girl near her age named Geri and I stuffed myself on rabbit and sauerkraut and other unidentifiable delicacies, all washed down with a heavy, dark beer. I was half drunk by the time Gil found me sitting at their table in the lazy French twilight. He carried us all home and put me straight to bed.

"Don't any of those people ever work?" I mumbled as he tucked me in.

"Grand-mère Baland says a nursing mother needs lots of beer." He petted my head and chuckled. "I think she has plans for you."

"Hmmm? To keep me drunk?" I snuggled down, peaceful inside. I barely felt the kiss he planted on me.

Not long after that, I found out where it was Grand-père Baland went with his hand trowel every morning. At the base of the hill was some land that an enterprising landowner rented to families in town for use as garden plots. The landowner supplied manure for an additional amount, and the town well and the runoff from the hill supplied water. Gil rented one of the squares for me and helped me till it and spade in the manure. We bought seed and sets, a shovel, a hoe, and a rake.

Later I found out that it wasn't normal or even acceptable for a woman to do garden work. Women stuck to growing flowers in window boxes. Garden truck was a man's job. For a time, I caused a lot of suspicious talk as I walked down the hill with my babies, carrying little Pete on my back like a papoose. Summer weather in Lorraine was perfect for vegetables, warm days, cool nights, lots of rain. I planted string beans and squash, bulb onions, sugar beets, potatoes, yams in Papa's honor, tomatoes that Grand-mère Baland tried to convince me were poisonous. While Nina dug with her play pail and shovel, Pete slept on a canvas mat in the shade of a small sycamore.

It wasn't long before the men in town got used to me out there with my children and my hoe. After a few weeks, Grand-père Baland even brought over a pair of wooden clogs that magically fit my feet. The shoes were bright yellow, freshly painted, comfortable. Gil got a big laugh out of me wearing them, clopping off to the garden plot like all the other gardeners in town.

I must have looked like the strangest French peasant woman in the world.

WHEN PETE WAS TEN months old, he gave up the breast. All by himself. Just decided it wasn't for him anymore and stopped nursing. I wasn't ready for him to grow up so quickly, but he was in a hurry. He learned to walk that fast, too. Never did much creeping. It seemed to me that he rose to his feet one day and took off, like he couldn't wait to follow Gil and Nina everywhere they went. Once he started walking, he was into everything, quiet about it, slipping up on you so that you would turn with a start that sent him off laughing. I always thought that if he was a devil, he was the sweetest one — like his daddy.

Gil wouldn't let me even spat Pete's hand in reprimand. He didn't believe in whippings of any kind, or even much in the way of punishment at all. He said he'd had enough of that for all of us and he didn't want any more of it in his life. I sometimes tried to bring to my memory the image of him in Weatherford that day, holding a gun on Ira Goodner, whacking him upside the head with it, kicking him in the ribs. And I couldn't make that picture match with the gentle man I lived with in France.

Pete never wore dresses. I made little plaid knee britches for him. I wasn't much of a seamstress, but he was growing so quick it didn't matter much. Gil brought home a pair of red suspenders and a little tweed cap, and Pete was the hit of the neighborhood. A sturdy little fellow marching along at his daddy's side. A living doll you could hardly take your eyes off of. Grand-père Baland took him by the hand on little walks and Grand-mère Baland made smoochy *tsk*s at him, called him *le petit monsieur*.

• • •

MEANWHILE, I STARTED YEARNING for another baby. I found I liked a little one at my breast and in my arms. Nina had already turned into an independent little lady, picking up after herself when she played, dressing herself, buttoning her own shoes. And Pete went right behind her copycatting everything she did. I needed another baby. By Nina's fourth birthday, it was almost all I thought about.

The idea of actually planning for a baby appealed to me. I had always just ended up finding myself pregnant out of carelessness or poor forethought. The idea suited Gil, too. Anything that meant a little extra lovemaking was just dandy by him. Besides which, birth prevention was illegal in France in those days after the war. Safety rubbers were an expensive black-market item and hard to get.

But then Gil caught a late-summer cold that hung on and left a cough deep in his chest. I made him stay at home and I tended him with hot packs and chicken soup. Once I got him well, I gave him a long lecture about taking better care of himself. He smoked more than ever, strong French cigarettes that smelled like burnt rope, and all day long he was breathing in foul road dust.

"Wrap a rag around your mouth," I scolded, "like the cowboys back home do."

He chuckled at that and pulled me into bed with him. "They all already call me Texas." He twined me in his legs. The sun had darkened his skin and the hard work had muscled up his arms. I ran my finger in the loopy hair there. He rarely ever had leg pain anymore, and his nightmares had stopped months ago.

"Well . . . I'm not going to have time for you to be sickly," I said. "Not if we want to have a new baby."

And I could see by the flicker in his eyes that he felt strong enough to get back to work on that. By October, I was pretty sure our efforts had succeeded.

Chapter Twenty-four

*N*INA SET THE FIRST doubt in me about Pete. It was the beginning of January, a month after Pete's second birthday. Snow was all over the ground and we were inside by the fire when she asked, "Mama, how come Pete don't talk?"

"*Doesn't,* honey," was my automatic answer. "It's *doesn't,* not *don't.* There's no use to speak poor English." And then her question jarred me.

I looked up at them sitting on the floor together, Pete in front of her. They had been playing quietly with the little tea set Gil had brought home from a trip to Metz he'd made with the road crew. And I had been darning Gil's thick wool socks, my mind on keeping him warm while he worked out in the weather. I watched Pete pretend to drink the imaginary tea from one of the cups, then give Nina his big smile.

In truth, it wasn't the first time I had thought that Pete ought to be talking, doing something more than gurgling and blowing bubbles. But I had been denying to myself that there might be a problem. Until Nina asked her question out loud. I remembered all the words she had been saying at Pete's age. She had been making sentences. The three of us repeated words to Pete all the time, words we wanted him to say first. Nina said her name to him over and over, and I secretly wished for *mama* to be the first one. And Gil, he pointed out everything. Sky. Tree. Car. Bird. House. Dog. Bug. Yet Pete just seemed to go on about his business, taking no notice at all of us drilling him.

"Girls are always faster," Gil said in answer when I shared my doubt that evening. "Calvin didn't say a word till he was nearly four. And remember how long it took Ding?" He turned a page in the magazine he'd been reading, took a sip of the plum wine he'd brought home. "Besides, Pete's got Nina doing all his talking for him. He doesn't need to say anything." But somehow I didn't think he sounded as forceful or convincing as I needed him to. We gave each other a look and he added, softer, "Don't dream up stuff, Sunny."

I went into the kitchen to check on supper. The fire in the stove had burned down, so I threw in some kindling to heat it back up. While I was doing that, Gil came to waver behind me in the doorway, his finger marking his place in the magazine, but I could tell that reading didn't have his attention anymore.

He said, "We'll take him to a speech doctor if you're so worried. They'll have one somewhere. Maybe in Bar-le-Duc or Nancy. I'll check around and see what I can find out."

I closed up the firebox, dusted my hands on my apron, nodded. I could see the doubt start in his face, too, though he tried hard to hide it from me. He came and put his arms around me. The magazine pages rattled behind my back. He rested his forehead on mine.

"And we'll probably find out he just doesn't know whether to speak in English or French." Gil smiled reassuringly. "Pete's fine, Sunny. He's just fine."

But no matter how hard Gil wanted it, or I wanted it, Pete wasn't fine. We had to go all the way to Metz to find a speech doctor, a German man who talked to us in beautiful English. He looked Pete over, checked down his throat, inside his nose, his ears, his eyes. He did some hand-play with Pete and then he told us that Pete had something called congenital aphasia. The way the doctor explained it, what those words meant was that because of some injury at birth, Pete couldn't learn speech patterns. It was simply beyond him. But I knew that wasn't so. Pete had come easy, with only a couple of hours of labor pain. There'd been no injury at birth. I had taken ether, though, so I asked if that could have caused a problem like this.

The German doctor just shook his head at me without really answering. "There's nothing to be done," he said. "Speak to him slowly and clearly. Be patient with him. He may learn a hundred words or so."

When we left there, Gil was red in the face. So red I got scared he might hit somebody, or explode, which he did, out in the car.

"That goddamn kraut-eater! Calling my son an idiot!"

I held Pete on my lap and he plucked at the buttons on my dress, unconcerned. I kissed his head. "That's not exactly what he said, Gil."

"The hell it isn't." Gil glanced at Pete. "*Can't* learn. Not won't, *can't*. Like he's retarded."

We rode in silence most of the way home. It was a long drive, took the rest of the daylight and into the night. Pete fell asleep and I went with him. We didn't wake up until we got home. As I carried Pete inside, he swiped big at his tired eyes and rolled his face against my breasts.

Gil went next door to fetch Nina from the Balands, but Grandmère Baland shooed him away, told him Nina and Geri were both sound asleep and he could come back in the morning. I put Pete to bed and Gil lurked in the doorway, looking in on us. And he kept on standing there, slumped against the jamb after I was done. He let me pass by, but otherwise he didn't stir.

I left him there and went to the kitchen. I sat down at the table, stared out the window to the dooryard. All I could see was my own reflection in the glass panes. I felt tight inside, and I thought of the baby growing in me, this one I had planned for. I pictured it in there. A sudden fright and nausea riffled over me.

After a while, Gil straggled into the kitchen, too, still silent and broody. He took down the jug of plum wine, swirled the liquid around, sniffed it. I thought he was going to hike it onto his shoulder and drink straight from the jug like the moonshiners back home, but he got out a glass and poured it full. He sat down with me at the table, took a big swig. The room was so hushed I could hear the wine swallow down his throat. Both of us watched out the window at nothing for a while.

"Kraut sonofabitch," he finally muttered, stuck on that one note.

My hand wandered down to rest on my belly. My voice had no strength. I couldn't seem to get it much above a whisper. "What've we done, Gil?" I said, and I felt his eyes shoot toward me.

"What do you mean by that?"

I glanced at him. I wanted to cry. He looked away from me, set the glass down on the table in front of him. The wine in the bottom seemed to catch light from the flickering gas lamp above us.

"I'm not going to listen to any bullshit about punishment, Sunny, if that's where you're headed. That God's raining down his wrath on us again. You're too smart for that. You know you are."

"But what if it is our fault? What if this new baby . . ." I swallowed hard. "Maybe we shouldn't bring another unsound child into the world."

He stood up so fast the chair clattered backward on the stone floor. I jumped at the sudden noise. He leaned both hands on the table, and I'd never had his eyes so dark and smoldery on me. "Pete is not unsound. I won't let you say that. If you do anything, Sunny . . ." His voice went low, almost dangerous. "If you go somewhere and try to get rid of this baby, I swear I won't ever forgive you."

My spine stiffened. He'd never used such a tone with me before and I think it shook him as much as it did me. He blinked first. The starch went out of his shoulders. I didn't say another word, just slid away from the table and went around him. I stepped out into the dooryard.

It was a cold clear night, a slip of a moon, stars all over the heavens. I didn't have on a coat. I hugged my arms and let the soft air slough the hurt and anger off me. I thought about that word *forgiveness,* what it meant, and how it went both ways. Maybe he watched me from inside. It seemed like he must've, because in a minute he came out, too. I smelled his cigarette, heard the quick intake of his breath as he smoked, but I didn't look at him.

After a few seconds, he said, "I don't care what some goddamn Heinie doctor says, Pete's not retarded. I'm taking him to Paris. To the American Hospital, where there's some good doctors. You can come if you want to. It's up to you."

That was all he came outside to say, and as soon as he said it, he went back in the door.

WE LEFT THE NEXT morning, still glum with each other. It made for a tense trip in that little popcorn car with two kids wallowing around for all those miles. The roads were rough and made me motion sick. But then I felt plain sick all that day anyway, sick in my heart, sick of everything.

It rained, a gentle rain, but enough so Gil had to raise the top. Then it was stuffy inside the car and Pete got irritable. I pulled him on my lap, where he burrowed and kicked like he couldn't get comfortable. By accident he knocked Gil's hand off the steering wheel and almost got a spanking. Later, an old farmer wouldn't move his one-mule cart out of our way. Gil cussed at the man, flinging out some ugly French with a flip of his hand, something about donkey shit. I didn't want to understand the rest. He drove hard, frowning, his cap down low on his brow, until we came to some broken tree limbs out in the road. Then he cussed some more and got out in the rain to tug and yank the deadfall off into the ditch.

Nina leaned over the seat, sleepy, wakened by Gil's bear temper. Above Pete's restless fretting and the car shaking to pieces, she said, "How come Daddy's so mad? Is he mad at Pete?"

"No, honey. He's just having a grouchy day, that's all."

She reached to twirl my hair. She liked to mess with my hair. "Pete tries to talk," she said, so it was clear she was aware of everything going on between us. "He moves his lips a lot."

Just then Pete grabbed for her shoulders like to drag her up front with us. He was full of his male strength and he almost succeeded. Nina started wailing, and Pete started wailing because she wouldn't come, and all that racket was going on when Gil slammed back inside the car, soaked to the bone, scowly. I felt the chill from him, too.

"Sunny, can't you do something with these kids?"

"What would you like me to do with them?" I snapped back. "Toss them out in the rain?"

We glared for a half second before our eyes skidded away from each other. We weren't used to this arguing. We didn't have any practice at it. We both clammed up with our hurt feelings.

It took two miserable days to get to Paris, and there was the Eiffel Tower looming up in the rainy sky, though the joy was taken out of the sight by our poor spirits. We found a small hotel near the river, on the Rue du Bois de Boulogne just down from the American Hospital. There were two narrow beds, flimsy mattresses, dingy gas lamps that hissed and stank and made Gil cough the night through. I hadn't thought to bring any quinine for him; I wasn't feeling generous toward him anyway. But during the night he hugged me up and in his sleep drenched me with his sweat. Not on purpose, of course. The bed was cramped and sagged in the center, so we had to sleep close. In the morning I felt awful, and guilty when I woke up wrapped inside his arms.

"Gil, wake up. Wake up." I shook his shoulders. "Are you getting sick again?"

He didn't jerk away, but just sat up calmly, groggy, and started peeling off his clammy undershirt. "It's hot as hell in here," he said, and went to push open the window.

The sulfur smell of the striking match came in with the chilly breeze. In the other bed, Pete and Nina stirred.

"I don't want us to fight anymore," I said. I had to work hard to swallow my pride, and it was a mouthful.

He glanced at me from where he stood by the window, then refocused on something outside on the street. The light coming in was weak morning light that turned his chest gray. I could count his ribs. His ankle-length BVDs hung low on his hips. Nina turned her head on the roll of pillow and opened her eyes. Gil coughed a little. Smoke flittered out his mouth and nose, broke apart in the air above his head.

"You're not going to say anything?" I was still struggling, flushing. Even my throat felt red. "You're trying to grind me down, aren't you? Trying to prove you can."

Nina sat up rubbing her ears, and Pete started up, too.

Gil turned from the window. "I'm not trying to prove anything, Sunny."

Pete rose to his feet on the bed then and I watched the front of his jammies blossom a bright yellow stain.

"Oh, good Lord, Pete," I said, scooping him up, but he'd already made a puddle on the bed between his feet. Nina shrieked and dodged away just before some of it flooded in her direction.

For a while we were thrown into a tizzy of tears from Pete, whining from Nina, damp rags from the washbasin, flinging out fresh clothes from the suitcase, and me giving orders, hurrying everybody, hurrying. In the middle of it all, Gil touched me— just a light, lingering squeeze on my upper arm, his eyes locking with mine, love in there again. It was like a big dark curtain lifted off us.

He pitched in helping me get the kids ready. And even though I could see he was still in a nervous mood, he started singing a silly rhyme song he knew to shut them both up. Nina groaned, "Oh, Daddy," yet in a minute she was singing right along, laughing. I couldn't help but laugh, too. They were horribly off-key. And then I noticed it, just like Nina had said in the car—Pete moving his lips. Moving them as he watched Gil's singing mouth, watched Nina's too, throwing up his little chubby arms and moving his lips like a guppy in a bowl.

"Look," I said, stopping everybody. "Pete *is* trying to talk." I could hear the wonder in my own voice. Nina and Gil both stared at Pete.

"I told you, Mama," Nina said. "He does that all the time."

My eyes lifted to Gil. "Maybe it's just something wrong with his voice box," I said, hopeful, searching. "Maybe something a doctor can fix."

THE DOCTOR WE SAW at the American Hospital was an Englishman. I was relieved, and I could see Gil was relieved, too. I did all the talking because Gil's cough flared up each time he tried to. The singing caused it, singing all the way here, and the rain yesterday, getting out to tend to those limbs in the road. He kept Nina backed up in his lap as he sucked on a hot cup of strong coffee.

Pete hollered loud as the doctor examined him. "There's nothing wrong with this lad's vocal cords," the doctor said.

"He moves his lips—" But I didn't get any further before the doctor interrupted.

"Take him into the other room and quiet him, please."

So the four of us went into the next room, a waiting lobby. There were playthings in a wire bin, but I couldn't interest Pete in them, not until Nina started fishing through the toys. Anything she did, Pete wanted to do, so it didn't take but a minute for him to get down on the floor with her. In a couple more minutes he was laughing again, though Gil kept reaching with a handkerchief to wipe at Pete's nose, the leftovers from crying so hard with the doctor.

One of the toys was a black wool dog on the end of a pneumatic hose. It seemed to be Pete's favorite, and in just a second he had learned how to squeeze the bulb on the end of the hose to make the dog hop on its hind legs. He laughed and gritted his teeth together, squeezed harder on the bulb until the dog jumped all the way off the floor and made a squeak.

"You think a retard could figure that out?" Gil reached into his pocket for a cigarette. I stopped his hand and shook my head—no at the cigarette, no at his question, too. He sighed and laced our fingers tight together. He shifted his hat backward on his head. I wasn't used to seeing him in a dressy hat anymore. It reminded me, for a second, of our first days together in Austin.

As soon as the white-coated doctor came in the room again, Pete started squalling. He jumped up and ran to bury his face in my lap. He grappled at me, trying to climb up, nearly yanking my dress clear off one shoulder. He was as solid as a bull calf.

The Englishman had another doctor with him, a French doctor, introduced to us as Dr. Laurent. He was thin and tall, had a sparse beard on his chin, trimmed neat. The Frenchman was going to do some special tests on Pete, but only one of us could go along. I noticed Gil start to stand up, but then he looked toward me and sat back down. I nudged Pete in Gil's direction.

"Go with Daddy," I said, but Pete didn't stop crawling on me for one second. He was in a panic, grabbing handfuls of my clothes and hair. Gil stepped in to unlatch Pete from me, swooped him up high. In his daddy's strong arms the crying stopped. Gil gave me a smile, thanking me for letting him be the one to go. I smoothed Pete's sweaty hand-wrinkles out of my dress.

They seemed to stay gone forever. Long enough to read a half dozen little books to Nina. Well, not exactly read them, since the words were in French and I could make out only a few of them. I invented stories to match the pictures and she got sleepy, leaning against me, sitting in the hard chairs they had in that lobby. I waited, wondered, worried the door with my eyes.

A woman came in with cups of water and some raisin cookies and I was grateful for the distraction. She was a nursing student from Belgium, and since she spoke good English, we visited awhile. I told her about my cousin being a nurse back in Texas, although I didn't mention that I'd stolen her husband from her. The nursing student told me about Brussels, where she was from. I remembered stories I'd heard about Germans bayoneting babies in Brussels, dragging people through the streets on chains, all I knew of that city. She'd been a child during the war, she said, and I wondered how old that made her now. I felt ancient, sitting there talking to her. Ancient at twenty-four.

Gil came in first, with Pete snubbing against his shoulder, and Dr. Laurent followed right behind. The English doctor wasn't with them. They came into the lobby talking in serious French. About Pete, I could tell, but I only caught maybe one-tenth of the conversation. They spoke too fast, and I envied again Gil's ease with the language. The Belgian girl left the room.

I listened for a while, impatient for them to include me. Gil kept having to clear his throat. I put my hand on Pete's back and he noticed me then, reached out for me, his chin dimpling in, snubbing harder. I took him in my arms and he tucked his head against my breasts. His tears got me wet.

"What?" I finally said, interrupting Gil and the doctor. They might've gone on for hours if I hadn't. Gil gazed at me. I couldn't tell what I saw on his face. He looked a little strangled.

"Pete's not retarded," he said. "He's deaf."

"What?" I glanced at the French doctor, who smiled at me. I clutched Pete tighter.

Gil kept that odd expression on his face. "He can't hear. That's why he doesn't talk."

My mouth went dry, eyes hurt, like all the water inside me was finally used up. This, I knew, was the truth, what was wrong, had been wrong all along. Everything fit, the moving lips, ignoring me when I called him. He couldn't hear me. He didn't know what my voice sounded like. I rubbed the back of my baby's soft, sweaty head, pressed my mouth to his little eyebrows. *Kiss it better.*

"As I was just now saying to your husband . . ." The doctor spoke in English so perfect it made me want to slap him for having left me out of the conversation before. I was tempted to slap Gil, too, for the same reason. "We have an excellent school for the deaf right here in Paris. Your son is very young, but we are fortunate to have new testing methods. We can discover things now at a much younger age. If you would like, I'll consult the administration of the school on your behalf. I work there myself several days a week, and I will take a special interest in your son."

"How did it happen?" I said, and Dr. Laurent gave me a confused look.

Gil said, "She means, why is Pete deaf? What's the reason?"

"Is it handed down in families?" That was what I really wanted to know, needed to know. I couldn't stop patting on Pete's back, like he was a drum and I was some crazy Indian mother.

Dr. Laurent said, "If there is a history of deafness, maybe yes. But your husband says you have no deafness in either one of your families, correct?"

The doctor glanced at Gil. I almost spoke out that Gil wasn't really my husband, that we were just pretending, lying to everyone. But the doctor's voice went on and on, like an echo in my head, all those ten-dollar words spewing out—*gestation, in utero, congenital.* After a while I couldn't listen anymore. After a while all it came down to was that Pete was deaf, and Gil was my cousin, and we had another baby growing inside me right now that might somehow end up malformed, too. I remembered old Lucien, the town idiot back in McDade. I thought of Aunt Prudie spouting Bible and Satan and willful sin. The skin on my neck crawled.

"I need some air." I shoved past the doctor with him still talking. I rushed by the nurses out in the hallway, down the marble steps to the pavement outside, Pete bouncing on my hip.

The sky was as hard and gray as slate. I could hear my own heartbeat, the breath whooshing through my lungs. I found a lonely bench and I let Pete down to the ground. I sat myself on the bench, sank my head fast between my knees, licked a tear that had pooled at the corner of my lips. I made myself breathe in deep till the dizziness went away.

In front of me, Pete squatted on his stubby legs and with his pointy first finger rolled a little black beetle into a ball. I watched him and tried to imagine his silence. Without the pop of the American flag above us, the pull cord clanging the pole beside the building. Without the birds chipping in the rhododendron behind us, or the clatter of the trolley going by on the street, the voices off in the distance, the hollow plop of a horse's hooves on pave-stones.

Pete found another beetle and rolled that one up, too, just as quickly as the first. Then he looked at me with his gentle, gentle brown eyes and tear-dirtied face. His head angled sideways as if to see me clearer, closer. And he smiled his daddy's smile.

Chapter Twenty-five

THE SCHOOL FOR PETE was expensive. So was our Paris apartment, and it wasn't half as big as the house in Clermont-en-Argonne. We had to carry everything up three flights of stairs, and the stairwell was spooky, walls peeling paint, a window with a spidery crack. One neighbor we had played the piano all day and night. At first I liked the music, but after a while hearing it all the time got on my nerves. Sometimes I envied Pete's quiet world.

In Paris, there were more people who spoke English. Our landlady did well enough to list out the rules for us to live by—no animals, no untended children in the stairwell, no late rent. Gil could speak to her in nice, polite French and get a smile, but I was half scared of her. I worried when the children played too rowdy. I always expected her to come stomping up those three flights of stairs to shush us down.

We had gas for the lights in the apartment, but the kitchen was a tiny nook off the front room with a stove that burned coal. The plaster walls were painted a horrible dull green. There was a bookcase gouged out beside the front door, and big windows that let in a cross-breeze. Someone like Aunt Dellie could've probably made a showplace out of it. But I didn't have the time or the knack. I hung my pots and pans from hooks in the wall and that was as far as my fixing up went. The only pictures were some Nina drew, and the curtains were white sheets thrown over rope rods. Pretty soon the bookcase in the front room collected everything from mail to loose change to caps and chewing gum. We weren't a tidy bunch. It just never did worry me much.

Pete was the youngest student at his school, and kind of an experiment. Just as he had promised, Dr. Laurent—or Jean-Louis as he insisted we call him—worked special with Pete, taking him off from the others, finger signing, putting Pete's little hand against his throat, or against mine. Jean-Louis said it was harder for the born-deaf, but he also said that Pete was bright and eager, so our hopes were high.

We all had to learn the signs. Nina, of course, caught on the quickest, while I was trying to learn signing and French all at once. But Gil, who had always had an easy time with such things, couldn't seem to get the hang of the sign language. He went through such low spells whenever he was at the school. The flat, unnatural sounds of the deaf voices bothered him, and how deeply the older students would fix on his lips when he talked. I could see he felt out of place, almost like it all scared him too much.

The school had the opposite effect on me. From Pete's first day I felt grateful, knowing this was the place where he would learn. Since I was there every day, the staff made me an unofficial helper, even with my poor French. But you didn't need to speak at all to wipe a runny nose, or bandage a scraped elbow, or hug away hurt feelings. It was the live-ins I tended to the most, because they had no family there. And I helped the teachers, too, holding up the picture cards while they made the signs, great big deliberate signs for the younger ones.

After a while, they found out I knew a little something about office systems. The secretary there was Jean-Louis's niece. Her name was Marivonne, and she spoke English as well as her uncle. Almost at once we became firm friends. She had an American boyfriend, an artist who lived a few blocks from us. He was from Indiana, had that twang when he spoke, which wasn't often. He made Gil uneasy. After a few weeks, Marivonne asked the administrator to pay me a little salary for my work at the school and he agreed to it. I was shocked and pleased, and also about five months along with the new baby. I couldn't think of a place in America that would've done the same thing for a pregnant woman needing a job.

Gil and I hardly talked at all about the baby coming. There was still too much soreness and sensitive feelings to, so we mostly ignored my ripening belly. The construction company had agreed to move him back to the crew at Épernay, but that was as close as he could get to Paris, and it was still eighty miles away. They put him on the maintenance crew as a truck mechanic, which he wasn't happy about, and the pay was less, but what choice did we have? We both agreed to do what was best for Pete.

Gil came home on Friday nights, getting in late on account of the long drive from Épernay, almost always well after the children were in bed asleep. I knew he was unhappy being away from us during the week. The company had a barracks-style place where he rented a bed, along with two Poles, an Italian, and a Swede. He said he felt like he was serving in some international army living there. And he hated his new boss, an Alsatian Gil thought had it out for him just because he was American.

I listened to all his complaints and tried not to feel guilty. I fixed him hot baths in the kitchen tub and gave him back rubs, smoothing out the knots there. I changed the sheets for him, dabbed perfume behind my ears, razor-shaved my legs, a thing Marivonne swore all the stylish Parisian ladies were doing. But I noticed him drinking more and caring less about his appearance. It was almost as if he'd lost some of his will with Pete's deafness.

Justine Theresa came early. The middle week of May and she wasn't due till June. The doctor couldn't say why she arrived early. She just got ready and she was born. Such a tiny baby — less than four pounds. Gil could hold her in one hand. When she cried she sounded like a little soft rabbit.

They made her stay in the hospital in a cradle with a heat lamp and I stayed right with her. I hated to be away from Pete and Nina, but Marivonne had a sister, Pauline, who agreed to stay with them. Jean-Louis stopped in to see the baby and to slap his hands behind her head. She jerked all over and let out a wail.

"*Voilà!*" he said with a nod and a satisfied smile. "*Tout va bien.*"

For the first few days she lost weight, and even though the doctor said that was normal, I was fierce about nursing her. Anytime she made a peep, I was right there to feed her, forcing her to take the nipple even when it made her mad. I wanted her bigger, quick. I vowed to do whatever I had to do. I would not lose her, couldn't even consider that as a possibility. And slowly, one gram at a time, she started to gain.

After a while her legs and arms stopped looking like string beans. She fattened into a beautiful baby, like a doll, skin as clear and smooth as china. She had three little blond curls that stood up on her head just like someone had finger-twisted them in oil. Her eyes were crystal blue. She reminded me of Isabel. Gil called her *ma belle Paree.*

The day we brought her home, she weighed in at five pounds.

As soon as we walked in the door of the apartment, Nina had to hold her baby sister. Marivonne had a camera. She took a photograph of Nina and Justine, Nina beaming her proud smile. Marivonne took one of me, too, still bloated, my tiny daughter in my arms. She got a shot of Pete sitting up smartly on his daddy's knee—Gil, all that luscious hair tumbling over his forehead, but gaunt and thin-cheeked, ill.

After Marivonne and her sister left, he poured himself two fingers of cognac and sat down with a cigarette. In our bedroom, I put Justine down in the crib and left Pete and Nina in there to play on the floor below her. Then I went to open the window in the front room to let the smoke out. Our piano-playing neighbor was at it, something classical that I'd heard so often I was beginning to hum it by heart. But before I could even step away from the window, Gil broke into a fit of coughing so real and rattling I slammed the window back down.

I stood there and watched him sputter and cough. He sipped at the cognac, sputtered some more. When the cough finally quieted, I said, "Gil, I want you to go see a doctor. Something's the matter, and I want you to stop ignoring it."

"It's just the weather." He'd gotten hold of his voice, but barely. He swallowed the rest of the cognac in one gulp.

"It's the end of June." I motioned toward the window. "There is no weather. It's clear and beautiful out there."

He refilled the glass and sat down on one of the little stools where the children ate their breakfast every morning. The stool was too small for him and he looked funny with his knees knobbing out in two directions. He tried to ignore me, but I stood right in front of him with my hands on my hips until he looked up.

"I don't need to see a doctor, Sunny." He let out one last throat-clearing cough, tried to laugh it off. "I'm all right."

I took the cigarette from his fingers, smashed it out in a tray. "It's these damn cigarettes. You smoke them one after another—"

"Ah, I love it when you cuss." He caught my wrist and pulled me toward him.

"I don't want to joke about this." I tried to push out of his grasp, but he held me tight between his knees. He laid his face against my breasts, pressed a kiss there. I put my fingers in his hair. "I mean it. I want you to go see a doctor. Send word to your boss and tell him you'll be gone a few more—"

"And give him a reason to can me? I don't think so, Sunny. He's been hunting an excuse to."

"Then see a doctor in Épernay."

He let go of me, nodded once.

"You promise?" I said.

"I said I would."

But he didn't sound sincere, so I made him raise his hand and swear it. He laughed at me, but he finally did it. We made love that night for the first time since Justine was born, and it took him forty minutes to get back his breath.

OF COURSE, HE DIDN'T go see any doctors. He made up one excuse after another—no money for such things, no time, he couldn't take off from work, the car needed a new radiator. I kept pestering him about it, but then he found some new patent medicine he swore cured the cough. He sipped at it all day long like a drunkard with a pocket flask. I recalled the nerve medicine Ira had plied me with after Richard was stillborn. I knew how easy it was to become dependent on such things, although I had to admit, the medicine did seem to help. No more fits of coughing, but he stayed as skinny as I'd ever seen him.

I went back to work at Pete's school. Jean-Louis gave me the use of his private office for nursing Justine. The administrator let me put a cradle by the file cabinets in the main office. Everyone seemed to want to help us out, and we needed the help. What with the hospital bill from Justine, Pete's tuition, and the rent on the apartment plus the bed in Épernay, our finances were stretched thin. My salary was only a pittance, but it bought a few groceries.

Justine became a sort of mascot for the whole school. The students would stop in to see her whenever they passed by the office, usually led by Nina, who had become a miniature teacher herself. She bossed the other children, even the older ones, and none of them ever seemed to mind. They all obeyed her.

Pete especially was curious about his new little sister. He made the sign for *baby* over and over, his arms cradled in front of him, whenever he saw her. Once he caught on to this sign talking, he started to learn fast. By his third birthday he already had about thirty words.

IN JANUARY, ON A Wednesday, with winter trying to tighten its grip on everything, Gil caught the early train in from Épernay. He didn't want to risk having car trouble on the road. It took him three hours and six stops to make it to Paris, where he used the streetcars to get to the American Hospital. He never trusted the underground trains. I think they scared him a little, being so far underneath the earth, reminded him of the war. All the way on the train to Paris, and on the streetcars, he tried to hide his situation from strangers around him. But they noticed, of course, the thin man spitting blood into his handkerchief. They kept clear of him.

The call came for me at the school. Marivonne promised to take care of the children and I gave her the key to the apartment.

Jean-Louis drove me. He claimed he needed to go to the hospital anyway. He didn't try to small talk or to console me or pry, and I was grateful to him for that. I couldn't have concentrated on any conversation.

When we got there, he went with me to the admitting desk, and in his quick, sure French asked the woman for Monsieur Lange. It still startled me to hear that name. Jean-Louis guided me down a hall, aimed me in the right direction, but he didn't try to come along. He gave us our privacy.

Gil looked awful, yellow and shrunken. I rushed right to his bed to smooth his forehead. He burned with fever. He took my hand, kissed the back of it.

"Sunny, sit down in that chair. I need to talk to you." He had to swallow several times. The medicine they'd given him had dried out his mouth. He gave me a tight smile. "It's TB." He said it softly, but clear. "That's what I've got. TB. The doctor says my lungs look like Swiss cheese."

I sat down hard on the chair. It plinked with my weight. My brain felt dull and mushy. I shook my head. He hadn't let go of my hand.

"And they want to examine you, too," he said. "All of you. The kids."

I leaned over on the bed, stretching to keep hold of his hand. "We don't have it. None of us are sick. You're not home enough to pass it on."

"I've had it for a while already."

"You knew?"

"Not that it was TB. I knew my lungs were shot . . ." He had to take deep, gasping breaths every few words. I wanted to hold my mouth against his and give him my air. "After they did the X ray, the doctor asked me what kind of gas I'd gotten into during the war. Just like that. Like he knew. I told him I wasn't sure. Phosgene, I thought, or a mixture like Green Cross. He said these ailments are showing up in gassed lungs. TB and asthma. Cancerous tumors."

He nearly choked. I patted his hand. I could've put my thumb and little finger around his wrist. "Ssh, Gil. Don't talk too much." I reached to straighten the hospital gown they had on him. "We're going to get you well. They can cure this now. They can. I've heard about it. You go up in the mountains, somewhere the air is thin and cold, and you stay there and take treatments—"

He made a grimace. "The sanatorium in Grenoble. The doctor told me about that. For rich people. It costs seventy-five hundred francs."

"We'll get the money. It's not so much as it sounds. It's . . . it's— what is it?" I said, trying to calculate.

"It doesn't matter. We haven't got it. Fact is, we're broke. It's gone. All of it. We've nickled and dimed it away."

At the other end of the ward, someone else was coughing. A nurse walked down the center aisle, looking all business. As soon as she passed through the doors, I crawled up on the bed. I stretched out next to him and I wound my arms around him. I nestled my head between his neck and shoulder. He smelled like sickness, like the hospital, like too much worry. The wheezing in his chest was loud and splintery, but I was still full of hope. I'd brought Papa back from the dead. If I could do that, then Gil would be a cinch.

"I'm going to get you well," I whispered. "You're going to stop smoking. And I'm going to feed you all kinds of tempting foods. We're going to get you well, Gil."

That night I wrote letters home. I made short work of explaining how we came to be in France and what our life had been like for the last four years, and then I simply begged. I didn't care if it brought American justice right to our door, I wrote to everyone. Papa first, and then Aunt Dellie. I even swallowed my pride and wrote to Aunt Prudie. I told her about the mountain cure and the sanatorium at Grenoble. I said Gil needed her, that it could mean the difference between life and death for him. Tears blotted and smeared the page. My handwriting was barely readable. I had to drink some of his cognac to get to sleep that night, and I put the babies in bed with me, all three of them. They were my comfort.

Chapter Twenty-six

THE HOSPITAL RELEASED GIL home to me. His doctor, a stiff and formal Canadian, handed me a packet of sanitary masks, the same as I'd worn when Mama and Papa took the flu. The doctor said, "Your husband should be checked into a municipal sanitoria, Mrs. Lange." But Jean-Louis had already told me about the public houses. He called them pest houses. He knew of other sanatoriums offering the rest cure, places not so expensive as the one in the mountains, one at Vittel and another in the south of France at Vence.

Gil had prescribed medicine to take, a tincture of opium. And he was to drink lots and lots of beer to help him gain back some of his weight. He needed milk and raw eggs. He was supposed to eat two dozen a day, but after the first full day of him puking, we gave up on the eggs. I didn't wear the mask. I figured if I hadn't caught the disease by now, I wasn't going to catch it. Somehow the children and I all X-rayed clean. But I moved Justine's crib in with Nina and Pete anyway and kept their door shut at night.

We tried to go on as before. I took the children with me to the school every morning. I left food for Gil to eat. I stuck plenty of beer in the cupboard. He was weak, but he could fend for himself. He read all day, stayed quiet. Color came back to his cheeks. The dark bags underneath his eyes lightened.

On the twenty-sixth of January, while I was at the school, Gil took the train to Épernay. He left me a note saying he had to work: *We need the money. We can't make it just on your wages, Sunny.* But he didn't last a week till he was back home again, driving the crippled-up car this time, sicker than ever, apologizing. He felt useless, ashamed of his disease.

"A puny, goddamn lunger," he said. "That's what I've come down to."

I put him right to bed with every window in the apartment thrown wide open. He needed rest, and he needed air, lots and lots of air. But when a spell of hard cold pushed through, I feared he might take pneumonia on top of everything else, or that one of the children might. He made me close up the apartment, but with the radiators running I noticed he wheezed more. He insisted I go on back to the school. All day long I worried over him, and with good cause. More often than not, I'd get home to find he hadn't eaten a bite since breakfast.

"I'm not hungry," he said. "But I'm taking my medicine."

That wasn't good enough for me. I fixed a bunch of sandwiches for him every morning, put in cheese and ham and butter and boiled egg. I bought fruit from the market: pears, bananas, and apricots, things Gil loved. Nina helped me with the sandwiches. She was almost six, wanted to help with everything. She stood on a chair and arranged the meat just so inside the bread slices.

"I can stay at home with Daddy every day," she said.

"No, honey, you can't. You have to go with me."

"Why do I have to?" she said, looking at me with those eyes, so blue and serious. "I can make him eat his dinner."

I studied her little face, touched her pink cheeks with the back of my hand. She adored her daddy, adored him the way I had always adored Papa. I could remember being her age, following Papa out to the fields before sunrise, sitting inside the cocoon of his lap in the evenings, wanting to spend every spare minute wherever he was. How I wished he were there right then, to tell me what to do.

The next day I left Nina with Gil. I made her promise to wear her mask. I tied it around her head. She was old enough to bring things to him — sandwiches, bottles of beer. She could take a five-centime piece and run down to buy a newspaper when the boy came by hawking. Gil read the papers to her in French. They spoke French to each other all day. They had pretend tea parties in French. They sang French songs. He gave that to her — those days, that language, the memories.

The first letter that came answering my plea for help had money inside, a check for one hundred dollars from Gabriel. He'd heard from Aunt Dellie of our need. There was a newsy letter and a snapshot of him and Letty on their front porch — happy suntanned Texans. The letter was all spread out on the table beside Gil's chair when I got home with the babies. The check was there, too, torn in fourths. My heart sank to see that, but Gil was furious with me.

"I won't take charity from Gabe O'Barr," he said, shouting as loud as he could with a voice getting weaker by the day. "How many more people did you write to for money?"

I confessed and I thought he wanted to hit me. Maybe if he'd been stronger he would have. "I did it because I love you," I said, and at least he stopped shouting long enough to hear me say that.

He didn't speak to me for two days, but he probably needed to rest his voice anyway.

The next letter that came was from the road-construction company. They'd had to replace him, but they sent him one month's wages as compensation, enough for April rent. It meant there would be no more paying of hospital bills for a while. Pete's tuition wasn't due again until September. By then I knew I would have Gil back on his feet. We would make do somehow.

The next letter came from Aunt Dellie, and I got to that one first. Another hundred dollars. I took the check to the bank on my way one morning. I stuck away the money and didn't tell Gil it had come. A letter came from the Grenoble sanatorium, too. Gil had underestimated their fee by ten thousand francs, but they had no available beds anyway. The one in Vence wasn't much cheaper. I waited to hear from Vittel, even knowing we'd need a miracle to send him away anywhere.

Early in March, Gil sold the car to Monsieur Durand on the fourth floor, our piano player. I don't know how they arrived at the deal they struck. Two hundred and fifty francs, about seventeen American dollars. The car hadn't been driven in weeks by then. When I came home, Gil was outside on the street, leaned inside the motor, while Monsieur Durand watched from the sidewalk. It gave me a lift seeing Gil in the sunlight, his head down in that car. But once he got the motor running, I had to help him up the stairs, one at a time. He bore hard on me, the breath storming out of him. Gil had always had a car. It seemed wrong somehow for him to be without.

AFTER SCHOOL ONE EVENING, Nina met us at the door with her finger pressed to her lips. "Sssh," she whispered. "Daddy's sleeping." She wasn't wearing her mask and I scolded her for it.

Pete was ready to play. He missed having Nina to walk home with. He grabbed her in a bear hug that made her shriek. I separated them, signed for him to play soft. He knew what I meant. He grinned guiltily at me. I put his mask on him.

I rolled Justine's buggy inside the front door and then I saw Gil, slumped in his chair, pale as whitewash. A half-drunk beer sat on the table beside him, a sandwich hardening on a plate. It took another few seconds before I realized the speckles on his shirt and down his chin weren't spilled food but dried blood.

"Oh my God." I left Justine inside the buggy, and she could already stand by herself. She started to fret, but I rushed to Gil, grabbed up his wrist. His skin felt like sandpaper. "How long—," I said to Nina, digging my fingers in for a pulse. "When did Daddy go to sleep?" I nearly shouted at her.

She looked ready to bawl. "I don't know."

I reached for his chest, his heart. I put my ear down flat and he opened his eyes. I let out my breath. Justine had started screaming. The buggy rattled.

Gil shifted, licked at his mouth. "What's the matter?" he said. He held his hand out to Pete, and Pete stopped staring long enough to put his hand inside of Gil's. "Was I snoring?"

"He's awake now, Mama," Nina said, and I could hear the relief ripple through her voice, too.

I dipped the edge of a clean diaper into the glass of beer and wiped at the blood caked around Gil's mouth. "Sit up," I told him. "We need to change your shirt."

He moved slow, and with a great effort. "Justine wants down."

"You have a headache?" I unbuttoned the blood-speckled shirt. The medicine had started to give him bad headaches. He nodded his answer.

Justine kept screaming. Nina went over to bear-hug her out of the buggy. They fell in a heap together on the floor and Justine shrieked all the louder.

I finished with Gil's buttons. "Did you eat?"

"A little angel peeled me a banana." He smiled toward Nina.

"You've got to eat, Gil. Have you had a lot of medicine today?"

He nodded. I pulled the shirt off of him. He was all brittle bones. The tattoo on his arm had shriveled from a rainbow to something like a roof without the house. His eyes floated like brown moons in his face.

Nina went and got a clean shirt for him while I tried to settle Justine down. She was greedy, nuzzling around at my breasts, seeming frantic, like it had been days and days since she'd had any nourishment, and she was as fat as a butterball.

Pete sat down on the floor with a paper drawing Nina had done sometime during the day. When Nina came out of the bedroom with Gil's shirt, she said, "No, Pete," then signed at him. He whined till Gil held up his wristwatch and let it swing back and forth, catching Pete's eye. Pete took the watch from Gil's hand.

"I'm sorry we woke you up." I opened my blouse for Justine's hungry mouth.

Gil trained his eyes on me and let his head fall against the back of the chair, the clean shirt limp in his lap. I held Justine to my breast and eased into the chair across from him. Even sick, he still loved to watch me nurse. He had always loved it. I think he secretly wished he had milk in his breasts, too. Justine made a big smacking noise and I felt my milk let down.

"She's a little pig," I said, and he smiled. "And she doesn't care where we are. All I am to her is titty."

He shook his head, his eyes bright with fever. "Breasts," he corrected, shaking his finger side to side like a schoolmarm. "We say *breasts* around this place."

I smiled. "I would feed you from my breasts if it would tempt you to eat."

A grin played at his lips. "That'll give me something to day-dream about."

In the other room, Nina shrieked at Pete and he came running out, laughing. He had one of her paper dolls. Its head was torn loose and dangled. I reached out to catch him as he went past me and Justine's mouth dislodged. She screamed immediately and I held Pete squirming in one arm. Nina came to pry the paper doll from his fingers. When he didn't let go, she walloped him on the arm till he did.

"Nina!" I said, hollering over Justine. Pete started to bawl, too. I sat Justine on the floor and bent to cuddle Pete. I signed that Nina was sorry, but he didn't see my hands. Big round tears spurted out his eyes and rolled down his face. Justine kept holler-ing, pawing at my open blouse. I looked across at Gil again, so shrunken in the chair, as helpless as these babies, and all of the sudden it was just too much for me. Too big of a load.

I sat flat on the floor, turned my back against his chair so he wouldn't see me cry. I put Justine on the breast again, to shut her up, and I hugged Pete in next to me. I laid my cheek on Gil's knee. His fingertips touched my hair, gently, like he knew what I was feeling. I couldn't hide it from him. He always knew me bet-ter than I did myself. I pulled his hand down out of my hair and kissed the back of his knuckles.

WITHIN A WEEK HE was back in the hospital. He com-plained that we didn't have the money, but I knew I couldn't keep him at home. He was worse, going down day by day, almost by the hour.

I talked to the head of the hospital. I pledged money to them that I didn't have, promised to get on a regular payment schedule again. I asked for a private room. I begged for one so I could keep the door shut. I needed it quiet, quiet enough so I could hear each breath Gil took. In ... and out ... in ... out ... I heard them all going out, gasping back in. I knew when they slowed.

Fever raged through him, fever that no amount of aspirin could bring down. They gave him opiates and he came and went with mumbling dreams. I stroked his cheek, his head, his neck with wet cloths. I whispered his name so he would know I was there. His legs and arms were spidery thin, face withered. He hardly made a lump at all underneath the hospital sheets. But when he was awake, his eyes still belonged to me.

Day and night I sat with him. Marivonne tended the children, days at the school, the apartment at night. I knew I could never repay her. My breasts dried up, ached for three days, and quit flowing. Justine had taken just fine to a bottle, Marivonne reported on one of her visits to the hospital. Her sister, Pauline, had come to help. I was grateful for that, too.

I couldn't leave Gil. I wouldn't. He might need me. He might wake in the night and need me to sit him upright so he could breathe better, or prop his arms on pillows to take the strain off his shoulders. Or he might need his medicine or a nurse. He might want to tell me something. Please God, let him tell me something.

I slept there in the chair with my head on the bed beside his hip, bent over, my back aching. I had to stay close to hear him if he woke up. Once he did wake me, his hand warm and limp, stirring in my hair. I curled his fingers in mine, pressed them to my face.

"You're better," I said. "I can tell you're feeling better."

"Go home." His voice was hardly there, a few puffs of air.

"Not yet, Gil. Not till you're well."

His thumb rubbed soft and listless against my cheekbone. "You should go home."

Later that night he had dreams. He moaned with them and it scared me, made me think he'd gone too far from me to get back. I crawled into the bed and lay against him. He felt small. I never had thought of him as small. I don't know if he knew I was there. Maybe he did. Maybe it was some comfort to him.

Afterward, the doctor told me it was blood vessels bursting in his lungs that finally ended it. They had a word—*exsanguination*. Blood vessels bursting quietly, silently drowning him in his own blood.

The day was the twenty-eighth of April, 1926. A sun-dazzled morning. Birds singing outside the window. Not a cloud anywhere. A Gil kind of day. He was twenty-seven years old, two months, and twenty-one days. I figured it out, counted it up. I wanted to go with him. I didn't see how I could keep on living. I didn't see how I would ever laugh again, or love anybody, or feel anything. I reached to close his eyes. I hated to. It was like closing a door you could never again open.

For a long while I didn't call for the nurse. I lay still beside him, staring out the bright window, remembering all our time together. It didn't seem fair that it was over, that this was all there was, just this. I wanted to get angry at someone. I wanted to scream or hit something. But there wasn't anyone that I could blame. Nobody to put a finger on. The war. The war did it, but that was too easy to say, and it didn't mean anything anyway. It had no meat and blood and bone.

I stayed there on the bed beside him till the fever in him grew cold. How quickly that happened. And when all the warmth was gone, every spot of it, I knew he was gone, too.

May 10, 1926, Instanter

Dear Sunny and Gil—

It is time now for you two to come on home. I have done
some checking, with Dan O'Barr's help, and the best we
can figure it, Ira Goodner never did report the two of you
taking off with your daughter, so it looks like you have
been hiding out over there all this time for nothing. That
man divorced you four years ago, Sunny, and Gil, you are a
free man too, so there won't be nobody standing in your
way. We have got t.b. clinics in Texas, and there is a school
for the deaf right in Austin, so for God's sakes use this
money I'm sending and get yourselves back where you
belong, where there is folks to look after you. Those babies
ought to be raised near family not amongst a bunch of
foreigners. Cable us as to when and where you will arrive
so somebody can be there to meet you.

Papa

June 14, 1926

Dear Papa,

I got your letter with the $500 check yesterday. I know that money was hard for you to scratch up, and I'm returning it to you. I don't need it now anyhow. I guess I should have sent a cable before. I did write a letter to you telling you about Gil and the funeral and everything, but I guess you didn't get it in time. The mail is so slow from here to there. Sending a cablegram didn't occur to me, but it is what I should have done, I see that now. All this time you have been thinking that you could still do something to help Gil and me.

It was a very nice funeral. They bury people in vaults over here, and Gil's has a little trough at the foot of it where I've planted some white geraniums. The cemetery is only a few blocks away, and they have got water spigots all around over there, so as long as you take a watering can with you, you can keep something growing. I like it there. It is real peaceful and pretty for just sitting awhile.

Try not to worry about us, Papa. Me and the children are going to do just fine. I know you probably just hate thinking of us alone in such a big city, but we have come to consider it our home. And we have got friends "amongst this bunch of foreigners." Pete is happy at his school and they have let me increase my hours there, given me more to do. I can take Justine to work with me, and the school where Nina will go come fall is nearby. My friend Marivonne is talking about moving in with us to help some with the rent. She is in love with an American painter who lives a couple of streets over. They will probably get married one of these days soon.

So see, Papa, we have got a life here. There are lots of Americans moving in and things happening all the time. It's not the sort of place for you, but Gil's here, and the children are settled, and it suits me after all. I can even speak a little French, if you can believe it. Please, don't worry about us. We are OK.

Take care of yourself and try not to work so hard. Give Ding a big hug for me. Say hello to the rest of the folks.

Je t'aime, Papa—

Sunny

P.S. Ask Letty to translate that if you can't figure it out. XXOO

ACKNOWLEDGMENTS

$\mathcal{A}$ LOT OF PEOPLE gave me their help and support and they deserve acknowledging. Most of all, thanks to Shannon Ravenel for pushing me to do something new, and also to Nat Sobel for his encouragement. Thanks as well to Susan Rogers Cooper, Denise Stallcup, and Marylyn Croman, dear friends, for being such faithful readers. Thanks to Jay Brandon and Tom Garner, my legal experts, and to everyone who helped me get the facts: Luellen Smiley of the Yorktown Library; Paul Morris of the Pierce-Arrow Society; Chad McCormick of the National Guard Association of the United States and Major Tom Weaver of the Historical Society of the Militia and National Guard; Robert L. Cox of the National Headquarters of the American Legion; Mr. Martin at the American Cemetery in Thiaucourt, France; Casey Morehouse of the Virginia School for the Deaf and Blind; Steve Gilbert of the University of Toronto for his expertise and knowledge of the history of tattooing; and to Dr. Charles Sanders, Tiffany Bonner, Fred Askew, Stephen Frodge, and, of course, my beloved, Charles R., for his endurance and his patience. If I've forgotten anyone, you know who you are — many thanks.

Books are produced in the United States using U.S.-based materials

Books are printed using a revolutionary new process called THINKtech™ that lowers energy usage by 70% and increases overall quality

Books are durable and flexible because of Smyth-sewing

Paper is sourced using environmentally responsible foresting methods and the paper is acid-free

Center Point Large Print
600 Brooks Road / PO Box 1
Thorndike, ME 04986-0001 USA

(207) 568-3717

**US & Canada:
1 800 929-9108
www.centerpointlargeprint.com**